Approaching the

Dark Age

Resonance

Approaching the Dark Age

Resonance

Copyright © 2009 Matthew Chivers

Original Cover Art by Matthew Chivers.

ISBN: 978-1-4476-7285-2

Third Edition.

Authors Website:

www.approachingdarkage.com

Authors Email:

matthewchivers@approachingdarkage.com

An Introduction

& dedication

This Introduction and Dedication section has not been proofed for grammar or spelling on purpose, to act as a testament.

So I have finally published my book. It has taken since the summer of 2005 until early 2011, and to be honest with you I never thought I would accomplish it. I have heard a few stories of authors taking more than ten or twenty years to publish a piece of literature...although six is a long time in itself.

Life can take many twists and turns, always knocking you down before you pick your sorry self back up and carry on till eventually you get to where you want to get to. I cannot help but feel apprehensive about releasing my work, perhaps it is too soon. The perfectionist inside of me wants to make my story %110 correct, every aspect from character development, to plot, and backgrounds, everything must be perfect!

Nothing can be perfected (as much as my other side keeps shouting yes it can) and there will always be a loop hole, or some clever berk would have had a better idea for that one scene, etc. There will be critics both good and bad, but that isn't too much of my concern, I'm just glad to have accomplished one of my dreams in life.

And that dream is now resting possibly (I hope) in your hands (not placed to the side with your toiletries).

I for one will cherish my story, as to me it's something inspired from everything I have experienced, loved to read or think about as a hobby and then to develop it within one of the dark halls and dungeons of my mind.

Always one attracted to both fantasy and science fiction, and I hope you, the reader, will enjoy the story based on these genres.

I've had many doubts and to be honest I still do. I had a faith in myself that used to be in abundance a few years ago, that isn't quite the same that it used to be now. I feel as if it's been stretched to the point of no return, only for me to wake up the next day to try and make something work, as for the last few years I've had a rough tumbling. Something I would not wish on any one.

I look at the world today and remember it to when I began writing the book, and I'm still undecided if the world is going to survive in the next century...or less.

In a way you could say this story is an alternate universe or what the possibilities could be, whether it's through pure fantasy or science fiction...pure escapism when we really should be doing something to heal the world, but perhaps I've already made my point so I'll stop. After all you're reading this to possibly forget about the troubles of the world (and I write for the same reason so were all hypocrites...awesome!).

The sequel has been written to this story, but it has yet to go through the perfectionism treatment like this book (don't worry you won't be waiting 6 years, more like 20).

When I was at the baby age where you should begin to speak, I did not. Turned out I was diagnosed by the doctors at the time (this was around 1986/87) with Aphasia. Therefore, I was thrust into this world with the inability to speak. The Doctors thought that I would remain a 'mute' and be unable to comprehend basic language skills.

All my friends in the pub would disagree of course, as speaking is something I like to do quite often! However, as you may have guessed from the last sentence, I overcame this at the age of 4 and then by the age of 5 I could pronounce of speak 2 to 3 words at a time – with long pauses in between the words.

Even today though my words may not always come out perfect, or I will say something that others may not know what I am on about until I further clarify what I meant. It isn't too bad, but it's a problem that will get easier with age.

This of course brings me up to the next problem I have suffered from since early child hood. Not only was I born with Aphasia but I also turned out to be Dyslexic.

Since a young age I wanted to write a story, trouble was at the age of six or seven and heavily dyslexic, most the words on my dad's computer...well...every word had a red underline. At the time I only wanted to write about me and my friends doing such and such an adventure (as you do at a young age).

Trouble was it angered me that I couldn't write or spell words, so needless to say I got angry at myself and stopped trying. This attitude dogged me for years (and still does occasionally), my brain just did not want to catch on, and, as I remember all too well, occasionally lashed out for apparently no reason at friends or family.

Six or seven years went by and after going to the Dyslexic Institute in Bath city while I was at Frogwell Primary School in

Chippenham, Wiltshire, I had managed to start properly reading and writing.

By the age of ten, I could quite happily read books designed for five year olds. For the first time in my life I could read and write (even it were 3 to 5 words at a time), and if I didn't by the time I hit Secondary School, life would have been much, much harder. It was a titanic milestone. Thankfully, now my spelling is above average but my grammar has something to be desired...

Of course going to such an institution for one or two sessions each week (that lasted only one hour each) over three years finally paid off, it crippled my parent's budgets however. My mother would not have it any other way mind you, for me to read and write it was an essential life skill, and if the governing body we had back then could not teach me to read or write then she would go elsewhere and make it happen. I despise people who claim dyslexia does not exist. Carrying on then...

So while I may bitch and moan in these pages that I have been given a cruddy hand by life I always think back to my mother. If it was not for her love and support for her baby (I'm 25+ by the way now mum) then my life would have been very different. I am very blessed to have parents that have stood by me for my whole life, giving me encouragement to keep moving on and to support me the way they have and continue to do so.

It was when I hit 17 that I sat in front of my computer thinking 'I want to write a book...' so I written the title of it and left it as 'Approaching the Dark Age'. I had no idea what I wanted to write, I had the urge, just not the idea's or rather the inspiration...so for a second time I gave writing up (second time...I try to make it sound like I did try! Ha!). A couple of years went by and I was 20 when I broke my hand at an accident at work one day.

So I quit my frustrating job, got home, sat in front of my computer (and at the time my bedroom was a tip from re-decorating, so I was living in my parents large shed for a good few weeks whilst I started on the story...oh large spiders how I miss you) and opened up a word doc to start writing. Since the second attempt a few years had passed and I finally had the inspiration to begin writing this novel.

I drew on many things ranging from my hobbies and life experiences (I have yet to experience the end of the world mind) to my friends, but also to write a book based on the future of this world, and if imagination snuck in then what would it really be like? My spiritual and creative nature took its course.

In those years (and today mind) I did nothing but keep telling my mates when we visited local book stores that one day my novels will be on the shelves whenever we went for a Saturday coffee, whilst always being dogged by some problem that prevented it from happening. The book itself or life itself. At the time it seemed like a dream, and every day when I woke up I kept feeling depressed because rarely did I have the energy as time went flying on by, and to be honest, in a way still does feel like that.

After getting the book professionally proofed I began to start creating the front cover you see now.

After many (eighty) odd different drafts I had created a front and back cover until I stuck with the one you have now. It took a lot of time and a lot of patience over the years, and wow, to me now, it's just awesome to look at and hold in my hands. We all have goals in our lives that we must reach, and I am now smiling that I am going in that direction.

I think the biggest trial was being unemployed for over a year and a half before finally finding employment again to get the money to publish this book (I sympathise with those out of work, bless you all and keep trying). I stare at it now, holding it in my hands, trembling with pride and joy. To me and what I have experienced, this is a mile stone that on a personal level has made me feel more centred at where I am meant to be in the universe.

So to this end, I would like to thank all my friends and family for carrying me when I needed it, giving me encouragement and advice and help when I needed it the most to get me through.

A special thanks to my mother and father for all the help, without you I doubt I'd be able to even write my own name today! Thanks for reading my book through, glad you loved it!

So once again, **thank you everyone**.

I did it, I finally did it.

So sit back and enjoy the journey...

Matthew currently resides at Langley Burrell near Chippenham, Wiltshire, England. He is currently working on the sequels of the Approaching the Dark Age universe whilst busy working as a hotel receptionist.

Chapters

1. The Tribals Encounter   1
2. Nightmare   15
3. Deeper Understanding   30
4. The Packs   45
5. The Unexpected   54
6. Ancient Battlefield   72
7. Forsaken Wilderness   89
8. Journey for The Hermit   107
9. Anunaki Council   121
10. Mysterious N'Rutas   142
11. Artefacts and Knowledge   159
12. Into the Glass   178
13. Dread Rising   189
14. Deceitful Plan   204
15. Safety of Meridia   218
16. Reunion   238
17. Release from Darkness   254
18. Grave Matters   265
19. Back from Dreams to Reality   282

Chapter One

The Tribals Encounter...

'If atomic bombs are to be added as new weapons to the arsenals of a warring world, or to the arsenals of the nations preparing for war, then the time will come when mankind will curse the names of Los Alamos and Hiroshima. The people of this world must unite or they will perish.'

J. Robert Oppenheimer

After the turn of the millennium, global warming reached an all time high. Wars raged on in many continents in the name of resources or precious metals. Economic crashes on a global scale were triggered, rich and poor alike were all affected.

Many protested for peaceful solutions while many were injured in the process as revolutions were taking place as a way to possibly solve their many spiralling problems. Where religion or church was once a place of sanctuary or solace, were now they were on the brink of collapse with many losing their spirituality day by day. Between the faiths there was bickering, arguments fought over petty differences, respect was lost repeatedly.

Gradually human beings began to realise that many were suffering causing great cost to both life and the planet. However, it was too late, too late to heed the warnings of the prophets who had appeared throughout the previous ages, their visions ignored or dismissed with laughter. Earthquakes ripped apart communities, countries, and great cities. Volcanoes unleashed their magma and shattered once lush and green landscapes with fire and brimstone, killing off many inhabitants of the landmasses.

Lightning storms raged across the planet destroying most communications, leaving the majority of the human beings powerless to know what exactly was going on. Tsunamis from every corner of the globe took over the coastal areas with an angry wrath.

Those who were unfortunate enough to live near the sea were stricken down from the great waves crashing all around them with no escape. Although the planet began its fated doomsday, many were surprised at what came at them from the deep recesses of the earth. Everyday life in the twenty first century ended. No more did humanity have luxuries to make their lives easier or safer. They were at the mercy of the planet in which few were spared.

Many years had passed since that day, and now on the outskirts of a ruined city were a sleeping group of humans known as Tribals. Peaceful and spiritual in nature, these travellers go from place to place, trying to survive against the elements or other humans. They scrounged day by day from any scraps or salvage, occasionally hunting in groups for whatever food may be available in the stricken lands. This particular wandering tribe were known as Larkham's Tribals.

Larkham was a holy man, or spiritualist, depending whom you asked that guides the Tribals that follow him, trusting in his spiritual intuitive abilities to get them through this dark period in which they lived. He is a guide of light to people who have lost hope, and so the Tribals turn to him for reassurance, hope and love in a world turned mad. On this particular night, many of them lay fast asleep, the air filled with snoring in their camp on a high hill, overlooking the ruined city below.

Most slept in either roughly patched blankets, made from animal furs or other such salvaged goods, like sleeping bags passed down from generation, to generation, mostly in a horrible foul smelling condition due to their age. Some slept in tents made out of such fashioned materials while others could only sleep under the stars and moonlight and depending on the season in either humidity or an unforgiving cold laced with frost.

Among the sleeping followers, one was awake and gazing towards the descending moon and the ascending sun that gradually crept up above hills, ruins, and clouds that littered the landscape from their hill vantage point. Moment by moment the stars that once littered the sky were gradually conquered by a blood red morning.

Maledream looked on as he had done for most of his life since he had ended up with the Tribals many cycles ago. First waking up in a sweat looking at the stars flickering brightly above, before watching what he loved best. The moon sliding down out of view only to be taken by the warm amber rays of the sun cutting through the sky like a soft brush with paint and paper. Sighing softly, he got up from his position, leant against one of the many stones that littered the camp from a ruined temple that had once stood on the hill.

As he watched the new day dawning, his head filled with more punishing questions to which he had no answers. At an early age, Maledream had suffered amnesia from some form of accident deeper within the city many cycles of the sun ago. Since then, he had suffered with troubling dreams or nightmares waking him most early mornings or late at night.

The sun when it came out, and was not being obscured by cloud or low mist, gave him some comfort. As Larkham always said to him, "your memory will come to you when you are ready and at the right moment." It felt that he was ready to remember, feeling something else was blocking his memory, helping to drive him insane with the same question he asked during his nightly dreams, awaking to find he was sweating and cursing with his foul tongue.

Meanwhile, the years passed and his quiet but slightly cheeky personality developed. He could still remember waking up in Larkham's arms as a young boy in the ruins below, the smell of fumes and shouting, haunting him as echoes from the past. Wounds seeping blood and a migraine was all that Maledream could remember. The day when his life was saved by Larkham, who nurtured him swiftly back to good health.

However, since then he was never one to care or appear to care, alienating people with his cheeky remarks or attitude towards other Tribals or, at times, becoming more introverted and keeping himself to himself. Not one for much conversation he was always a listener attending Larkham's oral tradition speeches given every few days or so during the mornings. Speeches intended by Larkham to inspire people through a tradition of stories given to him by his old mentors.

Even Larkham did not know if these tales were true lore or fiction, but never the less handed down the knowledge in hope it would someday be of use to the people that followed him. He walked casually up the steps of the ruined temple to approach a balcony that overlooked the ruined city from its vantage point in his dirty woollen clothes and patched together long coat. From there, any attack could be seen from a mile and was very safe from the killings carried out by other humans deeper inside the city.

Rubbing his blue eyes, he sighed then scraped back his dirty knotted hair causing him discomfort as the roots of his hair ached from being pulled so harshly. The breeze of the wind caressed his cheekbones as he strode out unto the balcony to watch the Tribals gradually awaking below, to chat, cook, and feed their empty bellies with whatever nutrition they had available.

Maledream never usually ate anything in the morning and left it until the afternoon, as he could not bring himself to eat scraps of food while the children in the camp looked at him with hungry eyes.

Guilt made him hungry most the time, however he was older and streetwise enough to gain food in the ruined city streets by bartering or stealing when he had to, just like everyone else. Gazing back down to the camp below Maledream noticed Larkham was gathering the children of the tribe for another one of his oral stories about the past and how damned the human race is, but of a much nicer tone than Maledream would describe himself.

'Who am I kidding,' he thought.

'They are just as damaged as the rest of us and just don't show it, they already know were all damned.'

Hearing the scrabble of children running up through sun lit ruined temple, Maledream watched Larkham steadily walking up the stoned stairway with the horrid little monsters in tow. They were making enough of a racket to wake up the ancient spirits themselves.

'Almost storytelling time, children,' the old man spoke joyfully, his dirty white robes catching the light as he strode out onto the balcony, where the cocky Maledream was stood arms folded with a smirk on his face directed at Larkham.

'Ah, I see Maledream wants to join in the storytelling then?'

'Don't count on it old man, you know what I think about your stories. I'm just up here appreciating the dawn of a new day...'

'Oh as always my son, but as always an amazing coincidence you're only up here when I am speaking of "old silly traditions," eh boy?' Larkham replied with a smile.

Still stood with his arms crossed, Maledream turned away from the Tribal leader, before uttering:

'Just get on with it,' to then send out a sigh towards the morning sun.

Continuing to smile, Larkham turned towards the massing children, raised his arms, and began loudly.

'Hush now children! I will begin to tell you my stories of old! And if you do not settle down, I will make this boring story last twice as long!'

Maledream grinned at these words.

'He brings it on himself I swear,' he thought.

Quietly setting down the children sat cross-legged in a semicircle around Larkham who stood in the middle of the open balcony while Maledream just prepped his ears for the latest story.

The children waited expectantly as they enjoyed these stories told most days unless Larkham was meditating or handing out advice to the Tribals. Quite often Maledream questioned how Larkham knew so much about the past considering no one here in the camp could barely read or write, and that even though Larkham is old, he isn't as old as his stories. When he quizzed the old man on several occasions, the Tribal leader could only reply "Try talking to the ancient dead, they know much."

Settling down Larkham closed his eyes and begun telling his dark terrible grim tale of blunt horrible truth, yet nothing could be hidden and all must know as to not provoke future mistakes.

'*Within a heartbeat, did the human race rise in all its splendour, and within a heartbeat did it break itself with self Pity, Hatred, and Lust. Within a Heartbeat, did the human race take from Mother Nature, and within a heartbeat did Mother Nature take back for what is hers. Deserted ruins, deserts, fields of lava and ice, graves, corpses, and maggots.*

This is all that is left now, for Mother Nature grew weary and tired of being gouged of her natural minerals, and being ripped at her throat by greedy, jealous tyrants of humanity starving for her precious liquids and metals. Tyrants above all else used, abused and raped her.

It was many cycles ago that our Humanity enjoyed its last united celebration of the passing of our ritualistic, rotationary orbit, around the Sun. The Polar Axis of the Earth changed, wreaking havoc on the land and inhabitants. The Waters took back the land, filling the lungs of many a creature. All across the globe did the water take life, but still some survived. One by One did the song of bird fall silent, and One by One did the screams and cries of anguish arise to fill the chorus of Vengeance.

Mighty, horrendous creatures, from the depths of old, rose up from the darkness of the great deep oceans, sinking great silver ships with no remorse. Neither man nor woman had ever seen such creatures that belonged to fairy tales or myths. Fantastic amounts of human blood were spilled into the Great Oceans of Earth, further coating the Great Mother with shame.

Nevertheless, the Behemoths did not stop there, the water allowed safe passage into cities close to shores, where they readily devoured the insect like humans hiding inside their grey stone towers, which the Behemoths ripped apart with great ferocity and ease.

They were not the only creatures to strike, for other terrible creatures of the deep walked upon the land, sea creatures which looked remarkably human, that were entirely thought to be the stuff of myth or legend.

Bearing sharp fins, spikes, and metallic scales did they wage war upon us, with fang and claw, killing the strong, and feasting upon the weak such as the young and old.

The Earth also wanted back its fair share and so mighty quakes erupted, engulfing many in hot flame and molten metal where some stood in its angry path. Humanities mighty buildings plummeted to the ground, swallowed completely by the earth. Homes were burned to the ground as fast as they were built, nothing but ash remained.

Nothing but a waste of moments within the greater scheme of things it would seem. One by one did the flickering lights of cities die and one by one signalling the fall of our kind.'

The Spiritual leader paused in the cold morning air atop from a ruined temple gazing out to the rising sun, watching the looming shadows growing smaller from the other various ruins scattered from the once existent and proud city.

Maledream's words disturbed the peace within the group as he spoke to wind up the old preacher:

'That's a nice story Larkham, but to tell the children all that at their age is well, it's just a load of crap. If you ask me, we done this to ourselves, not some cocked up version of a fantasy story. I wonder what their parents would say?'

The old man turned to face him, locking eyes with the young man. His matted grey beard was almost black due to the living conditions, his weary weathered wrinkled face did not look amused.

'Much to learn after his arrogance,' he thought, before replying:

'You just interrupted a very nice moment from your already known prattle! I would clip your ears, but at least you did not disturb my story telling...until the end for once.'

'Yeah, well I get bored with the same stories repeated every so often.'

'Well until you're old enough and far more mature than these children you're not going to hear another story,' Larkham said with a raised eyebrow, while some children covered their mouths to hide their chuckles at Maledream whom seemed caught for words.

'Now children please leave me and my son alone for a moment, go, and play outside,' Larkham said, the children did as they were told.

When they had gone, Maledream uttered:

'Your stories are nothing but old fools tales if you ask me, only things around this place are murderers, rapists, and beggars...that's a known fact by the way.'

'Well I'm glad you have gained the manners not to say such things in front of the children, Maledream. These youngsters do not need to fear the world we all do today, only to be cautious of it from my tales of old,' the spiritual leader said with concern.

'Yes, old man' he replied, turning his back to the Tribal leader.

'I want to know where you went the other day, you've found a few things haven't you?' Larkham quizzed, a concern lying within his voice.

'None of your business, I've been in the city.'

'Well, Maledream, I've heard from here and there that you've brought back some things into the camp. I'm just curious to know what they are exactly?'

'Look its nothing dangerous so nothing to talk about,' Maledream replied, turning to stare at his foster father directly in the eyes.

'I don't mind you going out from the camp but you know how I am against dangerous weapons,' Larkham said, still keeping a calm tone.

'These weapons of destruction only exist in your stories, old man. If you must know, I went off salvaging from the battlefield outside the city, didn't come across anything slightly interesting.'

'Please do not return to that place. I have warned you about it before Maledream,' Larkham said raising his voice a little.

'Look, I went to that forsaken place and saw nothing but rusted metal and bones littering the landscape. I have no idea why you fear that barren wasteland more than this city, it's safer in my opinion,' Maledream brashly replied without fear or consequence in his voice.

'Well it is your own hide at the end of the day, I should be thankful you do not drag anyone else into your stupidity' uttered Larkham after a brief silence, before continuing:

'Just remember who found you and nursed you back to health boy...'

'Oh not this again, enough of the guilt trip crap, old man, before you really piss me off,' Maledream replied with a sigh.

Larkham grinned at him, almost as if he had won the conversation.

'Well just remember that, if you do not have anything to share then...' before Larkham could finish, he watched the rude young man

walk casually past him, his eyes cast down at the dusty marble flooring.

'Don't care, I'm off to forage for more food, and maybe find something else that isn't the slightest bit useful or interesting, you nosey old bastard,' he said, adjusting the large sword underneath his long coat, making sure it was hidden away from the Tribal leaders eyes the best he could.

It was a nice find, and although Larkham could do nothing to stop Maledream from possessing it, he knew it would create more hassle in the end. He gazed at Maledream walking down the steps of the temple, raising his voice on the verge of echoing:

'It's a sword isn't it?' asked the old man.

Maledream almost stopped in his tracks but carried on walking, ignoring his foster father the best he could. Larkham sighed as he watched Maledream leave the temple shaking his head before turning his gaze to the rising sun outside the balcony.

'The boy needs to spread his wings,' he muttered.

Maledream travelled alone from the camp looking briefly at the families getting on with their daily lives. Most of the time it was not a life worth living, fear, and uncertainty always being a factor faced day-to-day such as when was the next meal. He entered the streets that seemed almost calm during the day. At night, it was far more violent, when most people came out who still lived in the city fighting each other under the cover of darkness.

'Life's not changed nor will it,' he thought to himself depressingly, kicking stones across the street as he walked farther into the city as the sun gradually rose above the broken ruins.

'That old fool believes we should all be fine if keep following him, and I don't see anything changing...spirits, psychics, and to top it all off he keeps recounting crap that probably didn't happen,' he moaned, kicking more stones in anger as he walked on grumbling.

He carried on in quick pace at sight-seeing through the near empty streets save for the beggars or refugees dotted about the place. Maledream was kitted out with salvaged and patched up leather, with a couple of rusty blades tucked inside his pockets, along with a handy sword that he had found recently in the "Forbidden Battlefield" of the ancients, the very sword that Larkham had referred to.

Also strapped around his waist was a very old but still working handgun with no ammunition, which Maledream had also salvaged. Warring people all around the city would trade for it. They were considered valuable assets, should you be lucky enough to find some. It was almost a form of currency for a month's worth of rations. A

woman's cry rang out and echoed down the street all of a sudden, halting Maledream in his tread. He keened his ears but could hear nothing. Moments passed by as he stared down different grey pastille streets and wondered if he was hearing things.

'Another murder or rape?' he thought.

He shook his head while sighing, staring at the dirt beneath his boots before again looking up again in surprise. A scream sounded again, the ground rumbled beneath his feet for a moment. His sixth sense triggered, his eyes wandered to the east towards an old ruined building overgrown with vines, a section of its wall crumbling into an adjacent river with a fierce crash.

Maledream at first began to walk slowly out of curiosity towards the building where the screams were coming from. Again, the blood-curdling scream sounded, he heard the woman shrieking and screaming repeatedly. His eyes watched beggars running away from the scene.

'What's wrong?' shouted Maledream to the beggars running away while covering their faces with clothing or not turning around to face Maledream as if their lives were in peril.

No answer was given as all went silent, but it's the most Maledream expected from the city people.

'Always the same,' Maledream moaned in anger.

Not a soul helped another, and the screaming was unbearable to his ears. He had to investigate. Stopping at the blocked entrance, he started to climb and scaled the walls to get some height.

'The scream is coming from in here, I wonder if the screams are because of the building falling onto some one?' he thought.

The screams then stopped. A chill raced down his back and his eyes widened as he secured his footing to stay quiet.

Something very evil was just beyond the wall on the other side and he could feel it with a fierce chill running down his spine. Looking to his right, he noticed a small window he could creep through so he went for it. Screaming once again echoed inside.

'Not liking this one bit,' he muttered to himself as he scrambled inside the window, which led out to a small balcony area overlooking the scene below inside the ruined building. He emerged while crouching noticing that the entire inside of the building was taken over by rich, slimy smelling vegetation that was lit up by the rays of the sun through the broken side windows. Almost losing his grip, he froze once again.

Peeking above the railing, Maledream gawped upon a huge looking beast with scales of every colour, vicious fangs, and spikes all along the forehead and down the creature's spine. In place of

fingernails, the large beast seemed to have large razor sharp claws, further adding to its terrifying large form. Standing a clear nine feet tall, the beast was trying to reach for the screaming girl hidden somewhere under some rubble.

He surveyed the area further seeing fresh corpses had been disembowelled, wearing the remains of garments and armour the likes of which he had never seen inside the city. Were they travellers? Rich traders? It was hard to tell how many people had tried to help the girl but it seems the humanoid lizard had made short work of them. His vision rolled back to the beast as it used its brute strength to move one huge stone after another.

The creature stopped with a groaning, croaking sound as it looked around as if it had heard something else. Maledream trembled and was frozen solid, he did not even attempt to move. Once again, the young woman screamed in terror, and so the reptile being turned again at the last pile of rubble.

'*Larszarish Zandrishth,*' Maledream heard in a strange a voice, it almost sounded like it came from the reptile being, only the beast had not opened its mouth. It almost broke through to the girl, its thick bony spikes on its back erecting as if it could not wait to devour the poor woman after slaughtering her like some wild pig.

Instinct took over and, before he knew it, Maledream's adrenaline was running faster than his legs as he slid down the slippery banister aiming to somehow help the girl.

Upon landing Maledream reached for the hilt of the blade he had found and clasped it firmly as he stared directly at the large creature with a terrified look. Standing still for a moment the beast turned its attention to him whipping its large tail threateningly, strike the ground with a heavy smack that sent dust pluming into the rays of the sun.

'**Help!**' the woman shouted as he held his weapon ready by his side.

Maledream felt a tightening in his chest and stiffening in his arms and legs, all symptoms he knew of a fear that was liable to make him useless to the hapless target of the beast. He tried to reassure her but his words came out weak.

'Don't worry...'

The reptile launched himself at the would-be warrior, shouting something that sounded like a laugh or a cackle. Locking gaze with the beast's large black eyes was like a reminder of an Ice Age that had never ended, its cold stare penetrating his soul. For a moment, he felt like he should die, the feeling was horrible and his muscles locked.

'Why didn't I turn back? Why didn't I just stay with the others and ignore my stomach,' he thought.

It was finally upon him and, with a mighty swing hit him directly on his chest with a quick powerful swipe of its hand, sending him flying a great distance through the air landing in a nearby large pool of murky water with a loud thud.

Maledream coughed, spitting blood from his mouth as he gripped on to the sword with one hand while clutching his chest with the other as sharp pains inside winded him further. The creature screamed, its eyes glowing red with unearthly energy as it gathered a fevered rage.

'I'm done if it hits me again, I might as well have served myself without a fight,' he thought, raising his blade off the floor scraping it across the shallow water. He breathed heavily in pain for a moment and then stared at the beast. Maledream strengthened his resolve for a moment to gain the courage within him.

'I'll give you a fight,' Maledream screamed at the top of his lungs to accept this screaming creature's challenge as he steadily stood himself upright, adrenaline and shock lessening the pain that seared through his nerves.

He ran with the blade ready to swing up. The beast closed onto him, Maledream swung. Sword and talons clashed against each other, echoing loudly within the large building.

'Whatever I do keep moving, it's slower than I am,' he thought as he darted in and out of the giant's huge powerful blows that threatened to disembowel the young man in one swipe.

It was much harder to do in practice as the Tribal ducked and weaved the best he could, scraping the heavy sword around as the strength within him was quickly subsiding. Breath was harder to catch with every swing, the sword weighed a ton for someone unused to heavy labouring. Despite this, several swipes of the blade caught the monster, Maledream almost feeling like a little progress was being made as he dodged another deadly slash from the beast.

Nothing could seem to cut this monster, however his sword was useless against its scaly hide as it rang out metallic hymns. Finally, the lizard caught him with another sharp blow to the ribs with its hard bony fist. Maledream went flying through the nearby stairway banister breaking his bones on the old stone. As he lay there, he knew he should try to get up, but he was losing consciousness from the pain, his eyes going darker, the dust shimmering against the light.

Loud strange laughter erupted from the being, its odd beak shaped yet almost human looking face snarling fiercely, many ancient wrinkles rippling down its scaly body from the neck down. The sound refocused Maledream causing his eyes to open and to stare into the beasts crazed eyes. A spasm of coughing took hold and he felt himself begin to sink back into unconsciousness, but then, just as his strength began to fade, he saw an image of Larkham's caring face before him. He closed his eyes for a moment and sighing with the pain that wracked him thought deeply for a moment.

'Sorry old man, you won't be seeing me again. Sorry for being a bastard all the time,' he regretted.

Maledream opened his eyes to see the image change into the beast that was stumbling over rocks and rubble towards him. It seemed all hope had been lost. He closed his eyes taking a last deep breath.

'Sorry stranger,' he thought, closing his eyes once more as the beast was upon him.

'Elin'shana dookilla shuen allina canshanna doom!'

A soothing voice appeared from somewhere causing Maledream's ears to twitch slightly out of his control. Waves of light as bright as the sun washed over him, the pain in his ribs disappearing almost as fast as it was created. His eyes fluttered and flicked open rapidly. Miraculously his wounds were gone within moments.

'What the hell just happened?'

With no time to waste he jumped onto his feet and over the banister to get away from the closing mountain of muscle that broke the wall he crashed into further to where he had been sitting moments ago, missing him narrowly with a swipe of talons as he jumped.

Landing on his feet, he turned to see the girl was out of the hiding place, with a raised right hand pointed at Maledream and carrying what looked like a strange wooden staff. Her green and purple robes were unfamiliar to him and in a dusty state.

'What the hell are you doing? **Run for...**' Maledream said, trying to catch his breath as the words barely escaping his throat.

The red haired green-eyed girl had a very pale worn expression on her face, more than usual for her kind.

She had a look in her eye that was somehow different. Spinning round Maledream deflected a very close blow to his face with his blade, and he was aware in that moment that the sword had changed. Now it was emitting a faint multicoloured glow but Maledream had no time to

examine it as the beast once again swung its mighty claws at his throat. His reactions quickened, the beast's swings almost appearing slower than normal.

Not only that but also his palms that held the blade felt strange, almost warm but also cold. It calmed Maledream down in some strange way. The Tribal ducked another swing from the beast, then swinging his blade with a counter strike, he hit the creature in its kneecap. With a howl of rage and anger, the beast span around punching Maledream with a great force sending him sprawling across the floor for many yards.

His patched leather armour absorbing some impact, the sword smashing and scraping into the ancient marble flooring of the building as he refused to let go of the blade, he coughed again as the punch almost smashed his ribcage for a second time round winding him yet again.

'Elin'shana dookilla shuen allina canshanna doom!'

Again the voice appeared, this time behind him as he regained his senses quickly. It was the girl, only this time the sword reacted a lot more strongly, the multicoloured glow turning into many bright lights that sprang up the blade as if it was a flame shimmering up its broad surface like waves on a shore.

'What's going on?' he thought, as he watched the hypnotic colours race up his long sword, letters appearing gradually as if the path of a moving flame darted across his eyes.

This seemed to stun the reptile shortly as it glared with blankness, and barely able to stand on both legs as blood poured from its wound.

It was long enough for Maledream to jump to his feet. Panting heavily he had a feeling this was his only chance to kill it or be killed, he arched his sword below the waist, and with all his strength he had left he sprinted forward holding his breath.

In the background, the repeated chanting seemed to build up his momentum, and increase the blade's power sending strength to his palms.

'Elin'shana dookilla shuen allina canshanna doom!'

Bringing his sword around and up in an arc, he thrust it into the shiny, unprotected belly of the reptile, helped by the momentum of the voice behind him. Small sparks flew, and for a moment, it felt as if the blade would hesitate to dent the creature.

The world stood still to Maledream. All went quiet in his head and the world around him. An explosion that sounded like thunder signalled the final blow, a bright light filling the ancient library for but a moment. Landing on his knees from the momentum that he threw himself, he stared at the large sword in his hands.

The hilt remained cool yet the blade sizzled with heat. Maledream slumped onto his ass catching his breath and closing his eyes as the last of the adrenaline pumped its way around his veins that caused him to visibly shake. On opening his eyes, he saw the beast toppled, split into two halves that squirmed from time to time as its dark red blood mixed with the puddles of water on the floor. Nearby, the girl lay in an unconscious state.

'Now I really do need to see that wise old man. I should have died,' he said, as he got to his feet, clutching at where his once mortal wounds that should have snuffed his life. Maledream stared at the large, bulbous, horned head of the beast, noticing that its eyes were staring straight at him creeping him out.

Raising the sword with both hands and lowering it harshly several times, he severed the head from the body just to be sure of the kill, blood spattering from each strike across the naked surface of the blade.

Its muscle was taut and its scales thick but eventually the neck gave way to the hot sharp sword that still sizzled in the surrounding air. He picked up the head by one of its horns with one hand, but did not stare again at the eyes.

'No one is going to believe this at all...except the old man,' thought Maledream, his eyes scanned for the young women to see she lay in an unconscious heap but seemed to be in no harm.

First Maledream wrapped the skull with some spare cloth and rags he had on him, securing it to his back after much frustration with trying to get it into a comfortable position.

'Now for the girl,' he thought. Walking up to the stranger whilst also adjusting his sword, he picked her up, slung her over his shoulder, and began to climb out of the ruined flooded building. Outside, he wiped the sweat from his forehead trying to understand what had happened.

Much he figured, would be explained in due time, he wondered all the same.

'Just who are you? And what was that?' he muttered.

Chapter Two

Nightmare...

'Vision without action is a daydream.

Action without vision is a Nightmare.'

Japanese proverb

Evening arrived within the Tribal camp as the sun set with blood red skies, the camp was getting ready for another cold night by lighting small fires dotted about the place. Much talk about Maledream and the new female visitor with red hair flared imaginations. Rumours and emotions were fired up about the strange serpent creature that Maledream said he had slain with a blade to rescue the young woman. Hours passed with nothing but the campfires for light sources as people gathered round them in circles gossiping about the visitor, and the serpent's head that had been rumoured Maledream carried with him.

People approached the fires holding out hands thick with dirt or dust, tipped with finger nails as dark as the abyss towards the warm orange rays of the burning wood that spat and hissed from time to time during the quiet moments of conversation. High above them and perched in darkness save for the faint moonlight was Maledream watching his people below in the camp conversing with one another. Occasionally the stink of burning wood would waft its way to his nostrils.

The only way for him to truly believe it was to show others so he could believe it. It was a strange feeling for him, something he did not expect to find in the early hours of the morning as the sun had risen on what seemed just another dull day. His mind cast itself back to the fight, a fight that seemed almost hopeless and should not have turned out like the way it did.

Averting and adjusting his eyes to the shadows, he stared at the serpent's head that he had unwrapped. It almost seemed like the worst nightmare come true for not just Maledream but for the other Tribals as well.

He thought about the red haired girl he had rescued, why, he wondered, had he leapt in to save her instead of running away, still there was something about her that reminded him of someone from long ago and it bugged his mind.

The girl's strange ability to heal his wounds that were certain to kill him made him think deeply. Strange uttered words seemed to trigger off the blade's secret power that he would never have known.

Strange colours and symbols had appeared across the entire blade. Magic such as this was the stuff of fantasy that lurked within Larkham's many tales. Guns were good weapons and far more effective at close quarters than a weapon such as a sword, so why was it made? What was its purpose? He had the faintest ideas circulating in his mind but could not come up with a positive answer.

He decided he would ask the girl how to achieve such effects, the likes of which he had never seen or known. Maybe it was something he could learn himself? Larkham had been with the girl since he had brought her to the Tribal camp. Maledream was certain Larkham could help her in some way just as he had always done with the sick of the camp with his healing ways. Why she fell unconscious, he would not know until Larkham gave some answers.

'People need someone to look up to in these dark times. I'm not the one they are looking for but I may as well pose,' he muttered, staring even more into the black eyes of the serpent creature's head as if talking to it.

He figured it would not hurt in the camp to explain the tale of fighting this creature, while showing them the sword and head.

After all, the Tribals were settled down by the fires and in one place. He got up from his perched position grabbing the head by one of its bony spikes. Adjusting the sword in his shabby scabbard, he made his way down the camp to act out as a hero.

It gave him a sense of purpose and for once, that made him feel something strangely optimistic rather than his usual pessimistic self.

Larkham sat in darkness with his eyes closed meditating as the girl stirred slowly in her sleep. Words escaped her lips from time to time until she finally stirred from her slumber.

'Who are you...you saved me stranger,' the girl muttered quietly to herself before taking in a deep breath and releasing a sigh as she slowly opened her eyes.

She took a while to check her surroundings as she sat up. Comfortable bedding was surely beneath her and it looked as if she was inside a tent of some sort, crafted out of old clothes and animal furs.

There was a smell of damp but otherwise it seemed a comfortable place to be. A poorly lit candle lit the area in front of her on the floor, slightly waving from the draft of cold autumn air coming in. The flap of the tent was slightly open and she could see night had fallen. Out of the darkness in one corner of the tent came a voice replying to her mumble.

'That young boy is also a lot of trouble here at our small refuge, young lady!'

She shrieked, clutching a blanket closer to her chest in surprise.

'Who are you!?' she asked.

A laugh that could only come from an old man replied:

'You are safe here, little lady.'

'Old pervert! Reveal yourself!' she exclaimed.

Surely enough out of the shadowy corner of the tent the spiritual leader Larkham appeared.

'Now, now, I did not mean to offend you, young lady,' he said softly reaching his hand out slowly and grasping hers softly.

'Naturally we have all been worried about you here in our camp. You have been out cold since Maledream found you, and rescued you from the "Beast" that he mentioned.'

Finally relaxing, after seeing no harm in the old man's loving eyes and the soft warm grasp of hands, she weakly smiled.

'Yes he did and I'm so very grateful. I have been on a very long journey from the West, with some friends...only to find everyone else's life and mine in danger after our long journey. We were looking for physical evidence of the old world such as books, scrolls, and anything else of value.'

'I see...well you have a lot to explain to me, young lady, if you will. Seeking such objects in a bleak destroyed land could only mean that you actually come from a place I have only dreamed about in visions...about the fight which my adopted son was caught up in, and what happened to your friends, please tell me you name dear child of spirit.'

'Angelite Rose,' she replied.

'What a pretty name, I am Larkham,' he smiled.

'So please tell me Angelite,' he continued:

'What happened?'

She felt apprehensive at answering having only just woken up, her last memories were of that young man with the strange sword.

She looked into Larkham's eyes wondering if he had a hidden motive, but then began to relax as intuition began to put her at ease.

'I have come to this part of the world for knowledge only hidden within books. I found an old ruined library within the city that I am guessing we are close to?' she asked.

'Yes, we are on the outskirts of this city. Maledream left this morning to get food from that city when he came across you.'

Angelite continued:

'I was with several others and we came across from the sea...it has been a long travel of around several weeks, close to a moon's cycle since we left my home city, Meridia...'

She was to continue but the old man coughed abruptly.

Angelite paused in her speech as she focused on Larkham, seeing him tap his chest slightly before replying.

'Meridia you say?'

'Yes?'

'So the spirits are right about this city...' he uttered looking down at the floor, one arm crossing to his opposite elbow while his other hand supported and stroked his bearded chin.

'Spirits have told you?' asked Angelite.

'Yes my dear, I am a man that has the gift of speech with the spirits. I lead my Tribals the best I can through divining the ether,' the old man replied with a brief smile.

'I see, there are quite a few of your kind within Meridia that have that gift, wise man,' Angelite replied, sitting up slightly from her bed, her hands clasping the old blankets tightly as her eyes widened.

'It is a very hard gift to use my dear but from the travels and through the cycles of years it has become easier, and it is within my dreams that they speak to me most, showing me images of a glistening city, a salvation waiting for the people I look after. It is a nice dream, and I simply find it unbelievable that someone from this city is actually here within my camp, yet from your garb I cannot question it for the answer lies in front of me,' Larkham said, his voice almost trembling.

'It is very much real, Larkham, I am part of an order called the Order of Spirit. It was an idea of mine to travel to some part of the ancient world, for you see I am a descendent from this city, from survivors over a hundred and fifty years ago that settled within its walls.'

'Very interesting young Angelite, so you are here as part of your Order to investigate the Dark Age lands?'

'Yes this is the first time I have set foot from the safety of Meridia's walls and ocean that surrounds my city. We landed far to the south and our objective was to collect anything of interest as we headed to the North to rendezvous with a port after our long travel. I

wish I had not for my friends that accompanied me were slaughtered by the beast within that old library.'

Tears swelled in her eyes. Larkham got up and walked towards Angelite, sitting on the edge of her bed to cuddle her for comfort. Long timeless moments passed as she cursed herself, the tears running into Larkham's sleeves.

'It's okay, miss Angelite,' he said, gently cradling her from side to side for a short time as she cried her heart out.

'I have known nothing like it...why did I leave my home.'

Half a candle burned away as she let out her pain since this morning. The suffering and the fear that she had experienced was like nothing else.

'Sorry,' Angelite sniffed.

'That is quite all right dear, I must confess it is hard to lose loved ones. It is quite commonplace in these lands, by nature, beasts or even us humans,' he replied.

'Thank you, wise man,' she murmured back.

'Sorry I should gather myself...thank you for taking care of me. I used a lot of my energy saving that young man from some nasty wounds. I could have done the same for my friends but that Anunaki beast crashed half the library down before I had any time to react,' Angelite continued.

'And within moments after the horrific screaming and...and...' she sniffed further, trying to hold in the tears and she hugged the old man tightly.

'The suffering my friends went through as I struggled underneath the rubble, stuck underneath them in almost total darkness save for a small hole that I screamed through at the top of my lungs. I screamed and screamed in horror as the beast started moving the giant stones with incredible strength. I felt scared, fear surrounding me running in all directions...' Angelite paused to catch her breath, using her hands to wipe away the tears off her cheeks.

'I thought I was about to go to the spirit world when the serpent was almost upon me, with only a couple more stones left to move. It was then I caught sight of a young man at the top of the library staring down. I screamed again. I watched him slide down a banister with such grace, landing on his feet at the bottom of the stairway saying "Don't worry"...it made my heart melt, and made me feel an inner calm with just those two words.'

Angelite sniffed, pausing again to catch her breath for a moment.

'I see...I wouldn't have expected Maledream to jump straight into the fray like that, as he often plays it safe and never seems to care, but I

think we both know differently,' replied Larkham with a smile, proud of his foster son acting with such bravery against all odds at such an ancient menace.

'Her voice must have struck a chord within Maledream sparking something deep inside his soul,' thought Larkham.

'Soon enough I managed to escape, and I was able to work my healing abilities on him. It was then that I felt another presence amongst us.'

'What was this new presence?' Larkham interrupted

'It was an old soul in our presence. You may not believe it, but I believe it came from his blade, it was resonating to my speech and the energy that I was focusing into brave Maledream,' she answered.

'I knew Maledream was keeping a secret from me, funny how a sword first came into my mind when I asked him about it this morning. This is the first time I've heard such a thing mind you, I know many tales, but never before have I heard of such a weapon,' he said raising his eyebrows over the thought.

'He used the sword well...it's as if he knew how to strike with it but at the same time I could see he was dumbstruck at what he was holding,' she continued, her mind trying to find an answer as her eyes hovered over nearby candles. Her hand lightly stroked her long hair behind her shoulders.

'I have not heard of such a thing before either...as I was saying before, this weapon glowed, many ancient runes and glyphs appearing on the side and before I knew it I fell unconscious as a bright blasting wave of energy exploded from the weapon...and now I am here,' Angelite finished.

'Sounds like quite a tale young lady...' Larkham replied, his eyes moving steadily to the rugged flooring.

'Where is this young man?' asked Angelite, watching the old man's eyes move to the earth.

'Perhaps he knows something else?'

'Perhaps, dear Angelite, perhaps, just as long as you're sure you have had sufficient rest to get up out of this bed,' Larkham smiled, slowly retreating off the bed and to the shadowy corner of the tent to pick up his wooden rickety staff.

His eyes gazed back into Angelite's for a moment.

'Well my dear, you get yourself sorted and we shall go find him.'

'Yes, let's go find him,' Angelite replied with a smile, her eyes slightly stinging from her tears.

Meanwhile within the camp Maledream was recounting his story to a large group of fellow Tribals that had just returned to the camp after foraging for food. They were eager to hear his story after a long trip.

'So, Maledream, what's this going around the camp that you've slain one of those terrible ancient creatures that Larkham talks about?' asked one of the Tribals, a tone of disbelief filling the air.

Many chuckled, they knew what Maledream was like, some had even branded him a thief and a coward.

'See for yourself,' Maledream replied, tossing the wrapped up head onto the floor. Roll by roll the head unravelled itself as it ended up at the feet of the Tribal who had asked the question. Many people gawped as they looked at the evil horned head.

'Get that cursed thing away from me!' one man shrieked, jumping back and walking away from it, almost tripping up over some wire and tent pegs as he stumbled.

Many other Tribals shared the same view and got up from their comfortable resting places, moving quickly away from its presence, but yet unable to take their eyes off it in amazement.

'I took it down with my blade,' Maledream continued, drawing his blade from the shoddy handmade scabbard.

'How on earth did you do it?' asked one and then another staring at the sword and at Maledream's frail size, many guesstimating the size of the creature by the sheer volume of the head.

He stood there for a moment not answering and only giving a small smile as he looked around those that had gathered. It was not every day that a creature from a story told by a teacher was actually the real deal.

'I defeated it, but it was a narrow victory,' Maledream said, the commotion quieting down as he spoke.

It was not like him to say anything, especially without being rude to others. He seemed sincere and people began to listen to him as he told the Tribals of the encounter.

'Were it not for the stranger and her strange abilities I would not be alive now,' he added.

'So why isn't your sword glowing now? For all we know you could have found this head lying around.'

Disbelief in the malnourished man and his ability to kill anything set in, all knew him, and were not inclined to believe him.

He decided not to argue, he had not the energy for it or to prove it. So many questions were being asked and put forward to Maledream it began to confuse him.

'Give Maledream a break,' another said, as the whole camp seemed to side with or against his account of the story.

'Either way I don't care what you all think,' Maledream said.

'Well what a surprise,' another voice said from the crowd.

The young Tribal man laughed for a moment, perhaps, he thought, he should start being nice if it would make people believe him.

'Right well I've shown you this head, and now you can all *keep* it,' Maledream finished.

The small crowd became quiet as they watched Maledream stick his blade back into its scabbard, and walked away from the light of the fire and back towards the small ruined temple. A silence fell again as the Tribals chatted quietly, many moving their tents and other sleeping apparatus away from the hewn head. His feet ached along with his arms and back, it had been a long day and even though the Tribals did or did not believe him, it did not matter to him. He had proven something to himself, opening his mind to what Larkham had been saying all this time.

'Perhaps all he says is true,' he muttered.

Staring into the night sky his eyes were transfixed by all the stars from the far away dark blue heaven above. The wind was calm tonight, and the moon appeared brighter than normal as sparse silver clouds drifted gently across the dark blue aura of the night.

'My tribe needs a person they can look up to,' he thought.

'I still can't believe what happened earlier today...who is she? What is she doing here? What the hell is she? I hope old man Larkham finds something out from that girl, but still, so much happened it went by so quick I didn't have enough time to take it all in.'

Maledream's thoughts vanished as he continued staring at the night sky.

Several hours passed and the people below in the Tribals camp had settled down for the night and were sleeping another night away in dreamland. He knew something had changed within him, had felt his spirit shifting from his usual stubborn stance to a new awareness. He had always believed he was there by fluke and nothing more, yet that voice had shaken him.

'Elin'shana dookilla shuen Allina Canshanna Doom.'

What did it mean? Why had his sword glowed with unearthly energies in the same way as the old man's walking stick during his meditations? What did it all mean? It is just a load of crap, surely?

Sniffing the air and stretching out his arms and legs, he continued to stare at the stars. Something was up, and he knew he would have little rest until he found some answers.

'Thought you'd be here my son,' a familiar voice came from behind.

Startled by the sound of a voice in the quiet of the night, Maledream turned to see Larkham had arrived with the extremely attractive young woman that he had rescued.

'Thought I'd never see you again old bugger...so what's the news?' he replied.

'Well, Maledream, we have a lot to discuss but I'll let Angelite begin as you can never keep your eyes open for more than two moments if I speak!'

'That's true old man,' the young Tribal replied with a chuckle as he continued.

'Well okay, it's nice to meet you...Angelite?' he said, thinking back to the time he seen her beauty in the daylight as he carried her away from the fight.

Angelite replied with a sweet tone and a smile.

'Yes very nice to meet you, young *warrior.*'

She caught him off guard.

'Warrior?' he scoffed.

'I do believe that you have the wrong man. I was just in the right place at the right moment,' he said.

'We have all night but I shall try and explain why I'm here and a lot more about what happened fighting that large being...'

Maledream's eyes squinted and a slight frown appeared on one eyebrow adding further to his confused look

'All right...well I'm guessing you will explain a lot of the questions I've been asking myself for the entire night, like for example telling me more about the reptile being. I always thought they were just something the old man made up,' Maledream finished, whilst Larkham just smiled at him.

Angelite glanced at the moon before returning her gaze back to Maledream. Suddenly, he seemed so young and vulnerable.

'Yes, Maledream, they are creatures which have always existed. They are here to prey upon the human beings left after the Great Catastrophe, which my sources say is just over one hundred and fifty cycles of the sun ago, but apparently they were thought of as a myth or legend to the people living in that moment...which we are still reeling from today.'

'Just as I have been telling you in my stories of old,' added Larkham, his voice uttering a deep concern.

Maledream put the information into his mind for the first time and re-accounted the stories of the old wise spiritual leader for a

moment.

'*Now I can't say they don't exist,*' he thought.

'So I shall continue,' she said.

'Since the arrival of the Dark Age, that destroyed our old but cultivated world and since nature has taken back what is hers, human beings have had a very special gift unlocked from within them. We still do not know how this happened. Excavations of 'Technology' from the past showed much intellect, but lacked our use of the powers that we have now such as Resonance or Magic.'

'Your beginning to lose me,' said Maledream, raising one eyebrow towards her.

Angelite lifted her right hand up and pointed it towards the night sky, while her left hand took out her staff from within her robes that was adorned with many symbols and strange looking runes carved out of the fine pure oak. Atop of this staff was a crystal containing strange symbols.

'I know you may not yet understand, but that comes in time. Now witness this gift,' she said, before walking a small distance into a circular clearing usually used by the old man to preach his traditions.

Still holding her right hand skywards, she turned around. All was silent for a few moments before she lowered her hand while outstretching the other smoothly and almost hypnotically. The staff's symbols began to light themselves up as if she was controlling them.

'Innanania triatus, sooulish contempas inan hispostitius,'

Angelite chanted, her eyes glowing a strange white that then changed to a soft purple. Maledream could hardly believe his own eyes and tried to doubt what he was watching but knew it to be true. Larkham watched and did not think much of it. To the old man it was nice to know that another human lived along with many others practising this discipline in their city.

Deciding it was best to ask questions later, Maledream stayed silent in awe of her craft and beauty. With more chanting from her lips, the floor around her lit in a bright radius around her feet with a golden aura with similar patterns snaking around various areas of the radius like a template similar to the letters on her staff covering the floor in an ethereal light.

Angelite finished with the words:

'Illafimia Denetus Shantanna Quialataluis Natu-aouri.'

Upon completion of the verse, a sudden burst of green energy erupted from the crystal on the staff like a green flame. Her long red hair flowing behind her as if gravity defying, the energy transformed into form and created a green bubble surrounding her much like a shield of energy, while the gold ethereal flooring seemed to become more solid.

The ruined temple balcony was moderately lit, as if three or four sources of moonlight were centred into the circle radiating outwards and touching much of the inside of the building.

'This is the power within us,' said Angelite in a husky voice.

'I can teach you how to find your energy, Maledream, and I can also show you a place that is being rebuilt as we speak by our kind where we specialise in such energy work...a place you may know as Meridia. Will you come with me?'

Angelite closed and opened her eyes slowly, enjoying the energy that she seemed to hold together with pure willpower. For the first time in many moons, the young Tribal was speechless.

'Yes he will come with you. It is far too dangerous in these parts for a young lady to travel by herself!' said the old man firmly.

'I can make my own mind up,' said Maledream.

'It will be a full moon's journey away and most of it will be travelling by ocean, but it will lead on to much more knowledge and enlightenment within the world we are living now. There are many new animals or creatures for you to see...well those that are left and those that are new along with other surprises for you,' she said smiling.

Her sweet voice was in sharp contrast to the power behind the energy that she released. Green and golden auras of power arched out like a rose or birds stretching their wings, unfolding in shape and fading away like a candle to the wind as it disintegrated in the soft blowing breeze of the chilled autumn air.

Short moments later the native plants around her grew in an instant to become lush plants and blooming flowers grew all around the three through the cracks within the building, much like Maledream had seen in the old library where he had fought that creature, except far more pleasant in smell. Her hair caught gravity again and falling strand by strand to the force, while lowering her staff to the floor and waving her palm over the crystal as if wiping it clean, once again shutting, and opening her eyes slowly. Within a quick rush, the energy stored in the symbols in the staff dispersed into the floor, whilst sweet smells of lavender filled the air captivating both Maledream and Larkham's senses.

'Anything else you would like to know?' she asked.

Maledream could hardly decide where to begin, there was so much that he wanted to know.

'Were you responsible for the strength that entered my sword? How did you heal my wounds? What were you doing in that old broken building underneath rocks with that lizard trying to kill you?'

'Hold yourself! Let me try to answer. I will begin with the sword. That sword you wield Maledream is an artefact of great power. It has crafted on it runes that can react to certain words, or energies, such as were displayed in the temple where you killed the beast. I can see it glowing even now. It has its own Aura, or rather a life of its own, and can be activated to such an extent that you can see it in this dimension, similar weapons are crafted back at my home, just not to your swords extent mind you! Where did you find it? It's strange to see such an object here.'

Maledream looked at his blade, now looking so ordinary, and answered her question knowing that Larkham would be annoyed that he had ignored his warnings.

'I found the sword in the ancient battlefield,' he confessed.

'Against my words of warning, It was only this morning I warned you again about that place,' Larkham's voice interrupted.

'Oh well I'm still here...and what else could I use to bargain fresh food with inside the city? All the gangs' trade weapons for food,' the young Tribal man sighed.

'That's not the point Maledream,' the old leader grunted.

'Angelite, please continue for both of us,' Maledream replied, ignoring Larkham before he himself started one of his rude speeches.

Angelite smiled at the two.

'To answer your other questions, as I said to Larkham, we travelled from the South in search of objects of interest such as books or scrolls.'

'So, "we travelled," are you referring those people I had seen were your companions?' Maledream asked, before realising what he said as he looked into Angelite's saddened eyes.

'He had to ask, the poor lady is close to breaking again,' Larkham thought with a worried expression setting on his face.

'Yes, they were travelling with me and were also from where I hail from,' Angelite answered, bravely pushing her feelings deep down.

'We carried on northwards till we reached this city in the day and had discovered what we were looking for. Then it all broke loose.'

'It's ok, I know,' he said, watching Larkham walk over to place a hand on her shoulder for a moment for comfort.

'So yes, we were going to keep travelling north to a port we were to rendezvous at.'

'I see, and this strange beast?' Maledream asked not knowing if the question would upset her further, yet wanting to take her mind off her friends.

'They are called Anunaki,' Angelite answered.

'It's the first time me and my companions had seen something like this, as like you, we only have some records of their existence.'

'Indeed young lady,' replied Larkham.

'It seems even today in the Dark Age lands, all peoples are still under the shadow of these foes of old.'

'You're telling me old man,' replied Maledream.

'I'm still having trouble at believing what has happened this morning, let alone witnessed, I'm glad you're safe though.'

'I am grateful, thank you,' she replied, finding the courage to let out a small smile, he responded in kind.

'There will be more time to explain when we are on foot,' she continued.

'I'll be leaving at dawn, and take the path set through the battlefield that Larkham has spoke of I am afraid. I know I said we have all night but I am feeling rather sleepy after showing you what I did, it drains me greatly,' she said.

'She's lying, she's still upset,' Maledream thought, staring into her glazed eyes.

'I'll accompany you Angelite, so don't worry and get some rest, guess this makes me your personal *warrior,'* Maledream said, hoping the words would perhaps lift her over the night, her reply was simply a warm grin and a nod.

Larkham looked on, nodding his head side to side.

'I wish I could come with you both, but it seems fate would keep me here with the Tribals where I belong, but I would say this to you both. Be careful,' Larkham said, moving to face Maledream square on to place his hands on the young Tribals shoulders.

'I sense that something big is going to awaken within you Maledream but I give you this warning which you must heed, so please choose now to listen to my words. Do not succumb to the temptation that does not belong in your heart, for it will threaten this young lady and everything you would strive for with your choice of freewill. You will have many battles to fight, some for your survival and some for your very soul's existence, but ultimately Maledream listen to your heart as I have said repeatedly. If it were not for the heart, we humans would not have survived this long, the incident this morning proves you have

a big heart and have grown from the small boy I have known to a proper man. You've always been a restless character my son, so go out into the world and find your true path in life, find your meaning and your purpose my boy,' he finished.

Maledream smirked, but did not have it in his heart to make fun of the old man this time. This was getting weird and too serious for his dry sense of humour. Gently, he removed the old man's hands from his shoulders.

'It is time for me to go, for a long time I have wanted to leave and this will give me the reason to go,' he replied, his eyes looking up at the moon for a brief moment before returning his gaze into Angelite's.

'It's as if this has been your call all along, Maledream,' Larkham added.

'I don't know about that,' he said, his head turning to the old wise man.

'All things happen in life for a reason, and I do not for a moment believe in coincidence,' said the old Tribal leader.

'You could be right, Larkham, but I think I'll wait a little longer until I have a final judgement on it. I do want to get out of this place, feels like I should be moving in some way.'

'In time you shall see, Maledream, in time you shall see. I for one believe in it, this fate,' Angelite added.

Maledream turned his eyes to look at the broken cracks in the marble flooring of the old temple.

'Well, we shall see what our trip brings,' Maledream said, staring into her eyes again, they seemed to make him shy away.

'Indeed, my boy,' Larkham replied, smiling at him.

'Right, well, we've had our short rest now. I'm going to grab what I need and what I can carry then we'll set off, after some sleep of course,' said Maledream.

'I'll let them get better acquainted,' Larkham thought.

Larkham nodded and bid farewell to them both before retiring for some sleep down in the camp below. Angelite strode forward to the balcony and looked up into the dark blue abyss and the twinkling formation of the stars.

Maledream accompanied Angelite calmly to the balcony.

'She's beautiful,' he thought, as he stood next to her looking at the night sky himself.

'Beautiful night don't you think?' she asked, as she stared at the stars and then to the city below them from their vantage point.

'Uh, It is,' he replied with a brief sigh before continuing to speak.

'Although I wish sometimes the destroyed city provided something more pleasing to the eye, the people in the ruined city streets far below outside the safety of this temple and hill are best avoided.'

'I know,' she said, as she turned her head looking at him, the new plant life creating pleasing smells to her senses.

'Where I come from is nothing like this place you all live in, disease is all but forgotten along with the dangers that still exist in there Dark Age lands,' she sighed softly as a means of expressing her pain for all those people without the lifestyle she grew up with.

'Well I would love to chat more,' she continued.

'But we shall both save it for the morning, I'm going back to the tent now, if that is okay?'

'Do as you please, you are a free person,' he replied, smiling and looking into her eyes. He wanted to know her better but knew he would have to wait until the morning. She filled him with excitement and intrigue somehow.

Chapter Three

Deeper Understanding...

'All truths are easy to understand once they are discovered,

the point is to discover them.'

Galileo

After showing Angelite back to her tent, he returned to his own tent, resting his blade on the ground, hardly being able to take his eyes off it since the incident earlier in the morning. He could see no visible markings etched on it, nor see anything that Angelite could apparently see on the dull metal.

'I don't get it, she said they exist in other dimensions?' he thought.

'How did she activate it? What is all this "energy" talk? I certainly felt something, more than physical, it felt more spiritual or something.'

An idea struck him. He leant on his knees and holding the blade in both hands began meditating out of curiousness and intuition, following the ways Larkham had taught him in the past. Taking in deep breathes he began picturing a vast ocean while sitting on a cliff near a beach, he filled the empty space with sea gulls flurrying high above him, while watching the waves below him bash the shores.

Storm clouds fast came in from the ocean and began raining down upon him. He loved the rain, it cleansed everything, and every droplet formed an ocean of vastness as he continued to visualise deeper and deeper. Gradually he fell from his physical senses and began to undertake a journey within himself. His concentration broke several times as other thoughts of his invaded his own mind, threatening to end his meditation.

Taking a sudden twist he found himself within his own imagination, his own vision of meditation, standing up within his dream wondering why he was not within his tent and actually within his little world now worried him. He could not open his physical eyes for now he was living in this place seeing through them, breathing the air and feeling the rain.

'Where am I? I'm living in my own dream,' he thought.

The clouds grew darker. Lightning appeared in the distance, followed by a swift crack of thunder rolling its fury across the sky. Rain hit him hard in the face, as his eyes gazed and wondered upon the unnatural sight before him. Loudly cracking behind him was a booming sound he was not familiar with. He turned around and wandered up the grassy perch from where he was sitting on the cliff.

Climbing over the muddy ridge in the now hard beating rain with wind as sharp as ice, he saw thousands upon thousands of human soldiers brandishing weapons of great power, and thundering war machines marching on for as far as the eye can see.

'Boom, boom, boom,' sounded the mighty machines, lighting the dark clouds with a great flare. Maledream's eyes following their tracer fire through the sky like shooting stars, to meet great towering Behemoths, much larger than the war machines the humans were using. The shells crunched into the few giant transparent insect creatures with little or no affect.

'What the hell is this?' he thought.

Death surrounded Maledream's senses all of a sudden, as he watched in horror as a Behemoth strode forward on its giant tentacle like appendages.

'Thump, thump, thump,' shaking the ground violently with its momentum before finally scooping handfuls of soldiers up in its mandibles, tentacles and claws ripping them asunder in nearly no time at all. Falling to his knees, and wide eyed he started to realise what he was seeing.

Just as in Larkham's tales, great monstrosities killing every human in sight, and not just one large creature but dozens that could be seen far into the distance on the horizon.

'*This isn't happening, this is my imagination,*' he thought in disbelief.

Looking behind him he witnessed something just as terrifying. Turning out in their ten's, then hundreds, and then thousands, were more of the reptile like creatures he had witnessed himself. They stayed on the beach as if waiting for something. Turning round once more he noticed the bloodshed battlefield was quickly emptying of the entire army of human soldiers, who were retreating away from the thunder of the giants as they smashed into the human war machines like rag dolls ending the thundering of their potent mighty guns.

Seeing what was about to happen, he started running towards the troops waving his arms around like a maniac, suffering from an overdose of adrenaline in the vain hope that they would see him.

However, he could not speak so he could not warn them. As if they were ethereal, they passed through him with no hindrance, leaving Maledream with emotional baggage as if he could feel the soldiers' loss of hope and darkest despairs of peril.

They were all afraid for their lives and did not know what to do next. With every spectre running through him, he staggered back as he recoiled from the emotions while trying to keep his footing while he stood in this confusing battle. Turning his head around in horror as events started to go into moments of slow motion, Maledream watched what the soldiers who died had had to cope with, no hope of life or no hope of living.

Certainly, there was no hope of winning against the impossible odds. As fast as lightning itself the reptile beasts pounced upon the broken men and woman ripping them limb from limb. They tried so desperately to take what they thought was cover and a chance to regroup while the armoured columns tried in vain to defeat the monstrous creatures with their mighty guns.

Soldiers fired their weapons into the horde of scales with seemingly no effect. Nothing but a tide of muscle and fins which seemed to retreat and flow like they were mimicking the sea shore itself on a sunny day, shimmering like rays of light through water, on top of all the blood and entrails from the men and woman who were lucky enough to make it to the beach.

Thunder and lightning flashed before Maledream's eyes with a defining boom. The weather was even harder, the clouds darker.

'*So much evil is being done on both sides, only death is the winner of the mortal,*' he thought, still unable to take his eyes off the massacre before his eyes. Maledream had a cold distinct feeling to turn around to witness the arrival over the hill of a stout looking leader of men.

He did not seem bothered by the death that surrounded them all as he strode forward and onward in metal plating, looking like a human war machine on two legs, shouting orders at the men and woman under his command with a stern bellowing voice. This man definitely looked a lot bigger and stronger than an ordinary human being.

Standing almost nine feet tall he seemed to be as big as the monsters himself towering over the ordinary troops. It caught his eye. Sticking out in this man's right hand was the blade that Maledream had found, except it was in a more pleasant condition. Wide eyed he watched as the giant among men strode forward and charged into the mass of scales and blood. Bursting with energy, the blade hummed to power and with many swipes, the commander cut through the beasts much like the Tribal had done when he had used the sword.

However, while Maledream could only use the blade in both hands, this large human held it in one fist. Maledream watched the giant man charge into the mass of reptiles, the blade turning ethereal as its sharp edges tore easily into the mass of scaly flesh that dared get within its deadly sweeping advances.

Those that got close to the man could not tear into his armour long enough to kill him or drag him down off his feet as the giant man swung and kicked. This man was indeed something that would exist out of myth. Maledream noticed that on the back of the big human's hood were some symbols that shimmered as they were hit by strong winds.

Soldiers roared their last defiant stand, trapped between gigantic beasts, thousands of scales, thousands of brutally torn corpses, and blood of the fallen. Tears began to stream down Maledream's eyes.

'How can there be so much death?'

The feeling of helplessness was overwhelming and he could not wake up from this nightmare.

Another strike of thunder and lightning blinded him for a moment, before turning back to see the brave human warrior being slowly swallowed by the horde of reptiles. One managed to get through to the large human, striking him off his heavy feet and with that, the blade flew high up in the air landing and embedding itself in the wet mud trodden ground.

Giant as he was among men, he was swamped upon in a daring sacrifice, a last stand. For a brief moment, Maledream thought he could hear a word upon the breeze in the madness pass from the man's lips.

The soldiers had all but been decimated, any wounded were eaten alive feverishly. He witnessed the dead or dying experience having their ribcages ripped apart with tooth or claw, eaten away, as if dining like greedy kings at a banquette. For the first time in this meditative state Maledream managed to let out a deafening roar which was followed by another thunderclap.

This seemed to gather the attention of all the beasts for miles around, their red eyes staring coldly at him with the moans of the dying growing smaller. Something told him this was now his own fears staring at him. He sprinted towards the sword, hoping he soon would wake from this nightmare. As he ran, he felt as if he were charging through cold air or water at a fast rate of knots. The sword was so close. Slowly but surely in this slow state Maledream fought with all his heart to keep going, stepping through the dead images of soldiers that lay before and under his feet.

All around him the evil presence he felt grew stronger and all the beasts closed in on him, they seemed however to be moving a lot faster than he could. As he drew closer to the blade, he heard the clouds roar with every footstep he landed, sounding like cracks of anger rolling from the heavens. Disfigured souls of the restless dead began grabbing at his ankles moaning and groaning to save them, while at the same time the reptiles were only several steps behind him.

Closing his eyes, he leapt with arms outstretched.

'Please grab it...'

Slowly, feeling the grip of the handle in his palms, he tightened his fists, the rain pouring down upon his hair, the wind slicing him with its icy touch as he opened his eyes. The angry black sky now rhymed with his heart, within each heartbeat a boom of thunder would sound from the black abyss above. Tearing the blade from the ground, Maledream held the blade up and whispered:

'Wake up,' with his last breath.

'No!' he shouted, as he awakened heavily panting in a cold sweat, his eyes dilated. Looking at the blade, Maledream promptly chucked it aside and crawled from his tent to wretch his bile.

It had freaked him to such an extent that he was tempted to pass out but something inside him made him refuse.

'No, No,' he uttered shaking his head.

For the rest of the night he hardly slept at all, shaking with his hands close against many lit candles, keeping the blade underneath blankets and out of his sight...

Glaring at the morning sun on the balcony, Maledream went over his dream before setting off with Angelite. Looking very pale with a serious look on his face, he thought back to the beach in this forgotten wasteland at the ancient battlefield. This was a place he had visited frequently lately, but only ever near the beach or the outskirts of it when he had been looking for old rusty equipment or weapons. That is where he had stumbled upon the sword, now held in his possession. He went through his inventory carefully, knowing that a long journey would mean travelling as lightly as possible.

Luckily, for him, that is what he normally did anyway.

'So much for getting a good night's sleep,' he thought, as he yawned before stretching his limbs. He had not slept after the nightmare.

'That bloody woman ready yet? It'll be the afternoon by the time we get anywhere,' he thought.

Maledream's knee gave in as he felt something blunt whack into

the back of his leg. He jumped slightly turning his head from the horizon to see Angelite with an attractive cheeky grin on her face.

He guessed that was a good enough reason to forgive her.

'Give it up, it's far too fecking early for that!' he blabbered in jest.

'You seem jumpy today, I thought I'd get your attention. I have been standing behind you for quite a while and you didn't notice!'

'Why, was I meant to?' he replied smiling back.

Crack as she whacked her staff on his ankle. Maledream let out a cry, comically rubbing his legs up and down.

'Good she seems to have calmed down from last night,' he thought.

'Silly man, you'll get more of it if you're just as disrespectful!' she laughed, leaving Maledream shaking his head with a smile on his face.

'So why are you in a good mood today then?' asked Maledream sarcastically.

'That old man gets it up after all these years?' he asked.

'That was uncalled for!' Angelite replied.

'Just thought I'd get even, I don't like getting hit, especially in the mornings.'

'Anyway...' Angelite put her finger on his lips.

'Let's get going then.'

Maledream gave her a nod, slinging his sword to his side and checking he had all his things such as spare hidden daggers, they began their journey.

Larkham watched the two leave with a blank expression on his face as the early rays of the sun beamed on him from the camp as the children approached him for another lesson in the morning.

'Look after each other you two, be careful,' he thought, as he turned to the children that tugged at his robes, smiling at them as if nothing were wrong.

Chatting away, they left the refuge of the Tribals and walked steadily down the hill into the city that was once again absorbed by the shadow of the buildings. They passed plants and other wildlife that had gradually taken over the brick walls. Birds of all varieties, now roosting in the ruins, were singing their songs of autumn mornings as the glow of heat touched their nests. It was very peaceful as the couple walked through the streets avoiding dangerous areas of the blasted city, from mainly the brutes or gangs that wandered the region looking for either loot, food, or any member of the opposite sex. Many human beings succumbed to primal instincts of survival that prevented them thinking with their hearts or considering moral issues.

They were the lost and the damned and did not care what happened as long as they got what they wanted. Along the way,

Maledream told Angelite about his disturbing nightmare that had left him unable to sleep.

'I think that whatever it was, you were definitely experiencing one of the many last battles, and your weapon was there, perhaps it is older than I thought,' Angelite's softly spoken.

'Yep, I think so, although it doesn't look anywhere as good as it did, but the power was released in the same way as it was during the fight with the beast.'

'I expect it just needs to be polished up a bit. After all dreams can be different from now in some ways.'

'I'll leave it how it is I reckon, besides I prefer the old look, doesn't look so valuable,' said Maledream.

'Things of shiny value get nabbed very quickly around here,' he continued, catching a breath of cold air, before adding,

'So how does all this 'magic' work out then? Because from my experience it is just a load of everything mashed in together to make some sort of sense but ends up confusing me.'

'That's a very good question, since from our early records back in Meridia it goes along the lines of energy called Resonance. Look at it how you will. I just view it as a free resonating energy which every living being possesses, and I personally call it the true magic.'

'So you're saying however you view it, people such as Psychics, Magic users, Spiritual healers, is all the same thing, and comes from just one source...this resonating energy?'

'That's right! Resonance, if you look up at the stars at night that is where it comes from.'

'The stars?' he queried further.

'The stars also have to come from somewhere,' she continued.

'Somewhere out there, in this great circle, or spiral of life, there emanates a sound, a Resonance so strong that it creates all the stars and more, above, and below us...do you get the idea? It's like a living heartbeat for all things.'

Maledream was looking into the distance, the conversation getting him deep in thought, but he refocused his attention. He wanted to know more.

'Please carry on, I am listening, even if it doesn't look like it ...so what does this energy look like exactly? From what I have seen so far it's like it comes from nowhere,' said Maledream.

Angelite stopped Maledream gently by holding his shoulder as she looked around for an example.

'You see that small puddle of water just by your feet?'

'Yes what about it?' he replied confused.

'This free energy has been named scientifically as atoms. Atoms are the force of, or carrier, of free energy. Everything you see, even you, are made up of these hollow atoms...so many that it is indeed countless.'

'Okay, so if they are so hollow, why do we even exist?' Maledream asked.

'Let me finish. I'm getting to that!' Angelite replied.

'All right, all right,' Maledream said, with a grin.

'These hollow atoms are locked with certain charges, called electrons, protons, and neutrons. Each charge or atom has the potential of changing itself into something else. Atoms are energy, and energy is never destroyed or disappears, it simply takes on the form of another energy or mass. Most of these "atoms" can change its frequency or energy field and are manipulated with the most basic energy of all...sound.'

'Sound? Let me get this right...so these atoms or energies can be manipulated by sound?' he asked.

'Yes, some sounds you cannot hear, but there are believe it or not many sounds that manipulate the known world and in fact the universe, however they are invisible to our "normal" senses.'

'So what does all this have to do with a puddle?'

Angelite knelt down picking up a dirty pebble, stood up whilst raising her arm above the puddle, and then let go of it, sending the small stone towards the earth gently hitting the centre of the water.

'Ripples?' he said with a raised eyebrow, watching the pebble splash the small puddle.

'Imagine that the puddle is such a round hollow atom and now imagine that those ripples are waves of sound.'

'Oh wow! That's quite clever actually,' he remarked, thinking he had finally grabbed the basic gist of what the priestess has been telling him.

'What these protons, neutrons and electrons do is lock that sound frequency into certain energies or forms, and countless atoms are what make you who you are, and indeed form the universe. The rim of the puddle you could imagine is that "barrier" locking that one puddle or frequency of energy into place. Energy only changes form, it is never destroyed so therefore this one puddle could change its frequency to look like or represent some different form of resonating energy,' she said.

'Sounds complicated, and will probably take me longer to better understand it, but for now I do see what you are talking about,' he said smiling.

Angelite grinned at him.

'I'm glad you do!' she said excitedly clasping her hands together like a satisfied teacher. Maledream continued to look at the puddle but Angelite tugged his shoulder to move on.

'Continuing on what I said, basically the centre of all this Resonance also connects all kinds of life and more together, such as spirits, ghosts or other beings which we can't see with our eyes, unless of course, we encourage the Resonance or energy or magic inside of us. We are connected heart and soul to everything else that exists, even if a person does not know it! That is what I find so fantastic...but still there is so much to understand...I don't hold all the answers.'

Angelite paused for breath and, while holding Maledream's hands, asked him a question:

'Are you sure that you are okay, Maledream?'

He let out a small sigh trying to conceal hidden confused thoughts.

'Man this is deep stuff,' he thought.

'Yes, yes, I'm just thinking about what you are saying...so what is the connection with the strange words you utter, and the runes that light up on your staff or this sword? That has something to do with this resonating stuff doesn't it?' he asked quickly.

Looking at Maledream's sweet looking face, big blue eyes, and rough stubble, she found it hard to answer his question, then realising what she was doing she let go of the Tribals hands, grabbing hold of her staff to leave him slightly bewildered.

'Yes, yes, it does,' she replied softly.

'I am still learning the 'arts' as it were and do not know everything but I do know a great deal from my hard research and from harnessing magic. Basically, Resonance works like this and because everything in existence is a resonating frequency, we can 'tune' into the resonating sound.'

Maledream raised an eyebrow replying:

'You're starting to lose me again, tune into Resonance? You mean like what you did last night with the different colours? Can you tell me more simply, please?'

She laughed loudly. Maledream wondered if there was something floating in the air, as she was acting strangely now, not that it bothered him because he thought she was unusual in the first place. In fact, that was the reason he liked her.

'Ok,' she began, as the pair continued walking:

'For example, a flame has certain energy, magic, or Resonance, however you call it. If you wanted to create a flame, then all you would

have to do, is to become one with that Resonance in order to use the power, magic, energy, that the flame shares. Everything is everything, all as one, am I starting to get you back on track? Remember what I showed you with the puddle? It takes a lot of mental focus to actually achieve this effect. I cannot actually do it without any flames nearby as the strain is too much for me until I improve. Some people are known to have this special ability and are called Pyrokinetics, the ability to summon flames without flame. Oxykinetics can control air as well for example. It is very rare for a person to achieve the desired effects without some sort of medium to work with in between. We call such objects reagents…that is why I use crystals as I believe they hold the key more than anything else, and the runes I use enhance the energy of both the person's mind, body and spirit to help further attune the desired effect that you want.'

'Now I am beginning to understand…still confusing but I think I'm getting the point of how it all works,' replied Maledream, adding:

'Let's keep going as we still have a bridge to cross and that takes forever.'

Angelite giggled and then went silent as the pair continued onwards through the deserted daytime city streets.

The sun was fast approaching above their heads, and bad weather loomed in the background.

'I hope the bastard weather doesn't rain,' he let slip with a slight hint of irritation. 'I'm not in the mood for that kind of weather.'

'Yeah it would be a shame. I am having a nice time on this walk, similar to when I was travelling here. I do feel a lot safer with you beside me.'

She looked at Maledream, who was walking with his hands in his coat pockets looking at the ground. He looked up and their eyes met. Maledream smiled.

'You know what? I can't remember when I've smiled so much.'

'Me neither,' she replied, linking arms with him while Maledream had his hands still in his pockets. They came to the bridge and started their long walk to the other side of the city.

The bridge had been made from steel and now stood rusting, looking crippled in places where it had bent as if large weights had whacked themselves against it. Birds that nested in between the girders flew high above singing their songs in the autumn sun enjoying the last bit of light before the dark clouds drew nearer to the ruined city.

The river that led out to the ocean was glittering in the sunlight, as the ripples of the river carried the flow of marine life within it. Vegetation had taken its roots on the bridge, which seemed to cling to

it from the river below, making it feel less like a bridge, and more like a fallen tree. They gazed on the scene as they walked silently, enjoying the great Mother Nature that surrounded them, the view captured their souls in tranquillity.

Maledream broke the silence:

'Can I ask you something? Why did you and your friends leave the safety of your home? It's so dangerous here, what was the real reason?'

Taking a deep breath, she replied:

'As I said last night, I was here with some friends from my home city. Some were bodyguards. I wanted to learn more about the Dark Age lands and to search for a place in this land, which held, from what I learned, much knowledge that needed to be recovered. Certain books, tomes, and perhaps scrolls or the like, anything that might prove valuable and which would benefit everyone...the truth is...I promised the Council back home that I would find useful artefacts. It was my decision alone,' she said, drawing a quick breath before continuing.

'Unfortunately we were not the only ones in that building and we were unaware of any kind of ancient foes within the ancient library. The battle erupted when the beast attacked from the water severely injuring my guards but, before I could use my abilities to heal them as I did with you, the creature brought half the place down, and luckily, I was just alive by inches under the rubble...by then it was too late to save them.'

Tears crawled down her cheeks, Angelite fought them back by wiping them onto her sleeve and stopped walking.

'It was horrific Maledream, I hate thinking back to their screams...they were good friends...'

'Well, they may not have known the danger involved but they did their best to save you. Yes they died but now they will wander the spirit realm...well that's how Larkham puts it...in a better place than here,' he replied, trying his best to comfort her with his words.

'You're right...may their spirits look after us...cannot help but...'

She sniffed, wiping the tears off her face as she continued:

'I wonder why things do happen. Sometimes I think it could be to help us gain knowledge. Knowledge has always demanded sacrifice, we just have to make sure we do not hunger for it too much, as our ancestors did in the forgotten days. I have found some books but not anything to do with what we have been talking about for most the morning and afternoon. I think I have found someone's journal, but we will have to wait until we get back to my home so my Order can decipher the language and make sense of it.'

A quiet moment fell upon the two. Maledream struggled to pluck up the courage to speak, not knowing what to say to the upset Angelite.

'What else can you tell me about where you're from? You just mentioned an Order?' Maledream's curiosity got the better of him, however, he hoped that taking Angelite's mind off the past would help slightly.

'Yes, I am a sister of the Order of Spirit. We mainly practice energy work and aid in any way we can for the greater good of my home city. We teach those that also wish to learn how to use Resonance or "magic," as I like to term it.'

A faint smile appeared on Angelite's face as she gained some comfort from remembering her homeland and reminding herself of the greater good she wished to achieve for her people.

'Certainly sounds like a good group you have going,' prompted the Tribal.

'Oh yes. We work well together and also link with other groups but you'll find out more when we reach my home,' she said.

'What is this city you keep speaking of? Is it a wall, a temple, or a cardboard box?'

Angelite smiled then giggled through the sniffing.

'No, it is not a cardboard box, you cheeky man. It is a beautiful city that is being rebuilt, even as we speak. It is roughly a full moon's cycle worth of travelling most of which we will be across the sea as I said last night, but all in all, a lot safer than the desolate place you have lived in. Have you been here all of your life?'

Maledream went quiet for a moment upon hearing this question. Half of his life he could not remember because of an incident. All he could remember for the past thirteen or so winter cycles was being raised by Larkham and an old friend that had probably now been killed.

He replied but changed the conversation again:

'Going back to my pointless existence isn't worthwhile,' he thought.

'What about the rest of my people? You say this place is safe, yet all my people are back there.'

His eyebrows creased and a subtle hint of pessimism settled in as he went off topic.

'Calm down silly man, I have already arranged a plan with Larkham,' she said, stroking his face and smiling.

Her red hair caught in the wind for a moment. They both stopped their pace while she gazed into his eyes and spoke into his ear.

'I have a way we can get them there in total safety without having to risk everyone's lives. As there are just two of us, we should be safe going this way as we are less noticeable to the many evil beings that

lurk in the darkness.'

He nodded in agreement.

'Now where were we?' Angelite continued.

'Ah yes, we are going to my home, it is called Meridia.'

'Not a bad name at all, I recall you mentioning it last night. We Tribals call it by other names though, like safe haven or sanctuary, well the other Tribals did, before now I didn't believe any of it.'

'You're making it sound like I've rocked that little world of yours,' Angelite softly teased. Maledream grinned.

'You could say that,' he jested, before continuing.

'We're almost on the other side now,' Maledream spoke, as if he could not wait to get off the windy death trap, no matter how beautiful the view might be.

Walking down the last segment of the bridge, the two sat down for a short moment to get their breath back from such a long trek.

'You know what...' said Maledream, once he had rested for a moment.

'You have taught me a lot, and the day is not over yet. I take it I will be learning more about this stuff? It's never fascinated me until now, maybe I needed to find a more interesting teacher than my boring old man,' he said, stealthily eyeing up Angelite with a grin on his face.

'You're never usually this open are you? I feel you have some depth about you, and you are quite bright. I think you would make an excellent student, and also an excellent protector,' she replied.

'Perhaps in the meantime, why don't we find ourselves something to eat? We have a long way to go across the last parts of the city, and then on to the ancient battlefield.'

Maledream looked deeply into her eyes as he spoke, he was unaware that memories of his dream from the night before drifted in consciously all of a sudden, giving him a headache.

He could not explain why but the pressure was great all of a sudden, his legs wobbling slightly as disorientation set in. Flashes of what he had witnessed still seemed to haunt him.

'What's wrong?' she asked with a worried tone as he fell to his knees gently for a moment, rubbing his forehead.

'It's nothing. It's nothing, just a slight headache.'

Kneeling down beside him, she put her arms around him, and held him tightly.

'It's going to be all right, okay?'

The Tribal nodded, struggling to throw away the thoughts but gradually and painfully resisting them in silence.

Where did this come from? I hope it doesn't keep happening, this

could be a pain in my ass,' he thought.

'Right, let me cook something up, I bet its hunger that is doing it,' Angelite said, whipping out a makeshift stove-looking device, some eggs, bacon, and bread, strangely fresh and plentiful in a container of salt.

'This will cheer you up! And add a little protein to you' Again he nodded before lying down as Angelite lighted her makeshift stove.

'They have contraptions like that all over the place in Meridia? It's been a while since I've eaten hot food, let alone stuff that looks and smells fresh,' he remarked, staring at her lighting the flame on the stove.

'This? Just a simple stove, but we do have many things that make our lives easier in Meridia...you could say many luxuries, I do not envy the existence your Tribe has had to go through. Once we are back in Meridia, I'll make it my priority to get your father and other Tribals back in one piece, I promise,' Angelite replied.

'You make it sound like one of Larkham's "high spiritual planes" that he keeps on and on about,' he chuckled with a slight grin, shaking his head side to side.

'Well I wouldn't go that far...but once you get there you'll probably feel slightly cheated, however you'll probably not grow so tired of it in some ways like I did before I left, you'll have more respect...'

'And now you're sitting on my side of the ocean, you look back and think how lucky you were, and now have a new respect for your home?' he said, staring into her eyes as the food began to heat up on her stove.

'No other way of saying it but yes you're right,' Angelite replied.

'I wouldn't worry though, you've been through a lot here, but when we get back at your home you will save many, many lives,' he replied, the words warming Angelite.

'You're right, that's our mission,' she said smiling at him with eyes filled with hope, and not the new found despair she had discovered since reaching the shores of the Dark Age lands.

'My old man had a saying for me "go with the flow" or, what he said more often was "your too laid back and a rude boy"...I prefer the first one myself,' he said, smiling back. Angelite giggled at the thought.

'You two are quite the comical couple aren't you,' she said.

'You could say that, I just think he's a daft old man most the time.'

'You love him all the same though,' Angelite said, Maledream giving her a strange look and not uttering a word.

'Oh seriously, you men all need to grow up and let your feelings out more often!' she said, slapping his knee with a grin.

He cried in laughter for a moment.

'Sorry, sorry...I'll shut up,' he said, his grin not dyeing down, and for that moment forgotten that his head ached and throbbed.

Soon enough the smell of food wafted through the breeze as he recovered by drinking some fresh water Angelite offered him. As he ate his food, Angelite offered some hands on healing. Placing her hands upon his shoulders, his head began to clear as he finished eating. To finish him off, she gave him a massage on his shoulders and back. At first Maledream did not know what to think when she got up and sat behind him raising his eyebrow.

'This some sort of mating ritual of something?' he thought.

He winced in pain a moment later, feeling her hands and fingers press into his muscle.

'Better?' she asked.

'A lot better thanks, what was that you did? I almost fell asleep...my joints feel a hell of a lot better,' he replied, moving his shoulders and arms around in circular motions, almost in disbelief.

'But we have to get going before it gets too dark, we've been sitting for too long I think,' he added.

'You're right,' she answered, packing her equipment away.

'Not hungry yourself?' he asked.

'No I'm fine...besides you're skinny and could use the fat!'

'What!? Come to think of it you're right...' he chuckled, remembering that he was rather skinny, but then again that was due to poor living conditions more than anything.

'I'll eat later, let's go,' she said, standing up and tugging Maledream's long coat as she did so once she had packed her things.

Chapter Four

The Packs...

'Relations are simply a tedious pack of people, who haven't the remotest knowledge of how to live, nor the smallest instinct about when to die.'

Oscar Wilde

In the distance, the sun began to set as if running away from the dark, bloodshed clouds chasing quickly after it. It was said to be a bad omen to see a setting red sun, warning of dangers. However, to Maledream, who had heard this from Larkham, he thought it was total nonsense. The ruined city, to him, was always a dangerous place filled with murderers, rapists, and beggars. Angelite remarked about the sunset, that it was a beautiful sight and was a beautiful way to finish off a pleasant day's walking while he wished he could share the same philosophy.

Maledream and Angelite set off through the ruined city that started to loom their terrifying veils of shadow across the streets below. A huge mass of dark cloud now threatened total darkness that not even the moonlight could penetrate as the sun began to fade until eventually disappearing. A huge storm was amassing and it could be felt on the light breeze of the warm air. Many lights started appearing from campfires or candles that littered the city like glowing fireflies, for the very few scarce humans left surviving or scrounging a living off each other. Uneasy and restless the nightlife was about to begin after sunset, and get far more interesting at night.

'We have two options,' said Maledream quietly.

'We can either find somewhere very safe and desolate to sleep, or the second option is to keep moving. I recommend not stopping around here for long and go with the second.'

Angelite questioned him:

'What makes you so uneasy and scared?'

'Trust me, bad things come out at night, and it's usually of the

bad human kind, not bastard lizard creature kind.'

'Well, we are both fairly exhausted and are in need of sleep, Maledream.'

'I know, but trust me on this. We don't want to be here. I'd rather keep going.'

'You're starting to scare me,' she replied.

Reaching out and holding her hand softly, he looked at her with a firm look of the eye before saying:

'We will be fine, trust me.'

Feeling reassured with him she nodded and they began walking through the darkest part of the ruins. Maledream whispered to Angelite.

'Be light on your feet, don't let go, and we will be all right.'

Quietly moving under the cover of darkness, the pair began moving through various broken and arched buildings.

The nightlife was certainly out, shouting echoed throughout the streets, while shadows of people passed by on the walls in the streets from the faint light of campfires that were a-light in rusty bins.

'Why so much shouting?' Angelite whispered.

'Usually fighting each other because they have no other purpose, preying upon the weak, mugging, raping, disembowelling, you name it and I would most likely say it's all here, utter chaos. We call them Packs,' he replied, trying to keep his voice low, while watching where he placed his feet on the rubble flooring as he led the way.

'You make it sound if they are a bunch of horrible hungry wolves,' she whimpered with a worried tone.

'That is what these packs are...nothing but bad news,' he said, while squeezing Angelite's hand reassuringly.

'You're safe with me, don't worry, just keep moving,' Maledream added.

In the distance, more echoes could be heard of the lawlessness that existed. Fighting, mugging and raping were rampant everyday life for the citizens that were left in the ruins since the Dark Age arrived.

Engines could also be heard starting up all around the streets as packs began raiding at high speeds on their makeshift bikes or other vehicles pieced together making hit and runs on each other for territory, food, and women.

Some packs had trucks mounted with many an array of weaponry in which to slay their opponents for table scraps.

The chaos could be felt, it lingered in the air like a foul smell.

'I've never seen anything like this before,' she whispered.

'I can't believe my eyes.'

'You had better start believing woman, because this is the real desperate struggle to a lot of people,' he replied.

'What's that noise?' Angelite asked.

'Shit, get down!' he ordered dragging Angelite with him to hide in the doorway of a ruined building.

They sank further into the depths of the building, taking refuge behind some marble pillars. Sitting on the floor, they peered out as the noise became louder. One of the pack gangs showed up twenty yards away, and looked as if they were waiting there for someone. Sitting on their bikes, they started chatting and yelling at the tops of their lungs while revving up their bike engines, swigging back bottles of a rough version of alcohol.

'*Great, this will slow us down,*' he thought.

'Is everything all right?' Angelite whispered underneath Maledream who was now covering her under his patched dark long coat.

'Yes,' he whispered back.

'I'm not crushing you am I?'

'Couldn't be better,' she replied.

'Good...quiet' he whispered.

His eyes scanned the pack's movements as he listened closely to their words. He spotted that this gang was the Ruthless Pack. It suited their nature and of course the painted symbols on the bikes gave it away in the faint lighting. Maledream would have no chance but to fight given this gang's reputation as one of the most feared within the city.

If it was one thing he knew about Packers, regardless of pack or gang, is that once they had found somewhere to settle, they would most likely get off their bikes and begin searching for scraps.

Deciding it was the logical choice of action, Maledream reached slowly for his sword trying to position himself on the floor, while balancing the large cumbersome weapon as his hands removed it from the scabbard.

Strength failed in his arms and, with a quiet gasp, his arm gave way to the weight of the blade in his awkward position, its tip striking the floor loudly. It was the worst possible moment for it to happen, just as the Packers turned off their bikes and stopped their lunatic-like shouting.

'*Shit,*' he sighed.

Looking up, he saw the pack get off their bikes, wielding weapons such as clubs, chains, knives and broken bottles. They had surely heard him as they stared towards his and Angelite's general

direction within the dark ruined building. Getting up slowly, he pulled Angelite off the floor and quietly hid her behind the dark shadow of another one of the old marble pillars in the shattered building to gain a little more distance.

He pulled his hood over his head, he didn't want any survivors to see his face otherwise he would seriously be in more trouble than now. Preparing himself, Maledream stood ready to strike with arms raised for a high to low blow in an arc across the torso. Angelite watched, her eyes were like a scared feral animal as she clung onto her wooden staff, drawing her own hood over her head.

'Who's there?' shouted one of the pack members.

'I heard it boss, right big clang it was, sounded valuable if you ask me!' came a reply from one of the other Packers, the voice high pitched and whiney.

'I know what you heard runt…Come out and face us like a man, you little girl! We won't hurt you…we'll just smash in your knee caps…'

A loud roar of laughter from the individual that said those words ensured, the pack followed their leader's laugh, and then stopped when he did, showing a great fear and an odd respect for their leader.

Angelite squeezed Maledream tightly and began whispering her words of magic quietly, praying to come to no harm. Maledream stood motionless however, his arms still raised, his head bowed slightly down with the hood draping over his head ready to fight.

'Something's telling me you're hiding behind these shadows and pillars!' the Pack leader snorted.

The Pack started spreading out into the darkness surrounding the couple's position, searching for them, making as much unnerving noise as possible by banging their weapons and roaring at the top of their voices.

Maledream knew he would have to fight, there was no other way to escape. One of the Packers was nearby, gradually stepping closer and closer. He whispered to Angelite:

'Whatever happens, Angelite, stay here…'

The Packer came round the corner making a racket and accidentally clouted Maledream in the head.

Maledream responded by giving a flurry of sweeps with his large blade. The Packer stood no chance, as he cleaved his head clean from his neck. With grace, he stepped back into the shadows, the sword seemingly feeling lighter now. Surprisingly, the other Packers did not notice the noise. Again, another Packer walked closer this time stopping and just out of range of Maledream's sword swipes.

A few second later, the Packer shouted:

'Leo's dead boss, cut up he is!' A roar of noise filled the ruined building.

'Crap,' Maledream thought.

'Find him,' yelled the pack leader. In less than a breath, torches were lit and the lights flooded the ruins leaving few shadows to hide in.

'No more fun and games! Time to die...no one gets away with killing even just one of us.'

With a leap round the pillar, Maledream took down the nearest Packer in one large mortal blow across the spinal column, but in doing so revealed himself to six more of the gang, plus the pack leader in the mass of lit torches.

'Get Him!' shouted the leader, and in no time at all, they all came for him.

He lowered his large blade for another swipe. The attack was very fast and swift, as they came clashing against his sword, some of the blows he had to duck and weave over and under. Maledream was in a flurry of defence against all odds, but he knew he could not keep it up for more than a minute before his arms would give way to the weight of the sword. Parrying a blow, he quickly dived through the mass of bodies before spinning around, swinging his blade around the Packers' ankles, cleaving them from his legs in one swoop.

He then raised his sword and brought it down firmly across the ribcage of a runt as fast he could possibly swing. With a squeal and shriek, it signalled one down and five to go as the blood from the main arteries sprayed his blade and face as he punctured them from behind. Twirling to his left and right, he fenced off another three swings clumsily before getting his sword wrapped around by a runt using a chain very effectively, and with a tug Maledream lost his balance and went flying with the sword into a pillar knocking him into a daze. He closed his eyes and witnessed something he did not expect to see...

He was experiencing a flashback to his dream, Maledream could see himself with his back to the sea and cliff face, staring at the commander wielding the sword in his dream. The giant of a man stood before him, his facial features clouded by the shadow of his hood.

A loud voice cut through to his mind.

'Retrinumun,' echoed inside his skull, the blade's hilt humming slightly within his hard gripped hands.

Maledream did not understand as he stared at the tranquil scene before him...

Opening his eyes, the Tribal shook his head, not knowing what he had just witnessed within the blink of an eye. With every ounce of strength, he pushed himself from the pillar swinging the sword loose of the chain and cutting through it like paper.

He charged through the mob as if he were ten men.

'I'm not going down!' Maledream roared with defiance as if filled with a new energy, to which he could not explain.

Exploding into life, the sword cracked with power, flashing like rolling thunderclouds across the surface of the metal for a moment, the energy banks inside the weapon gradually awakening and charging. Raising the old blade above his head and bringing it down upon another Runt Packer with a satisfying blow, he severed the attacker's skull in half, cleaving its way through the rest of his body. Still they came on, with more blood lust. It was as if killing them made them even stronger and more blood crazed to die.

Fighting was a lot harder, even with the power from the blade. He found it difficult to wield its power and concentrate on everything going on around him. At the same time, chains, broken bottles and knives, were all trying to gut him as he dodged and parried, not helped by the thick long coat or loose leather armour that he wore. Going around in circles, Maledream flung himself behind pillar to pillar, leading them away from Angelite and in turn being chased by the Packers weapons ringing out as they struck just behind him trying to cut him down.

'Get that adrenaline running, pack! Makes the meat taste better!' yelled the Pack leader, letting out a bellowing laugh.

Maledream's boots slipped on a smooth marble slab causing him to crack his face on the ground but still he gripped the sword tightly.

The silhouettes of shadows from the Packers on the nearby walls showed them all jumping in for the kill. They piled on top of him, slowly overpowering him by sheer numbers pinning him to the ground as a pack of wolves would hunt down a deer.

'We're going to enjoy gutting you like a pig,' one of them hissed into his ear.

Maledream's eyes widened as he realised that he was about to die.

'No,' he yelled, his voice echoed louder than the entire ruckus inside the ruins.

Maledream's sword activated and, as bright as the sun, crackled into life and suddenly the Tribal felt he had become something else.

'Retrinumun,' he roared, producing the word of a strange language in response to the humming of the sword.

His eyes glowed with unearthly ions that seemed to flare energy in the air, and in a great explosion of bright energy, the Packers were viciously flung into the walls, half disintegrated from this strange force while Maledream leaped to his feet.

'My turn next,' shouted the voice of the Packer leader.

As he approached, Maledream could see he was far taller and more muscular than the others that Maledream had just defeated.

The Tribal tried to stand to meet this new threat but his knees buckled and he fell to the floor, gushing blood from stab wounds caused by the pack.

He began to lose consciousness as the pain from his wounds became unbearable, causing his body to feel exerted and stiff.

His mouth dropping slightly as he tried breathing desperately for air. His eyes glanced at the blade to see its surface grow dull again.

'Not so hard now are you?' scoffed the Packer.

'I'd have more chance fighting a chicken and losing than to your runty ass,' the pack leader roared in laughter.

Maledream's sword glowed dimmer as if it was part of his own life force, his eyes beginning to dilate from loss of blood at an increasing rate as he struggled to calm his heart beat down that sprayed his life away onto the cold dust covered ruins around him.

'Angelite...' he murmured.

'Ha! There ain't no Angels where you be going shit head,' shouted the Packer leader bitterly.

'You're going to hell, boy!'

'I think not,' shrieked Angelite.

'What's a little girl going to do huh?' the pack leader snorted, as he gazed upon Angelite holding one of the Packers torches in one hand that was left on the floor. Angelite started to focus with the burning embers, her eyes reflecting the white and orange glow of the fiery stick.

He grunted:

'What's this trickery foul **Witch**!?'

Angelite said nothing and instead raised her free hand and started to twirl it around the naked flame that started to follow and dance with every passing action as if building up strength. Her voice echoed as her eyes began to burn a bright violet.

'You're not killing him, and I'm not a little girl.'

Taken aback from Angelite's way to manipulate fire, the pack leader was starting to lose his cocky edge.

'You're going to die foul Witch, but not before I desecrate your cute body,' he shouted whilst grinning madly, charging towards her in a fit of muscled frenzy.

She let the final energies pass through her hand which gushed out into the swirling, dancing flame causing it to super combust into the air in front of her. The last sight he saw was a glow of solid white flame turning into an inferno before his eyes, engulfing him so quickly that he had no time to run for cover.

Maledream lost all consciousness as the blast knocked him over and the heat wave passed over him. His dreams taking flight as all sight turned to darkness and then to a white haze. Angelite ran to him as he lay unconscious upon the floor.

'This can't happen again I won't allow it,' she said defiantly.

Speaking some incantations quietly, she clasped her hands together as she knelt down beside him. Her hands began to glow a green and gold that became stronger in colour as her voice rose in volume. Fate lines upon her palms began to glow a brilliant white as she placed her hands upon the Tribal. Maledream had lost too much blood, in danger of dying from his many mortal wounds. For a moment Angelite feared she had been too late as the resonating magic seemed at first resistant. With a sigh of relief, Angelite watched as her efforts were having an impact.

The cells on Maledream's body reacted to her Resonance, the wounds were sealing back up, leaving only faint scar tissue. An hour had passed as Maledream lay still in the dark, Angelite remained staring at the many shadows. He breathed quietly and occasionally snored. Angelite panicked even more as she held her hand against his mouth from time to time.

'Wake up, Maledream,' she said, quietly nudging him constantly. Eventually her efforts paid off as his eyes began to flutter.

Waking up and returning from the white area within his mind and without knowing what exactly happened. He dozily glanced at Angelite with her hands on his chest.

'You were almost lost,' she said quietly, staring at him with a purple glow in her eyes.

Maledream attempted to get up but soon fell down on his knees again letting out a moan.

'Your wounds are sealed up, but I cannot replace the loss of blood, your body will gradually gain strength again.'

Butting in, Maledream added:

'We don't have time...we have got to...move,' he said, groaning as he forced himself onto his feet using his blade and Angelite to help steady his balance.

More chaos echoed down the streets. As they were in no position to fight, they had no option but to run.

'To their bikes,' he spluttered in a hurry to get words out.

Quickly, they searched the Packers for keys and then rushed outside to find the bikes.

'Do you know how to work one of these?' Angelite asked.

'Kind of...haven't ridden one for cycles, you'll be okay, get on the seat,' he ordered.

She got on the back of the seat while Maledream got on the front, inserting and twisting the keys while putting his foot down on the peddle, starting the bike, revving it hard.

'Hold on, tighten your arms around my waist,' he shouted over the noise of the engine.

The pair sped away at high speeds darting through the streets, managing to avoid rubble. They darted through pack territories that threatened to crash them as they dodged firebombs, rocks, and gunshots.

'Faster, faster!' shouted Angelite, even though she was terrified as she clung on for dear life.

'I'm going as fast as this piece of crap can go,' Maledream shouted back, adding:

'Hold on...' as he screeched the bike's brakes to a halt only to face a dead end of an alleyway.

'Shit,' he muttered.

A shot rang out from the building above them, puncturing the rear wheel tire, Maledream instinctively drew his blade, while grabbing Angelite to one side behind him as they got off the bike. A strong searchlight blinded the two of them as a voice shouted at them from above.

'Is that who I think it is?'

Maledream could only hope it was not someone who he had ripped off in the past as he raised his eyebrow and breathed heavily as sweat dripped from his brow.

Chapter Five

The Unexpected...

'None of us knows what the next change is going to be,
what unexpected opportunity is just around the corner, waiting a
few months or a few years to change the tenor of our lives.'

Kathleen Norris

A familiar voice from a long time ago came from above. Maledream tried to match the voice to someone he knew but he was too busy struggling to stay on his feet from the loss of blood.

The voice called out again:

'It's Neveah, come on in quickly.'

'Neveah? No, it couldn't be he's...dead?' Maledream thought.

As he spoke, the light from above dimmed slightly and was not so painful to look at. Without hesitation, the pair advanced to the door that opened on the side of the ruined hotel building.

They stepped through a doorway into darkness and heard a loud clunk as a corrugated iron door shut behind them, a dim red light switched on above the door to reveal two dodgy looking male individuals side-by-side, armed with what looked like pole arms strapped to their backs.

They wore sewn together scraps of leather forming similar coats to Maledream, with the exception that chain mail or other plated pieces of armour protected vital areas. Both had strange hairstyles similar to the style adopted by members of packs. Maledream hesitated. Were these men friends or foes?

'Up **here**,' shouted this Neveah character from above a flight of stairs.

'Go on then, he won't wait all night,' one of the guards muttered.

'Well, why don't you help a lady out and help me carry him up! He's too weak to move very much!' Angelite yelled at them.

Looking at each other and then at Angelite and then back again, they grunted at each other before both helping Maledream up the stairs.

'Quite a lady with a back bone,' the guard said cheerfully, showing a small smile.

'Don't get many women like that anymore that's for sure,' the other said.

'Thank you,' said Angelite.

'No problem,' the guards grunted.

Reaching the top of the first flight of stairs in almost total darkness, they pair were led into a room lit by many candles.

Maledream could guess who the Pack Leader Neveah was by seeing him sitting on a badly torn and burnt couch with others smoking a pipe full of tobacco that made his mouth water.

Tobacco was usually a treat for the leader of the pack, and handing it freely was seen as a blessing from a saint to a peasant.

It had been a while since the Tribal had that privilege.

The room was a shambles with old electrical equipment and various other unused objects scattered around the room collecting an obscene amount of dust and dirt from the decades, perhaps, centuries that they had lain there. Such objects were considered useless unless you could kill, eat, or burn them.

In the centre of the room, next to the two crippled couches, was a table stockpiled with weapons and ammunition, and on the right side racked on the wall were plenty of knives, swords, and other weapons for close quarters' combat, some of which had not been cleaned after gutting some poor individual. By the broken glass window was the man with the large gun that had blown the bike's tire out, ever watching the perimeter the pack had set in the street below.

By the side of him was the giant stationary searchlight that had been used to blind them. The power seemed to come from a humming machine down the hallway a few doors away, with power leads running to it. Smells of fuel could be whiffed in the building meaning that a rare portable generator was responsible for the false lighting. Such a generator was considered the most sacred gift, it was such a rare find within the city.

Sitting the couple down, the guards returned downstairs leaving them with a room full of people they did not know save for Neveah, whom Maledream did barely recognise. He glanced at Angelite who was looking very uncomfortable with all the rough looking men and one rough looking woman staring at her.

Neveah was wearing an eye patch covering a blinded eye. His head shaved with a few cuts, and a carefully shaved goatee.

'So can I offer you buggers something to eat or drink? Water? Meat? Bread? Thin air?' Neveah asked.

Maledream's memory rushed to him, flickering through his mind ignoring Neveah's homely patronage and blurting out a question.

'What...happened to you?' the Tribal asked as his memories of his younger years rushed back into his mind at an alarming rate, hardly believing his eyes in shock and awe.

'Aye, we shall move onto the history lesson after we have discussed drink and food, you both look worn out.'

'Worn out isn't the word for it. Water would be good,' muttered Maledream.

'I'll second that,' Angelite's sweet voice uttered, as quiet as a mouse.

With the raise of his hand and a snap of the fingers, Neveah's gang members handed them flasks of water.

'Drink up, it's the cleanest and freshest source we have,' taking a giant swig Maledream drank it in a few seconds. Neveah laughed.

'Thirsty?' Angelite just sipped it slowly, still feeling uncomfortable in the room.

'So, is this your woman, Maledream?' Neveah asked, almost causing Maledream to choke on the water.

'No...No!' Maledream said. Angelite nodded 'no' as her reply.

'Bit of a long story, Neveah, but I'll tell you later on,' Maledream replied.

'Fair enough...does this lass have a name?' asked Neveah.

'Angelite,' she spoke up quietly.

'Angelite eh? Well nice to meet you,' he replied, smirking.

'So before you question me again and now that I have been introduced to this young lady of yours, Maledream...I shall explain my disappearance from all those cycles ago. Do you remember when we were attacked many, many seasons ago at all?' Neveah asked, leaning forward from his seat slightly.

Looking dumbstruck, Maledream paused before answering,

'Kind of, I lost a lot of my memory, and can't even remember my parents too well...I was adopted by Larkham and his Tribal refuge group, by fluke I still remember a fair bit of you from our teenage moments, but that's about it. I assumed you were buggered by the Packers or worse.'

Neveah exploded into laughter and forced a smile on Angelite's face.

'It seems your humour has kept you alive thus far my old friend...I can't tell you how good it is to see you, it must be the fates or something' Neveah bellowed shaking Maledream's hand.

'It's good to see you again, Maledream. I lost all hope, and no I wasn't buggered, I'll tell you what happened.'

He paused to puff on his pipe full of sweet smelling tobacco.

'If you can remember, or at least try, we and our families were on our way to the north to this "new" safe haven further up in the cold north or north west, that is when we crossed this city, and this is where I remained, but you disappeared, Maledream, and I was unable to find you. Fate it seems has now reunited us,' he added with a smile.

'I'll just take your word for it,' replied Maledream.

'I would like to remember the past but I would also like to talk about the present. You have built yourself quite an empire here,' Maledream said.

'I have gone through much struggle,' Neveah proceeded.

'To reach where I am now I had to go through much hardship, much bruising, and the lost vision of my right eye.'

He lifted his eye-patch to reveal a hole in his skull where the eye should be, making Angelite feel slightly light-headed at the gory sight.

'Now let me introduce you to my present crew members. This guy here is called Crazy John and when he gets going in combat you'll see why he gets the 'Crazy' tag,' he laughed.

'But in all honesty he is always crazy.'

Crazy John menacingly looked at Angelite with a smirk as he polished the many knives, forks, and spoons set upon his lap. She felt uncomfortable looking into those maniacal eyes of his, they seemed to match his sinister smile. Staring at Crazy John's topless torso, Maledream asked the question:

'Why is his chest caved in?'

'I don't know. I've never asked...I never do, but I am sure he was dropped on his head when he was a toddler' Neveah chuckled.

'Ok who's next? Ah yes, here is a brute called Pixie. Before you ask, don't ask about that name or how he came by it. All I can tell you is that he loves his hand to hand combat almost as much as he loves his trusty gun.'

Pixie spoke in a light polite tone towards the couple.

'My pleasure you two, you will be safe with us,' Pixie smiled, his goatee wrapping itself slightly across his stubbly face. His largish appearance was the same as Neveah's, except there was no muscle to him just girth.

'You sure don't sound like a brute,' Maledream chuckled, bringing a smile to all faces in the room.

'Well met, appearances can be deceiving, I was once a refugee myself, not a Packer,' Pixie answered respectfully, stroking his goatee

and large sideburns as he slyly winked at Maledream.

'Hmm who else, ah yes, Boris here, only female in the group but is considerably crazier than Crazy John when she gets going and...'

'If you value your balls, Neveah, you had better think to finish off what you're saying wisely...' Boris butted in.

'You see what I mean, do not mess with her,' he said with a grin.

'She and Crazy John here are madly in love of course, and fight harder because of it as well, shame we can't all fall in love and fight harder eh?' Neveah continued.

'Well the last member over here is called Reckless, I would say the most "sinister" if I do say so myself...isn't that right, Reckless?' he added.

Reckless said nothing as he sat clutching the rather large gun.

He looked over at Angelite with cruel iron eyes making her feel compelled to look away from him.

'All in all it's a very tightly knit group. There are others of course but they are either somewhere else in the building or outside scavenging because it's their turn. In this room now are the men and woman whom I have known and fought with side by side for over many cycles of the sun and moon. Others come and go...the two guards who let you in downstairs are new, just started a while ago now, at the request of Reckless, still don't know what to think of them.'

Neveah looked at Reckless and Reckless looked back at Neveah, both with questioning inquisitive eyes. Reckless replied in a low toned voice that only just managed to sound louder than a whisper:

'They are fine, boss.'

'Well we shall see I want no back stabbing boy,' Neveah replied.

'As I said boss, all is well,' said Reckless.

'Aye it had better be,' said the Pack leader, glancing deeply into Reckless' dark eyes for a quick moment before turning back towards Angelite and Maledream. Being a leader of a gang meant Neveah had to ensure he maintained his position as top dog. He could not allow to be seen as weak, it would take many years for any new member to gain his trust. Assassinations were rampant in the city, with power viciously switching hands all the time.

'So, anything else you want to know, Maledream? Angelite?' The room was so quiet that Maledream could hear the hiss of wax burning faintly from the slow burning candles and the wisp of the wind outside.

Breaking into the conversation, Angelite spoke up:

'So do you like this life, Neveah? Does the rest of your pack like it here?' she asked politely.

'Hell no little lady, if we had a choice we would move.'

Neveah got up and strolled towards the dark broken window, peering out of it with his hands clasped gently behind his back looking out into the desolate city from his vantage point.

'If you seek solace from this life, then there is one option you can take. Join me and Maledream as we journey back to my home, perhaps a destination where you were meant to go many cycles ago?'

'You mean the "safe haven" we've all heard rumour of?' Neveah queried in disbelief at what the young woman was saying, but for a moment fell silent when he took full notice of her robed attire as he turned around from the window to face her. She was indeed dressed strangely, and her clothes were of the finest silks that he had seen for a long time.

'Yes, it is my home, called Meridia,' she answered.

'The safe haven that you speak of is called Meridia?' asked Neveah.

'What proof do you have it exists, this Meridia? It's a strange name, do you really believe it could be a sanctuary for us?' he added.

'We have all heard the rumours, they are a load of bollocks' Boris interrupted, also unconvinced along with the many others in the room who broke out a chuckle or shook their heads at Angelite.

'Well I'm going to find out, you lot can stay here and keep killing each other,' Maledream spoke up in her defence.

'Aye, is that so old friend?' said Neveah.

'Yeah, look at what she is wearing for instance...have you ever seen silks as fine as this?' Maledream asked.

'They do look rich, and very odd' Neveah replied, asking:

'But what other proof do you have? You can't expect us to risk life and limb with you two, the Dark Age lands are filled with worse things, give us some good proof and we might consider it' Neveah asked.

Slowly rising bravely off her seat Angelite said 'Sit down and watch and I'll show you my proof'.

Maledream settled down to watch. Neveah passed him a tankard of ale and a pipe of tobacco.

This'll be good,' Maledream thought, drinking the tankard slowly whilst taking a drag from the pipe.

'I say we could do with a lot more light in here don't you?' Angelite said.

Withdrawing her Rune chiselled staff from her hooded cloak and robe adorned with symbols, she held it aloft and pointed the attached crystal towards the middle of the room.

'You may want to move yourselves away from the candles,' she said. In no time at all the pack retreated to the walls of the room, dragging their broken couches with them.

Angelite asked for quiet so she could concentrate. One by one the runes began to light up from the base of the staff then gradually reached the crystal.

'Flamash, Flamash, Flamash, Gionistisa triatus.'

For a moment the candles in the room flickered and grew darker, Angelite continued to chant her power words...

'Flamash, Flamash, Flamash, Gionistisa triatus.'
'Fire light the beacon, fire be my light, fire be my guardian.'

She sang in song enthralling all that looked upon her as Angelite worked her Resonance. One by one, the candle flames grew brighter once more.
'Fire be my Sun, Fire by my creation, Fire give breath to the Ether.'
'Flamash, Flamash, Flamash Gionistisa Triatus.'

Energy from the runes on her staff glowed with a soft amber colour, while the crystal turned into a fantastic array of multiple colours radiating a deep glow. One by one the candle flames placed all around the room led a river of hot swirling gold, snaking through the air at unimaginable angles until gradually circling around the crystal on Angelite's staff creating bright rings of fire, dancing and licking the air as it did so, lighting the room as bright as day. Hair floated on end, and loose clothes began to tug towards the rings of fire as if they had some sort of invisible gravitational force within the hot rings itself focused around the crystal.

'Like a droplet of water to the ocean, like a candle lit flame to the sun.'

'Elin'shana dookilla shuen Allina Canshanna,
Flamash, Flamash, Flamash.'

Finalising her spell, the rings of fire exploded into a nova of Ether disappearing from the room, shocking her audience as they covered their heads before continuing to watch.

With that, the rivers of hot swirling candle lit gold reversed like a slow vortex, leaving the room as it once was, dropping hair and clothes to the natural gravity of earth once more.

Lowering her staff, she looked around the room, uttering: 'Convinced?'

'That was strange witchcraft,' they all said similarly with frightful looks and glares towards the young women in disbelief.

'So she's a cursed Witch?' Crazy John spoke up.

'With power like that, that's one woman I wouldn't mess with' Boris joked as she grinned at her fellow female.

'Aye, I think that might be all the proof we need...' stammered Neveah.

'If she was truly a Witch, she would have incinerated us right now, and this is the first time that I have heard or seen of someone using such power by singing it like it were a craft,' replied Pixie.

'I agree people with those strange chaotic powers can't control them as well as Angelite just did,' added Boris.

'I've seen and killed many of her kind, but she's different,' said Crazy John.

'So have I, this one's different alright,' said Boris.

'Not to mention she doesn't have any skin mutation or the likes, her robes are of the finest textures, and her Witch staff is quite alien yet intriguing' Pixie said.

'Pardon me for asking, but what do you mean by Witch?' Angelite softly spoke up. The group in the room fell silent for a moment, reluctant to answer.

'Aye little Angelite, Witch's in this city can do weird things what you just did yourself. They are chaotic, distrustful, and have strange destructive powers that have been known to wipe entire Packs out. We stay away from them the best we can in case they curse us with foul magic's and make our skin rot...we don't know too much about them, although as Crazy John and Boris just mentioned, they have had a couple of encounters with them,' Neveah answered.

'Yeah, mean sons of bitches boss' Crazy John replied.

'But she doesn't look like one, she's in way too good a condition,' Boris said, staring at Angelite's robes.

'As you can see, we are quite fearful of such powers...if this were any other Pack, they would have most likely slain you by now,' Pixie said.

'I see,' Angelite said, wide eyed.

Reckless remained speechless and not sure what to say as he eyed up Angelite with distaste.

'Thing is,' she continued:

'I'm not the only one in my home that practices it. There are many of us that do, we have existed in peace for over a hundred and fifty cycles and have only ever used our arts for defence, learning and healing.'

'Aye Angelite, as Pixie said you could have melted us where we stood or burned our place down. Now I ain't saying we'll ever trust your strange Witchcraft but, you're not insane, and when I was younger me and Maledream were with families and friends heading for this safe haven before we got separated by a battle, and we knew of magic like that...and I know of all the stories...' Neveah replied, looking at his group with his one good eye.

'So, what do we do then, great leader?' Boris asked.

'Okay, we take the hint that you come from some place of wonder though...who here will join me with Maledream and Angelite? This lady here is living proof that this place exists,' said Neveah.

While sitting down, the pack started eyeing each other up, whispering and nodding amongst each other to gather there various opinions to come to an agreement. With that, one by one they rose to their feet.

'I will come along for the ride,' Pixie said reassuringly.

'I'll join you,' said Boris. Other similar responses came from the Pack.

'Me too, better than this shit hole right? As long as there's killing to be had on the way,' said Crazy John, raising his arms with clenched fists in the air looking at everyone else with his continued mad grin.

'I will...but we all need to remember that this witchcraft is dangerous,' replied Reckless, lowering the high atmosphere.

'And why so, runt?' replied Neveah in turn, his one eye staring coldly at the new recruit.

'I am beginning to think that you have all lost your minds, she is dangerous,' Reckless continued in a sombre tone.

'I'm sure miss Angelite here is more than able to help us with her abilities,' replied Neveah.

'Even so...I don't trust Witches and neither should any of you...how do you know she won't turn on us once we are out of the safety of the base? Maybe she will turn us into dust one by one with her ability to control fire! Burn us alive in an instant!' Reckless barked angrily, pointing his bony finger at Angelite, his voice rising in fear of her.

'That's enough.'

Neveah raised his own voice, slamming his fist into the small

table. He feared Reckless' words would kill his pack's enthusiasm.

Neveah wanted a way out of the city, but needed a good reason to leave the safety of their territory to make such a journey. Now that Angelite and Maledream was here, he could see a possible way out.

'I will not hear anything else about her...I am well aware of stories of witches or odd beasts in this world, and I don't see this sweet girl doing anything like that runt! So shut your mouth before I smash it in with the butt of my pole arm,' Neveah barked back.

Reckless seemed fearful of the Pack leader, resentment clouding his eyes in the gloom. Neveah spat on the dusty floor as he turned to each member of the group examining them in turn to make sure he had not lost his respect.

'Then it is settled, you two shall not travel alone. If we meet trouble, we shall all fight side by side,' Neveah said in confidence.

Angelite seemed hurt by the comments but tried to show no weakness as she sat back down next to Maledream.

'Isn't this fantastic, Maledream?' Angelite said, only to discover him sleeping.

'Looks like he is in the clouds busy counting animals. I'm surprised the commotion did not wake him,' Pixie said quietly.

'*He lost so much blood,*' Angelite thought, stroking his face and let out a reassuring sigh of relief.

'At least he is now getting some rest,' she said quietly.

'Must have been one hell of a day,' replied Neveah, pausing to look at all Packers, thinking about the arrangements needed to move out.

'We shall leave in the morning after gathering up our supplies and weapons. You're also in luck as we do have some mechanical transport covered and guarded downstairs, that should speed our journey up greatly.'

'Thank you,' Angelite replied graciously, adding:

'I cannot thank you enough for your help. I feel scared yet safe with you all here'.

'Heh...that's fine miss...' Neveah replied.

'I do have something to say though,' she said hesitantly.

'We must travel through the ancient battlefield which rests just outside the city.'

At hearing this, Neveah and the other Packers glanced at her and a swift silence fell across the room for several moments.

'You do know what can lie there if we are unlucky and cross them,' Pixie replied in a disturbed low tone.

'I am not sure what you mean, however there is no other way around the sea and water...what do you mean unlucky and cross them?' replied Angelite, raising her eyebrow at them all.

'I'll tell you about it tomorrow, we should be fine though. After all, we live our everyday lives fighting in this battlefield of a city, so what does it matter if we cross this fabled battlefield and shit hits the fan?' said Neveah.

'One question, Angelite...can you show us the way?' Neveah added.

'Of course, when we get going,' she replied.

'Okay then. Everyone rest now so we can get up nice and early to make the preparations, whenever you're all ready,' the Pack leader ordered.

Nodding in silent agreement to each other, the Pack stared at the candlelight's deep in thought...

Eventually, they fell asleep, taking turns at being sentry in the hideout during the night. Angelite stared out at the broken walled window into the sky above. Still growing darker were the ever-menacing clouds that started to drizzle down its cold depressing sorrow. A cold draft was creeping into the room while the light spell of rain spitted in Angelite's face as she stared upwards into the heavens, feeling drained from her use of potency but still unable to sleep, finding the rain almost refreshing as it touched her skin. Perched on the window, she started thinking back to the safety of Meridia.

On her lap, she held the journals taken from the ruined library. She opened one and began trying to decipher the text that appeared to be written by a poorly adept hand, whereas others were clearly printed by technology from a forgotten time. There was no noise now from outside to disturb Angelite as the city slept now after heavy blood was shed. Occasionally, Angelite glanced away from the journal to Maledream who lay snoring away on the couch, while also some pack members were sleeping soundlessly on the opposite couches. Angelite quietly stepped off the window to tiptoe to Maledream's couch in the dark room.

Suddenly, someone grabbed her, covering her mouth with a filthy hand. Panicking, she tried calling out, only to sound a pathetic whelp, while struggling with her arms and legs at this unseen force. Her eyesight fell to darkness as a blindfold was hastily applied, her wrists and ankles were tightly wrapped in rough skin cutting rope. Something told her it was more than one person as she felt another groping her breasts with a harsh squeeze against her will, hurting her greatly

physically and emotionally as she continued to struggle for freedom. A harsh tasting, foul smelling rag was shoved into her mouth while another rag was wrapped around her mouth.

'The more you struggle, the more pain you're going to feel wench...you move too much and we will cut your throat,' a croaky whispering voice uttered.

'You're ours for the taking,' another croaky whisper uttered.

Angelite struggled as much as she could but it was no use. She was quietly dragged away from the room out into the hallway, over rough hard stones and objects cracking and cutting her head as she was dragged along helplessly until being thrown into a dark room.

She landed on her face to be kicked by a hard leather boot, the strike landing on her cheekbone as she muffled a scream.

'We think you weird types are not good for business,' the voice whispered sinisterly.

Another kick landed into her stomach taking the wind out of Angelite as she struggled to breathe through her nose.

'In fact we think the world's a better place without people like you. What can you hope for in this place? Huh?' a different voice whispered.

She then felt feet kicking her from many angles while being struck in the head with a blunt weapon.

'Your staff feel good bitch? Huh? This safe haven does not exist, you filthy snake woman!' another spoke angrily.

Tears were streaming through the blind covering her eyes creating a rainfall down her bruised face.

'Your kind deserves to be cut up and sliced up...but not before we use your warm body first,' the voice said, a tongue licking Angelite's tears off her cheeks. She could not believe the amount of pain she was suffering, all she had was some powers over which some people seemed to hate and fear in this part of the world.

Angelite was picked up and tossed into a nearby wall, to then be beaten on the legs by her own staff.

'*I don't want to die,*' she screamed out in her mind.

She was finally led to rest, only for the Packers to start ripping and tearing her clothes. They began to start groping her as she could barely struggle with her hands and feet that were bound tightly, almost making her feel claustrophobic.

'*Not like this,*' she thought.

A voice sounded outside the room.

'Over here...' a voice uttered outside the room in the hallway, suddenly they stopped.

'What was that... **who's there?** one of them asked signalling for everyone to stay quiet, as they did not recognise it.

'You two check it out,' one ordered.

Angelite caught her breath back, but dared not lose consciousness. She was scared stiff, her legs tightened to try and stop the would-be rapists before they started again. The draught seemed to be the only peace she could muster in as it cooled and comforted her.

Kicking her again on the floor one of them uttered in her ear, 'Stupid whore, you're still going to die.'

Applying pressure on her neck while continuing, the voice said: 'You ain't catching your breath back witch.'

Angelite violently coughed as she desperately tried in vain to breathe as the big cold fingers firmly wrapped around her throat.

Outside the gloomy room, struggling of some kind erupted, and could be heard down the dark hallway.

'I'll stay with the bitch, you two go and see what's going on,' a voice ordered.

After a moment of hesitation, Angelite could hear the two leave the room saying:

'Save us some, we want our fair share of that beaten Witch.'

'Don't worry,' replied the man, holding his hand tightly over Angelite's throat.

'There will be plenty of holes to fill,' the voice finished with a sigh as if close to climax. Angelite felt a cold steel edge come into contact with her skin as the stranger held a knife to her throat.

'Move and I'll slice your jugular, bitch,' the voice spoke coldly.

Once the other men left the room more struggling could be heard, metal against metal sounded with the cries of the two men, signalling their quick and swift defeat down in the dark, dank hallway outside the room. Angelite prayed and prayed it was someone coming to help her as she breathed as quietly as she could.

'Maledream is asleep, who could it be?' she thought.

The stranger stayed motionless for a moment trying to hear anything within the darkness of the room and hallway.

'If you want a job done, do it yourself,' the angry voice bitterly said, releasing his hand and knife from her throat. Angelite breathed a sigh of relief the best she could through her nose catching her much needed breathe back.

Lying on her back, the tear soaked blindfold fell slightly covering her nose allowing her eyes to adjust to the gloom of the cold damp room. The sound of a weapon being released from a strap caught Angelite's ears and then her eyes as the dark figure drew out his

menacing looking pole arm that had many sharp serrated edges.

'*No it can't be Neveah,*' she thought, remembering that the pack leader himself had something like that design.

'Show yourself assassin!' the angry man spitted furiously.

Stepping around the corner and pulling back his hood revealed what looked to be the face of Maledream brandishing his sword, covered in warm blood, panting heavily. It was then that the Tribal spotted her form on the floor in the darkness.

It was difficult in the gloom but from what Maledream could see Angelite was covered in bruises, blood, and assuming the worst had already happened was raped and killed as he stared at her ripped clothes for but a moment.

'*I'm too late,*' he thought.

His hands gripped onto the handle of the sword with anger rising through him a fury rising in his eyes.

'You're going down, Reckless!' Maledream screamed.

His blade activated to the anger in his voice, lighting the runes in the colour of crimson almost setting the sword itself on fire as ether burned through the air making a low, whispery, hissing sound.

'Will see, looks like your no stranger to Witch craft yourself,' Reckless replied, happily not caring for death or victory it seemed.

Maledream's sweeping blade clashed with the Packers pole arm. The two started the dance of death with blades and equal skill.

Toying with him, the Packer used his lighter weapon and fast reflexes to hit Maledream in the head with the butt of the pole arm, Maledream staggered for a moment before swinging around to lurch the blade forward for the Packers head.

Too slow, it seemed, as Reckless parried Maledream's blow aside before threatening his head with a quick sharp sweep that Maledream ducked narrowly as he regained his composure.

Another clang sounded as the two squared off their two handed weapons against each other in a lock of wills. Anger grew and festered inside Maledream's spirit and thoughts raced through his mind of what they had done to Angelite, fuelling him like an unstoppable engine of wrath.

Releasing a quick kick, he hit the pack member square in the crotch and then elbowed him in the face faster than Maledream thought he could strike. The light given off by the sword made the room glow a dark red as silhouettes of their shadows danced to the glow of the blade as if it were blood dripping through the very air. Reckless hit Maledream again in a quick swipe across his chest.

The deadly looking pole arm was narrowly deflected, and absorbed, by his studded leather armour and thick coat.

'*Not a moment for a mistake,*' Maledream thought, as he backed off to gain some quick air into his lungs before jumping once again with his blade that rose then fell against the Packers pole arm with more menacing sounds of metal against metal ringing through the night air as the parries of deflection carried on.

Maledream was growing tired of fighting as his blood supply did not quite catch up with him, and the scuffles in the hallway where he had dispatched Reckless' accomplices did not help.

He brought down his sword once more, but he was not fast enough to plant a solid killing blow on the Packer, who quickly rolled and darted to the sides, leaving Maledream's sword to ring out loudly against the brick wall besides Reckless.

Both men had the eyes of killers, one for retribution and the other for the sick pleasure of inflicting pain and death. Reckless swung around his weapon with finesse and expertise that kept Maledream parrying or dodging with his heavy blade, as he continued to struggle to counter attack on the rare occasion.

The Tribal parried one blow after another until he found the chance he was waiting for. He dashed his large sword towards Reckless' pole arm, trying to disarm him after locking them only to feel Reckless' feet trip his own. Falling forward and losing the lock of weapons, Maledream's blade lodged itself into the wall of the room with a thwack of concrete.

'*Shit,*' he thought, as he regained his balance. The pole arm had narrowly wedged itself beside his right ear as Reckless made a clumsy mortal strike, luckily missing him, who was trying to pull out the sword that was now stuck. Maledream gave up trying to free the sword and reached for the two daggers concealed within his coat.

Spinning around with both rusty knives, he made quick strikes towards the lanky Packer who twirled his weapon around faintly parrying each of Maledream's strikes.

'*This guy is a flimsy wall of iron,*' Maledream thought, as he thrust one rusty dagger towards Reckless' chest, blocking it as expected, while holding the other dagger Maledream jumped quickly onto the pole arm's shaft, taking the Packer off guard as he thrust the dagger hard in the back as he jumped over his head landing onto his boots.

Twirling around as Reckless winced in pain and gasped, Maledream spun on his crouched feet slicing the back of Reckless' kneecaps hard with his rusty knife causing the Packer to roar as he spun around trying to hit the cocky Tribal.

Grabbing the pole arm by the shaft after dodging the sweeping blow, Maledream used all his strength to twirl the maniac in a circle. He then released the Packer but jumped up to kick him harshly in the chest. Maledream flew a short distance backwards towards his blade still lodged in the wall. Reckless on the other hand could not keep his balance and fell backwards onto his ass.

The Tribal gripped his blade once more trying to free it. Reckless taunted him with all his strength as blood filled his lungs he yelled:

'Not fast enough are you? To be honest that bitch of yours was crap, I've had better...' he laughed, coughing blood all over his chin as he barely picked himself off the floor using his large two handed weapon for balance.

Believing the lies Maledream roared in anger, ripping the blade out of the concrete with gritted teeth. He turned and charged towards the Packer swinging faster and faster in a flurry causing the Packer to block multiple blows or dodge several well-placed mortal shots as the weapon seemingly lost its weight, Maledream became more focused on his object for revenge.

Sparks and molten metal flecks flew off the pole arm from the heat of the blade, slowly battering the shoddy weapon's poorly made frame and style whereas Maledream's ancient looking blade certainly felt no pressure whatsoever against it.

Maledream span around on his feet swinging the massive sword as if it were a club. With a huge power, he let out a scream, ploughing the crimson glowing blade into Reckless. Crimson energies leapt up from the old sword. Blocking the blow, Reckless' pole arm snapped under the power of the sword, and with that, he felt a huge force from the swing of the weapon that drove him through the air with a fantastic flash of crimson light, exploding from the blade, hurling the Packer through the wall of the old grey apartment room.

In a fantastic display of dust, Reckless flew like a crippled sparrow to the world outside. He spiralled in the air before plunging down to earth into the deserted streets below. He screamed his last defiance at losing the fight before there was a finalising squelch and crunch of his lost existence as his head hit the solid cold and wet concrete.

Silence fell as Maledream wandered up to the new hole in the side of the building, gazing down upon the shattered Packers corpse, his blood mixing with the rain that began to fall from the dark sky that went with his now current mood. He watched as a few hidden scavengers came out from hiding within the darkest shadows, tearing off the old Packers clothes and armour and even fighting over the

corpse for a source of food. Falling onto his knees and screaming at the sky, Maledream chucked his sword down before clenching his hands.

Gritting his teeth hard and letting out a quiet moan. He did not want to stare upon Angelite's battered form. He had only just met her and had taken a great liking to her. He breathed hard, catching his breath from the second fight against many in one night, the rain drizzling on his forehead, cooling him down as his head span.

'Humph! Humph!' a muffle came from behind. Turning around in disbelief, he stared into her living eyes.

'Angelite!' he shouted, joyfully getting up and running to her, sliding on his feet, skidding on his kneecaps. Unbinding the rag around her mouth, he took off his long patched coat to cover her and keep her warm.

'Maledream, thank you,' she whispered into his ear.

Clutching her hard and cuddling her, he sighed with relief, the anger within him dissipating quickly with every moment.

'I showed those bastards Angelite, I showed them. I'm sorry I fell asleep...' rushing his words.

'Silly man, it's okay, all I have suffered is a little beating and bruising, I will be...fine...' she whispered, but then fell unconscious and slumped in his arms.

Rubbing his cold bloodshot eyes, he picked her up in both arms and rested her on a nearby couch before gathering his sword and her staff and taking a seat by the side of her using some clean cloth to wipe her blood off her face. The Tribal could not understand why he himself was so upset, he barely knew her. Maledream could not put his finger entirely on his feelings.

'What happened here? What's the noise all about?' Neveah said, as he entered the room with a bright lamp shining pale light into the room.

'There are a couple of dead Packers of mine outside! What the hell happened?' he asked, several more armed Pack members walked in behind him.

Getting off the couch and stepping forward, Maledream gave him a cold hard look before Neveah noticed what had happened to Angelite as his one eye gazed around the room.

'Take a wild guess,' Maledream answered, lifting, and waving his blade towards Neveah with the Packer blood still not wiped from the blade. Stunned for words, Neveah stared at him blankly.

'Now get me some nice dry clothes for the lady. I'm sure you have more than looted weapons in this place. Hurry!' he ordered sternly.

Neveah nodded and, with a raise of his arm and click of his fingers, the loyal Packers left the room to get dry clean clothes, and any available heating they had.

'I'm sorry, Maledream,' Neveah said, looking at Angelite's crippled form. He rested a reassuring hand on Maledream's shoulder.

'It was that Packer called Reckless...he's splattered on the pavement below or worse from the scavengers...' Maledream said.

'Aye...let the bastard rot,' Neveah replied as he wandered over to the hole in the wall.

'What the *hell* did this?' Neveah said quietly as he inspected the damage with a creased brow.

Chapter Six

Ancient Battlefield...

'In peace the sons bury their fathers,
but in war the fathers bury their sons.'

Croesus

In her dream, Angelite found herself walking through green fields and dark green forests listening to the wildlife in full flow. Upon walking to the edge of the green forest, she saw Larkham standing before her.

'Do not succumb to the Temptation which does not belong in your heart, for it will threaten this young lady,' he said, before disintegrating into thin air developing into a dark mist, enveloping her slowly, crawling into her lungs...

Waking up she could smell some sort of chemical assaulting her senses, hear a lot of noise, and felt incredibly tired. She opened her eyes to find she was sitting on a broken armchair covered with a blanket.

She was aware that Maledream and Neveah were there and that they were being carried on some sort of mechanical transport. Angelite closed her eyes again but listened to the men's conversations.

'The people whom adopted you are called Tribals to us as you know, many Packers hate and fear such people...many Packers are superstitious. I try and find members who aren't muggers and killers, but obviously I can't see what their hearts are truly like until something like last night happened...we aren't a bad pack, we are just survivors in a way, trying to find peace in this war zone,' said Neveah.

'Why are there so many bad people around? If I had my own way I would wipe the lot of them off the face of the planet,' Maledream cursed.

'You're starting to sound like someone who'd believe those stupid myths about the planet turning on us humans,' Neveah chuckled.

'Perhaps the planet was right. It's the people that have turned this earth into a shit hole of a world,' Maledream said, looking at Neveah before looking back at the deserted cityscape.

The big city began to look smaller as they travelled further and further. They were in a large vehicle capable of carrying around fifty passengers.

A strong smell of diesel fumes filled the air making Maledream feel sick. Added to his discomfort was the state of the vehicle that looked like it had been crafted together badly, leading to a bumpy ride. At least it was keeping them dry from the rain seeping in from the heavens above. Angelite thought back to her dream while listening in on the conversation.

'Do not succumb to the Temptation which does not belong in your heart, for it will threaten this young lady.'

Thoughts started to circulate in her mind.

'He is too angry with himself and the world, it threatens to consume him,' she thought.

'He even used his anger on the sword...without knowing...'

'What did you call this thing again? What are we riding in?' asked Maledream.

'We call this beauty the Battle Hammer!' Neveah replied proudly.

'Battle Hammer?' Maledream laughed aloud.

'What kind of name is that?' he scoffed.

'Trust me when you see this beauty fire up to full speed and full power, you'll understand why, even the deck above us is sported with weapons so there's no problem when it comes to fire power, and you should see it's ramming power.'

'I'll have a look later. Meanwhile, I'm quite content sitting my ass here on this comfy chair, besides it's pissing down with rain, and I'm not in the mood to get damp.'

'Aye,' replied Neveah before they sat in silence.

Several hours went by as they snaked quickly down and up the old broken weed overgrown roads. The gears were loud as the driver changed lower gears to higher gears revving the powerful engine up and down the hilly land until they reached the flat surface of the ancient battlefield.

Angelite awoke once more after drifting off, Maledream and Neveah remained seated looking out of the half-drawn shutter windows in silence. Faint rain pattered against them.

The priestess tried to move but felt pain in her stomach making it slightly difficult, as the hurt had not yet healed from the night before.

'I hurt,' she moaned.

She was aware the two men were smiling at her.

'Up at last I'm glad to see,' said Neveah, as Maledream picked up her clean robes that lay beside him.

'Had them cleaned to the best of our ability,' Maledream said.

Angelite looked at what she was wearing, and it certainly was not her clothes. Blushing, she was stuck for words.

'No need to worry,' spoke the two at once.

'We didn't look. Boris changed you...honest!' they grinned, both trying to be comical in a way to take Angelite's mind off the night before.

'You could have fooled me...'

The sweet blush quickly vanished as she asked:

'Anyway, how far away are we from the battlefield?'

'Well it shouldn't be too long now. We have been on the road for a while now so we have to be close,' replied Maledream.

'That's when we are going full throttle through that place,' said Neveah.

'Why? It's not that dangerous, only difference is I went when the weather was fine a while ago.'

'Not when the sun isn't shining mate, around there they say the shadows themselves rise up and take the unwary. They don't like the light, that's the rumour in the city at least.'

'What are these shadows you speak of? You sound like my old man with his warnings about the place,' asked Maledream, wondering if Neveah himself knew.

'They come from a place between what the ancients used to call "The Heaven between Heavens", 'Angelite butted in.

'Aye, well whatever you call them or wherever they are from I don't care much just as long as we and my crew make it through in one piece. Besides it make more sense to me to think that they were soldiers who died horrible deaths in the hell hole we need to pass through. At least that is the common theme going around the different packs back in the city. There are far worse rumours from the brave Packers who go there to salvage most of the weaponry we have, but to them it is a dangerous living. Just as dangerous as trying to survive fighting other humans I guess.'

Neveah spoke in a low tone as if he were afraid someone from the battlefield might hear him. He looked grim as his one good eye peered out through the window into the horizon. Struggling over the pain and holding onto her stomach, Angelite drew a breath, slightly coughing from the fumes of fuel and then let out a sigh.

Maledream's eyes fixed on her waiting to hear any knowledge that she had on such things.

'These beings are not entirely made of shadow. They are just solid enough to appear to be made of shadow, and they hail from a zone, which nestles in-between the dimensions on many planes, as far as what I have learned back at home at Meridia. They create a feeling of dread, and fear, and feed off such emotions to sustain themselves in our physical world...a sort of syntheses.'

Maledream felt Angelite was giving himself and Neveah information that could be valuable if only they could understand it. Even after her tutorial on Resonance yesterday, Maledream still did not know enough about the dimensional factors.

'So did the ancients call the shadow creatures' home "The Heaven between Heavens"?' asked Neveah.

'Yes we think so, records contain written accounts of such beings being witnessed when the world was different back in older days. They seem to be more solid now and can show themselves and kill now the world's rifts have opened on major energy points on the planet after nature took its course.'

A dark mood fell upon Neveah as he struggled to comprehend Angelite's words. To him most of it was superstition or myth, tales from a fearful city.

'You mean when the "Axis" changed at the poles, from what Larkham was talking about in one of his everlasting speeches?' Maledream questioned inquisitively.

'Yes, when the Resonance change occurred. Do you remember we discussed this yesterday? Anyway, these beings can take many forms and are often beings that have never ever lived a life before, and so desire to take a life to feed themselves and their ever-growing hunger for such energy, such as emotions for example. They could attack you in your dreams, or even take control over your body and mind, which is known as Possession. They are addicted to life essences.'

'Sounds like a nasty bunch to me,' Neveah replied with a frown etched on his forehead.

'One good thing is that they hate any sort of light, at least we have that going for us,' he added.

'Not if this weather persists,' said Maledream, his eyes staring at the rain that was falling so heavily that it was drowning out the noise from the engine.

It was indeed getting chillier within the Battle Hammer as cold winds set in stealing the warm air from the vehicle.

'Not to worry though,' Angelite said.

'I've got ways to rid them if ever we encounter any, if I can manage to pull off the spell that is. I've not actually had an opportunity, let's say.'

'How are you now?' asked Maledream.

'I'm getting there,' replied Angelite.

'I've been using the healing techniques I learned to ease the pain, its working but it takes a little time to heal. A drink of water might help if you have any?'

'Sure thing,' Neveah replied, handing Angelite a water flask, drinking it quickly.

Proceeding to get up slowly, she made her way to the Tribals seat to sit next to him, hugging him tightly.

'Thank you for last night, Maledream,' she said, kissing him on the cheek. The act made him grin, turning his head away in embarrassment.

'Uh No problem,' he replied with a grin.

Neveah laughed heartily at the sight with his muscely arms crossed.

'Let's go up on deck and let Angelite change. Besides a little wind and rain will...cool you down,' Neveah laughed loudly, putting his hand on Maledream's shoulder. Getting up off his seat almost as if he were in a hurry, Maledream nodded to Angelite and then walked up the metallic staircase with Neveah in tow.

'Oh and Angelite,' Neveah said, as he put his foot on the first step.

'Sorry about last night. I'm truly and deeply sorry for what happened.'

'Thank you, it's not your fault,' she said.

Nodding he gave her the thumbs up then headed upstairs to join his old friend. Sporting many weapons, the Battle Hammer was certainly crafted out of many hours of hard labour. Inches of iron and steel from various other vehicles were crafted onto the large chassis to make it some kind of mechanical beast.

Some parts rattled as if they were about to fall off. All in all Maledream felt it was a very comical looking vehicle, he just hoped it could protect them if trouble hit them. Packers were sitting around on stools with sheets covering them from the rain, smoking pipes and swapping tales about past adventures, or just telling each other rude jokes and enjoying the travel.

Among the Packers, he could see Crazy John, Pixie, and Boris huddled around each other discussing the situation and taking shelter under a sheet the best they could from the downpour.

Maledream and Angelite did not know many other Packers, but in time were sure that they would learn their names. The Tribal simply lifted his hood over his head and gazed out over the distance.

'Certainly a beast isn't she!' shouted Neveah above the wind, rain, and sound of the engine as he stood next to Maledream on the iron girding leaning on the thick metal railings at the front of the vehicle.

'Yeah not bad at all,' replied Maledream.

'Quite a daemon,' he jested.

'Aye, this baby can take anything on, although believe it or not, a lot of Packer gangs deeper in the city have mechanical beasts twice the size of this one, I'm pleased you look impressed,' said Neveah.

Falling silent once more, the two looked out into the dark distance, the battlefield was almost in reach.

'You ever get that feeling Maledream when it feels like where you are at the moment is meant to happen? Seeing you and Angelite should have shocked me a lot, but it didn't. You ever get that or know what I'm talking about?' Neveah asked.

'Sometimes, usually I just go with the flow because it's a lot easier for me that way, thinking requires too much energy sometimes. Back at the Tribal camp I spent way too many hours thinking about life, now I'm experiencing it,' replied Maledream.

'Man, I'm starving,' he added.

'We have some fresh fish in the decks down below if you fancy a snack...well not entirely fresh, some smell like shit but that can easily be chewed away and spat out or even cut out with your huge sword,' Neveah laughed, slapping Maledream hard on the back almost knocking him over the slippery cold railings.

'No thanks, Neveah. I hate fish, especially the kind that could kill me if eaten,' Maledream replied, rubbing his now tender back.

Lightning flashed and thunder boomed in the tearful clouds above, cutting the tranquil landscape in front of them while growing unnaturally dark causing them both to stop their conversation in awe.

Angelite finished donning her clean and freshly stitched robes. She looked out of the shutter window at the dark looming clouds spitting lightning bolts from the heavens filling her with a childhood like energy making her want to inspect them closer on the deck above. Grabbing her staff, she steadily made her way up the metal staircase covering her head with her hood as the rain flooded down from the sky like an angry waterfall.

'What's going on?' she asked Neveah and Maledream.

'Glad you could join us, we were just admiring the view,' answered Maledream.

Nature's drums of war resounded again and again periodically, lightning arching across the clouds.

'Not far until we are almost upon the battlefield. After we drive through it Angelite, which course should we take next?' asked Neveah, staring at her clean sewn green and purple robes.

'Uh huh, keep heading this way,' said Angelite, pointing in a northern direction.

'Aye, no problem some hills lie that way somewhere I've heard,' Neveah said.

'Yup!' replied Angelite. Boom, another crack of thunder lit the heavens, the wind was gradually picking up blowing the Packers' rain covered sheets, creating little whipping noises as the air caught them.

Maledream could see the battlefield appearing before them. For a moment when the light flash caught his eyes, he thought he could see something odd in the distance.

'I feel a great presence coming,' muttered Angelite.

Neveah joined Maledream looking out into the distance, the lightning flashing their eyes once more. A pale expression sank into their faces as they gazed at something clearly.

'Battle stations, Packers!' Neveah roared, raising a clenched fist into the air signalling to take up arms.

'Fire up all the lights we have,' he added.

All at once, the loyal Packers got up and armed their weapons.

'Neveah, the torches are damp. They won't light!' uttered Pixie.

'These things are hopeless, you can't even burn skin with them!' Crazy John added, trying to keep a barely kindled torch by keeping his palm millimetres above the tiny flame.

All fell silent. They could hear the banging rain, occasional thunder, and the noise of the engine but their focus was fixed into the distance. Shadows were moving across the ground and starting to come in from all angles as the Battle Hammer ploughed through the edge of the battlefield crushing bones, rusted metal and stone on its monstrous tracks. Many failed Packer expeditions could be seen on the horizon in the distance, evidence that many had not succeeded on their journey.

They could see many vehicles much like Neveah's own Battle Hammer lying on the battlefield.

'It's the shadows. There is not enough light to keep them away,' Maledream said. There was a tremor in his voice as he watched some in the distance close in on them.

'Can our weapons kill these beings and send them back into that black "dimension" they belong to, Angelite?' Maledream asked.

'If they are solid, then I don't see why not. They will have to be physical enough to get to us, just be on your guard!' she replied, going through the words in her mind needed for a spell.

Trying to learn them was a mission to her, the energies she could transmit was easy enough but without the right words it could turn messy or prove hard to control.

The shadows began moving in-between, disappearing and reappearing between the flashes of lightning keeping up with the speed of the Battle Hammer.

Within several heartbeats, many shadows rose from the ground forming different shapes and sizes, some human looking in appearance but some faster ones moved with demonic speed.

Forming four legs, they looked like some sort of hellhound, running faster than the Battle Hammer, telepathically barking inside the minds of the living like raving dogs. Everyone looked at them instantly feeling a sense of dread. Fear and terror dragged down their hearts as they stared into the shadow creatures' dark red abyssal eyes.

'Do not fear them! Do not dread them!' shouted Angelite.

'They will only grow stronger if they can feed off your dark feelings!'

Gunfire erupted as the Packers lost their nerve, shooting at the darting shadow beasts that barked in retaliation. As they closed in from all directions, their eyes burst into strange red fire as they fed off the humans fear. Drawing his blade Maledream got ready for any other little surprises that might creep up on them, while Neveah drew his pole arm. Angelite held on to her staff with both hands.

Pixie started firing blindly at them with his automatic rifle, the bullets seemingly passing through the shadows' existences. Crazy John and Boris delved into their clothes to whip out many knives that had been hidden completely until now. Lightning flashed once more in the harsh beating rain. For a moment, the shadow beasts disappeared from the light, but were next seen even closer when the gloom returned. Maledream could feel something behind him as his body shivered with a sudden sensation of pins and needles.

Turning around he watched a shadow beast jump high into the air, with all four paw like appendages ready to strike Angelite down. In a split moment Maledream raised his blade in one hand while pushing Angelite down with the other, striking the hound in between its firelight eyes as it flew down, cutting the shadow in two before it disintegrated in the air like ash. Passing through it as if it were nothing, Maledream buried his sword in the metal railing sending sparks flying through the wind.

'Hey watch what you hit mate!' said Neveah, hating to see his beloved Battle Hammer get scratched.

Looking round, many other beasts had the same idea and had already jumped and latched onto the side of the large mechanical vehicle, climbing up the metal monster screeching their terror to encourage more fuel to sustain their existence.

Many Packers had already given up shooting them, as it seemed to have no effect, instead, they withdrew their trademark pole arms of their gang slicing the creatures with length of arm as they unnaturally climbed up.

'Do something, Angelite, and be quick,' Maledream shouted above all the noise, while helping her back up to her feet.

'If you can stop them getting to me, then I might have time to think!' she replied.

Many of the beasts were now hopping over the top deck from side to side, trying to lop off heads as they flew past. Some beasts succeeded in knocking over an unwary Packer off the deck, who was then devoured in mid air by many of the floating beasts before what was left of what they were wearing could hit the floor, their souls it seemed were even devoured as the beasts barked with excitement at finding such rich spirit. Terror filled the pack and they screamed for their lives as they battled with their weapons or dropped them from the sheer unbelievable sight. Crazy John and Boris cut through them with ease without the emotion of fear, other Packers nearby were not so fortunate with their willpower, as the screaming banshee like shadows continued the assault.

Some were helplessly pounced on, and instead of being dragged off the vehicle, the shadows corrupted them as they ate their souls, possessing their bodies to fight and kill the humans. The whites of the eyes glowed dark while the beasts' eyes shone through the retina like a red fire seeping into the wind, turning their weapons to bear on their old comrades.

These were easy targets for Pixie as he blasted at the red-eyed frothing maniacs who were once his friends with one arm holding his automatic rifle, the other his pole arm. He could do nothing but cross his heart with one arm and blast through them with his gun arm automated weapon.

Bullets rang through the air tearing the flesh and bone of those Packers now possessed. Once their bodies were destroyed, the Shadow being rose to try for a new piece of fresh meat to possess jumping from vessel to vessel. Neveah's pack numbers began to dwindle, and if he did not destroy their fear then they were destined to be doomed.

Neveah spun around cutting through four of the beasts that tried toppling him all at once with great cleaves. Graceful blows and solid arms insured that he could give a quick defence and counter attack with quick reflexes, lopping them in halves in a whirlwind of hits. His one eye had no sense of fear in it, only an iron will.

'Do not fear these beasts, they are nothing,' he shouted at the top of his lungs.

'Fight you mongrels!' he yelled, his words and actions inspiring his pack to fight harder.

'Why can some Packers kill them while others can't slice through them,' thought Maledream, as he chopped another in two as it threatened Angelite who was knelt down on one knee trying to concentrate from all the noise.

'It must be the fear,' he continued to think as he watched the battle for their lives continue on top the deck.

'Fight, Fight, Fight,' roared Neveah, as he once again tore another beast down in one swoop of his giant weapon.

'You've all fought worse things, Pack!' he yelled, swinging his weapon again with the great strength of a bear, bringing another shadow down from mid air, burying it in the metal grating before it exploded in a plume of silvery ash.

More and more Packers gradually started to overcome their fear of the red-eyed beasts and were now standing more of a chance as their fearless leader showed even greater feats. Roaring with vengeance for their lost Packers, they began fighting with a renewed vigour and boosted morale.

Crazy John and Boris sliced through the air at the shadows that threatened their unity. Almost like a Dance of Death with blades, they performed a great deal of acrobatic feats with quick and fast accuracy.

Pixie used the last clip he had, and seeing more of the shadows coming for him had no choice, and just like the other Packers, reached for his pole arm and began to slice through the daemons like a raging maniac. Maledream looked out in wonder while the battle raged on.

'Don't tell them what is in front,' a female voice uttered inside his mind, sounding very much like Angelite.

Confused for a moment, he wondered what she meant. He could see her standing on her own, her robes and hood moving in the strong winds. Out in the distance he saw a large mass of shadow gather from the ground, snaking into the air like tendrils, almost reaching into the clouds to spread out over the sky as if they were poisoned veins.

As he watched, the tendrils of shadows began spiralling towards earth, circulating like a tornado, growing larger with every moment.

'*Tell the driver to keep going,*' the voice soothingly told Maledream.

'I'm not leaving you!' he shouted amidst the noise.

'*Trust me, just do it,*' she replied.

'*I'll be fine.*'

Suddenly, Maledream felt a great force knock him off his feet, throwing his blade from his hands to land in the grating and sending him flying over the side. His foot luckily caught some of the rough metalwork on top of the Battle Hammer, unable to flee as the shadows beasts gathered round looking for the next kill.

Banging his head on the open shutter on the driver's side window, he shouted:

'Keep going,' noticing after that the driver was nothing but a lifeless corpse, and the accelerator trapped by its bony foot. Hearing a shriek from one of the beasts, Maledream twisted his head around to see one coming straight for him...

Angelite was focussing her energy. Her eyes lit up like the sun as she spotted three more shadow beasts flying straight towards her. She raised her staff, stepped one foot forward, and raised her hand towards the shadows, keeping her staff back to build up the energies. Closing her eyes, she called within herself her inner flame...

'Illumani' Penetrana Sheol dagadan, Illumani' Penetrana Sheol dagadan.'

Shrieking for the kill, the shadows were almost upon her but they shifted slightly from the energy fluxes surrounding her. Resonance energy snaked its way up Angelite's arm to her palm, lighting her fate lines as she released her power. It took the form of a barrier of light that lit up like a ripple in water as her spell bore life.

The beasts were trapped as the energies held and shackled their twisting forms in one place. Their eyes blazing terror and screeching from the burning light of her pure spirit that she used as a weapon against the beasts, entrapping them with a faster Resonance than what they were made from.

Spinning around Angelite held her staff in both palms, her robes and cloak flowing in the wind and rain, swung the crystal tip in the centre of the rippling light roaring with all her might.

'Be gone from this plane,' Angelite shrieked.

Hissing defiantly one of the three shadows exploded from the inside out, shattering in silver dust before catching the wind and taking flight, its embers passing through the battle on top of the deck. Spinning on her feet again, she swung the staff at the second shadow beast roaring her defiant attack once more causing great and vast energies from the crystal to explode into life and shatter the second shadow with the same result.

Twirling her staff in a circle, she finished off by swinging the staff once more straight into the third creature's belly causing the crystal to let out a burst of multicoloured light, fully releasing the power inside it. Now no longer binding the creatures, the shield of rippling light dissipated to the strong whistling winds as Angelite waved her hands across it as if to say thank you, her hand brimming with flowing ether of green and gold auras. With brightly lit eyes, she gazed out to the huge abyssal shadow storm they were approaching and once more took the one-foot forward stance holding her staff skyward...

Maledream stared into the beasts' eyes as it closed in for him, as he struggled to loosen his trapped limb. A roar sounded from above signalling Neveah's entrance as he swung his long weapon into the shadow below with skill and precision, severing the creature in two and narrowly missing Maledream's head. He could not help but break into a cold sweat as his heart raced, his body bouncing with the vehicle as it crunched over more terrain.

'Grab hold,' Neveah yelled, the Tribal grabbed onto his pole arm for dear life as the Pack leaders great bear-like arms swung him up in the air allowing Maledream's foot to loosen as he did so.

'Be more careful next time will you?' Neveah uttered.

Landing on the deck and picking up his sword, the two nodded before turning around to see Angelite take on three of the shadow beasts. Gawping, the two looked at each other as the embers of energy flew past them from the disintegrated shadows she blasted into the high heavens.

'She's damned good,' said Neveah, itching his eye patch for a split second.

'Now everyone, protect Angelite,' Maledream yelled.

'You heard the man,' Neveah roared.

What was left of the dwindling Packers gathered around Angelite the best they could while fighting back to back against the seemingly limitless hellish shadow hounds. Onwards the Battle Hammer charged, gaining speed from the stuck accelerator in the cockpit. Maledream side by side with Neveah took to the front of the juggernaut to cut at the shadows that dared interrupt Angelite's concentration with swift blades...

As the Tribal drew his sword up above his head to drive another shadow hound away with a swipe, he found himself somewhere else within his mind again. Surrounded by nothing but green grass and blue sky, he heard Larkham's voice sound from behind him speaking his words of wisdom.

'Use the power of the elements, use the energy of the sky, and use the energy of the beating drums.'

Hearing the words inside his mind, Maledream watched a dark cloud forming above him booming with thunder. Lightning then spat from the cloud striking his sword within his hands, ringing out as if steel was striking against steel. Humming above him, the sword spoke as if it had a voice of its own softly glowing to its words, his spine feeling a chill running down his back, hairs standing on their ends across his entire body.

'Retrinumun, Retrinumun, Retrinumun.'

Maledream had heard these words before when he had fought the Packers in the ruins back in the city. Glowing and humming the sword spoke more:

'Retribution, dispense it well' it sang...

Bringing his blade down in seeming slow motion, he awoke from his vision as the sword crackled the energy of ions down its surface. As he stared into the shadow hounds' hellish eyes, his soul lit with fire, and he shouted out the words of power.
'Retrinumun.'
A resonating booming power sounded, his blade bursting into life as charged energy coursed up and down the sword as it appear to awaken. He thrust the blade into the incoming shadow hound, splitting the beast into fantastic light fragments as the swords resonating power released in an instant. The rain evaporated in the near vicinity of the old weapon as if the blade was the sun itself.
'What the hell was that?!' Neveah asked as he stared at Maledream in shock and awe at the weapon he possessed.

'I'll explain later,' Maledream responded, just as shocked as Neveah was.

'More of the beasts,' yelled Neveah, burying another beast into the cold steel surface of the Battle Hammer as he looked again into the distance with his one good eye.

'Bloody vultures,' Maledream replied, seeing hundreds of the shadows running with demonic speed towards them.

Guided by an intuition, the Tribal moved to the forefront of the deck, placing his right foot on the railing, the wind threatening to take his balance as the rain pelted him hard in the face.

Lifting the two handed blade above his head and spoke to the sword, as more thunderclaps sounded lighting the sky above.

'Retrinumun,' Maledream said, not knowing what to expect.

Swinging his blade down bolts of raw energy shot from the ground around the Battle Hammer ringing his sword for but a moment.

In mid swing the Runic weapon itself channelled the ions forth, shooting out bolts of pure energy at the approaching masses of shadow, first striking one, then three, then thirty, splitting into the gathering like a chain reaction arcing out as it were the lightning rolling across the clouds in the sky itself.

'That's sorted them mate,' Neveah spoke in a daze as he wondered what kind of weapon Maledream was using, but he had spoken too soon. The large tendril shadow storm was almost upon them as they carried on speeding towards it. Maledream repeated the steps he had just performed but the blade grew dull and was once again a lifeless piece of metal within the palms of his hands.

'*Why isn't it working again?*' he thought, looking on in worry.

'Come on mate, pull off that trick again, that gigantic crap stands no chance,' Neveah jested.

'I don't know, I've tried but it's not working now, I have no idea.'

A mighty roar sounded from the dark abyssal shadow, causing all the remaining shadow beasts to disappear into thin air, phasing out as fast as they faded in. Looking down at the floor over the corrugated iron railings, the group could see them all converging towards the storm as if to join it.

'This will be difficult,' Angelite muttered as the Packers began to catch their breath, the rain cooling them down in the fast winds.

Ideas were running through her mind to find a way to overcome the shadow storm. She knew her only hope was a very strong light source.

Maledream kneeled on one knee from exhaustion, looked on, and then asked Neveah:

'Is this it?'

'Looks that way,' he said, his brow creasing with worry.

Breaking the silence Angelite stepped forward:

'Get back, what I am about to do is dangerous give me room please.'

They stepped back off the front of the Battle Hammer's pointed deck letting her take the lead. The very ether around Angelite began to shift and distort as her magic flowed around her, white orbs began to circle her person frantically but gently. She started her chant as she channelled the energies within her...

'Illumani' Penetrana Sheol dagadan, Illumani' Penetrana Sheol dagadan.'

'Elin'shana dookilla shuen Allina Canshanna Doon Mitsubargui shui.'

Raising her staff towards the grey heaven above, the runes on her staff started to uncontrollably spit excessive energy as the force of the influx of Resonance was more than it could handle, but still she carried on.

'Bring me sun, bring me light, and bring me fire to burn this plight.'

'Illumani' Penetrana Sheol dagadan, Illumani' Penetrana Sheol dagadan.'

'Elin'shana dookilla shuen Allina Canshanna Doon Mitsubargui shui.'

Her eyes glowed with an unearthly violet colour that spat out ethereal Resonance. She started to use herself as another spell focus, sending great amounts of energy into the crystal that began to overload it, the runes spitting ions into the surrounding air around her with pure, but very unstable energies. Cracks began to appear on the crystal, lines of orange light began to grow more strength with every passing moment until it could not contain no more. Exploding with a loud shattering sound as if it were glass, the crystal fragmented but did not fall with the force of gravity.

Instead, the fragments floated around what was left of the core of the crystal surrounded by multicoloured energies surrounding each piece, circulating with speed in clockwise and anti-clockwise directions.

Popping up out of thin air were darting silver particles surrounding Angelite with similar motions to the fragments of the crystal that travelled well with the orbs of ectoplasm light that surrounded her.

'She's going to kill herself if she keeps this up, she can't control it,' yelled Maledream, and before he could stop her Neveah held him back with iron gripped hands.

'Just stay back mate, she said it was dangerous,' he shouted. **'No, I won't let it happen.'**

Wriggling free with adrenal strength, Maledream pushed himself past Neveah, reaching out to grab her.

Sound was for a moment drowned out as Angelite completed her spell. The air stood still before all the glowing of the energies fluxed and flashed, the silver particles surrounding the fragmented crystal atop her staff. An almighty explosion of gold and greens shot out from the crystal blowing back Maledream, Neveah and the other Packers to the back railings of the Battle Hammer.

Wind in her hair, the rain beating her in the face, Angelite twirled and swung the staff with tightly gripped hands towards the sky. The energies raced through her body, overloading the runes, causing them to burst one by one as they travelled through the energy banks, disintegrating them until they reached the crystal core. All eyes were keen as they watched a beam of silver, green and gold shoot from the crystal tip snaking and entwining into the sky forming a comet racing through the clouds at incredible speeds.

At the same time, the floating crystals shattered into a hundred pieces, the force of the blow knocking Angelite to the floor in a crippled heap, even denting the iron girders she stood on as if she was stomped by an invisible force. Looming out to the Battle Hammer were menacing tentacle looking shadows reaching to snuff the life out of the last living members on the fast moving mechanical beast.

Hurtling into the clouds the magical energy mass disappeared, and for a moment in the last fleeting seconds, the group feared it was too late as they sped towards the wall of swirling shadow. Thunder boomed heavily, followed by lightning strikes beating down into the dead battlefield lighting the entire sky brightly.

'Look up,' shouted Neveah, barely able to boom his voice with so much racket from the thunder.

Swirling around above, the clouds began to twist opening a gap in the sky rather rapidly, unnaturally growing wider and wider against the wind's direction and against any law in nature. Revealing a blue sky and what looked like a small brightly lit star gradually starting to fall to

earth again. Deafening screams from the Shadow Storm forced most of the group to cover their ears. Not Maledream however, who ran full speed towards Angelite lying on the floor.

He did not know whether she were alive or unconscious but he was damn sure of getting to her in time before anything else could get to her first. Blood started pouring from his ears as the screeching became unbearable, drowning everything else out. The star of magic exploded into a brightly lit nova sending a shockwave through the swirling dark clouds, rippling like a pebble to water to clear the sky for several miles.

Rays from the sun raced faster across the ground overtaking the group with speed as the clouds dispersed leaving a ring of blue in the sky, the shadow beings swiftly disappearing or bursting into dark puffs of ash and silver as the sun hit them. Ending its screeching, the Shadow Storm began to retreat from the sky, causing a violent wind to buffet the mechanical transport as it created a large drag, almost taking the Packers, Maledream and Angelite along with it.

Burning their skin softly with a brilliant warmth, the sun shone upon them, while the Shadow Storm retreated into the depths of the dark ruins from where it had sprung, only for the Battle Hammer to totally decimate the spot as it charged through unrelenting with ease, causing many to fall over from the impact. Running down the iron steps into the lower deck, Neveah grabbed the dead driver, then shoving him to one side to slow down the transport. Maledream shook Angelite gently:

'Come on wake up!' he yelled.

Slowing down and finally resting to a halt, Neveah ran back up the stairs, barging through the Packers that had gathered to see if she were dead. Putting his ear to her mouth and his hand on her chest, Maledream listened as all fell silent, a faint breath graced his ear.

'She's alive,' he said, sighing with relief.

Roaring in victory the Packers celebrated as Neveah put his hand on Maledream's shoulder in the now glorious sunshine that enveloped them all.

'She'll be all right mate, put her downstairs to rest.'

Maledream agreed, leaving the Packers above deck to count the remaining survivors and check the total damage.

Chapter Seven
Forsaken Wilderness...

'Animals do not need to question because they know the world, they can feel it, the nature of it. Humans question their Nature because they are the only creatures that have disconnected, separated themselves, from nature's roots.'

Author

Grinding to a halt, the Battle Hammer coughed and spluttered like a sickly person. Black smoke plumed from the hot cracks on the engines surface, the smell of unclean burning oil lubricant from the engine filled the nostrils of all those around the Battle Hammer. Crazy John inspected the engine the best he could with the pack survivors. Neveah watched, hoping that they could repair his mechanical transport. It was bad news. The cam belt had snapped, the engine radiator coolant was wasted, and the pistons were cracked.

Even if they had the repair kits they needed, it would take several days of constant work and hard labour to get the engine operational again. A bigger problem presented itself when the Packers found that even the fuel tank had caught a leak, and some of the tires on the front section of the vehicle were just grinding metal, whilst the rubber was all but worn away by heat or punctures and even the iron tracks were loose.

The armour plating of the vehicle, as thick as it was, needed a lot of repair work. The pack seemed disheartened at the sight, not looking forward to travelling on foot in possibly dangerous lands, their only knowledge coming from rumours, myths, or legends.

'This ain't good boss,' Boris said, chucking the last of the supplies on the top decking down to the group below.

'Aye, our baby's shafted,' he replied, letting out a long drawn out sigh shaking his head.

'Think I can safely say we ain't getting her going again,' Crazy John added, wiping his oily hands onto a thick putrid rag.

'On the bright side we did get through in one piece,' Pixie replied as he polished his rifle.

Neveah stared into the green lush wilderness before them, trying to put conceivable dangers to rest in the back of his mind for now. He could not show weakness or despair at the sight of losing their only safe transport from the elements on this long trip. His one good eye followed the plume of black smoke trace itself into the sky above, his left hand wiping some sweat and oil grease off his brow for a moment in the heat of the sun.

The last of the Packers took all the supplies they could carry and the group started heading into the depths of the forest away from the battlefield. Neveah could only give the orders of pressing on regardless, hoping that his men would not be deterred by stories such as Witches haunting the green wilderness or vicious animals that could walk upright like men.

Usually Packers would not enter the place because of superstition, rumours, legends, and fears that surrounded the tranquil landscape. In contrast, the Tribals avoided such lands because they respected the strange spirits that inhabited the wilderness. Both it seemed were now breaking their own rules or superstitions.

'Can't believe we made it after all that weird crap,' said Neveah.

'If it wasn't for dear Angelite, I don't think we could have made it at all!' added Boris's feminine voice. Neveah looked at Maledream expecting a reply of some sorts but he had nothing to say.

Pixie spoke in his polite voice:

'Indeed it is so, poor lady, although our pack has dwindled severely, only thirteen of us left after the count.' They looked back onto the battlefield.

It was hard to believe they had made it through at all from the amount of men that lost their lives, not just physically but also their spirit essence too. The thought of that turned Neveah's guts giving him depressing feelings about it.

He turned around to see Maledream staring at Angelite's unconscious form.

'She'll be all right lad, don't let it get you down,' he said, gazing into Angelite's sleeping eyes and then turning to the deep forest lit by sunlight, the rays of the sun shining through the thick green lushes.

The Tribal looked on with the rest of the group as they stood gazing at the tranquil land before them.

'What do you think is further in there?' muttered Maledream.

'From what I've heard I can't say, because I don't know for sure...' Neveah replied, his voice ushering a concern.

'Maybe we shall find out?' asked Pixie.

'Aye, maybe, but I think its best we try to find another way,' said Neveah.

'It could add more days to the journey if we do mate, Angelite knew it would be safe otherwise she would have told us not to go this way.'

'But even so…I wish she would wake up,' Neveah replied, staring at her.

'She looks very weak, and her staff is in pieces. None of us here know how to repair or even craft such an item. I've never seen anything like it in the city,' Boris replied.

'Well, don't worry about it now. Let's just start trekking through this forest,' said Maledream.

Nodding Neveah bellowed to the few remaining Packers:

'This way Packers the safe haven isn't far away now.'

A slight cheer from the pack arose before they picked up their equipment and food from what they had salvaged from the Battle Hammer and began advancing further into the glimmering strange woodland wilderness. The Tribal walked behind the Pack with Angelite in his arms. The sun and sky were now bright from Angelite's spell and reminded him that she had managed to control nature.

The place was alive with wildlife, from insects to birds, and seemed peaceful and untouched by anything evil, easing Maledream's deep and dark thoughts. Much banter was being talked of the things the Packers had undergone back in the city, and they seemed happy to have swapped the grey walls of suburbia for the green walls of the countryside. It seemed the Packs' superstitions were gradually easing the further they ventured in.

'So Maledream, we gonna talk more about what happened to you and your family all them cycles ago?'

'Not really in the mood now, Neveah. Can't you leave it for some other moment?'

'Aye, I know you don't want to talk mate, but you ain't helping yourself…'

'Listen, I don't know myself Neveah, so I don't know why you're bothering to ask. All I can remember is some stuff about our childhood, but I can only remember you, no one else,' he let out a sigh before continuing as if all were a blur to him.

'All I really remember was something along the lines of a very long journey…' he said.

'And then since over ten, maybe thirteen cycles ago even, I was picked up by Larkham and his group like some lost black sheep.'

'Aye, I know it sounds depressing, but I can help you remember who you are, mate. I may look like some kind of ugly ogre but I ain't all that bad,' he said, laughing to lighten the mood while wiping the sweat from the heat of the sun off his roughly shaved bald head.

'Pity there isn't any breeze, all the trees soak it all up it seems,' Neveah said.

Maledream looked down at the dry earth.

'Nor has the rain touched the ground here.'

'It is quite unnatural but then again, nothing seems natural as of late,' replied Neveah, softly grunting as he walked over a small grassy slope as he gazed at the earth.

'Right, well get on with what you have to say Neveah, as I know you'll just keep bugging me until we get back on the topic,' Maledream said.

'Aye, so be it, well all those many cycles back we came from a place far down south, from a place that not even I can remember now as it has been a long time. A place apparently worse than the city and more like near those damned lizard beasts, from what I remember we lived in a place that was overrun by these sick beings intent on killing every last one of us. We and our families...or what was left of family or friends back then we managed to get away and travelled far from water. You could say that water is a curse nowadays. We travelled on foot for hundreds of days avoiding danger at most turns until,' Neveah paused for a second.

'I know what could jog your memory! Eventually we came across four robed travellers, who themselves wielded blades which looked similar to the one you carry...except I don't know if their swords did what yours did earlier.'

'What, or who were they?' Maledream quizzed.

'Who were those four robed figures? They had blades much like mine?' he added.

'Aye, as I said, similar like yours. It was they who told us of this safe haven, but they didn't agree to accompany us. They were very aloof, didn't talk much, and had some sort of weird symbols on the back of their hoods...somewhat circular, with other strange symbols. Funny thing is these men had some sort of animals with them...can't remember what they were called now but they had four legs and long necks and were built rather largely, much like the strange large men themselves. What was also stranger was that you could not see their faces, it was as if their features were covered by shadow from the hoods they wore. No idea who they were but they talked little from what I remember to the Elders in the group and pointed us in the right direction you see, you remember anything at all mate?'

An eerie whistling of wind passed through the leaves in the trees giving Maledream a cold sensation up his spine thinking back to his dream, before replying:

'No,' he lied, not mentioning his dream, wondering if the hooded figure was perhaps linked to Neveah's memories.

'Well maybe it will come back to you but, as I was saying, these four characters pointed us in the right direction and we set off on a difficult trek through dead grasslands, dead burned forests, mountainous terrain. I'm surprised you can't remember anything mate it was quite a journey! Built up our legs like they were nothing but muscle. Seeing this forest here is a nice welcome site compared with everything else I can remember.'

Maledream wiped the sweat off his head carefully, the cool breeze returning to the group as they pushed deeper in the forest under the cool shadows of the leaves.

'Those blades they had were something else which they carried though. You seemed quite drawn to them, you went on, and on about them until you drove us mad. But it was something to talk about and we were all a little curious ourselves. Those travellers even had teeth and other mementoes from the many beasts they had killed hanging on chains from their necks. Some of these chains were finely crafted and woven with the finest metals you've ever seen. They even bore one ring on each hand, all glowing different colours as if they had some sort of magic about them. Quite dark characters they were but it was quite a misconception of who they were if you get my meaning?'

Pausing for breath, Neveah looked at Maledream, continuing:

'Got off the point slightly, but I was hoping you might have remembered something as you were enthralled by those strangers and their swords and other various bits and pieces. I thought you might have remembered something.'

'I'm sure it'll all come back to me eventually,' Maledream breathed heavily.

'So what about this sword of yours? How the hell did you come across something just as weird as Angelite's spells? It's had some Packers asking questions and I don't know what to tell them,' Neveah said.

'I have no idea what it is, but I found it a while ago on the battlefield, except a bit closer to the coast.'

'Shit, makes me want to go back and find something like that myself!' Neveah joked.

'I've no idea what sort of power its capable of doing, scares the crap out of me, but it's saved me a few times now...first time I seen its power was when I first met Angelite the other day, saved her from something called an Anunaki.'

'Anu-what?' Neveah asked as his brow furled slightly.

'Basically a giant walking lizard...almost decapitated me, if it were not for Angelite saving me with her strange gifts I wouldn't be here now.'

'Ah, so she saved you then,' Neveah chuckled, adding:

'Figures!'

'I prefer to call it team work...' Maledream said with a smile.

'So back to my original point, when she healed me, it seemed to awaken the blade and within moments I managed to fell the beast.'

'Aye quite a tale Maledream, after all I've seen I believe you...only ever heard of those bastard lizards in legends though. To hear you defeated one with that sword of yours, it just sounds so unreal yet also believable. If I hadn't of witnessed use that sword myself, I would have said that you were taking the piss,' Neveah replied.

'It's one thing to hear of them in stories, but to see them with your own eyes. It's large black eyes petrified me down to my very soul, it was about twice your height as well,' Maledream said, shaking his head and remembering the fear he felt fighting the beast.

'Twice my height? Shit mate, you got to be pulling my leg?' Neveah chuckled shaking his head in disbelief.

'Let's just pray we don't come across one. It's scales are thick and they are crazed beyond belief...if it weren't for the sword it wouldn't of fallen,' Maledream replied, Neveah staring into his old friends eyes for a moment and could see the fear of it deep down within him.

'Anyway, let's rest, it's been a long day, and we've walked a few miles.'

Neveah ordered the rest of the Packers in front to sit down on some fallen trees. Laying Angelite down in a comfortable sleeping position, the Tribal stroked her head staring at her wondering if she would ever awaken again.

'It's a shame our Battle Hammer died on us. I'm severely grieved Neveah, I put so much of my heart and soul into that piece of rusted crap!' spoke Crazy John sparking off some conversation amongst the quiet Packers of the group.

'Aye, it's a shame but what can you do, eh? We didn't have the fuel to make it all the way to this safe haven. We knew we had to walk, but not this early on that's for sure,' Neveah replied, scratching his eye patch and wiping his forehead.

'This forest gives me the shivers, it has gotten a lot quieter too Neveah,' said Pixie, looking around anxiously as was the rest of the Pack.

'Hmmm nothing we can do, except kill anything that has a problem with us being here. Anybody heard anything about this place?' Boris asked.

'No, apart from some myths surrounding it which we've all heard of in one crappy bar after another,' replied Neveah.

It seemed that no one had gone this far from of the city. The land was totally new to them, and with only rumours of beasts and Witches it certainly did not lighten anyone's mood.

'Plenty of lumber around if we want to burn something,' Crazy John said as he sharpened his knives with a thick whetstone.

'Aye, but don't you touch crap...no telling what's watching us and what'll get pissed off if we do something like that,' the Pack leader muttered.

'Not much chance of that happening Nev, we'll need heat later on,' Boris replied, Neveah eventually nodding.

'Aye, don't want to freeze at night either,' he smiled.

'It is a weird place, never seen so much green everywhere and seeing anything else human in this place is like zero to none or something,' said Pixie.

'Well let's have some munch, and then we'll continue, I don't like being sat down for too long. Never can be sure who is watching, if anybody is there that is,' Neveah uttered.

Falling silent, everyone seemed paranoid that something was looking at them from the trees around them. All were ready to fight if they were charged while they were eating, drinking, and resting but nothing came for them. The occasional twig snapping in the forest or a quick rush of air alarmed some of the group for a moment, until a sigh of relief sounded at it being nothing.

Maledream lay down to rest after placing Angelite down carefully. He was thinking about Neveah's words hoping some of his memory might return.

'So tell me Neveah, what else happened? How were we separated and from what?' Maledream asked.

Drawing in a deep breath Neveah continued to enlighten him the best he could while sharpening the blade on his pole arm with a thick whetstone that created a swift flow of sparks.

'Well...' Neveah continued:

'We blindly set foot in the city during the day but as we travelled through at night all hell broke loose. We weren't prepared for the

trouble we met in the city.'

'You mean that's when we first met this Pack culture?' Maledream elaborated.

'Aye, anyway to cut a long and bloody depressing story short we got separated as we got lost in the fights while trying to flee in panic. I was caught with my back against the wall facing a few big Packers. One of them stood out before me and thrust his weapon towards me trying to gut me. In a heated rush, which I can barely remember save the blood afterwards, it was clear I had swiped his blade across his own neck. There is more to it though and I'll try and fill you in on most of it.'

Neveah stopped talking for a moment, his hands still as he looked into the surrounding forest thinking he heard something.

Maledream turned his head himself but could see nothing.

'I see,' Maledream replied quietly.

Neveah continued:

'Since then I have taken charge of these guys and all the fellow people. It's how pack groups work as I'm sure you know. You take out the biggest brute who leads them all and you become the Leader. But facing the loss of my family and friends and not knowing the way I decided to take refuge in that bloody place. For many cycles of the moon and then the many seasons I gave up on almost everything except leading a group of Packers. I soon learned the ways...some members I did not like, especially how this new culture to me reacted. It was not in my nature but I found myself caught up in their way of life but refused to bow down to it...carefully and slowly crafting a group of friends I could rely on. I'm thankful for my physical strength, Maledream. At times it may not have been enough but I pride myself over my ways more than anything else in this blood soaked world.'

Neveah paused again while he examined his blade to check whether he had sharpened the blade too much or too little.

Adjusting his stroking of the stone against the edge of blade of his pole arm, he continued with his story.

'I never did find out what happened to you, Maledream, and I presumed you were dead like everyone else I knew or loved in the attack. It's great to see you made it. Come to think of it I shouldn't be too surprised as you were always good at hiding especially in the shadows. I wonder how you lost your memory and how you can get it back. Perhaps if I give you little snippets from my memory, it will help you. Oh, we did have a good laugh back then as you were always a comedian.'

Sighing the pair sank in thought for a moment.

'Hmmm it is a hard one isn't it,' Maledream muttered quietly under his breath.

'I can't remember much but I do have dreams or nightmares sometimes of some things, sometimes I think it's my memory trying to tell me, but to be honest I go with what my adopted old man said "Only look in front of you, never look back". I see wisdom in those words in some way. Even Angelite has helped me take my mind off wandering in the past and I do want to look forward not back if you get my meaning. I don't think my past matters terribly to me anymore. I just want to find safety and begin a journey of learning safe away from everywhere else. I think it's time I started growing up properly and stopped being an annoying fool like I usually am.'

'Aye, but it what makes you, you Maledream. Remember looking back allows you to reflect and change and it makes you a better person. Things happen from moment to moment but it's all a learning experience for the spirit in all of us,' Neveah replied.

'You're starting to sound like Larkham, Neveah, with all this bloody wisdom, it must be contagious. I do remember that you were chosen to be a leader when you were younger.'

'Ah see your memory is coming back mate! Yes I was going to be chosen to be a spiritual leader back in those days, but that was before we had to face the violence of the city. I have tried to reach out to the few Packers here who do agree with me, but only my closest Packers mind you...the ones you killed back in the city were rotten apples, but you get them occasionally and unfortunately.'

'Indeed, old friend, indeed,' Maledream said.

'Anyway, as I was saying, once all my friends were dead I turned into a barrel of hatred...for a short time. I hurt from losing everyone I cared about or even loved. I met one woman, but sadly things didn't turn out the way I hoped,' said Neveah.

'Really? Who was this woman, mate?' Maledream asked.

'Aye she was nice...' Neveah's eye seemed to water at the thought of whoever she was inside his mind.

'I'd rather tell you some other time, pisses me off just thinking about it too much. Anyway, as I was saying, I was a barrel of hate and then after my woman I became worse, and then after a many brutal pillaging I began to grow tired and weary with this hate lingering within me. Since there was no one around for spiritual guidance like I was used too, I had to contemplate things myself,' Neveah said, pausing for a moment to look at his Packers talking in their own conversations.

'It was an endless cycle Maledream but now from the last few cycles of the moon I began to feel more tranquil in myself. Some of the

other Packers have too. Something was different we would all say. I sometimes wished things had turned out differently and that we had reached this safe haven in the first place. I always used to say to my fellow Packers that one day we would search for it. Back when you and I was younger, mate, our group leaders told us that everything in life was planned as if it were all a great big spider's web. And that coincidence only existed for the most ignorant of humans...I thought until yesterday that it was all a load of old shit...and then you reappeared from the shadows, my old friend.'

Neveah paused for a moment to fill up his smoking pipe, the crude tobacco smelled nice on the breeze.

The Pack leader continued:

'And now I have no doubts, perhaps life is all planned even with our choices. Maybe there is some sort of strange stalemate or something, you know sort of like a balance...I don't know, maybe...makes you think doesn't it mate?' Neveah asked Maledream, who had his chin resting on the knuckles of his hand deep in thought.

'You are right, something strange certainly is up. Don't know about you but I think this place is bringing a lot of peace to us all,' replied Maledream.

'Aye, you're right. It is.'

They finished talking, instead listening in on the group's conversations, blowing pipe smoke into the breeze around them as the Packers dished out food, water, or alcohol.

Maledream shut his eyes for a moment to catch some rest rather than eat. It had been a long day, but now he was enjoying lying in the sunlight relaxing as the breeze caressed his face.

After they had finished their meals and drink, the group began their journey through the forest once again. They crossed over many brooks and streams of water within the huge, what seemed to be, a never-ending woodland as the sun began to set creating a more gloomy mysterious atmosphere.

The light wind blowing through the leaves of the trees created eerie sounds making some of the Packers feel nervous so they kept their weapons ready for any sign of attack from anything hiding in the green wilderness.

'We're going to have to set up some sort of camp soon Neveah,' said Maledream.

'Yup, we've earned a good rest...what the...you all see this?' asked Neveah.

The group had entered an ancient grove containing a large giant oak tree that had many extra different warped roots leaving and joining

each other at the base. The leaves seemed to have an autumn gold about them as if they glowed within the last of the dying sunlight. Maledream sensed a very large amount of pleasantness about the spot and felt extremely safe.

It was similar to what he had felt when Angelite had done her spell in front of him and Larkham back at the Tribal camp. It had the same feel of raw energy that was pure of heart in some way. What was more unusual about this large oak tree apart from its size was the base of the trunk was separated into three parts each joining into a centralised point like some sort of pyramid.

Its bark had unusual swirls and symbols etched onto it. Yet on closer inspection had not been carved by any known tool and seemed entirely natural, as strange as it appeared. Entering slowly the pack surveyed the peaceful, quiet area with stern eyes and tightly held weapons. Ears were keened as Neveah raised his fist to halt the group. Moments seemed to disappear as the group focused on seeing and hearing.

'Well don't know about you but this place is fairly safe looking everyone. Let's sit our asses here for the night!' a satisfied Neveah said.

Cheering, the Packers began setting up their skinned tents with renewed vigour just so they could have at last a nice quiet sleep with what seemed no disturbance, even from other Packs. Slumping Angelite gently to the floor, Maledream stretched his aching muscles high in the air, letting out a huge breath of relief before setting up the tents with the rest of the group. Night soon fell and the moon shone brightly through the leaves of the great mysterious oak tree, lighting the camp in a soft silken vale of faint cosmic blues. Burning its soft embers of light, the camp fire they had lit from dead logs and dry golden crisp leaves kept the group warm in the cold chilling breeze wafting steadily through the woodland landscape.

Around the fire, many of the Packers chatted but some felt it difficult to relax in such an alien environment. Packers took turns parading around the perimeter of the circle just in case something was spying on them. Gradually as the moon reached the highest point in the dark blue starlit sky, they began to start their well-deserved slumber as the group bid good night retreating to their tents, as their own ember in their spirit grew weary and tired.

Maledream could not sleep however and was troubled by a headache. He rubbed his forehead and walked around before settling next to Angelite in her tent.

'Why don't you wake up, Angelite?' he whispered.

'It's been a while now...'

Crackling softly with slight hissing and popping the campfire began to subside. The air began to feel colder.

'Won't this pissing headache just bugger off!' he said quietly, groaning again as he covered his eyes with his hands rubbing them intensely.

Opening his eyes Maledream felt a cold wet sensation on his back. He noticed that the circular area around the oaken tree was starting to grow a frost up the trunk of its bark. Unsure of what he was seeing, he crept closer to see moonlight shining on this white blanket oh frost that had seemed to come from nowhere.

Around the circular area were stones, standing several feet in height that began to glow with many arcane symbols that hummed and flickered with energy, many vines that covered and camouflaged them grew and floated upwards in an anti-clock wise direction around the clearing.

Maledream felt no fear in what he was seeing or feeling so he did not reach for his weapon and instead continued watching looking to see if any other Packers or Neveah was awake.

'You bring weapons of war, stranger. This is the forbidden woodland retreat and this is also a sacred grove you are desecrating,' a sweet soothing voice, much like Angelite's own, whispered in Maledream's mind.

'Who are you?' he returned quietly.

'We are the warders, the protectors, the most sacred, we look after this forbidden forest. You have trespassed. What good reason do you have for setting feet within the Sacred Circle?'

Spheres of ethereal light slowly floated from the leaves of the great oak tree, floating high above as if they were many droplets of snow yet to hit the ground. Shaking from the cold, he replied:

'We came from the city...and seek a place called Meridia. This woodland was in our path and we did not mean to offend, whoever you are?'

'I sense death surrounding you all, give us a reason as to why I should not banish such vile creatures back into Mother Earth's oceans? Or let the ground you stand on swallow you whole to feed this Great Oak?'

Clenching his hands, he barked back at the lights in frustration:

'Do not dare threaten us for we have not done any wrong to you or this woodland,' Maledream said, his mind thinking back to what Larkham once told him to say about freewill with spirits.

'We are free spirits and have freewill,' Maledream asserted.

The voice did not utter a word after the Tribal' anger lit his

sword slightly, creating a pale crimson glow around the crystal clean sheets of frost on the ground.

A few moments passed before the voice uttered once more.

'So I see you have a weapon lost from ancient times, young one. Very intriguing if we do say so ourselves, but please stem your anger in this peaceful sanctuary,' said the strange voice.

'We have not done anything wrong.'

The voice ignored Maledream's defence, instead, the strange voice changed topics.

'And you have brought along a very spiritual being with you, Angelite is it?'

Maledream gasped in amazement as he looked back into the tent to see many white pulsating orbs hovering above Angelite.

'I think it is time we revealed ourselves.'

The white orbs began to glow brightly before a shriek rang through everyone's minds, disturbing the Packers from their slumber.

'What the hell is that?' Neveah yelled, coming out of his tent and covering his ears. Similar responses came from other Pack members.

The shriek faded away disappearing back into the dark foreboding wilderness.

'Don't draw your weapons,' Maledream ordered as he gazed at the pack unlatching their pole arms.

'What the hell is all this frost? And what is with those lights?' Neveah muttered, wandering over to stand next to Maledream.

From the opposite side of the great oak and in the pale glowing light of the moon, several strangers entered the circle drawing closer to the group. Their tread seemed to freeze the floor beneath them, yet caused the very wildlife around them to sprout poison ivy and thorny vines instantaneously.

They watched the first stranger approach into full visibility within the camp. She was a young woman with long black coarse hair, wearing a full-length shimmering white robe as if it were crafted out of thick spider silk.

As the frosty dew set upon her garb, the lights of the Orbs lit it with a shimmer. The stranger's robes seemed to imitate frozen spider webbings that one would see on cold frosty mornings. The woman was wearing a circlet on her forehead, which had been carved from fine tree-bore. It was decorated with many gemstones placed within individual holes that glowed a cosmic blue.

These hummed with energy that seemed to emanate its own cold

spell upon her eyebrows. It looked as if she was cold death itself.

Two similar women appeared dressed in similar robes but without the circlet. Instead, both held staffs that looked very warped. Amongst the Packers could be heard whispers that the stories about Witches haunting the forests to be true.

'My, my, three beautiful shrieking women, just my lucky night,' Neveah said, clearly not amused by the high-pitched voices, showing no fear to stem the morale of his pack.

'How very rude,' she replied, adding:

'However, this is not a time to teach you manners. You wish to know who we are and I shall tell you.'

A sinister cold smile raced across the woman's lips.

'Forgive me for such a rude entrance at this moment of night, you have not only disturbed our Sacred Grove, but you have also desecrated it by burning dead oak. The spirits of nature do not look on kindly to those that disrespect this most natural spot of beauty. I and my companions here are the Witches of this Sacred Oak Grove and follow in the footsteps of many generations who have protected this place.'

From around the Grove eyes of night creatures caught the group's attention, glaring at them from all around, their eyes glowing soft showing greens and reds in the pale moonlight.

'So you are guarding this sacred site? May I ask how you know Angelite's name?' queried Maledream, not sure on the Witches motives.

'There is much we know, we merely wish to help this unique soul,' the lead Witch replied.

'You have changed your tune all of a sudden Witch, first you threatened us, and now you wish to heal one of our companions? What exactly are you playing at?' Maledream asked.

Gracefully walking up to the Tribal, the Witch put her cold finger on his lips with the creepy cold smile emanating from hers. The cold touch relaxed him almost instantly warming him slightly inside.

'I am the Witch of the Spirit of the Earth. It is my duty to protect this Grove. There are many, many others but you shall not see them here in this deep forest. All groves are sacred places keeping the world healthy and in full flow with the energies of Mother Earth. We here guard it in hope of atoning for what our ancestors' atrocities have done in the past. That sword you carry has seen much evil, and killed much evil but it is not the only one. There are many others used for balance, some used for evil.'

She paused, staring at Maledream's sword as she circled him, her stride stirring thoughts of ghosts of apparitions by how she moved with a smooth elegance.

'We felt the very air thicken with an ancient taint this afternoon...to prevent you using it more we also aided Angelite without her knowing, thus saving your lives on the battlefield of old. If it were not for us you would not have made it here, it is simple fate that you managed to stumble onto our grove,' she said.

'So you're saying you're responsible for almost killing Angelite?' Maledream said angrily.

'If it were not for us as I said, you would not have made it. We watched you fight the evil on that dead plain with courage. We helped you because we pitied you,' she said.

'So you almost killed Angelite in the process?' replied Maledream bitterly.

Neveah watched as the two were close to arguing while the other Pack members watched silently with twitchy fingers.

'Aye how did you witness us fighting? The battlefield is many leagues back to the south,' Neveah asked.

'We have our ways, large man. The same way we found out Angelite's name,' replied the Witch.

Maledream and Neveah looked at each other and shrugged.

'Well all this spying hasn't gotten you anywhere yet, and I'm still trying to comprehend your motives...' Maledream said.

'We shall discuss more soon. But for the moment, let us heal her before her soul is too diminished to be saved.'

Silence fell as they watched the spirit Witch push past Maledream and then Neveah with the other two Witches in tow.

Racing underneath Angelite white orbs carried her out of the tent, glowing, and humming brightly underneath and around her leaving a trail of neon light in their flight paths.

Angelite floated through the air until she descended to lie underneath the Great Oak while the three strange spell casters sat down in a triangle around her, laying their hands on her chest, overlapping one hand onto another while the group watched.

The Witches did not speak and the entire group could hear was the slight humming from the surrounding Orbs, as they floated or raced around, over and under the roots of the Great Oak.

Many creatures appeared within the area, although they were not solid and appeared more as spirit forms. There were cats, wolves, and crows, their eyes glowing in the pale reflection of the eerie, pale blue light of the moon. They seemed to be drawn to the small ritualistic ceremony for Angelite. A mist began to seep in from the darkness of the forest as more of the spirits began to show, adding to the chill and

the strange atmosphere filling everyone.

'The spirits that heal are here, it is up to nature herself in the realm of spirit not this earth plane of existence. These creatures of this ancient world will decide,' said the lead Witch.

Maledream was getting edgy and even though the frost was as cold as it was, he was breaking a slight sweat on his forehead. A reassuring Neveah put his hand on Maledream's shoulder.

'It'll be okay mate,' he whispered to him.

'Let them get on with it. I don't think we want to mess with them, no telling what curses they can inflict us with.'

Howling, the wolves stepped forward, their fur coats were either pristine with white, black or grey while some looked as if they died a painful death as remnants of tattered flesh and bone hung from some who had not done so well in their former lives on earth.

If it were not ethereal, Maledream could have passed out from the sight. To him he could imagine the strong smells of their rotting flesh. Others in the group were weary but stayed very still, the Packers tensed with terror and superstition at what they were witnessing. Some gripped their weapons tightly or jumped in a surprised fashion as the ghostly animals walked straight through them.

The wolves sat around the Witches as if they themselves were communing with the spirits. They stayed a short while and then began howling again, which seemed to be their signal to retreat to the outskirts of the grove. Once more, they took their places in the darkness of the undergrowth watching with cold eyes.

Next came the cats, many in number, and many variations, from big to small, fat or thin and some looking like rotting carcasses. They squealed as they approached the inner circle and stood before the Witches. Like the wolves, they then returned to the undergrowth, their eyes beaming at the group as they passed between and under their legs, causing some members of the group to freeze or jump in fear.

The spirits of crows did not move and instead their cawing cries sounded from the trees, their beady little eyes glowing dark hazy blues. Maledream eagerly waited for Angelite to recover, his impatience growing, as nothing seemed to happen.

'How long now?' he muttered clasping his hands together to try to keep them warm as it was still very cold.

'Quit your worrying mate, it ain't going to speed anything up,' said Neveah.

Maledream tried to be patient as he and Neveah watched closely to see what would happen next.

'So mote it be,' the Witches uttered in unison to the spectral

sprits, the orbs racing through the Witches' crown chakras. Energies were manifesting through their arms and into their hands flooding Angelite with healing golden energies of spiritual constitution.

Singing with hums and sighs as they worked their healing on Angelite, the group could only watch and stare in bizarre amazement at what was exactly going on. Dissipating from their cold gentle hands, the Orbs stopped flowing through the channelling coven of witches, and so the ritual ended.

The old woodland spirits such as the wolves, cats, and crows sank back into the moonlit darkness of the forest. The mist began to subside and disappear from the Sacred Circle, giving back a little more warmth to those that were shivering.

Slowly and gradually, the mysterious orbs raised Angelite from the ground once more, elegantly twisting her form through the air against all laws of physics to her tent and rested her there in her original slumber spot. The lead Witch leaned on her staff, looking at Maledream for a moment.

'You wished to know how we receive our information so I will tell you. Larkham...you know him, young spirit?'

'Yes,' Maledream replied sternly.

'He has told you about communing with people such as ours, but you would never listen to him...we communicate with him on the astral planes, now a part of this "Earth Plane." You still have much to learn, but then again so do we all, isn't that right?'

Getting confused by her riddles he merely nodded, and pretended to know what she was babbling about.

'In basic terms, young man, we communicate with him and many other spiritual leaders across this strife ridden and sick planet. It is through means of travelling through this extra dimensional existence in spirit that we can find out such information or keep an eye on certain people, people like you and Angelite.'

'So you have been watching over us for some time then...a request from Larkham perhaps?'

'He did ask, nicely I may add, if it were not for him you would be surely doomed...but your fate lines did not and will not end on that battlefield or any yet to come but you never know.'

She laughed loudly, toying with the emotions of those who were scared of them.

'However...' she continued in a low tone.

'We do not possess the means to fix your dear Angelite's staff, or rather the crystal, for such an object you will have to travel high to the mountain ranges to the north and seek a hermit called N'Rutas who

dwells in a secretly covered glade, covered by a waterfall. Be aware travellers for she shall have a task at hand for you to accomplish before she can gift you such a sacred stone or staff of the mountains.'

Looking weary Neveah butted into the conversation.

'Aye and what will she ask of us, Witch of Spirit?'

'How am I to know? I know her, and she does not give willingly without a favour especially for such artefacts that she hordes like a dragon in a den,' she said.

'So, are we to find this waterfall to the north on the hills easily?'

'Of course not,' she laughed cruelly.

'Have faith and follow your best judgements, it is not easily missed, if you can follow the correct clues.'

'Aye, damn you and your riddles Witch...but we are thankful, and I thank you on behalf of Maledream and the pack for helping Angelite,' Neveah spoke graciously.

'Now that's how you talk to your elders,' she said.

'*Elders? They look as young as us,*' Maledream raised his eyebrow thoughtfully.

'You can stay until morning. May the spirits protect you, and dare I say you have our blessings. We must go. We have spent too long talking. You had better be gone before the sun hits its highest point in the heavens, for we do not like lodgers...and Maledream...give Larkham our warmest welcome when you should encounter him next.'

She finished by darting symbols across her chest and then to the air before turning her back on them and disappearing back into the darkness of the Grove. Many Packers sighed with relief, and many began to talk about the rumours of Witches haunting the forests being true.

'Wait!' shouted Maledream.

'When will Angelite wake up?' His voice echoed through the dark recesses of the forest but there was no reply.

'Great didn't expect that. I did expect more...I have a feeling this won't be the last time we cross her and her coven,' he added.

'Relax, mate,' replied Neveah.

'I'm sure she will wake in the morning. Now let's all go and get some well earned rest. This cold is starting to bite my fingers and toes just standing here with these weird Orbs flying above us.'

'Think I'll feel much better when were out of here,' Boris said amongst the idle chatter.

'This trip is getting stranger every day,' Crazy John added.

The group settled down again to sleep but Maledream stayed awake, reflecting on what he had seen.

Chapter Eight

Journey for the Hermit...

'On a long journey of human life, faith is the best of companions, it is the best refreshment of the journey, and it is the greatest property.'

Buddha

Maledream awoke to find Neveah yelling in the cold morning.

'Cowards!' he cried with enough anger to wake even the dead.

'Are we under attack!?' Maledream shouted back, trying to find his weapon in a dreary panic.

'The bastard Pack left us!' Neveah growled like rabid beast, punching a nearby tree with his fists repeatedly.

'What?' Maledream quickly replied jumping to his feet outside the tent looking around in bewilderment.

'Where did they go?' he asked.

'Who knows but they swiped all our food...and I am so hungry mate I could eat even this great blasted Oak!' he said, stomping his feet hard into the ground.

'I'm going to personally cut off all their bollocks!' he roared once more. Taking notice of his surroundings in the early morning in the grove, Maledream noticed that the Orbs were gone, although his senses told him otherwise. The ground was wet and moist and no frost was to be seen, save on the Great Oak that had silken frosted cobwebs still dangling and shining from the warm sun through the leaves of the surrounding forest.

'At least they didn't take our weapons, but their balls are still mine,' Neveah spoke in a calmer tone, although there was still anger in his deep voice. Maledream was relieved to find his sword and other equipment still present.

'Well they haven't taken my sword,' before he could finish his sentence, both Maledream and Neveah heard a sweet voice utter to them.

'What are you boys squabbling about?'

Angelite was awake sitting upright and rubbing her eyes.

'Whoa!' The two men cheered.

'You're awake at last little lady!' Neveah said with excitement, the pleasure of seeing Angelite squashing his annoyance about the morning's surprise. Maledream rushed to her, grabbing her hand and squeezing it tightly.

'We thought we had lost you,' he said, smiling at her.

'No, no really I'm okay. I just feel slightly tired...and thirsty,' she replied, her voice dry and croaky.

'We can't help you with your thirst for the moment I'm afraid. My Pack has buggered off, along with the last amount of food and drink we had,' Neveah said, looking around to see which direction they may have gone.

'Let's not worry about that for the moment,' she said, and then asked:

'Where are we? I feel a very strong Resonance about this place, it's comforting.'

'We stumbled across it after we reached the edge of this forest, which we are now quite deep in. We came across a bunch of these Witches, or that's what they call themselves, and this grove is their 'sacred' grove apparently and we had trespassed.'

Angelite interrupted.

'Yes, as was intended!'

'Come again?' asked Maledream.

'It was arranged before we left your Tribal camp with Larkham. I should have told you but I did not count on falling unconscious.'

'That explains a couple of things,' replied Maledream, his voice filled with relief.

'I counted on you having a plan anyway,' Neveah replied with a smile, roughly scratching his eye-patch once again while Angelite continued:

'It was arranged, and I did intend to lead us this way through the forest counting on meeting these mysterious Witches that Larkham had told me about, he assured me they were nice.'

'We have a little quest we must accomplish for you first, Angelite,' Maledream said.

'Your staff broke when you cast that mighty spell that split the clouds in the heavens, and also the crystal stone you used also shattered. We have all the remains or as much as we could physically gather in a ragged bag for you, but also something else you might like to hear is that the Witches helped channel or rather force energies through you when you cast that cloud breaking spell,' Maledream said.

'Oh my, that was what the major influx of energies was! I did not know. I knew I had help but the help of these powerful Witches? How did they know?' she asked.

'Aye, that's what we asked them, they wore scantily clad robes and weren't like any Witches I met before, except for you of course,' answered Neveah cheekily, his arms crossed and his eyebrow lowered in deep thought over the events during the night, before continuing:

'They did not explain much and some of what they explained we could hardly understand, not least my pack, but apparently they have their ways through this Astral Plane of existence where all is spirit but not spirit and it was all rather confusing...especially for Maledream' Neveah sniggered shortly afterwards.

'I'm not as dumb as I look! Just because you're hungry you don't need to take it out on me,' Maledream retaliated.

'Only joking mate!' The atmosphere was picking up as the sun gathered its position in the sky, now above the silver clouded and red skyline.

Although neither sight nor sound was present from the animals that should be living in such a vast forest, it felt more alive than it had when they had first entered. It was almost noon by the position of the sun, and so the three of them began preparing to leave.

'I have learned of such techniques, used by the Witches, back home in sanctuary. This Astral Plane...I shall talk more later about it for now I think we had better get going to find some water. I can hardly open my mouth!' she sorely and quietly spluttered, sifting through the bag containing what was left of her staff.

'Right, well, let's pack the tents up and go hunting for some fresh food and water,' Maledream said.

'Aye, I hear that mate,' Neveah replied, ripping his shoddy tent down with one arm snapping the already bent and dented metallic pegs holding it in the ground.

A cycle later and all was packed. Neveah stopped trying to track his mutinied Packers and instead focused on his stomach, cursing once or twice while on the move about his pole arm and the betrayal of the Packers.

Maledream followed Neveah while helping Angelite's tired form walk through the deep green woodland. The two men enlightened Angelite on how the Witches had appeared, what was said, and how they had performed a healing ceremony to heal her spirit, finishing with how they had been told how to fix the staff.

'We have to travel far to the North up the hills and keep a look out for a...um...'

'Glade, Maledream, a Glade,' Neveah butted in.

The Tribal sighed and smiled.

'It is covered by a waterfall apparently if I'm not mistaken,' Maledream continued.

'They did not say how long the journey would take even if we find the right place. Apparently we need to "follow our best judgement" and that could prove frustrating,' Maledream added.

'Only to you,' laughed Neveah, turning around and punching Maledream's arm lightly.

'Someone is in a playful mood today. If I wasn't helping Angelite walk, I'd gladly kick your ass!'

Neveah did not reply but instead continued to laugh as they walked north through the lush forest.

After travelling several more cycles forward and after many breaks for a rest, the three companions gradually came across a river. An oak tree had fallen across the water serving as a useful bridge.

'Well, looks like we have some fresh water at last,' muttered Angelite.

'Aye and it looks mighty fine,' replied Neveah, his steady eye checking the open surroundings of the riverbank across the other side hawking for any potential threat or game that could be hunted.

Angelite sat down on the grassy bank while Maledream filled his empty flask with the clean sparkling river water before examining what lay on the riverbed.

'What...are these?' he muttered.

He had put his hand in the water, disturbing the fine dirt creating a brown mist in the unspoilt water. Dragging his hand back up, he opened his clenched fist to reveal many different crystals in his palm.

'Wow, look at these crystals,' he said aloud, sticking them in front of Angelite's weary face. She ignored them and instead snatched the flask of water from Maledream's other hand to drink it dry within a few heartbeats like a thirsty animal, then wiping her mouth and lips dry she finally spoke:

'Oh my!' she said with excitement.

'What are they?' he quizzed staring at the different colours.

'They are very unusual crystals. They look pure, and as I said very unusual but I guess this place has many more secrets,' she said, examining each one and noticing how perfect they were in shape.

'This one is an emerald, and this one, and um oh my, I can't remember what the rest of them are, but I do think a lot of them are different kinds of quartz crystals...very useful! If you boys can wait a little while longer, I'll have a quick swim to try and find a good sized

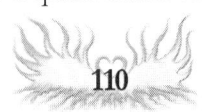

one for a new staff.'

'You expect to go swimming in your clothes?' questioned Maledream.

'Of course not,' she said as she started to disrobe.

'You can't do that!' he said, gawping and finding it difficult to avert his eyes.

'Watch me, if you want, but if you do I will not forgive you for it! Besides I need to drink more water while I'm at it, and have a good wash, I feel so filthy.'

'By the spirits,' Maledream muttered, slapping himself on the cheek. Neveah did not say a word but laughed at the pair with his arms crossed as he stood upright, still looking around like a hawk towards the distance.

'Well if you stay here Maledream and watch over Angelite, I'm going to try and find us some food over this tree bridge on the other side of the bank, won't be too long.'

Maledream nodded with a blush on his cheeks.

'Don't be too long mate, I don't know what she'll tear off next,' he laughed.

'You cheeky man...'

Angelite was totally stripped down and facing away from the two men with her long red hair covering her coxes. She turned to the two men with both heads averted and said:

'Don't be too long, Neveah, and Maledream don't look!'

She raised her arms, took a dive to the water, as smooth as a dolphin, and disappeared with a splash.

'Well if that wasn't an invitation I don't know what is...' said Maledream. Neveah laughed once again before waving at the Tribal as he began crossing the log bridge...

Reaching the other side of the bank, Neveah's eye caught footprints in the muddy bank to his right. On closer inspection, he could see it was the trail from his Pack's tread.

'Just wait till I catch them,' he said gritting his teeth.

He began to run through the green maze following the fresh tracks in a hypnotic fashion, his breathing now heavy from the heat and lack of breeze, sweat dripping off his forehead. Eventually, after following the fresh tracks, he found himself in a clearing, to find a bloody scene before him. Trees were battered and blood stained, pole arms were stuck halfway through the trees as if a battle had taken place. He could see the remains were from his Pack.

Catching his breath and wiping the sweat with his spare hand, he caught a strange scent on a burst of soft wind.

'Smells like flowers,' he thought.

Keening his ears, he froze. A humming noise sounded from somewhere but he was not sure from which direction.

'Where's it coming from?' he muttered.

Neveah's good eye spotted one of the nearby trees had a pole arm buried in its thick brown bark. Gently walking over and treading over the tracks softly and slowly he examined the battered condition of the weapon.

Ripping the pole arm out the bark he carefully laid it to rest on the floor, trying to think of what could have happened. Hearing the humming faintly he looked around to check for danger, the humming stopped again.

'Could have sworn I felt a breeze then...where are their bodies? Where is the rest of their cursed blood?' he thought.

He carried on examining the tracks, but all they could tell him was that a battle had been fought and his Pack had disappeared. He noticed different bullet casings lay on the earth, and from what he could see the Pack had been attacked from all directions.

The wilderness itself must have masked any gunfire that was used in self-defence. A disturbing sense of paranoia slowly seeped into Neveah's mind as he scanned the forest and deep green foliage in what was possibly one of the deepest parts of the forest.

Strange tracks or markings that did not look human were seen to have entered the small clearing where the Packers were fighting back to back. Scorch marks brushed the surrounding oaks in the vicinity with many bullet holes also etched into the thick bark. Neveah inspected the bark and could see that the wounds on the trees were recent, with sap running down the open seeping wounds.

The scorch marks looked as if they were made by a fire strong enough to have set trees alight, yet they seemed to be controlled in one area, as if it were a focused energy of some kind.

'Perhaps the Witches used similar magic to Angelite?' Neveah wondered. His senses heightened as he struggled to come to terms with what he was looking at. He reassured himself that the Witches would not have attacked them as they had offered safe passage last night, once they were told to leave the Grove and never speak of it again. The scent of flowers caught his nostrils once more, along with the soft wind. Humming once again rang in his ears but this time getting louder and louder.

He looked in all directions but remained on his knees as he prepared his pole arm to meet the danger that appeared to be coming closer. He could not see it but could hear and smell it.

Neveah wished Maledream were there to back him up with his enchanted sword. He was aware that the breeze was picking up behind him, bringing in a stronger smell of flowers. He tensed his muscles but kept his legs loose for a quick reflex for any moment. Catching the sound of the leaves and breaking branches above him, he realised then that the threat was not surrounding him. It was above him.

A split heartbeat sixth sense reaction caused him to move without a second thought as he dived to his right side raising his pole arm in a wide arc at the attacking foe from above. A splitting crunch sounded as if he had sliced through bone. Neveah rolled to his side before jumping to his legs raising his weapon in a defensive parry position to clearly see what was stalking him. Chilling cold ran down his spine as he stared upon the huge yellow and black striped flying beast.

'Looks like a giant wasp or bee, no wonder there was a smell of flowers and the sound of humming,' he thought.

The creature flew wildly after the blow across its carapace but it had only suffered a scrap and soon refocused on Neveah, raising its abdomen preparing to strike again with its many barbs.

Its wings created a cyclone of wind in the vicinity shaking the trees with its giant wing span blowing leaves, branches, mud and dirt at Neveah, as he struggled to retain his balance against the sheer force of the false wind. Still he held his ground like an iron wall. The giant beast charged, its mandibles dancing around its bony thick furry skull as if wanting to devour him.

With all his strength underneath its pressuring great wings, he thrust the point of his pole arm into the giant creature's exoskeleton covered thorax resulting in a satisfying crunch as he split its surface.

The creature reeled in pain, its wings slowing down as it came crashing down threatening to squash him underneath its weighty body.

He rolled to one side to deliver a final killing blow with his weapon in a deadly high arc slicing through its thin wings as it hit the floor. It was not fast enough as Neveah brought the death it threatened him with to the creature itself. First, he sliced off its great abdomen in several quick hard crunching blows severing it from its thorax and head. Finally, to put the beast out of its misery, he brought the weapon to bear on its head severing it from its thorax. Neveah stomped on it with his giant boot, thinking it may have been this strange beast that killed off his Pack.

'Fucking bugs, those Packers were mine, question is what you did with them all huh?' he muttered.

The smell of flowers was becoming stronger. More humming was apparent and closing in on his position.

He looked up to see more beasts were coming, many of whom looked bigger and more menacing than the one he had killed.

'Shit, ain't I glad I sharpened my weapon yesterday,' he said steadying his stance once again for another charge.

Nudging another pole arm on the floor with his boot, he picked it up with his offhand staring at it before looking back up at the charging beasts from above. Neveah swung at the creatures as they attacked. His fury was absolute as he swung both the pole arms like a whirlwind of anger.

Meanwhile, Maledream was leaning on his back while Angelite was diving for more stones. Looking at the blue sky with his arms crossed behind his head, he relaxed. It was then that memories from his childhood began coming through to him. A person he knew long ago with long red hair flashed into his memory, his eyes widened as he sharply sat upright looking for Angelite.

'She reminds me of somebody, that's why my feelings are mixed perhaps?' he thought.

He stared at the glinting water as the sun shone upon its surface, reflecting the hypnotising colours from the different minerals glittering under the thin layer of dirt that covered them. Before he had met Neveah way back in his childhood he knew he had met a young girl, all he could remember was long red hair, which Angelite shared. Emotions stirred deeply in his heart.

'Is it her?' he asked himself. Then muttering:

'Who was she? Why in my childhood?' he asked, losing himself in his mind.

He was interrupted all of a sudden, as Angelite emerged from the water, holding some large quartz crystals in her arms that barely covered her naked breasts.

'Put them away woman!' he cried, staring for a moment before remembering to look the other way.

Only laughter could be heard for a reply. Soon enough Angelite clothed herself again.

'You can look now, Maledream,' she called, a cheeky flirtatious grin wrapped around her cheeks.

'About bloody time! Neveah hasn't come back yet so he must have found something interesting.'

'Aye, Aye!' she heartily spoke, mimicking the Pack leader.

'I feel much, much better after the swim, my hair's clean, my skin's clean, that water has worked wonders with all those crystals underneath its surface! And...'

Maledream got up on his feet quickly, distracted by something that appeared near them.

'What is that on the fallen tree?' she muttered to him quietly.

'Appears to be the first sign of wildlife I've seen around here if I'm not mistaken,' he said.

The creature had long hair and a furry silver grey mane.

'It looks like a wolf,' said Maledream.

'There were some at the Witches' grove last night, but they were some ancient spirits.'

'I thought wolves were extinct in the Dark Age lands?' she said.

'I guess we thought wrong,' he replied.

The wolf's eyes locked with the Tribal before raising its head up high to let out a long and large howl.

Maledream drew out his sword, as he was not sure what to expect from a creature long thought to be extinct many cycles ago.

Angelite crept behind him also not sure what to expect. Finishing its howl, it turned tail and began to run in the direction where Neveah went.

'Got your stuff ready?' Maledream asked.

'Yes,' Angelite replied.

'Good, because we have some catching up to do, right now! Neveah could be in trouble.'

The pair ran as fast as they could across the fallen tree and onto the other side of the forest to chase the strange wolf.

Its howling continued yet it kept pace with them through the undergrowth of nettles, brambles, and roots that threatened to trip them at any moment.

Blinding them every moment was the noon sun beaming through the fast pacing autumn leaves as they ran after the wolf.

Then the howling stopped to be replaced by the sounds of humming and the wind wafting through the trees. Stopping in their tracks, they both began to listen.

'That humming is strange,' Angelite spoke loudly.

'It's strange indeed. And can you smell flowers?' asked Maledream.

'The breeze is stronger here. Can you hear the wolf? It's howling again.'

'I hear it,' replied Maledream as they began to follow the wolf again.

Breaking through the clearing, the two witnessed Neveah swinging two large weapons around like a maniac against the strong winds with many gashes across his torso and arms fighting gigantic wasps or bees.

Grabbing his sword instantly and ripping it out of its shoddy scabbard, Maledream joined in the fray.

'I'm coming,' he yelled, trying to be heard over the strong winds. Angelite stood back hiding behind a nearby tree, hoping the gigantic insects would not see her. She hoped she would not scream but she had a phobia about flying insects.

Neveah swiped his weapons against one of many of the beasts shearing its wings clean from its thorax and sending it crashing into one of the many surrounding trees. Roaring as loud as he could, he continued his blood rage of survival against more of the attacking insects. Maledream ran towards one of the flying creatures, while lifting his heavy sword up high waiting for the right moment to strike.

Neveah battered another away from him landing it onto the floor, its buzzing noises signalling the pain as its antennas raced around its skull like a confused headless chicken from the blow to its head. Just then, Maledream found his right chance to take it out. Jumping onto the crashing creature's abdomen, he swiped his blade in a low-arced fashion striking the creature from behind and right through its body, thorax, and head spraying its blood as his sword cut right through the bony exoskeleton of the creature.

Landing on his grip-less boots and panting as hard as he could from the amount of energy he just exerted, he struggled to remain on his feet. Maledream wondered how Neveah could have carried on after a few swings from holding both pole arms, let alone his own one. Regardless he carried on into the fray while Neveah skewered another of the flying beasts against a tree with one arm and then sliced it into three pieces with his other hand as if it were paper but Maledream could see he was weakening greatly.

His attention was drawn to another attack. He spun on his feet and dived to one side to avoid a great barbed stinger from an abdomen of one of the great flying beasts. It came at him again, faster than he expected for such a huge creature. As it threatened to impale him for a second time, Maledream's hands gripped tightly on the blade ready for the attack. The beast rushed towards him but Maledream timed it at the right moment to roll to his side while slicing the beast's abdomen in half, causing it to recoil and flutter like a confused moth hit by a hand.

Neveah diligently brought his weapons to bear on the crippled creature, relieving Maledream for a moment. The humming stopped. Nine beasts lay dead scattered around and severed in many pieces.

Any survivors had gone. Returning to its natural state, the wind had died away. Maledream watched Neveah fall to his knees and then keeling backwards breathing heavily, covered in gashes, with a lot of dust sticking to his drying wounds. The Tribal became aware of Angelite's hand on his shoulders and said:

'I think Neveah needs some attention, Angelite. Could you work your healing hands?' he muttered.

Nodding and without saying a word Angelite reached into her backpack, getting clean rags to wrap around Neveah's wounds, as he lay on the floor exhausted. She placed her hands on his chest and began murmuring her resonating incantations to help with the healing processes.

'These things are quite something aren't they? I didn't realise they got bigger than my fingernail,' said Maledream as he examined one of their bony, yet furry heavy severed heads with his hands.

'Guess we learned something new and deadly about this place,' replied Angelite, her eyes closed but still able to speak as she channelled the energies through her conscious mind. Neveah did not speak, only moaned for water occasionally as he slowed his breathing.

'I think we had better leave here soon before more of these giant pests threaten to take our lives again,' Maledream said.

'Wise decision,' a strange voice entered their minds.

'Who said that?' he asked. Angelite and Neveah looked around also to see if there was any one around.

'Didn't you hear that voice?' Angelite said, the two men nodding in reply.

'Who are you? A Witch?' Maledream said aloud while lifting his heavy sword up high looking in all distance directions of the forest.

'Show yourself! I bet it's you damned Witches messing with our minds. I would not put it past you.'

A growl could be heard in the distance, silencing him with a chill.

'Please be calm I mean you no harm. I am here to help you three out as a favour I owe to the Witches of the Grove in this forest. You could say I am one of the few remaining species of my kind.'

Maledream relaxed his sword arm.

'Species? All right come out and show yourself, whoever you are?'

Motioning to the others to stay quiet and still, they all waited. A huge, grey, and white coloured wolf came through the undergrowth and appeared in the clearing.

'You're that wolf from earlier?' said Maledream, the three all looking confused.

'Yes,' it replied within his mind.

They were a bit surprised that the voice came from an animal, Angelite had freaked Maledream out before by doing it herself when she was casting her magic but never before had he communicated with a creature that could talk with its mind. He glanced behind him to see a frightened Angelite hiding behind Neveah's bulky form, his one remaining eye looking at the wolf with a constant stare.

'It was I who warned you with my howls that your friend was in need of assistance. He would have fallen if you had not reached him in time. Those Vasps can kill by just grazing you in a matter of moments...it is good you were not stung.'

'Vasps?' Maledream asked getting closer to the wolf and locking his eyes with it.

'Yes Vasps,' it replied.

'These are not merely insects...these are gross mutations.'

'How the hell can that mutt speak to us?' asked Neveah.

'I'm a wolf not a mutt,' Silver replied, his voice not amused by the remark.

'This place gets weirder by the minute,' Neveah said.

'He looks so cute!' Angelite said finding the courage to move from Neveah to stroke the large wolf.

It seemed to grin with its mouth before continuing:

'For now I wish to tell you that you have escaped a terrible danger. Vasps contain venom said to be as strong as a viper's sting, like the snake, but enough about these filthy creatures, you three must follow me if you would like to reach N'Rutas. We don't have enough moments to waste right now. We must hurry before more return.'

'All right, if you say so,' replied Maledream, staring at Neveah who merely shrugged. Holstering his blade in place and making sure he had everything, he turned to speak to Neveah and Angelite.

'Let's get going then,' the Tribal added.

Neveah sighed, saying:

'Just when I was relaxing,' stretching his body and muscles in every place imaginable from the exhaustion.

'More running I suppose,' said Angelite.

'I guess we could just walk quickly,' Maledream replied, smiling.

'But we have got to hurry. The sun is starting to slide down the sky rather quickly now.'

Before they set off Neveah gathered the Packers' broken pole arms, weapons and torn rags from what was left of them tied them all to one tree in memory of his Pack.

'You were bastards, but you were good men, I shall honour you to your ancestors,' he muttered quietly.

One final check and the three adventurers were ready to set off following the wolf to the north, hoping that it was not one more fatal trap that would be too costly, and luckily, for Neveah they were travelling at a walker's pace.

'I will take you through a safe passage in this dense and formidable dark part of the forest. There are some places here that even the Witches cannot claim back because of evil taints,' spoke the wolf elegantly walking beside Angelite.

Darkness seemed to cover this part of the northern great forest as they waded in further, yet the smell of pollen floated on the air with the occasional hum of wings fluttering by above the forest canopy to much aggravation of Angelite's phobia as she squealed from time to time.

'So, wolf, just to break the ice a little, can you tell me your name,' asked Maledream in a quiet whisper.

'You may call me Silver.'

'Silver, quite a catchy name for a wolf with shiny silver looking fur,' the Tribal replied.

'Indeed,' replied Silver, as he carried on leading the way.

Feet aching and after much sweat, the group of four finally reached the edge of the darkness of the fallen part of the forest.

Maledream, Angelite, and Neveah followed Silver down a steep slope to a waterfall.

'We're almost there at last!' shrieked the priestess in excitement.

'All right, keep it down woman,' Neveah said, watching where he put his footsteps on the way down the slope.

Silver jumped down effortlessly bounding from one muddy ledge to another, twisting, and turning through the air while the three human beings struggled to keep their grip. Maledream found the going very difficult, constantly slipping in his shoddy boots.

'Just around the corner, you will know what to do and how to reach N'Rutas as I'm sure the witches instructed last night.'

Just as the group finally reached the bottom of the slope wiping

the mud and dry leaves stuck to their footwear.

'Great, he's disappeared,' said Maledream, the others looking around confused.

'Your right where did he go?' asked Angelite.

'Aye, strange mutt,' Neveah replied.

'Any idea on what he was Angelite?' Maledream asked.

'Not the slightest idea...he is the first of his kind I have encountered, his unique thought waves are something else indeed,' she said.

'You're telling us,' Neveah added.

They settled down to rest. Behind them was the slope they had climbed down. Ahead were the sounds of the waterfall, which seemed to be coming from around the corner of the cliff face.

'Well forget about that strange creature for now. We must move on and find this N'Rutas person to see if she can fix Angelite's staff' said Neveah as he wiped his brow.

'I hear you on that one mate, let's get a move on,' replied Maledream, before they headed around the corner towards the waterfall covering the entrance to the glade mentioned by the Witch.

Chapter Nine

Anunaki Council...

'When men began to increase on earth and daughters were born to them, the divine beings saw how beautiful the daughters of men were and they took wives from among those that pleased them...It was then, and later too, that the Nephilim appeared on earth - when the divine beings cohabited with the daughters of men, who bore them offspring. They were the heroes of old, the men of renown.'

Genesis, Chapter Six

Thousands of blood red and black candles lit the dark abyss of the triangular chamber where a meeting was to be held, flickering shades of dark colours lighting the gigantic tomb beneath the surface of the earth. The race of the Anunaki who had come from within the great catacombs and deep underground cities were already high on the hot smell of sulphur.

Looking down on them from above the seats of power were obelisks of great snakes, Anunaki Kings, and Queens of old, as ugly as the gargoyles hanging off arches of churches in the old human civilisations. Filling up the chamber were many Anunaki in blood red robes, hoods barely covering their bulbous large heads as they floatingly walked to their seats. These were known as lesser Anunaki. They had skin of a greyish texture and were far smaller than the 'warrior' type that Maledream had fought and defeated.

The second group of Anunaki that entered the triangular chamber bore robes or rich purple. Their skin was a darker texture than that of their grey kin, brown in contrast. This signified the age of this breed of the Anunaki compared to the grey breed that were still considered young, even after living over several hundred cycles of the sun. Sitting down and conversing among themselves, they waited for the high Council members of the black cult to enter as they all took

their seats speculating on why they had been gathered together. Rumours were plenty and scattered throughout the large candlelit chamber. Sure enough during conversation between the red and purple circles of the Anunaki Chamber, the black robed Anunaki entered, bearing gold rods or staves with snakes intertwined up the shafts of these ceremonial instruments.

Black obsidians represented the two eyes of the golden snakes, while a third jewel, an amethyst, represented the third eye in the middle of the snake's golden skull. Wearing robes of the darkest black, they truly looked like creatures from a dark abyss.

The presence of these powerful figureheads could be felt. There were only thirty-three of them but they had the power to break both the Red and Purple factions of the Anunaki sects alone and were greatly exalted and feared because of their immense powers.

They bore on their heads a third eye that burned with a purple haze as if the eye itself had an aura of its own, situated in the middle of the skull in between the two usual eyes. The black-robed Anunaki had gone through a ritual to lose their normal eyesight in order to be reborn anew with just this one eye.

It had taken many ceremonies of great sacrifices in order to obtain such a token of respect. The third eye itself, to the Anunaki represented one vision, and only one vision. You cannot be, they believed, be contradicted if you only see one truth, one vision. Their original eyes were gouged out, soldered shut, never to be opened again.

On their heads on these highborn Anunaki were bone spikes protruding from their skulls as if they were rays of a sun, representing enlightenment and illumination to knowledge and power that lesser Anunaki could only dream of. Their skin was of the darkest reds, greens, and blues looking far more exotic than their grey and brown brethren in the younger sects within the cult of the Anunaki.

There was a mass of hysteria within the blood red halls of the Anunaki Council as rumours had fast circulated that Relic weapons had been rediscovered and activated. Wild accusations and conspiracies were directed at all parties as the pace quickened to know what exactly was going on.

'Before the Royal Highness enters, I would like to address the seriousness of this matter,' echoed the voice of Ganzath, leader of the purple sect amidst the voices of the six hundred council members that soon quietened down.

'This weapon has great power as we all know, but from our reports through the astral planes it is a mammalian that has it in its possession. We must discuss how to take back this sacred blade,' he

said, his tongue rasping the air before him tasting the very heat of the hall.

'Your words are weak, Ganzath,' shouted the grey-skinned, blood red robed leader Tunzuulizh, causing most in the council hall to listen amidst the outburst.

'Every single one of us here knows we must attack, attack, attack, take back what is ours. We are giving too much time for the scattered mammals to reunite, forget this weapon for now...for all you know it is just an old story. Ages past created by the cursed Creators in ancient days, bah...it has no meanings to our magnificence!'

Yet more squabbling between the factions ignited faster than an inferno, the halls barely keeping the echoes to a minimum.

'What does the most revered Black Sect have to say to this? This information cannot be wrong! It is a lost Relic weapon! We must take it back!' exclaimed Ganzath, hissing his forked tongue towards Tunzuulizh of the Red Council.

'**Enough!'** echoed the thirty three highborn Anunaki in unison, the fear from the two lower factions could be heard and duly fell silent before one of the Black Council came forth into the centre of the council hall slowly and elegantly walking, a bemused look etched on his brow.

'Who is that master Tunzuulizh?' a new young blood Anunaki asked him in a whisper behind him.

'That is Quetolox initiate...' Tunzuulizh hissed quietly, adding:

'It is said he is the oldest living Anunaki...can you feel his power? It is strangulating, is it not, initiate? They say he is over millennia old.'

The Initiate nodded in turn with a scared rasp.

Quetolox looked in all directions with a slow rhythm beating in his one eye, his ceremonial staff clanking the marble floor of the great hall created an echo to be heard on the deaf crowds of the council members present.

His one eye glinted like gold from the thousands of burning blood red and black candles as he took his residence in the centre of the great hall. Robes rich with silver and gold were draped from his tall slender form from many ancient discovered and stolen treasures from the surface world that intertwined with rich exotic colourful feathers of ancient birds that were centuries old, yet were well preserved.

He almost seemed like he was royal himself, and was the most trusted servant of the royal bloodlines who regularly sought his council.

No one dared dispute his wisdom without calculated thought. Scanning the room, he hissed his tongue, relishing the feel of the heat against his scaly hide.

'Before we talk about such matters in front of her royal highness, I will command you all to watch what you say as always, she does not like bad and ill news,' he said, his one eye glowing with a red haze of fury for but a moment, the candles close by blew as if wind were touching them.

'We have captured some mammals on the outskirts of the large woodland maze. That is a known fact, however any more rumours of a "lost weapon," have no backing as of yet.'

Some of his audience were confused by these words, as they were convinced that rumours of the weapon being found were true.

However, it would have been madness for anyone to question the Black Sect for fear of being unfavoured.

'We know what is good for you all...for your security,' he hissed licking his scaly lips.

'We do know however that some mammals still exist fighting each other in ruined cities or the wilderness, they will kill themselves off one by one like the stupid Cattle they are. Don't you worry about that, however, there are some Cattle that are connecting with the higher dimensional energies and these are our main targets. We must not let them unlock powers that they have gained since the birth of our glorious Dark Age.'

Whispers could be heard across the entire hall in controversy over the news that had just broken. Quetolox continued:

'Some of us here know about the secrets of blood...to speak that these Cattle can share our power is, well, quite unfathomable to say the least' he sighed.

'However it is true, the alliance we had with their ancient ancestors, I do not like to speak of them, but it must be said. These Creators, the highborn equivalent of the common Cattle we have today. Back in ancient days, our species mixed with their blood to create the Nephilim. Blood can be unlocked by any means given it the right symphony or note, lesser brethren. There are still members of the mixed race on the surface above but they have chosen to ally with the Cattle using their composition to stay hidden from us. They as far as we know are few in number and always have been, and they too are our targets.'

He stopped speaking, bashing the butt of his staff into the marble and stone floor to intimidate his audience, to put an end to some whispers.

'Of course this mixing of blood was a mistake and has not been allowed since. However, the damage was done and I tell you all that we of the thirty-three Black Council will look after you so there is nothing

to worry about,' he hissed.

Quetolox's eye scanned the council room slowly.

'Now for other matters to speak of...Ah yes,' he continued.

'As I mentioned before, we have found Cattle within the fallen forests and they will be brought before us later before the great feast with her royal highness the dragon queen...for now they are being pleasantly tortured for information regarding these false weapons of a...weapon? It is our understanding that it does not, and will not exist.'

Ganzath was angered at these words so he snapped at Quetolox:

'I do not believe it!' he shouted, slamming his bony hands on a nearby ornate marble table.

'We have heard reports that it was used on one of our most victorious battlefields of the new age, and that it split the sky open to reveal daylight from the dark clouds.'

Quetolox gazed at Ganzath of the Purple Sect, his ancient scaly hide wincing around his third eye in anger.

'As I understand the situation, this was not a blade that could do such a thing, there was too much Ionic activity to get a sharp image from our Blood Adepts. We do however have several images from the feedback before it was cut off by another presence in the plane...this I shall share with you as I decrypt the information before you all now.'

Quetolox waved his arm and, at once, ancient marble doors slammed open revealing an alien-monitoring screen that defied gravity floating forth into the central hall being pushed by small grey Anunaki in what looked like white lab coats.

The screen was made of pure quartz crystal, while the edges were adorned with many smaller crystals, mainly Amethysts, connected by a form of crystalline wires and conduits. It was heavily decorated with gold and silver but was also covered with dry blood in places that enriched the image of the dragon gods, to bring favour unto the chosen ones, the Anunaki.

Placing the screen within the centre, near Quetolox, the Anunaki lab coats pushed several switches creating a high pitched whirring sound. A moment later and the large screen floated high into the air above Quetolox, and positioning itself so all in the hall could see it.

'Now I will decipher the images again stored within the crystalline information maze which was stored there by our Blood Adepts,' Quetolox said, wetting his dry scaly lips with his tongue whilst staring above to the blank quartz screen before him.

Crackling broke the silence as the screen activated. Ions of electricity hummed with a fast upbeat rhythm across its surface, its ancient architecture of technology activating the many Amethyst

crystals along its edged gold and silver surface as Quetolox linked to it with his psychic power.

'It is close, very close...ah here it is.'

Quetolox let out a sigh of relief as his eye began to get bloodshot from the throbbing power he was channelling through it.

'This is all we have, a short moment of them fighting the netherworld shadows of the hidden dark dimensions which I shall play now.'

The whirring came to a stop, replaced by a sound like a flock of angry birds mixed with interference of radio waves as a holographic image shot down out of the screen suspended in the air. The Council watched a small moment of the battle where Angelite battled three of the shadows from a long distance. The vision skipped and then they saw her use her staff to open the heavens.

Quetolox was in a deep inner meditation while sifting through the psychic data, but still conscious to remember and attain the information.

'Wait...there is something else...something I missed.'

The breaking news got most Council members gripping their seats fiercely, their eyes straining at the holographic images for any hidden meanings.

'The staff that breeder wields...but...there is another individual.'

The holographic images flickering through back and forth, rewind play, rewind play, Quetolox was certain he was missing something.

'There!' shouted Ganzath, pausing the revered one on a certain frame in the holographic image.

'That is blurry but as you can see it is a blade! Wielding the ions of the sky and shooting them forth on the battlefield!'

Tunzuulizh raged with his own Red Sect's opinion.

'What tripe! Do you not know anything? That is ionic interference, your conspiracy theories do you no favours Ganzath. You are imagining things. All you can see are energy bolts from that staff wielding female breeder. As our Lord Quetolox has said, these are targets for extermination and nothing more.'

The hall was a mass riot of opinions from every faction member present as tempers were heating.

'I am more concerned about that female breeder,' Quetolox's voice boomed above them all.

'Whoever crafted that staff, whoever it was...there is a traitor within our ranks. Such knowledge could only be possessed by us, or possibly a Nephilim.'

Many Council members fell silent, wondering if who among them had betrayed them, such was the paranoia present in the chamber.

'Crystals are a valued commodity, and of course they are most common upon this planet,' Quetolox continued in a rasped husky voice.

'Also, they are the sacred substance that links the dimensions. Of course, we do not possess the Silicon in our own Blood structure. These offspring Cattle do because of the ancient days which is why they can be especially potent adversaries when using such objects, such as channelling ethereal energies through them.'

Quetolox's eye was burning a deep crimson that also had an orange glow or aura as he continued to channel the holographic image with much thought power.

'Thankfully, there are only a handful of the Cattle that know how to channel such energies which we have had the right to farm since the dawn of creation,' he hissed.

'But she...the breeder...we must not kill her yet. We must try and follow her steps and see if she is related to any more Cattle we do not know about on the surface above,' Quetolox rasped in irritation.

'When we have our chance we will annihilate the rest of the unlocked bloods of Cattle, that breeder, will be sacrificed to our highness. Her blood will be drained and drank, but only after the feasting of her soul and supple weak and warm blooded flesh,' he spoke articulately.

He laughed while stamping his staff into the marble stone floor, enjoying his image of the thought of the blood soaked ritual.

The Council Hall erupted in cackles and sinister grins upon the Anunaki as they dreamed of the powers and illumination that would be granted for the capture of such humans.

'So what is our first priority?' asked Ganzath to the council.

'We need to send scouts to the last known areas perhaps? Or link more Blood Adept spies into the hidden dimension to try and find them?' Ganzath suggested.

Tunzuulizh interrupted:

'We need an army! We need to assemble the once great army of the Dragon Elite's. That is, by far, our only way to achieve this...messing around with spies in the astral plane can take a long process, we do not have any more time to waste.'

Both the Red and Purple robed sects started bickering amongst themselves once more, all suggesting a solution.

Quetolox continued to scan the data entries stored within the quartz crystal thinking something was missing.

'We do not possess the power to summon such an army that size without the permission of new breeding initiatives. To produce such a hungry elite that you speak of Tunzuulizh. Resources are pushed as they are!' raged Ganzath, before continuing:

'In case you have forgotten, the last army of Anunaki Soldiers turned mad themselves because of flaws within our Blood Engineering. They consumed far too much energy, and in turn burned themselves out to the point of death.'

'You know not what you speak of you fool,' Tunzuulizh argued back, Ganzath continued however:

'The ones that are left straddle the surface and are the last remnants of these soldiers which are now hundreds of cycles old. While it is useful that they still hunt the annoying Cattle to live on, they only now serve themselves in madness until they are slain. You know that they do not age due to the extensive stem cell activity within their brains and spinal columns, and for our purposes, they are next to useless. To send another army of that size is impossible because we do not have enough sources to support such an army after victory. Until more research is done into the possibility of renewable bio-logical fuel for such a new type of soldier then your idea is stupid folly.'

Tunzuulizh knew Ganzath spoke the truth but decided to enlighten him with new information that came to light.

'I do not doubt your *old information*,' Tunzuulizh hissed.

'However, now we have made many breakthroughs in newer blood technology where we can program the blood to draw in the infinite dimensional energies by harnessing the potential of light matter coexisting with the resonating energies that travel through many of the Chakras which are in turn linked to the blood and cells of the body. Once we have refined this technique you can all expect an army that can never die of old age...or consume themselves any other way. This is the renewable energy source that we can use to program future generations, and it is just around the corner, then we can start to colonise even other worlds increasing our expansion **for her most Royal Matriarch!**' Tunzuulizh roared with the echoes of his Red Sect behind him.

Ganzath rose again, slamming his hands on the marble table:

'Yes and, as you said, we cannot wait for this "newer" technology. Anything the Red Sect has promised is a farce, much like your face, this is not the first time you have promised us all something new,' he snarled fiercely.

'New ideas for plans and initiatives is what we are meant to come up with to better our kind, as unlike your Purple Sect, we actually get on with some work,' Tunzuulizh laughed.

'Work...don't even make me spew my own bile, or even laugh for that matter,' Ganzath spat onto the floor.

'You have no guts Ganzath, since you've gained leadership of the Purple Sect you have turned it into a weak sickly parasite...your Sect has done nothing but turn down improvements in the aid of progress, and as soon as this rumour about a "relic weapon" began springing up, you're all over the subject voicing your opinion,' Tunzuulizh paused.

'What are you trying to say?' Ganzath replied.

'That you are traitorous scum!' Tunzuulizh spat back onto the floor, the whole chamber exploded into an uproar.

Ganzath seemed to quieten the room with what he said next:

'We must act...you are right...but going to war and taxing our precious resources cannot be the only option available to us. If we discovered a new Cattle civilisation then yes perhaps a new army would be needed. But they are so scattered and leaderless they are already killing themselves off for us, sparing us the work to totally eradicate them from the planet in the great cleansing program that was started before we were even thought of in our enriched incubating catacombs.'

'Get on with it I tire quickly of this,' Tunzuulizh interrupted, the Red Sect smirking and quietly laughing behind him.

'Tunzuulizh, what you are referring to is the great army that actually failed after wiping out most Cattle in the latest war when we crushed them all to near extinction. Let me remind you of our history, how we had huge ocean behemoths under vast mind control programs to help squash any resistances...how we judged the right moment to strike...how we caused the planet to swap polarities leading to great floods, eruptions and tsunamis to also crush their communication networks. That is when we first used half breeder Anunaki, the Nephilim, inside their governments to create infighting, instability and miscommunication or misdirection worldwide. It succeeded more than our armies after they exhausted themselves. After the great victory we had no need for either the shape shifters or neo-soldiers that you want to reignite.'

He finished feeling the history lesson was a good reminder of the past transgressions. Quetolox shuddered as he delved deeper into the hologram, the ghostly visages of every action and moment was sifted through repeatedly, he was close to what he wanted and at any moment, he would break the news to the rest of the Council members present. He chose to speak about the current matter at hand.

'Yes and using the Nephilim was a mistake. I am the only oldest living Anunaki here and I saw it firsthand. The rebel shape shifters then decided to join with the Cattle, they had discovered our pure strain plan and chose to hide for fear of getting purged,' he sighed.

His voice dry, his wrinkly forked tongue barely able to lick moisture around his cracking scaly lips as his body dried out even further from the heavy channelling.

'That is why we cannot risk such contamination again, it upset the royalty for near on or over one hundred cycles. We are right in that we need to act, however we must be patient. If we mess up this time, then we will have more than Resonance wielding Cattle to worry about.'

Discussion was high along with the Council's appetite to learn more of the hidden foes.

'What about hunting for traitors? We cannot allow any newer technology to be publicly available yet as it may be leaked to the surface world. We need to keep it all a secret if we are going to keep one hand above the Cattle and pull the strings first,' Ganzath uttered, raising his hand and pointing his scaly, pasty finger at all Anunaki within the council halls.

'We need to form a strategy, an offensive plan is what is needed, we all know this, just accept it,' Tunzuulizh urged with his war mantra.

Quetolox siphoned through the data at a faster rate, destroying all barriers that had hidden data behind more data, flowing through it as if he were one with the crystalline pathways.

Most Anunaki were arguing amongst themselves to what the best course of action could be to take notice.

The Anunaki Lab coats monitored the information on smaller hand held quartz screen panels monitoring Quetolox's mental levels.

Their instruments crackling with a form of arcane power as they sifted their scaly fingers across similar holographic images that were buttons or ancient symbols existing on the panels they held.

They were more like ants then reptiles by the way they moved and interacted with the devices in unison.

Now was the moment to finally break the silence:

'I have intercepted a vision, right before the lightning swept forth across the battlefield,' Quetolox hissed with agitation.

'I will relay the findings now...'

The monitor hologram crackled to reveal what happened within a certain individual's mind, the thought waves spoke out from the ancient quartz.

'...the power...elements, use...energy of the...use the...beating drums.'

All the Anunaki racked their brains trying to understand what this could mean, and who or what it was.

Quetolox spoke aloud:

'I have narrowed it down to a male Cattle who had this vision...its name is Maledream in their foul tongue. This I have dissected from the amount of voices, confusion, and fear surrounding these Cattle on that archaic contraption they ride. I will need the translating thought formers to go over these words in the laboratory banks. I am afraid I cannot decipher all this babble myself,' he said.

His eye glowing with a dark crimson of hate, he raised his voice to a shout as he stumbled on another clue that he had overlooked.

'What is this?' he questioned aloud in an angry tone.

'This cannot be.'

His rage distorted the holographic image that he was unfolding before his eye. Thousands of candles within the Council Hall began blowing themselves out and relighting themselves like a beautiful opera as Quetolox could hardly contain his demonic fury.

Many Anunaki in the Council hall were frozen in fear at any backlash from this powerful legend.

'What is it, gracious one?' asked Tunzuulizh with unquestionable fear within his voice, his forked tongue rapidly hissing like a scared panting animal.

Quetolox's power could be felt and seen as he started to glow like a black abyss even worrying some of his own Black Sect, who shuffled uncomfortably in their seats.

'It is...It is a lost Relic weapon.'

He shuddered as the Anunaki lab coats as they locked on to the image and froze it, intensifying the holographic image for all to see in the great council hall. Maledream could just be seen in the distorted image using the deadly blade that had been crafted ten ages past by the Creator race during the first war of the dominant races.

'I have seen that once before, but believed it to have gone missing forever, and now those Cattle have it. Nevertheless, it will be okay children, we will capture that forgotten blade finally. Perhaps even present it as a gift to her Royal Highness.'

Many whispers were abounding now in all sects while Ganzath stared across the Hall with gleaming black eyes, standing with a arrogant posture, a smirk present on his face towards Tunzuulizh. Feeling defeated, Tunzuulizh withdrew into his seat whispering more propaganda on how to undermine the Purple Sect with new ideas.

Quetolox announced:

'So is it settled? We must do two things. Kill that Cattle and sacrifice the breeder. We cannot be hasty however, there are no places they can easily survive, however we cannot lose track of them. From information gathered from interrogation, we know where they were last seen so perhaps we should send out small scouting parties to try to find them. Once we do that we can follow them and complete another objective which is to try and discover if there are even more breeders like this Cattle who can wield the resonating energies.'

Quetolox's anger subsided at his own well thought quick plan, the dark energies surrounding him slowly disappearing.

'We should not worry about the blade though, we have many more weapon variations in our vaults which cannot ever again be touched, but there is no known way to destroy these weapons, but rest assured it is something we are always researching. Be aware that her Royal Highness does not know we have such things locked away. I suggest we keep it that way.'

Tunzuulizh got out of his seat, deciding to ask more about the situation, his eyelids twitching with some anger and resentment.

'What of the ancient Relic weapons? There is no history of them save for a few scraps of it...what of the vision this Maledream had while using this potent weapon? We thought such things were stupid myths and only now do you say they exist,' he finished with a shrug to all the council.

'There are currently around twelve to thirteen such weapons to our knowledge all look quite ordinary save for a few on the outside, but within they have their own life forces...such dimensional weapons also bear runes upon their surfaces when activated, all are unique and were created by weapon smiths in darker days, youngling. And yes I did not tell you for it is for your safety,' hissed Quetolox.

Many of the council members talked quietly amongst themselves about the new information becoming known, the Red Sect were reeling from a crushing defeat of egos from their military plans and operations.

'Then please share it with us Lord,' urged Tunzuulizh.

'I shall, young one. It was over twelve thousand cycles of the sun that the first great neo-mammalian civilisation sprung forth...alliances were great and true between many races, not just the Creators or Nephilim mind you, but others, before we crushed them for our own empire,' creases formed over his scaly lips as he smirked.

'Genetic engineering then was at an all time high, and breeding programmes were well under way showing us how we can manipulate Genesis Structures between unique races...and it succeeded. We discovered that, on the inside of a mixed being, you could have a neo-mammalian trapped inside an Anunaki body, effectively. They were better days when we as a race lived upon the surface of this world.'

Quetolox laughed, croaking at the humour of such terrible but true nonsense, before continuing:

'We were not forced underground by the great old cataclysm, it was by the Creators during the war over twelve thousand cycles ago. There were problems with the politics, sanctions on Genesis Data and Dimensional Energy Data, you get the picture,' croaking to clear his throat he continued again:

'Alas we were forced underground and, soon forgotten over the millennia, that is when we used our knowledge on Genesis Structures which we researched with the Creators millennia before, and other forgotten races, to interbreed with the Cattle above and to infiltrate them, much like we did over a hundred years ago. We created lies upon lies that the ignorant Cattle believed over many generations of their life spans. Of course we have longer life spans than those who were half Anunaki, half Cattle, so we were able to still direct the proceedings in secret over many lifetimes to the "fake" world leaders, still thinking of the fury of the past which burned us for revenge.'

Ganzath interrupted:

'Such great information, my lord, will indeed enlighten many here today who did not know our past.'

Many nodded in agreement, Quetolox replied calmly:

'We teach the true knowledge, my brethren. We must keep the faith loyal to the one true entity we serve, her Royal Highness. I shall continue. Genesis or Blood was our secret weapon...while the Cattle's ignorance worked tenfold, we were secret, and we were gods of these Cattle. We were called "The Sheppard's" or "The Almighty Ones."'

He grinned as he remembered the times during the human's Dark Age hundreds upon hundreds of years ago.

'When the time was right, we used the stupid Cattle against themselves, severing communications and causing confusion. The time was right to send our armies out of the deep oceans and cracks of the earth's crust using secret underground tunnels and facilities to full effect. No one was expecting to be attacked by forces from underground. During this purge, the weapons of bane were used. Listen carefully. The Creators were great scientists and crafters, who researched many advances into blood knowledge, applying their new thinking to make the Relic weapons,' stamping his snaked rod onto the marble floor again, he continued:

'They built them so that these intelligent weapons could harness the true powers of the Resonance frequencies, turning the user

wielding such a crafted weapon into in all accounts a god of the sorts. But to apply a weapon that needed to be held meant that the weapons could not be turned into long range weapons as the shells that fired would lose their potency once they left the vicinity of the being wielding it, they were only crafted for close quarters' combat, which is a blessing in some ways.'

Clicking his fingers, Quetolox paused for breath, while the Anunaki lab coats brought over to him a chalice poured with warm blood carried on an exotic feather pillow.

Picking it up steadily with a slight shake, his tongue licked feverishly at the contents until not a drop remained, the feeling of the rich haemoglobin racing down his neck gave him a quick boost of ecstasy and then euphoria. Many Anunaki licked their scaly pasty lips at the sight, wanting some for themselves.

'At the time, we had the dimensional technology that they needed,' he relished.

'And we wanted to trade some of this for most of their blood advances, but it was almost successful until something went wrong. We do not have the ancient accounts to tell us what happened exactly, but we were denied the technology that would have allowed us to construct these weapons linked to genetics before the war over twelve thousand cycles ago. Of course, we could not use them due to a specific hidden composition we ourselves do not possess in our blood pool...only the corrupted ancestors of the Nephilim have any possibility of accessing it with their own blood. Thankfully those in the past who wielded such weapons of bane could never use them to their full deadly potential as the true Creator bloodlines did and so whenever we had an outbreak or discovered such a weapon being handled by the lesser Cattle we hunted them down easily each time, even though it is worrying that.'

Tunzuulizh narrowly interrupted, too much of Quetolox's annoyance:

'Are you worried that one day such Cattle will be able to use this weapon to full effect, my lord?'

The silence of the council was broken, hysteria flying out of control of the accusation.

'Yes,' Quetolox replied.

'It is a possibility that the puny Cattle could activate it to full effect. We do not know the full dangers of this as scraps of records were lost during and after the Great Conflict. I would not like to imagine the consequences of such devastation, we worked hard to reduce the populations of the mere Cattle. Let us not allow them to rise again in vast numbers. If they were to discover how to unite and assemble before us, this would be an enormous problem. With such knowledge of Resonance, they could wield vast power. Knowledge is Power.'

Moisture escaped Quetolox's scales as he closed his eye, the holographic image above him shattering like glass and stardust as the feed of energy was cut.

Taking a deep breath, he stretched his tight muscle tissue from all the tension within the council hall before continuing to speak:

'We must not let this happen. The key to prevention is ensuring that there is no weapon to cause us problems. We will concentrate on Maledream to find out if he has such a thing. Another focus for our interest must be the female breeder that can wield Resonance through crystals. We must discover how she could attain such technology or artefact from the world above without Anunaki assistance or handed down knowledge.'

Quetolox paused while blinking his one eye around the room as if he were sifting through all minds of the council members present before continuing:

'Enough debate, younglings.'

Quetolox raised his staff and in one swoop cracked his rod over a nearby Anunaki lab coat in his anger. The blow broke his skull and skinny neck, killing it instantly. Its large brain lobes spilt across the council floor. He stood on one of the large opal black eyes and continued with his plan of action.

'We shall send standard scouting parties onto the surface immediately. We will tell her Majesty that we need to increase our blood banks so she will authorise such an expedition to the surface.

'Our main objective will be to find and contain information or whereabouts of any such Anunaki technology or peoples that still exist on the surface in hiding. We have a many Blood Adepts at our disposal. These do not use "genetics" to hide their features but rather use illusion to cover their own face by harnessing heavy dimensional energy. As you all know, they are powerful in the Resonance Arts and are extremely potent adversaries for these Cattle if they were to come across them. Not only that but it will be a lot easier tracking the Cattle by using these certain Anunaki...they can "smell" if you like to call it that, their spiritual essences. Now soon the Royal Highness herself will join us. After this assembly, the forces will be dispatched.'

Finishing with a hiss, Quetolox looked at the remaining labs coats, which then in turn started clearing the mess he had made. Satisfied with how the proceedings had gone, the red, purple, and black orders began quietly chatting about the findings and results.

Behind the Black robed sect, was a door similar to the one that the lab coats had used to enter the room. This door had noticeable differences with imagery. Exotic plumes of feathers, mostly blood red in hue, were attached to its ornate ancient marble surface, while snakes golden snakes adorned the door.

Many crystal stones were embedded into its surface. These shimmered as if they were water reflecting the sunlight or moonlight from the countless lit candles lighting the great council hall. Precious gems that glittered mimicked the star systems within the galaxy, all glowing lighter and darker in power and hue. Behind the door came the sound of a screech, the signal that the Royal Highness was approaching.

The sound she made echoed into the council chamber with an impressive wail as if it were some huge terrifying beast of old coming from an ancient depth or dark void.

'Quick she is coming, get rid of that quartz screen, get rid of it!' Quetolox ordered.

The lab coats quickly turned off the machine and pushed it out of the hall. All fell silent as they waited for her Royal Highness to enter the room and take her seat behind the Black Sect to do business. Quetolox sighed and hissed his forked tongue.

'Not long now my Royal Highness, not long now,' he thought, turning to stare at the royally sealed door that began to hum and shake.

The exotic feathers began to wave from the vibrations of the shaking door. The many crystals began to glow in several colours snaking from the bottom of the door gradually coiling themselves up through the many crystals representing the stars and planets of the galaxy. It would look like an impressive display to anyone but the Anunaki.

Moments later, starting from the bottom, the crystals ignited with a dark green and yellow flame travelling upwards as if to signify the purge of all the stars and planets ritualistically until it reached the top.

The door began to open but, at first, all that could be seen were the Queen's Royal Guards who towered over her. Their muscles bulged beneath ceremonial gold plating that was adorned heavily with thousands of intricate symbols that were so small it was a hard job to even start counting them.

These beasts looked similar to the one that Maledream and Angelite had encountered within the ruined library. However, they were far more muscular and taller, and had many sharp razor spikes or bones protruding up their arms through the gaps of the gold plate that they wore.

These particularly royal guards were almost as powerful and venerable as the Black Sect and were a breed of the Rarest Anunaki you could get. Some even carried banners of royalty with many snakes and serpent gods of old mimicking ancient battles upon the banners. They seemed to flutter even though there was no wind.

Fanning out behind the Black Sect, the Queen came into view and all could see she was dressed in pure white robes. Her frail form moved as if she were afloat with ease from walking, her white robes covering her long arms as she swiftly took her position behind the most loyal Black Sect who would do anything in their power along with the Royal Guardians to protect her at all costs.

'Kneel,' Quetolox ordered, he himself kneeling down to face the most Radiant one. All followed his lead.

Pulling back her hood, she revealed herself. Her skin was that of an Albino Anunaki, a trait only available in the Royal family soup. It was considered godhood to the Anunaki.

'Welcome, my Royal Highness,' Quetolox said with a fine tongue.

'How was your visit with our allies?' he asked.

'It went well,' she said, her voice gently rasping with her tongue, her deep dark eyes appearing like a far distant universe within which there was a glow of the stars.

'They have had reports on the surface that many of the precious feeding grounds are almost out of stock. I hope you will please me by telling me that you have found a way to make up for the loss of meat and blood,' she said, her reptilian eyes staring at the Council present.

'Yes, that is so, but those reports are not entirely accurate your Royal Highness. We have a feast prepared and awaiting for you, and upon your orders your bloodbath can and will be brought forth to you. We have information of livestock on the surface that have found a refuge somewhere within the mountains and green mazes. With your permission we can start culling them and breeding them for more resources.'

The smile of his plan burned within him. Quetolox was used to lying to Royalty.

'One day, I will achieve true godhood,' he thought.

'Good,' she replied, adding:

'Keep them in a cage.'

'Now, I would like the feast to begin.'

He smiled and thought to himself:

'Yes spoiled brat, you will get your precious sweet feast.'

'Of course, my Highness, it is a pleasure,' he replied.

Withdrawing from the centre of the council hall, Quetolox finally rested upon his seat with the rest of the Black Sect.

'May the feast begin,' the Royal Highness spoke aloud.

The doors, from which the Quetolox's lab coats had walked through, once again slammed opened to reveal human beings, stripped down to nothing but their bare skin, being dragged along by Anunaki soldiers by iron chains with sharp curled iron spikes safely embedded into their ankles, wrists and necks.

The rough dragging from the strong Anunaki soldiers caused the spikes to dig even more into the soft human flesh, gouging deeper holes into them just for added insurance that they could not escape without ripping off half their flesh, muscle, and sinew.

Leading the soldiers was a taskmaster called Lazzathrish, who day by day took delight at capturing more Cattle and torturing them to get their adrenaline running, just to add to the taste of the meat.

His appearance was that of a soldier Anunaki, instead of brandishing ornate gold or silver armour he wore the skins and muscle from deceased humans that were mummified on his scaly hide to keep it fresh for as long as he lived, to symbolise his deeply respected role.

Blood was staining the marble floor at a fast and impressive rate as some humans that struggled too much pierced their own jugulars or main arteries spilling their life essence onto the floor in screams of agony. The blood ran in between the gaps of the marble floor to form intricate patterns and symbols, now exposed to sight by the flowing liquid. Screams from both males and female humans filled the room with terror, as they saw the strange creatures. It was a true nightmare for the human psyche to behold seeing hundreds more Anunaki in the chamber.

'Look at these worms,' the Queen hissed, her Albino skin taking a shade of red from the glowing candlelit blood forming in the centre of the council halls.

'We, my dear people, are the rulers of this world, and always have been, if it were not for your loyalty and support we could not have unfolded our agendas thus far,' she said.

Her eyes glowed with a turquoise colour for but a moment, before the marble centre of the council hall collapsed in itself to create what looked like a bath that was slowly filling up from the draining blood.

'And now once again, I shall bathe in their blood while the sacred ancient ones watch over us all, and we receive their mighty boons,' she said aloud for all to hear, over the screams of the humans.

Pulling the one hundred or so humans around that were either dead or still alive the soldiers one by one began hacking a leg on each human to cripple them to the floor.

After much bone snapping and cracking, tearing of muscle, sinew, and flesh, yet more blood filled the bath. The Royal Highness walked through the Black Council, and through the chained human beings, towards the inner sanctum of the council hall to take her place in her ritualistic blood bath.

Among the throng of victims was Pixie, one of Neveah's Packers. He was terrified but refused to scream, even when his leg was cracked and snapped open. His chains were rusty and he knew they could not hold him. What could he do? He hazarded a guess that the albino lizard in the white robes was some sort of important person or guest.

'Just one chance at perhaps capping her out, I am going to die so I might as well die trying', he thought.

His eyes could see the larger reptiles that pulled them along on chains had weapons he was familiar with.

'Great, pole arms,' he thought.

The screams from his fellow humans were unnerving to him, but he tried to remain focused. With a broken leg, he would have to make one ditch attempt at killing the white Anunaki.

'May I bathe in the holy blood, in the presence of the God's,' the Queen's voice echoed, her frail robed form ghostly walked towards the pool of blood in the centre of the hall.

Pixie could feel his heart racing as he finally let his burst of adrenaline flow from the anguish and fear that filled the room.

'Rot in hell you bastards,' he shouted.

Grabbing the chains that bound him, his muscled arms pumped and bulged, he strained for but a quick moment, breaking the bonds that held him.

Letting out a war cry amidst the mayhem, the naked Packer charged towards the nearest guard to him. Shoulder barging the large creature to the ground he ripped the pole arm free from its scabbard on the back of the giant beast. Swinging the weapon across the Anunaki's neck, he killed the giant reptile in one blow, the soldier roaring a last defiance as its life was no more. His weary eyes looked straight into the frightened Queen who could not believe that Cattle had such strength.

'One's escaped!' shouted Ganzath, among the hundreds of voices that filled the room to try to warn the Queen.

'Stand together and fight!' Pixie yelled to his fellow prisoners, while staring eye to eye with the white frail lizard that was but ten paces away.

Encouraged by Pixie's success, the humans began to fight back, dragging down the vast large soldiers of the Anunaki to the ground in quick numbers, ignoring wounds they had suffered which had been replaced with hope, fury, and vengeance.

More guards rushed in from the great marble door while many council members began to flood to the centre to swamp the Cattle and take down the large human intent on killing their sacred bloodline.

'You're mine,' Pixie yelled at the white robed lizard.

His muscles pumping blood with the fury of molten lava itself, his skin breaking sweat as he drew close to his main target. He could no longer feel the pain in his leg from the chemical reactions in the brain that had gone into self-defence last-ditch attempt for survival. With hands gripping the pole arm, he jumped towards the white lizard, prepared to kill her without pause.

'Enough!' shouted Quetolox, his eye burning fiercely and with such fury that all the candles in the room were snuffed out as if a huge gust of air waved itself over them.

His one eye beamed onto the troublesome Packer with speed and precision. Suspended in mid-air and in mid-swing, Pixie was frozen by his power and could only move his eyes.

'So close,' he barely worded from his paralysed form.

Many of the soldiers and council members started tearing from limb to limb the hundred Cattle to put a stop to any assassination. The slaughter began but it was unofficial and the ceremony for the Royal Highness was ruined. The Anunaki gnawed and started to eat the living flesh of the living humans biting into them as they screamed with defiance or terror. Some were lucky enough to pass out into darkness never to re-awaken in the earthly conscious state.

Stomachs, hearts, and other organs were torn out of the still living humans, witnessing themselves being eaten alive by the ferocious beasts. The Queen was escorted from the slaughter, fears that something else might threaten her life further. Quetolox was unhappy and sighed as he looked at the naked Cattle wielding the weapon, now gripped tightly by Lazzathrish who pushed Pixie before him.

'What of this scum, my lord? More torture? Shall I keep him alive with food supplements directly attached into his stomach so he can survive more torture at his displeasure, my Lord?' he hissed delightfully at the strong specimen.

'You can have all the fun you want with him now. I have accessed the fool's mind and now know of some troublesome breeder woman that exists in the green maze,' Quetolox said.

'As you wish, master,' replied Lazzathrish.

'Assemble the Forces,' shouted Quetolox.

'We shall act now, or forever be damned for eternity! For the Queen!'

A cry of war sounded within the bloody halls of the council filled to the brim with blood, flesh, and bone. Excitement could be felt at the opportunity to deal with other Cattle like Pixie who did not fear their masters and, in fact, were ready to attack them.

'Thanks to you, human,' Quetolox muttered quietly.

'I have all the excuses I need to do what I want with the full consent of the council and the royal family,' he thought.

Quetolox eyed Pixie inquisitively before letting the slave master take him back to the torture banks.

'Fools all of you,' he thought.

Chapter Ten

Mysterious N'Rutas...

'The most beautiful thing we can experience is the mysterious.

It is the source of all true art and science.'

Albert Einstein

'Well, here's the entrance,' Angelite said, standing before the one hundred or so feet of falling water.

'I don't bloody see it, all I see is water,' replied Maledream.

'Aye, and all they had for us to go on was "follow your own judgement" or some crap...so very helpful,' said Neveah.

'Come on boys, let's head around the sides so we don't get wet and try and find a way in,' Angelite replied.

They began looking for an entrance enthusiastically, after a while their efforts slowed and they wondered if this entrance existed.

'I'm stumped,' exclaimed Neveah, he sat down on a nearby damp rock scratching his scalp staring at the falling water as it joined the river.

'It should be here somewhere,' said Angelite.

Nothing but weeds, roots, and ivy were seen surrounding and snaking up in-between the cracks of the rocks as the group looked up upon the drenched surfaces.

'What signs did the Witches actually talk about?' asked Angelite.

'Search us...they were a mystery,' replied Neveah.

'Well that Silver was pretty certain it was here,' said Maledream.

'For all you know that wolf might be getting the rest of his pack while letting us wait here like stupid, sitting wild animals searching for an entrance that doesn't exist,' Neveah said with a laugh.

'Well if we can't find the clue physically, maybe we will have to delve into the realms of the spirit,' Angelite said.

'It might be something we can't see normally so if you two wait here a minute I'll go and sit down somewhere more comfortable than a rock and meditate for an answer.'

'Well if it's another option then I say of course Angelite, just don't stray too far from us okay. I'll keep watch along with Maledream,' replied Neveah.

Maledream nodded at the priestess as she stared at him, her eyes beginning to change colour.

'How does she change her eye colour?' Neveah asked the Tribal quietly.

'No idea, maybe it'll be something she shares with us some time, I've only ever seen her do that when she is beginning to focus,' Maledream said.

'Aye, possibly.'

They watched Angelite settling on a dry, grassed area further up river. They could see her removing the new crystals from her bag and holding one up to the sun, admiring the purity of the quartz crystal chunk glistening and refracting the rays of the sun within its core and on its surface. Then she held the crystal near her heart and began to meditate.

Maledream leaned against a rock taking off his thick heavy coat and baggage while he rested more comfortably in the hot sweltering heat of the sun, even the waterfall near him could not cool him down.

'Well, mate, looks as if we just have to wait, perhaps that wolf will make his way back soon,' said Neveah.

'I'm sure will make some progress. I'm counting on Angelite to find a way,' he sighed.

'Aye,' Neveah said, wiping the last of his sweat off his forehead with a dry rag.

'Well at least we can relax for a moment, this little adventure of ours is quite straining,' Maledream said, crossing his arms behind his head and looking blindly upwards towards the water crashing into the pool below.

'To be honest I needed it, those damned bugs took a lot from me...how did they get so huge I wonder?'

'Silver said they were a mutation somehow, don't ask me how, I'm not even sure what mutation means. Larkham would probably know but he isn't here so I can't ask,' replied Maledream.

'Aye well at a guess, he probably meant they weren't normal insects but altered in some way. I hope I never see them again. Those things were damned hard work. The deafening noise they made was unbearable to say the least, noisy shits,' Neveah looked over to Angelite and nudged Maledream to look as well.

'She's still at it,' said Maledream smiling away at her.

'So are you two actually a couple then, Maledream? I've not had the balls to ask this yet, but you both seem to.'

Cutting him off, Maledream brushed in quickly:

'No! Course not! You know the story. I only met her the other day.'

'Yeah sure mate, whatever you say,' Neveah bellowed with laughter.

'No joking! We aren't...it's a long story but yeah, came across each other when I found her being attacked by one of those strange reptiles. I killed it, anyway, I'm sure I've told you all of this?'

'Refresh my memory mate,' Neveah said with a smile:

'We have all day.'

'I won't go all the way back into it, but Angelite does remind me of a girl I knew a long time ago, it's not necessarily Angelite herself just a very old memory.'

Maledream began scratching his rough stubble as he thought about it.

'I cannot remember anyone back then, mate, here were a lot of us travelling back then in older days. I've forgotten most people except for the ones close to me. You were a child that mixed with everyone back then, well not a child but a teenager. Feels like an age now,' added Neveah.

'Hmm it has been troubling me inside...that's why I think I'm so fond of her even though we barely know each other, like it is some sort of connection, which is really deep but I just can't put my fingers on it.'

'Right...deep connection and fingers...I'm afraid you won't know how deep she truly is until you stop using those fingers and use the real stuff!' Neveah said holding back a laugh.

'Yes...NO!' Maledream replied punching Neveah on the arm.

'Full of innuendo today aren't we' Maledream said smiling and shaking his head at him.

'Ha ha...aye' Neveah replied.

'Perhaps it is something you need to work on, mate?' he added.

'Seems so,' he smirked as he looked at Neveah.

'I'll get there in the end I suppose,' he said.

'Aye, you sure will mate, keep working on your memory, it will all come back. Try not to worry about it too much. We have a long journey ahead of us.'

'Agreed,' Maledream nodded softly, staring back up at the sky and then back again to Angelite.

'Just wish I knew more,' he finished.

Both men settled back into silence. Moments later, they were disturbed by a noise, something was approaching them.

Gathering their weapons quickly and rushed from the rocks ready to take on any threat. A figure was charging towards them.

'We're going to kill you!' screamed Crazy John.

Maledream and Neveah lost balance at the surprise, falling backwards trying to swing their weapons away from each other as both landed in a heap upon the large rocks.

'Damn you, crazy bastard!' Neveah shouted, whilst Maledream looked on in bafflement before lying down on his back groaning from the shock of hitting the stones hard. Boris appeared behind Crazy John with a smile on her face.

'You bastards,' yelled Neveah.

'You're both alive!?' he asked in surprise.

'Of course, although from what we have seen deeper back in the forest it appears a big ruckus went down. I'm glad only Pixie led those Packers in a different direction from us,' she replied in her buff accent.

Neveah and Maledream just gazed at them in wonder.

'And to think I fought extra hard to avenge you bastards, looks like my pack is still alive! What the hell happened for a start? Why did you all bugger off this morning? Most the food and equipment was gone when we woke up. I thought you had all buggered off like a bunch of cowards,' Neveah asked, his anger quickly subsided, as he had no real energy for it.

'We left a note somewhere for you, unless of course you missed it carved into one of the trees,' replied Crazy John, pressing a dagger against his fingertips.

'No we bloody didn't find a note instead I found a bloodbath across a bloody damn river!' Neveah said.

The relief of some of his pack still alive comforted him.

Boris continued:

'Well we carved arrows on tree bark to point which way we went. You should have seen them but I guess you didn't?'

'Indeed, my friend, indeed,' humoured Crazy John, he stared at Neveah scratching his scalp.

'We left early to save time in getting out the forest, but there was a forked path, we didn't find much on our travels except broken old ruins and an impassable field of stinging nettles, which we weren't brave enough to wade through. Not to worry, Neveah, we heard fighting of some kind...gun shots...from the direction Pixie took and led the rest of the Packers but when we got there, we found nothing but dead giant insects chopped in half, and some of our weapons wrapped

around a tree. We found some tracks and we followed them.'

'Nice story on how you found us, no idea what happened to the equipment and rations though?' asked Neveah.

'No idea chief,' answered Crazy John.

'We let the rest of the Packers look after it because we were travelling light, you know our style. We don't do heavy,' added Boris.

'Of course,' nodded Neveah.

'What else could I expect from my best assassins?' he said.

'Pity that we lost the provisions though. Now we have more people and so need more food.'

'Well let's just hope Angelite knows a way to find some. I'm starving,' groaned Maledream, still lying down on the dry rocks and sparse patches of grass.

'Aye, well it's good to have you two back, the more company the better,' Neveah said.

The group sat near Angelite and watched her.

'Wonder if she's making any progress?' Neveah asked.

'Probably, although she hasn't been the same with her powers since that dark day yesterday, and she relied on her staff to do the things she did,' answered Maledream quietly.

'Sure saved our asses,' said Boris.

'She is some woman, even if she does seem a bit physically weak. She's full of energy,' she added.

'Aye,' Neveah agreed.

Gradually the group began settling down discussing the day's events in more detail and what obstacles they had overcome and what obstacles could be facing them before they found the safe haven known as Meridia.

Meanwhile Angelite was in a deep trance. She had focused her breathing patterns and had focused her inner energies connecting to the very Resonance of the cosmos. Her mind and spirit became one. Moments passed slowly as if all was becoming still and stagnant, as if time no longer had a bearing of age.

Slowly her mind gave in losing the sensations of her body as she entered a clearing of light in the ether. Her first vision was that of the stars and comets that raced through the void of space. Her second vision was that of the earth itself from high above as she gradually fell back to earth once more in her meditation. Everything she saw had a glow or Aura resonating around it from the clouds to the terrain below her.

The Resonance emitted incredible feelings of sensation free of fear, hate, greed, and all the badness that existed in her life.

'Clearly the Resonance of this crystal is helping,' thought her higher self of being, she felt as if she was floating.

'Now, spirits show me a solution to my problem please.'

Before her third eye's sense came an ocean from the horizon in her meditation. It reached her at an impossible speed but to her it did not matter. It was like a fantastic dream she was witnessing with her spirit. The water swirled and changed form until it became the waterfall near her and within the vision, she saw the way to pass it. As soon as she had found the solution, she felt herself slammed back into a conscious state of being.

'We've got to go now!' shouted Maledream as he shook her around like a rag doll, her eyes barely opening after such a deep trance.

'The Vasps are coming back, we can hear their wings,' she heard him say as she opened her eyes.

'Right, okay, give me a moment,' she said, hurriedly scrambling off the floor to brush past Maledream. She saw Crazy John and Boris but ignored them for the moment and treated them with a recognising nod.

'Everyone follow my lead. I know what to do,' she said eager to go before the Vasps returned.

'Right, well we have all our stuff together so just do your stuff, Angelite,' said Maledream, keeping his sword bound to his hands.

Gradually the humming started to grow louder.

'Well here it goes everyone get ready.'

Angelite concentrated and held the crystal close to her heart and chanted:

'Kinanan Worshiphia Cunadun Valore Demanenor Kinesis.'

Her words became more powerful as she continued chanting, feeling like an age to the group who watched her and the approaching giant swarm of Vasps in the distance. The stress of their auras could be felt as Angelite struggled to channel even more energy from the crystal to help her as the medium.

'Spread this water, show me the path, show me the way, and give us safety...reveal yourself hidden frame.'

With that, she stepped forward, the group watching her every move intently like a flock of crows picking at a corpse for the slightest

chance of living. By now more than a hundred Vasps were filling the sky and preparing for the strike.

'They look pretty pissed off to me,' said Crazy John.

'Aye, shut the hell up!' Neveah replied.

'Don't know about you but I don't plan to be lunch, I haven't even eaten anything myself yet! I'll be damned if they're getting their pincers on my ass!' Neveah yelled with defiance.

Maledream gripped his sword harder and gritted his teeth like everyone else at the sight. He turned around to see Angelite's hair beginning to float on end and some form of energies coming from around her feet, causing ripples to form on the river. Calmly moving the crystal away from her chest, she knelt down slowly placing the crystal just on the surface of the water. A pale blue light shone from the crystal rippling the water to such an extent that it disturbed the dirt lying on the riverbed.

Shrieking from sheer power, Angelite forced energies through her and through the crystal moving the water within the river to create a path for her. Gradually the energies of the light blue crystal moved upstream creating a bigger rift in the centre of the river until it reached the waterfall.

Winding up the wall of water the energies reacted with it to light up runes on the rocks, etched upon their slippery moss covered surface. The surrounding area trembled with power like a small earthquake parting the waterfall to reveal an entrance about half way up its height.

'*Climb and hurry,*' a voice said to Angelite inside her head from an unknown source.

Closing in, the noise emanating from the Vasp's wings started to sound deafening.

'**Climb!**' shouted Angelite.

The group all followed her through the parted river by jumping over the water's edge to reach the middle where it was seemingly dry as if no water had touched the bottom of it.

'I'm going to break a leg trying to climb that thing with my boots!' shouted Maledream, barely able to make a sound from the humming as he ran with the Packers and Neveah trying to catch up with Angelite as she started to scale the centre rock face quickly.

Neveah helped the Tribal on his first step and then helped Crazy John and Boris. Following last and keeping his pole arm out, Neveah's muscled free arm helped to keep him going. Angelite reached the top peering into the darkness of the cave. She looked back down seeing Maledream in tow followed by the others.

They were making great progress until the Vasps started their dive-bombing run covering the once sunny area in shadow.

'By the spirits' she gasped with a look of horror on her face.

Maledream looked back down feeling slightly nauseated from the height he had climbed followed by a large shadow and a huge amount of humming as he stared up seeing the large squadron of Vasps closing in on them.

He had to climb the slowest, letting Boris then Crazy John climb past him as he constantly slipped on the rocks while trying to hold all his equipment and sword together in one piece. Blood pumped fast as everyone's adrenaline kicked in at the fear of being caught off guard to be killed or worse. Neveah caught up with him trying to speed Maledream up by pushing him.

'Hurry up, damn it! They're close, just don't look back,' Neveah yelled as hard as he could.

Maledream nodded and continued to race to the top gripping the wet and damp chunks of rock as hard as he could, scared to death that at any moment he could slip back to the floor or be picked off by a hungry Vasp. He was near the top when a Vasp struck. He felt a piercing sensation on his ankle and was being tugged hard as the Vasp tried to take him. Neveah swung his weapon wide knocking the giant beast away as he cut into its hypnotic wings. The Vasp reeled in pain, screeched, and let go of the Tribal as it fell heavily to the rocks below.

Crazy John reached down and pulled Maledream up to safety within the cave where he lay groaning in pain clutching at his injured ankle.

'Give Neveah some covering fire,' shouted Crazy John nudging Boris. Nodding she pulled out a large silver pistol, cocked it, and began to let loose with a hail of lead, the shots faint compared to the noise of the wings.

Neveah had almost reached the mouth of the cave followed by several Vasps out of the hundreds that made them sound louder from the echo of the tunnel behind them, as the group gazed out towards the swarm.

'Have some of this, you bastards,' Boris screamed, shooting the ancient pistol towards any Vasps that threatened Neveah as he crawled up with adrenaline pumping furiously through his bulky muscles.

The bullets cut through the thick hides of the giant insects with ease felling several of the large beasts with near on accurate aim. Angelite had her eyes shut hard and her hands covering her ears. Crazy John had his daggers out ready for anything that wanted to get into the

cave. Neveah launched himself up in one last go to make the top clutching the mouth of the cave and clambering in with another helping hand from Crazy John.

'Right let's go, run!' he barked furiously.

Neveah picked up Maledream who still clutched his ankle from the bite, blood pouring out of the cracks and holes in his footwear. Boris helped Angelite up to her feet and proceeded to pull her harshly.

There was a roar at the mouth of the cave, the entrance shook and the floor trembled as the secret entrance closed and the waterfall collapsed back on itself, crashing down upon the slain beasts below carrying them off down the river.

Silence fell within the short depths of the deep black abyss while the group crawled further into the cave. Gradually their ears healed from the excessive ringing in their ears from the beasts' deafening wings. When they felt they were safe, the group lay in the darkness catching their breaths and regaining their strength.

'Looks like we made it,' said Neveah his voice heavy and slow.

'Looks that way,' replied Maledream, wincing at the throbbing pain in his ankle.

'Aye...and you're lucky you still have a foot mate.'

'Telling me...anyone got a light?'

'Not a problem, I've got an ancient one here, as long as it still works,' replied Boris.

Fumbling around she delved into her leather pouches.

'Found it,' she said, repeatedly butting the small hand torch on the walls of the cave, gradually blinking on and off weakly until finally the full beam switched on with a final hard clunk.

'There we go. Is that all right for the rest of you?' she asked as she shone the beam at each of them in turn shortly blinding them.

'Aye,' replied Neveah, stretching his aching muscles, the light creating a ghostly silhouette of his shadow in the dank moist cave.

Crazy John sat in silence with both sets of eyes closed and breathing calmly enjoying the moment of rest. Angelite stared into the darkness, trying to pierce the abyss with her vision. Turning around she felt it was her turn to speak.

'I think we had better press on. N'Rutas' place must be close now,' she said.

'Aye, let's go everyone,' replied the Pack leader.

Neveah helped Maledream to his feet, as he needed the support for his bitten ankle. Angelite got up by herself now that she knew she was safe from the flying beast. Boris led the way with the flashlight, brushing past Crazy John as she did so.

'Looks like this cave hasn't seen much use in a long time,' said Crazy John as the group moved in a single line deeper into the darkness with only a small light to guide them.

'Aye, looks it,' said Neveah, adding:

'Never been inside a dark place inside a rock before, well a natural rock that is, not like the city buildings we lived in.'

'It is very peculiar,' said Angelite, her hands gently passing over either side of the cave walls feeling every groove and damp surface to try to get a feel of the area.

Brightness grew at the end of the tunnel while cold fresh air brushed the group's sweaty skin. As they waded deeper into the cave it started to widen up gradually showing the real age of the underground network as stalagmites and stalactites grew bigger and bigger until eventually Boris stopped as she entered a huge cavern.

Her light seemed to increase as it refracted upon a whole field of different types of glowing crystals of all shapes and sizes lighting the entire area of the cavern like a beautiful rainbow. The group was in awe at the splendour of the ancient cave and was stunned into total silence. Angelite could hardly keep her excitement contained as she clasped her hands together to her lips.

Auras of multi-colours took over the shadows as the group inched forwards gradually. As they moved, the flashlight continued to increase the crystals illumination of the cave.

'It's beautiful,' muttered Angelite.

'It is like these crystals have never been touched by light. They are making me feel more rejuvenated!'

'Aye, I'm starting to feel like my old self again surrounded by these bright stones,' replied Neveah.

'Crystals, Neveah! Crystals! Not stones!' Angelite replied

'Alright woman calm down! Stop getting so excited,' Neveah replied heartily, smiling at her.

'It is a sight to behold though captain,' Boris replied.

'I think I preferred the woods,' Crazy John said with a mad grin.

'Say that again and I will boot you back outside with those beasts,' Neveah replied shaking his head.

Stalagmites and stalactites could be seen everywhere inside the cavern, lit and shining brightly. Water that exited from the cracks in the ceiling trickled down the stalagmites, gently filling pools below.

'It looks like we are not the first ones to have walked into this place,' said Boris, shining the flashlight on some old toys near one of the pools of water.

Walking closer and inspecting deeper inside the huge cavern filled with ancient pure crystals, the party of adventurers stumbled upon more things that had been abandoned by previous human beings. Old rusted weapons, rotted items of clothing, but no bones or any existence of anything that died. It was as if any humans that were here had found a way out, possibly deeper inside the cavern.

Angelite walked back to a poorly looking Maledream who was still being supported by Neveah. His veins were slightly raised on his neck and his skin began to take a green tinge. Maledream could barely keep his eyes open it seemed he was now unaware of his surroundings.

'I don't feel too good, I feel like I'm on fire,' he said, his legs gave way causing much concern to everyone else.

'You need to rest mate,' said Neveah.

'You're not heavy but I think it's best if we sat you down for a while.'

'I'm sensing something,' said Angelite, she peered over to the pools of shimmering cavern water.

'Bring Maledream this way, let's put him in the water. I bet this will help him, I think he may have been poisoned by the bite,' said Angelite calmly.

'Aye woman, come on mate. Watch your step now,' Neveah said.

Angelite took off Maledream's boot, her nostrils met with the stench of unnatural rotting flesh. It was so bad that it even cancelled out the fresh air that flowed through the cavern.

Neveah just grinned and bared it as he looked at the festering green wound that spewed yellow pus where blood should be leaking.

'I don't feel too well...' Maledream said weakly.

'Just hang in there you will be fine. I'm just lowering you into the water now, alright mate?' Neveah's large arms helped Maledream in the multi-coloured pool of water. Maledream's foot went in, and at first, nothing happened. The group watched on silently to see what Angelite herself could do.

Grabbing the crystal she had used for her spell to open the cave entrance, she said a silent prayer trying to use what little energy she had left to use her healing abilities to try and cure the poison within Maledream's bloodstream.

Mustering the strength he had left, Maledream took off his heavy coat letting it fall to one side. He removed the latch upon his scabbard. The blade fell loosely into the pool as his strength failed him.

He noticed the runes upon the surface were illuminated as it slipped out from its shoddy scabbard.

'That is strange,' said Neveah.

'It's like the sword's reacting with the crystals...' remarked Angelite as she watched the crystals within the vicinity react almost instantly to the blade.

'I think it's because it is linked with them, like any of us here,' replied the priestess, her eyes focusing on the runes.

Maledream slipped further into the water his hand lightly brushing the hilt of the strange weapon.

'The water...it's warm,' Maledream said, closing his eyes and floating in the clean crystal water as he felt the weakness leaving him.

The ancient blade let out a ringing noise as it submerged in the pool, humming with power and life as it connected with its owner.

'I'm going to try healing him,' said Angelite, dunking her hands into the water. Green and gold energies began to glow from the palms of her hands. Her eyes widened and pupils dilated for a moment as her thoughts went into overdrive.

'I'm not the only one healing him...' she said barely above a whisper.

'How do you mean?' Neveah asked raising his eyebrow.

'I can feel the sword is healing him because he is injured, but not because Maledream has control of its power. It's must be because the crystals are singing to the sword and in turn it is singing back like they are a set of musical instruments, like the crystals are hitting a certain sequence or notes in order to activate that power.'

'You mean like the thunder and lightning back at that old dead battlefield?' asked Neveah, watching the crystals and the runes on the sword glow almost in sync.

'Yes...like it mimics the surrounding area, the state of being of the person carrying it, amongst many other possible things, but yes, I believe so. It needs Resonance to activate, but it only does it on certain frequencies it seems. I've seen it glow a dark crimson when Maledream was intent on revenge back at your old place, and before that Maledream seemed to use it to devastating effect on a beast of old.'

'Aye he mentioned something about a lizard,' Neveah said.

Angelite turned her head to stare at Neveah in the eye.

'Yes, in the blink of an eye he moved just as fast as a lightning bolt as he struck it down. At the time I was healing Maledream from the vicious beating that he was receiving from this beast and it seemed my powers awakened some of the swords potency.'

'Hmm,' Neveah grunted.

'Well I couldn't care less, it's still a powerful weapon either way, even if it does look ancient and deceiving,' said Crazy John.

Boris continued to scan the area picking up old dolls, which almost fell apart into dust as soon as she touched them, still listening to their conversation and generally keeping a look out.

'Aye, I second that, I don't quite understand enough of it yet but I'm sure I will later when we get out of here and find that woman...she can't be far now,' replied Neveah.

The conversation around Maledream faded to faint echoes as he lost consciousness. His body wracked with a fever so high he wondered if he would survive.

'You wielded me once before Maledream, and once before you unlocked me, and once again you can unlock me.'

The entity spoke to him.

'We are connected.'

Maledream was unable to talk or think back to it as he felt the humming within his palms grasping the hilt of the blade gently. The sensations of weightlessness were overpowering and he felt that he could lift from his own body. Colours dashed in softly flowing lines within his eyelids as the song and chorus of the blade within his mind soothed his body and spirit. The burning sensation inside his ankle started to leave him.

He opened his eyes to see green and gold energies racing in front of him and dancing on the surface of the water. The Tribal could see more runes upon the blade than had been there before yet somehow they seemed familiar. Now he felt the sword was alive and had become part of him bringing him extra strength as it filled his mind with song.

Maledream decided it was time to break out of the trance. Blinking once more, his vision was restored as if he had known how to control it all along. He noticed the sword now only contained its original runes.

'I feel...better,' he said with a strong voice.

Although unknown to him, everyone had witnessed some sort of transformation. They had watched Maledream's blade glow with a new colour of silver, amazed by the humming lights of the runes on the sword.

'Thank the spirits your alright,' said Angelite, her hands gliding to Maledream in the pool to hug him briefly.

'Thank you,' he said, turning around in the watery pool of brightly lit crystalline cavern water that now seemed brighter than ever

due to the potency of the blade's ancient awaken powers.

His eyes gleamed with a deep ocean blue as he stared at the surroundings and the company he kept. Everything seemed brighter to him, almost a small glow surrounding everything for a few moments as his eyes adjusted to the surroundings.

'Aye, mate, and by the looks of it you're all healed up! All thanks to Angelite!' Neveah said, patting Maledream hard on the back.

The Tribal smiled before saying:

'You have to stop making it a habit.'

'Let's get you out before you catch a cold next,' she replied.

'Let's drink this water, and take some with us. It will help us on our way,' said Boris pointing to another pool nearby.

'Aye,' replied Neveah, emptying the flasks of the normal river water onto the floor to get this crystal water all batched up.

Maledream put the sword back into its rough shoddy scabbard. Piece by piece he took off his clothes to dry them.

'Look at that, you skinny runt! Not a muscle on your scrawny body,' Neveah said with a laugh, Maledream was indeed a lot thinner than what his baggy clothes suggested.

He smiled as he looked into Angelite's eyes, causing her to turn the other way and blush shortly with an awkward smile wrapped on her face as Neveah carried on poking holes at him.

'All you two do is get naked,' Neveah chuckled, Crazy John and Boris eyeing each other up at the odd comment.

'Well we might as well press on then...' Crazy John was interrupted by the most peculiar laugh or cackle further down the cave.

'What the hell was that?' asked Boris.

'Sounded like something is close to dying up there,' Maledream said.

Neveah cracked his knuckles together.

'Me and John should investigate first,' Boris suggested.

'Not going to happen,' Neveah said bracing his weapon.

'We're safer in numbers, we stick together. No telling what that was,' he added.

Maledream finished donning his damp clothes and boots, and with a swift nod, Neveah began to lead the way down the passage.

The cackling echoed continuously over short periods as they made their way further into the brightly lit cavern. Turning a corner, they stumbled upon a crippled looking old woman and knew they had found the source of the cackling. Her features were wrinkly and weathered, so much so that it was impossible to see any real detail even from the front as she stared smiling at the group with a gentle yet

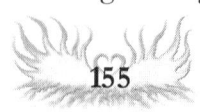

happy smile. Neveah asked:

'Are you N'Rutas?' while scratching his scalp.

'Maybe...' her voice was husky yet gentle as the wrinkles wrapped their shape around her moving lips almost hypnotically.

'We were sent by the Witches back deeper in the forest outside,' Maledream replied.

'So it seems young one,' N'Rutas said before continuing:

'Forgive me for all the hiding and all the secrets of this place, but to prove who you are takes more than just words to me, you must complete challenges and obstacles. There are many things I hide from to stay safe' N'Rutas said in a playful tone, the group believing her words.

'Even though we risked death?' replied Neveah.

'It appears so, but my messenger has already given me all of the details, so relax.'

N'Rutas stared at Maledream and then Angelite.

'You must be Angelite with that red hair,' she cackled, limping closer towards her.

'And I know what you seek, young girl,' N'Rutas let her arm reach towards the priestess' back pack, slowly dragging it off Angelite's shoulders while staring eye to eye with the young lady.

'You had a staff that was created by my kin, and in fact it is one I made myself if you did not already know, young lady?' she asked, peering into the bag to see the dusty fragments of the staff and crystal.

'I didn't...kin?' Angelite replied with a gasp, her words barely escaping her mouth as a confused frown set upon her face, the comment also raising brows within the group.

'*What a strange woman,*' Maledream thought, both he and Neveah looked at the others whilst shrugging.

'I am guessing you were gifted that in Meridia. It has been a while since I have been there but I myself have been busy. I shall tell all once we have reached my hut and fed your growing bodies! I can sense hunger festering within you all...follow me and I shall stuff you all up!'

'You hear that? Food!' shouted Neveah in excitement, raising his fists in the air.

While the others looked forward to fresh food, Angelite made sure she walked beside N'Rutas so she could ask her some questions.

'N'Rutas, did you know we were coming all along?' Angelite asked.

'But of course dear, I have many ways like the Witches you and your companions met back deeper into that forsaken forest. Burning the wood to stay warm and such, I know all about it.'

N'Rutas' body shifted back and forth as she cackled.

'Then again that shouldn't surprise us. You lot always seem to talk without opening your mouths. I don't understand it,' said Crazy John.

'You are quite lucky my children, not much longer now until you reach Meridia, as you new age people would call it. It was another name before that, but I am sure Angelite's teachers will tell you that when they give you a tour of the place. Anyway, where are my manners? I shall tell you what this place is. Ahead of us used to be one of the biggest volcanoes at the turn of the new age. I took refuge there at the start of this Dark Age and rather turned that volcano around after it fell dormant into what it is now...a basin paradise of rich greens, pastures, and animals. The earth has inside it precious life giving minerals for the use of us that live on the surface, and I was able to use these to transform the place,' she said, cackling at her own expertise.

'Transform the place?' Angelite asked.

'You'll see child,' N'Rutas assured.

Slowly the group followed this strange and eccentric old woman as she continued to speak of the group.

Angelite was constantly on the heels of N'Rutas noting down anything important that was being uttered.

The group gradually approached the light at the end of the tunnel complex. After travelling through the refreshing crystalline passages, they all had a renewed vigour of energy, although still their stomachs rumbled as their acids started to devour them on the insides.

Fresh mountain air slowly brushed through them as N'Rutas led them into her home. Upon exiting the lava duct and entering the mountainous glade, the group stopped in awe at the beauty of the place. Gasping at the amount of lush green grasses, many variations and kinds of trees and other such foliage and flowers that went on for as far as the eye can see. Leopards, wolves, buffalo, tigers, lions, deer, and many other creatures lived in what seemed like harmony.

Birds flew above in and out of the misty sparse clouds that populated the ocean blue sky. In the distance and gradually as they eyed up the area they came from, the group noticed even further that the sides of the circular basin reached further into the sky and encapsulated the whole glade, as if it were a barrier of rock.

Even in the distance, the sides of the volcano looked like far away mountains. Stones with runes lit upon them were dotted about the landscape, humming with different colour energies and chiming many faint but distant sounds as if resonating to frequencies on a constant basis.

Angelite instantly fell in love with this place of wonder.

'I cannot believe that you have conserved some of the rarest animals on this planet, N'Rutas! How on earth did you manage it?'

N'Rutas cackled once more before turning to smile at Angelite and then said:

'Mind over matter, my dear. If I were to tell you, I would be here all day! And you lot need feeding...perhaps another time when we meet again.'

N'Rutas led the way through the slightly forested areas as they followed a cobbled path from the mouth of the exit of the crystalline cave towards their final destination to her hut.

Neveah, Crazy John, and Boris remained silent but their eyes took in everything around them. To them, it was not possible that such a place could exist next to so many dangers that existed outside of the mountainous walls of this volcano basin.

Maledream looked on in deep thought.

Chapter Eleven

Artefacts and Knowledge...

'The eye sees only what the mind is prepared to comprehend.'

Henri Bergson

Reaching her hut, N'Rutas opened her wooden door with a subtle push, its old stone hinges creaking against the old wooden framework. Enriched herbs surrounded her hut with crushed and ground crystals strewn like a fine dust over the ground where they were growing, keeping the lush exotic plants thriving on the energies.

'Keeps them strong and healthy these crystals do,' N'Rutas muttered as she scuffled inside the hut, waving the others to follow.

'Please make yourselves at home, I'll be right outside picking some vegetables and fruit I need, not to mention spices as well! I hope you are all vegetable and fruit eaters?'

Neveah spoke out, his stomach raging:

'I fancy some meat if you have some, N'Rutas, Aye?'

'Tough,' she replied, giving him a sly wink, her wrinkly eyelids almost collapsing down her nonexistent cheekbones.

'I know what's good for you young ones and this food is enough to keep an army of ten thousand soldiers going for weeks,' she said laughing.

'That will be fine, thank you kindly,' Angelite replied, smiling softly at the old hag.

'Now that's manners,' N'Rutas replied, smiling back at the young red head.

'Please sit down, make yourselves comfortable, and rest. Those crystals in the cave can dull your physical senses somewhat and make you feel strong when in fact you are as tired as sin! So rest children, I'll be back at dusk.'

Moreover, the old hag left the group in the hut. Most of them were happy to rest but Angelite wandered around, keen to learn how N'Rutas lived. She could see mortars and pestles strewn all over one table in the corner of the hut, surrounded by grounded crystals and ground herbs that had not yet been swept up from the floor.

Different variants of crystal or glass bottles were also present with strange glowing liquids inside them.

'Is it me, or does this place looks bigger in here than it did from outside?' asked Boris.

'Outside, it seemed like this place was under need of being rebuilt before it collapsed,' she added.

Neveah laughed.

'Aye, it does look shoddy woman, but from the looks of it outside and from what I've seen around this place, I wouldn't be surprised if this thing could withstand ten thunderstorms all at once.'

Crazy John peered outside the ancient glass windows, focusing on the deer and other meaty creatures that were grazing just a few metres away, not even sure himself if he could wait for N'Rutas to come back with just vegetables and fruit.

'Don't any of you feel slightly cheated?' asked Crazy John.

'Maybe slightly,' replied Boris.

'I think we'll all feel even more of that once we reach Meridia,' Maledream said resting his arms behind his head shutting his eyes to relax.

'I reckon so, and it sure beats surviving and killing back in the city,' said Neveah.

'That would be a shame,' Crazy John said.

'You drag us down with your pessimism then there will be problems,' Maledream replied angrily, one eye flipping open to stare at Crazy John.

'Calm it down you two before I hit you both,' Neveah bitterly replied.

'I want no fighting, had enough of that shit back in the city. Keep your dark thoughts to yourself Crazy John, and Maledream, calm it down,' Neveah said.

An awkward moment of silence fell on the group for a moment, Maledream falling fast asleep on the woollen rugs that softened the hard stone cobbled floor beneath him with no care.

'This place has a good, spiritual sense,' said Angelite going off topic.

'It makes me feel safe. I suppose the pungent smell of herbs adds to its charm.'

'Aye, woman, well, it could do with a fire but there doesn't seem to be anything we could use to burn except perhaps the hut, but I think the old hag would have more than our balls on a plate, to add to the vegetables and fruit she's been talking about most of the trip,' Neveah heartily chuckled.

Angelite stopped exploring the hut and settled down beside the rest of the group who were sitting in silence, recovering from their journey while the retreating sun began to set into the dusk. Then she remembered the old journals and books she had retrieved so she moved to one of N'Rutas' oaken desks.

She struggled to decipher the symbols of writing to the best of her abilities and intuition. Some of it made sense yet some pages, especially from some books such as the journals she discovered, were sometimes vague or not the information she was looking for.

Although, from what she could decipher at the time of the writer jotting it all down in his or her old book, there was a time human nations from all continents had been at peace before the Dark Age arrived. She sighed as she studied the writing, more and more immersing herself with the languages of old. Taking a break, she smiled when she looked at Maledream thinking how brave he had been.

She could see the sword and his bag slumped by his side while he snored slightly but quietly. Looking at other members of the group it seemed the rest also joined Maledream in catching a wink or two.

It was then that Angelite noticed that there was strange looking round objects suspended in mid-air just above Maledream. The orbs resembled planets that were either crafted from wood or crystal hanging from poison ivy that crept through the cracks of the thatched ceiling. Staring harder, she started to recall what each planet was, while noting the positions of the planets and their formations.

'Certainly an intelligent woman lives here,' she whispered to herself, while staring into the centre of the orbit of all the planets where the sun should be, but instead there was only a crystal that was latched into position roughly by thin but much taut string.

Peering onto N'Rutas' other wooden benches, Angelite also spotted maps, very old brown maps that if touched could fall to dust.

As she walked closer and upon sharper inspection, she saw different star constellations on several different maps, while also noting positions of certain parts of the world, which had symbols of either pyramids or more bizarre types of symbols inked upon their ancient paper surfaces.

Very peculiar drawings of the earth's continents from the other maps were of great interest to Angelite.

'The world's continents were destroyed or changed, could this be the old map of the old world that I'd hoped to find in that old library?' she asked herself silently.

She gazed on new maps made by N'Rutas, as if she had been creating and piecing together what the world looked like now.

She felt a hand on the back of her shoulder startling her.

'Finding my work interesting, dear?' asked N'Rutas.

Calming down, Angelite replied:

'Yes...very,' she said, sighing with relief.

N'Rutas shifted besides Angelite and began speaking over her work.

'I have been alive for hundreds of years now dear, or cycles to you and your kin. And it was back then at the turn of this Dark Age that I found who I really was, and who was using and controlling me.'

Angelite did not have a clue what she was talking about but could not take her eyes from her face, she hazard a guess.

'I have read of beings that have lived as long as you,' replied Angelite.

'You said Kin earlier back in the cave...could that mean you're a Nephilim?' she asked.

N'Rutas stared into Angelite's eyes, and then slyly morphed her pupils into the shape of a reptile before returning them to their original human form.

'Yes, you are a bright one aren't you? I can see why your mentors cannot wait to see your full potential. However, do not run before you can walk. You still have many decades left. I am...well let us not use that old useless and senseless word, as far as the people who made up that name it no longer exists now, only in memory it seems. I am what you would call a half-breed, a polymorph, a shape changer, a shape shifter. Although I prefer my old crippled human form rather than my scaly hide, I find that I chaff too much in odd places,' N'Rutas cackled.

Angelite gasped, ignoring the gag.

'So you're an Anunaki? You're a lizard as well?' she asked.

N'Rutas smiled.

'Yes, although we are few and far between us now, and I use my abilities of shaping Resonance and deep, deep knowledge to preserve what life I can, hidden away in this dead but alive volcano, my child.'

Angelite thought hard before asking another question:

'So how come I couldn't sense you were one, N'Rutas?'

'My dear, it is because I have the best of both worlds, even though I am shunned by both, except perhaps in Meridia of course, but there is still prejudice that exists within many humans and so I remain here, and visit across the ocean whenever I can when the need arises. Last time I went to Meridia I dropped off this staff for you, child, because I knew we would meet today, and that was...hmm twenty-two cycles ago? Yes, yes it was if I remember correctly.'

'Fantastic,' Angelite replied.

'It seems as if it were written in the stars,' Angelite said as if it were a fateful omen.

'It seems so, dear Angelite, although I pictured you with short red hair, not long red hair. Although perhaps it is not the right moment yet, my abilities are fading, young one. I have lived for hundreds of years and I feel as if now I am coming to the end of my life. Which is why I need to tell you a few things about the path you must travel, but even that I feel it is not yet time to discuss your journey further...end of my tether...' she muttered, for a second forgetting what she was saying. Angelite held her hand and said,

'Please, N'Rutas. You must help us, my navigator died while we were on our mission and I cannot read maps well. Guess we can't be good at everything?'

N'Rutas gripped Angelite's hand.

'It is okay my dear, things happen, some bad, some good, you must learn to respect it. Besides, if we were all good and perfect where would it get us? Meridia isn't perfect in itself, as I'm sure you'd agree dear, but it is a step forward, that is certain, although I won't be around much longer to see it reach full fruition.'

'I guess you are right,' Angelite replied while staring at the maps and notes strewn across the tables of N'Rutas' workbenches.

'You are indeed a very old being N'Rutas, and being around you I feel more connected with everything, even being here in this great round glade in this sleeping volcano. I feel hope.'

'Indeed, child, hope is what we all need,' N'Rutas said, smiling.

'We will talk again but I must feed you and your companions who all seem to be sleeping rather heavily. We must be ready because I feel something dark coming...so it is best if I make you the food, and then give you the present that I have been crafting for many, many years, knowing this day would come.'

Angelite's eyes widened and stammered:

'You have made me a staff? That is a bit too much, N'Rutas!'

'I know that you will need it, but it isn't just any staff. I have placed some of my power inside it and some of my knowledge too. Of course, you will have to look after it, however, it should not break from resonating energies if that moment ever does arise. It is a...well let us call your new staff Catalyst shall we?'

'That is incredible, N'Rutas. I am honoured!' Angelite raised her voice in excitement, almost stirring the group nearby.

'I thought that would put a smile on your lips dear, now I shall prepare the food, and also prepare you afterwards for where you have to travel. First a little more light, it is getting rather gloomy outside now

the sun is disappearing.'

Angelite hugged N'Rutas while thanking her further for the gift that she would receive after dinner, the old hag responded with a chuckle.

N'Rutas hobbled around the hut lighting many handmade bees wax candles, which thanks to their different colour dyes emitted odd and bizarre glows as they burned. She had prepared the meal by the time the rest of the group had awakened.

The group gorged themselves, some did not like the taste but did not argue over their stomachs that ached, moaned, and groaned. Gradually, as they finished, all of them joked and bantered while drinking some fresh spring water from N'Rutas' taps. Spirits were higher but sadly, the group knew deep down this would only last tonight before they would be on the move again.

'That was some fine grub, N'Rutas. On behalf of everyone thank you for your hospitality, otherwise we would surely have died from hunger,' said Neveah, wiping his mouth after drinking.

'It is not a problem. You are more than welcome,' she replied.

'But now I must be serious with you…I will lead you to a passage that will take you to the shore but, before the shore, you have obstacles ahead of you. Once, you have reached the seafront, look out for a group of people related to Meridia who are called the Watchman and they will let you travel by boat across the new ocean, well, it is new now, but let not that concern you or I'll just be confusing you all. Angelite knows what I mean very well, as that was the rough direction she was leading you.'

She cackled before gaining a little breath.

'You will have to head North West from this volcano,' N'Rutas continued.

'You will have to travel across another barren wasteland, although this wasteland is rife with a hidden danger lingering in the air. It is called radiation, and if smelled or touched can make you ill for a few days or a lifetime, until gradually killing you. If you were unlucky, you would suffer for months. Do not worry, it's levels are now quite low, but it is still dangerous. Angelite will look after you. The main danger I want to warn you about is that there are still ancient Anunaki that inhabit that dead land. Be on your guard, you will all have to leave in the morning, and you will also be accompanied by Silver, the wolf.'

N'Rutas coughed, clearing her throat to continue:

'Now where was I? I shall explain a bit more about the "radiation". In the olden days, before the Anunaki from under the earth's crust came and attacked your race, there were weapons of wondrous power. Powerful weapons of destruction that could rival the power of the sun high in the heavens, they could turn human beings, or in fact any living being to ash, and wipe out entire cities in one mighty blast.'

The group drew closer around N'Rutas to hear her story.

'These devices were used against fellow human beings over trivial affairs or, of course, to support manipulated agendas by governments wanting power over other human beings or natural resources. This led to escalating affairs that were going to happen eventually, and this is before the axis of the earth changed too. Not that much later, just a little though. Many prophets from the Mayan culture, tried to warn of doom, but were frowned upon because of trivial meanings, or dates. They carried with them sacred crystals of wondrous power that resembled human skulls and were thought to have been crafted from the mind back then, which is true of course young ones now that the world has changed differently it's hard to say it can't be possible. They were also the masters of "time," or the "stars," it was said, even though time does not exist. Only a constant...they had knowledge handed down to them by the Anunaki thousands upon thousands of cycles ago. They used to worship the Nephilim or Anunaki who, and made sacrifices often to the "Sky Gods". Truth be told they were lied to by the Anunaki, during that period. These skulls were gifts from the people that came from the sky, children, who we are all related too, the race that created human beings and Anunaki alike, the Creators themselves,' she continued:

'The wise holy men or shamans who knew this also possessed knowledge of the stars and how the world would come to be and come to pass, which even now, from the relics I have saved here myself and from the knowledge they knew, everything has gone according to plan. You will learn more about the skulls when you reach Meridia but for now I shall tell you how the Anunaki did not manage to posses them, and how even now, civilisation is starting anew just as intended.'

N'Rutas coughed again, drinking more spring water.

'The Maya knew what was coming, after all they were the masters of knowing the "future" or rather the constant. They have secret sects that still exist to this day, hidden away in a few secret places. As I was saying...the Mayan shamans knew of the plight of what was to happen, and they decided against the will of their masters to disperse their people to help the human race for millennia to come. They evacuated their entire civilisation, as if they disappeared overnight. This was because the shamans wanted to preserve the knowledge of the crystal skulls for the better of humankind. They established other civilisations on the continent, leaving clues and even some forgotten artefacts. Soon the populaces even forgot where they come from themselves save for some false history here and there for the younger generations to swallow up. In keeping secrets, they were covering their own tracks and preserving their people and their secret knowledge that was handed down from the people from the stars to which we are related. Therefore, as you see, young ones, there is a lot to learn, and much I cannot teach you in one night. You might not realise it now but I have given you all very good, true history.'

Drinking more spring water, she could see the bewilderment in the group's eyes, some understood what she was saying, but others did not. Angelite knew what N'Rutas was talking about, after all, coming from Meridia, she knew a lot of the history of the Old World.

'It is all valuable,' replied Angelite in awe at N'Rutas' wise words.

'All I can say, children, is that the Maya were very famous for disappearing, leaving many scholars of old confused to why they all disappeared at once. Some speculated that they all died of a disease but there was no trace of them to be found. Surely if they all died of disease then they would have at least have left many bones behind as evidence...but it was not so. When you have the vast amount of knowledge I have collected for generations, you can easily derive a conclusion that precious knowledge was protected in the form of artefacts. By fleeing, they ensured that their secrets were safe until they were needed.'

Neveah scratched his eye patch, before staring at everyone else who seemed to be deep in thought, where as he had no clue. He was a Packer, plain and simple, fighting was his strong point, not knowledge or learning.

He could not care less about a civilisation that had existed long ago but still he tried to listen. Maledream was fascinated, imagining a great culture that had existed with these strange crystal artefacts that N'Rutas described.

'Before you go on your journey tomorrow, be sure to take the bags of food I have supplied you with, and the water also,' she chuckled, her skin wrinkling like a pebble to water much like a rippling effect as she did so.

Maledream spoke up:

'It sounds very interesting. But, surely if these ancient people saw the future or the constant, how you put it, they should have stopped the trouble, shouldn't they?'

N'Rutas replied:

'They believed that you could not stop the inevitable and that you should not even try, besides, many alternate states can happen in a constant, it's what makes reality so linear and easy to manipulate. After all free will is the universal law, for both forms of dualities such as good and evil. They possibly felt the world needed to open its eyes to see that human beings should appreciate each other and work towards a common goal. An evil threat would serve as a means to unite the people. Whether the Maya also wished to start a newer civilisation, I do not know...but they knew this was what they had to do.'

The group was silent and in a deep contemplative state about the tale. An ancient race of people called the Maya was news to them and even then, most of them except Angelite did not know any history of the world. Only the Dark Age lands that they had been accustomed to all their lives.

Maledream had heard some of Larkham's stories but he had forgotten them. He wished now that he had paid more attention to the old man. N'Rutas took deep and silent breaths.

It was the most she had talked about for many cycles now, and her age was finally showing. She knew she did not have long left to live on the planet. She felt it was soon going to be her moment to pass into another dimension and leave this one.

'Now,' spoke N'Rutas quietly.

'I think it is time to give you your staff Angelite...and then Maledream I must speak with you about that sword of yours.'

N'Rutas hobbled from the centre of the room to near the corner of her hut near where Angelite was observing much of N'Rutas' maps and other such arcane notes.

She lifted the wood on the table to reveal a long object wrapped in leather and tied with strong, thin rope. The wood creaked as if it were about to break from the age of it as N'Rutas closed the wooden desk gently and hobbled back to the centre of the room.

'Use this in the Radiated Zone dear to protect yourself and your companions. As I spoke to you earlier, Catalyst shall look after you very well,' she said, gently passing the wrapped staff to Angelite who handled the package with great care.

'Go on and open it, dear. You have made it this far. Tell your mentors back home that you are ready for your next trial in your Spirit Order.'

'Thank you,' replied Angelite, barely containing her excitement as she gently opened the tight rope like it were a winter solstice.

Angelite unravelled the staff that shone bright glistening silver and seemed to sing as the leather brushed down its surface as she held it upright. Symbols were joined to symbols very intricately which were in turn leading up the shaft until it reached the top where a Swan sat completely made from strange metals but was so finely crafted itself, that it did not seem to have any markings on it whatsoever.

'The animal is known as a Swan my child, a beautiful creature, the name derives from old languages to mean "song" or "sound", quite apt for a talented individual such as yourself. Human works of art used to show supernatural beings called angels, bearing such wings on their backs. They were considered, at least in art form, messengers for the old god's, the Creators. To spread the conveyed word of sound or the likes, and as the ancients once said, the first word was sound, and they would be correct on that assumption today,' said N'Rutas, her eyes and smile beaming like the sun towards Angelite's excited expressions.

'Yes, it's beautiful! I don't know what to say, it's incredible,' she remarked, stroking the new pristine staff with joy.

'It has the power of resurrection my dear. It is a power not to be used lightly. Once used it will take a month to recharge itself, and it must be done in the power of a full moon...this is, of course, a safety caution in case this staff ever falls into Anunaki hands...living underground will mean it will never see the moonlight.'

N'Rutas cackled at the thought of the Anunaki trying to use its power. The group smiled at Angelite seeing her so happy obtaining such a gift that would no doubt help them along the way.

'It also has much of my power stored inside it. You could say that the staff is more powerful than I am, and if you are in a dire need, the staff will help you dear Angelite, and turn you into a force that few could destroy. You will know when the time comes to use it. All I can say to you now, my dear, is to remember mind over matter when it comes to crystals as I'm sure you will understand when you age...and now for...'

N'Rutas paused and stared towards Maledream for a split second and then to the blade next to him.

'That blade, boy,' she said, stopping for a moment to take a drink of water.

'What about it?' Maledream asked.

'I have not gazed upon one such as this for a long time. Where did you find such a dangerous thing?'

'Dangerous? I found it several moons ago, kept it hidden from my adopted...well Larkham. Found it on that old battlefield back from where I came from near the city, when the sun was out and baking me.

Didn't know anything about the shadows we came across until recently.'

'I am sure you would not have done, Maledream, not many people have a stroke of luck like the one you do have,' she cackled.

'That weapon, it must have been left there after the battle and thought lost. It is not rare for that to have happened since the Dark Age arrived, it's very commonplace for it to happen in fact. Do you wish to know where it came from and who crafted it?' N'Rutas asked.

'I guess...I'm not really interested in the history of it. All I can say is that it has helped me sometimes, and even shown me several things, which scared the hell out of me at first. It usually activates when I get angry, although it has used lightning somehow. I really wondered how I didn't die from such a force to be frank with you,' Maledream replied.

The old hag shuffled closer to Maledream on her crippled legs to where he was sitting to get a better look at the sword.

'It works when you are in tune with it, boy. You seem to have the same frequency it likes to work with. There are two ways you can use items or crystals like this. You work either with them or against them. Crystals are life forces too,' waving her hand just above the blade, she shut her eyes and seemed to absorb herself within the weapon's own consciousness.

'It was crafted by one of the Nephilim, or maybe even perhaps before my kind...maybe the ancient ones from the sky, the Creators. This weapon is slightly better in calibre I would say than the staff I created. Incredible.'

Her wrinkly eyelids overlapped themselves, as she delved deeper, while her eyes rolled back into their sockets. She gasped for a moment and shook her head as if refusing to tell the group something about it.

'Although it is severely aged and in need of a huge recharging... that explains why it is very...choosing of when it wants to use the resonating and surrounding frequencies as a weapon. It does have its own consciousness, very strong in fact. Yes it is like the other twelve Relic weapons, these weapons were made by a higher dimensional power...my skills aren't what they used to be.'

She rolled her eyes back into the right positions in her skull as she slowly opened her eyelids.

'Damn, now I wish I stopped by in the battlefield to get me one of those weapons, if you say there's more of them,' Neveah said with a chuckle.

'These are dangerous weapons, and can be used by skilled Nephilim or human beings alike young ones, although they are designed so the Anunaki cannot use them or their potential power so

easily. They are Master Creator Weapons. And if used are potentially stronger than the weapons of man that obliterated this earth.'

Neveah quietened down, as the old hag still seemed quite serious.

N'Rutas sipped some more water and then shuffled to a seat in her rocking chair. She sighed as she sat down.

'All this standing up and running around! You lot are terrible,' she said, smiling to lighten the atmosphere. She closed her eyes for a second as if she needed to recover from the strength of the blade. The group sat around her.

'Those weapons were made for the planet, another gift just like the sacred skulls. There was once a legend that claimed there were other planets just like ours, and that we were the thirteenth. Many objects were made to celebrate another life on another planet in the universe.'

She sighed, thinking back before continuing:

'Once back thousands of millennia ago all was bliss. Eternal peace existed because no life was apparent until an entity called consciousness grew, and it is this consciousness that binds all things and beings alike in harmony to what it is now. The relics were made to represent a time, almost thirteen thousand years ago, when all the races agreed on peace and prosperity, under the watchful eyes of the Creators. It is then that knowledge was sky high and everything seemed possible without being hindered or damaged by another living being or by the world itself. However, it was not to be. Other planets, if they have not suffered the same fate as us, have reached a point now that, in legend anyway, where they live at an everlasting pinnacle. I think it is what the Maya knew themselves having being gifted the knowledge as a second chance. The crystal skulls and the weapons were gifts, part of a second chance, perhaps.'

'The weapon you have with you, Maledream, was crafted more than thirteen thousand years ago when the first major war on this planet erupted. The Creators, as they are known, made them with the subtle excuse of art, creation, and celebration. In addition, they could foresee what was to come through logic, and so made them into superior super weapons. These weapons once destroyed the greatest city on earth because of over use of them, and to this day are either captured by the Anunaki never to be used against them again, or lost and carelessly thrown away or sold away unknowingly. For you to find one Maledream, and actually use some of its force, shows that even after many ages, they are still destructive weapons.'

She began coughing which caused the rocking chair to creak.

'So, what should I do with it?' Maledream asked.

'I would say destroy it, but that is impossible, my child,' she replied with a slight husk.

'For you to find one suggests that some secret society had been carrying it with them for many ages, handing it down, until it ended up on that battlefield as its final resting place. Moreover, as to the rest of your question, I would advise you not to overly use its power. It is not evil as such, but humans are easily corruptible and can turn hands as fast as you can blink. It is wise not to use it unless you know you can get away with using it, especially when the Anunaki are around. But if the only option you have is to fight then you have to protect yourself until you reach Meridia,' she said sighing deeply.

'You will know what to do with it, child, when the moment arises. If the Maya could have foreseen this moment then it cannot be all bad. Another thing about your weapon is that it is crafted in the same way that I constructed Angelite's new staff, Catalyst, except as a relic it is particularly gifted and has its own consciousness. Metal...rare metals I might add...and crystal are what makes your weapon so potent, Maledream. Angelite's weapon has not been designed for war but I did ensure that it would help to protect her. The metal comes from the Creators, not much is left of it now mind you, but it is very potent stuff, which cannot be smelted down, you have to bend it to your will. That is the secret of crafting such powerful, indestructible weapons with this dimensional alloy.'

Maledream looked at his sword, fascinated by what he had just heard. Once the earth had been a peaceful place, yet all he had known was how to fight and how to survive. He guessed a little more fighting would not hurt if it put humanity back on its toes.

'How could I recharge the weapon?' Maledream asked.

'Meditation, my boy, or of course, wait for it to wake up gradually the more you use it' she answered swiftly.

'I see...it would explain something to me then...'

'Please go on child,' N'Rutas asked.

'Well the night before me and Angelite left Larkham and the rest of the Tribals, I decided to meditate with it, something that Larkham always believed in and I thought I would give it a try. I had a vision I could not wake from and I saw a huge battle taking place...this sounds so crazy but from what I have seen it cannot be...I was staring at humans and Anunaki fighting each other. Huge war machines that the humans were driving had deafening booms going off, my head felt every pounding from them. There was a storm, lightning was erupting from the sky and, and well, too cut a long story short I had to run to the blade that this man with a strange symbol on the back of his hood

was carrying. It was flung away from him as he was swallowed by a horde of those...Anunaki. This man was something else, taller and bigger than Neveah unbelievably and was wearing this powerful armour too. I jumped at the weapon with the beasts closing in behind me fast and then woke up in a sweat. There's one more thing, occasionally this blade seems to mix its mind with me and shows me things to open up its power somehow.'

The Packers eyed him up and then looked at the blade. Neveah could not help however to butt in.

'Bigger than me you say? That takes a lot of beef to get as big as me I know that much,' Neveah laughed, flexing his arms while doing so.

'It's true, mate,' Maledream said, with a weak grin.

'Come on, children, calm down,' ordered N'Rutas.

'I expect that man was a member of one of the secret societies that guarded the blade. I am not sure who that man could have been, maybe one of my kind...perhaps the symbol would help. Jot it down here for me please, Maledream,' she said, passing him an inkpot, parchment and a wooden ink pen.

They all watched as the Tribal sketched the round symbol on the floor.

'Hmmm a bit rough, but that will do I suppose,' cackled N'Rutas with a raised smile from her weathered skinned wrinkles.

'Do you know what it is?' asked Maledream seriously.

'Hmmm,' she murmured.

'I think so...it has been a while since I have stared at it. I will need to think about it and talk to you about it again.'

'I see,' said Maledream who now felt foolish for talking about this vision.

He had been so sure that it was important, but if N'Rutas could not remember what it meant or what it stood for, for that society or sect, what could it mean? He racked his brain while N'Rutas carried on speaking to him.

'It is difficult, my boy, but do not let it get to you. You're still young,' she cackled.

The conversation was boring Crazy John so he got out his various weapons to polish them, much to Maledream's annoyance.

Not that anyone could blame him for being rude, he did not have a clue what N'Rutas was talking about however.

All he knew was the language of the smell of food to satisfy his hunger, and that of blood being spilled.

N'Rutas continued her advice to Maledream who looked even more troubled about the blade as his eyes were lost in its dull surface.

'You dreamed of lightning my dear Maledream, when you were meditating, and so you charged it with the Resonance of the storms I am guessing. All you have to be is the medium or the charger of the weapon whenever you can manage it. That is all you need to know. Now, all of you must get some rest because I especially need it. It has been fun talking and gifting you knowledge but I am too old to stay up this late. If you should wake up and find me gone, do not worry. I have a lot of animals and trees to attend to. I have prepared water, bread, fruit, and freshly steamed vegetables for you all in six packs. Maledream, you will be carrying Silver's meat.'

Neveah butted in:

'Hey, how is it that we have to eat greens and the wolf gets away with eating damn chicken?'

The old hag laughed at him.

'He can't eat greens, fool...now stop whining and be grateful you got something to eat before I clip your ear! Or your remaining eye...'

Maledream laughed at the insult.

Angelite and Boris giggled and smiled.

'She had you there, captain,' Boris said while saluting Neveah, who just murmured about it not being fair that N'Rutas had favoured the wolf.

'Anyway children, good night, your food rations are just on the table behind you.'

She got off her rocking chair, limped passed them and hobbled up the stairs of her hut to her room.

'Well, what an eventful evening,' said Crazy John packing away his weapons.

'Aye, it was mate. We can all get some good rest on these thick soft sheep rugs too...nice and warm they are.'

'Yup,' replied Angelite.

'Although I think I will stub out the candles except a two or three. This place has a nice glow to it with the candlelight,' she added.

'Whatever you wish sweet, but I'm hitting the sack,' replied Neveah as he took off his worn footwear, wrapping himself in the comfort of the wool on a nearby chair.

Crazy John and Boris slept next to each other and were wrapped up warmly as they shut their eyes and began to dream.

Angelite put the candles out bar two of them that were near where N'Rutas was sitting on the rocking chair.

Sitting down next to Maledream and placing the staff next to his sword, she gazed at him as she leant over his head as he gradually drifted off to sleep with his hands behind his head.

'Hasn't even taken off his boots, terrible man,' she said, then smiling at him. She took the liberty to remove his boots off the clean thick white rugs, noticing they had already left brown marks.

'No manners either, oh well,' she whispered to herself as she rested her head on his chest listening to his heartbeat.

She then looked up to notice the Tribal had one eye open staring at her with a small smirk on his lips. Her heart then raced as she stared into his blue eyes that reflected the two candles in front of him. He broke the silence softly.

'You all right?' he whispered.

She stared deeper into his eyes before realising he wanted an answer.

'Yes,' she whispered back, her arms finding their way around Maledream's neck and chest as she cuddled up to him.

'Are you sure?' he asked again.

'Couldn't be better,' she answered back, squeezing him tightly.

'Good,' he finished, shutting his eye and letting out the sigh of a worn traveller as he put one hand on Angelite's hand and one arm around her waist.

'Good night,' she whispered.

174

Chapter Twelve

Into the Glass...

'I do not believe that civilization will be wiped out in a war fought with the atomic bomb. Perhaps two thirds of the people of the earth will be killed.'

Albert Einstein

The next day, early in the morning, the sky was thick with red clouds tinged with silver as Maledream stood outside the door of N'Rutas' hut. His ankle ached slightly from the day before where he had been bitten but it was only slightly niggling him. As he waited, he scratched it until he felt better.

Around him, he could hear a variety of birds chirping which seemed to heighten in chorus as the day became brighter. Fresh air from the healthy trees and grass gave him strength. The country air seemed natural to him. It was such a contrast to the bleak ruined city landscape where he had lived for most of his memory.

'I wonder what it would have been like to have lived before where we are now,' he thought, sitting down cross legged on the cobbled stones just outside the door watching more animals dance and gallop in the distance. He imagined the world had once been like this glade before the destruction had set in on the planet.

Over in the distance walking on all fours following the cobbled stone path of the hut appeared the familiar figure of Silver, the wolf. Smiling to himself, Maledream waved towards him. Angelite joined him and placed her hand on his shoulder.

'You up already?' asked Maledream.

'Well I wanted to enjoy the morning while we still can before we head off, it's a nice day, despite the clouds in the sky.'

'Well it doesn't look like it's going to piss down today, so we have that going for us at least. Hey, can you see who is coming?'

'Ooh! It's that wolf again!'

'Yup.'

They began gently bickering, and were so busy focusing on each other that they failed to notice Silver was sitting next to them until he began scratching his hind leg.

'*Miss me?*' he said to both of them, startling Angelite as she stared at the big silver wolf.

'Of course! How are you this morning?' she replied.

Maledream just smiled and looked into the distance.

'*I am fine but we had better be on the move. It shouldn't be too hard once we have passed the radiated zone.*'

His telepathic voice was reassuring as it was deep and pleasant to listen to.

'Okay, let's get the others up and be on our way,' she said.

Soon enough, after much swearing and cursing from Neveah as Maledream kicked him to wake him up, the group packed the rations that N'Rutas had prepared the night before along with the bottled spring water.

Everyone was in high spirits as they all felt their hard journey was nearly over. Angelite stared at the remains of the melted candles, reflecting on what the day might bring. She felt her intuition mixed and confused, perhaps it was just her senses being clouded, or dulled, by the glade itself. She could not decide on the answer.

'Aye all, let's make a start,' said Neveah aloud, standing with his backpack on both shoulders, his halberd resting on his right shoulder looking at the group and then towards Angelite.

Approaching her, Neveah muttered quietly:

'Are you okay, lass? You've gone silent all of a sudden.'

'I...I am fine. I just feel a little dizzy, in the spiritual sense, I guess.'

'Aye, I've had that feeling, but just remember to keep yourself grounded woman and you'll do all right.'

He put his hand on Angelite's shoulder to reassure her.

'You are right, Neveah. You do have some kind of spiritual leader in you,' she said. Neveah laughed heartily at the comment.

'Some have said that in the past, Angelite, even Maledream, maybe when it's the right moment I'll try and take it up,' he said with a grin ,while turning to the others who waited outside the hut admiring the view as it got brighter.

'Let's **move out!**' he yelled as he exited the hut with Angelite in tow.

'**Aye, aye** grand leader,' Boris yelled back just to humour him. With Silver leading the way in a slow trot, the humans followed him closely as he led them North West.

Maledream kept himself to himself, focusing on the cobbled path. Staring up he could see the clouds were still sparse but their darkness was beginning to lighten as the sunlight gradually passed through them as the sun rose into the deep blue sky.

The group was silent save for the sound of their footsteps and the small noises made by animals in the grass and trees.

'There are so many animals here that I have never seen before,' said Boris.

'Aye,' replied Neveah, watching the creatures.

'That is why N'Rutas stays here and looks after them,' said Angelite, walking with her staff gently tapping the floor as she walked along the cobbles.

'A lot of them come from many parts of the world, far and wide. This is a utopia for the animals, much like Meridia is for us. Very few, except the birds, survived the arrival of the Dark Age with its destructive wars,' said Angelite.

'This sounds a bit dark coming from you, Angelite. Are you sure that you're all right?' asked Neveah calmly and curiously.

'Hmm, I'm only being realistic! Perhaps I do feel weary,' she said.

'Fair enough but if anything is troubling you we are here for you, Angelite, just remember that,' replied Maledream.

He was a little concerned for her, but just thought she was tense and nervous about the coming day.

'*We are almost there now,*' Silver's voice popped into everyone's head making Crazy John and Boris a little uneasy.

Soon enough after walking in the cool breeze, the party, led by Silver, entered another lava duct entrance that would bring them North West outside the mountainous glade. Angelite's new staff called Catalyst glowed soft silver by itself in turn illuminating the crystals on the passage floor.

As they walked, Silver spoke to them:

'*The place which we will be passing through is quite a sight. Those giant insects you fought last noon were mutated by this radiation, and it has forever changed them but not killed them.*'

'You mean those Vasps?' replied Maledream.

'*Yes...this place can either change you, or kill you. To you humans it would do the latter.*'

'Which is why N'Rutas gave me this gift, to shield us,' replied Angelite.

'*Correct,*' Silver said.

They made steady progress as they navigated their way around the huge passages and huge multi-coloured crystals, not speaking but dwelling on all that had happened to them so far. The air was fresh, the smells of clean water that had been purified from the rocks was welcoming in the dampness and glow of the cave structure.

Silver paused raising his head and taking a big whiff with his fine nostrils. Stopping instinctively the group wondered what was up, as Silver's mane seemed to fluff up.

'What's the matter?' Maledream quietly whispered.

'I think we have company ahead...an Anunaki, the stench is definitely that of scales,' Silver's thoughts raced through everyone else's.

'Guess we had better get ready to fight,' said Neveah, slipping his pole arm from his shoulder into his spare hand holding it in both arms.

'Crazy John, Boris, protect Angelite in the shadows, myself and Maledream will take its attention.'

'Speak for yourself. I'll be right behind you,' answered Maledream.

Having fought one before with Angelite, the Tribal still put his victory down to luck. He was thankful that he was in good strong company this time.

'Sounds like a good plan,' said Silver.

'I'll help wherever I can.'

'I'll think of something to do,' said Angelite, barely audible.

'I'm not fully attuned to...'

Before the priestess could finish her sentence, a mighty roar echoed through the cavern cracking several frail crystals, stalactites, and stalagmites, causing them to cover their ears.

Water began dripping above the party as they looked upwards towards the cracking ceiling of the lava duct as the beast ahead continued to roar. Suddenly, they realised that if they did not make a move, then they would not make it out.

'Charge!' yelled Neveah barely above the roar.

Maledream following him into the darkness of the unlit crystals ahead while the party could barely keep up save for Silver also running on. The three of them disappeared into the darkness, their feet echoing loudly as they charged.

Moments later, they could hear metal against metal echoing up the tunnel, shaking it and causing the roof to crack further from the noise. First Silver flew back out of the darkness, landing into Crazy John, then a second later, Maledream flew back into Boris and last came Neveah shouting as steel against scale echoed in the tight cavern.

'Bastard,' he yelled, before also slamming into Crazy John and all landing on the floor leaving Angelite at the back wondering at what had happened. The crystals now lit enough of the darkness ahead within the range of the staff Catalyst to show a gigantic warrior Anunaki that was twice the size of the one Maledream and Angelite had fought and slain.

It seemed unnaturally bigger in some way. Rotten scales hung off the Anunaki Warrior as if it were already dead. Its eyes were barely visible and its snout almost hanging off. Pus spots and sores the size of fists were scattered all over the sickly creature as it roared again. Terror raced through Angelite's heart as she gazed upon the grotesque being which blocked the entire tunnel leaving no way out.

'I told N'Rutas that this passage should have been sealed long ago,' Silver's telepathic voice raced.

They heard the sound of crumbling from behind them as the cave started collapsing. Water rushed past Angelite's feet. Maledream, Neveah and Silver stared as the water trickled by.

'Now I have an idea' she said, gripping her staff while smacking it deep into the water underneath her feet.

She began a quick verse of magic from her vocal chords.

'Valui ad satanam in computatrum meum invocandum.'

At first her voice echoed, her eyes began to gleam with a deep frosting blue. The staff's runes and the little Swan on top of the staff glowed as did Angelite's eyes, her red hair raised as she channelled energy into Catalyst.

These actions seemed to anger the gigantic monster that was coming closer with each heavy step. Everyone began to sweat at the sight of the beast as it closed in towards them.

Angelite crouched on the floor and began shooting energy from the fingers of her free hand as soon as they contacted the water flowing past the party on the floor. The blue energy quickly dissipated into the liquid and the surrounding cave. She was testing the energy, ready to unleash it at the right moment.

'What you waiting for?' Neveah yelled as he looked at her with a harsh rigid frown.

'Okay,' she panted, unleashing the energy and controlling it with her new staff.

The water that gathered around the group and the gigantic beast was now enough for what Angelite wanted to do. She shrieked at the beast, her voice seemed to activate the summoned energies turning the

water instantaneously into iced spikes that shot into the beast so quickly that they penetrated the thick scaly hide.

It was a remarkable sight as the beast was mortally wounded, impaled by the gigantic icy barbed trap Angelite had utilized. Its blood froze almost as quickly as it seeped from its many wounds. Screaming in agony, it started flailing its arms and gigantic tail it into the walls and roof of where it stood before it rested and died in a mangled state.

'**Run!**' shouted Crazy John.

'**I ain't getting squashed!**' he continued.

'**Aye!**' Neveah replied.

Bobbing and weaving through the gigantic iced spikes and the huge slain creature, they ran as fast as they could from the caving in structure behind them, not to mention the water from above that was in hot pursuit.

They headed for the light at the end of the tunnel. Silver leapt out of the tunnel first, hotly pursued by the rest, as the mouth of the cave collapsed behind them, weakened from years of weathering. Boulders fell, sealing the entrance forever.

'We just made it,' Neveah said, catching his breath, while wiping the sweat from his head.

'Yup,' Maledream replied.

'That beast was a lot bigger than the last one me and Angelite came across,' he added.

'*I am not surprised,*' said Silver's mind.

'*It is the radiation over there,*' he nodded his head towards the distance from over the small cliff face they were perched.

'*Remember what I said about the Vasps? The same thing occurred with that Anunaki. I thought there were none alive out here but I have not ventured deeply enough it seems. They are more resilient to many things and still surprise me.*'

Not uttering a single word, the group gazed upon the shattered sandy landscape before them.

They could see giant, circular, glass spikes reaching high into the sky. Below them, in the distance, were mountains and towers that were curved as if hit by a mighty blast sending them in all directions from the centre. Some areas of the tall glass spires were lit brightly by beams of bright sunlight, acting like a prism as the multiple colours created a glowing aura across the landscape.

It seemed to give the dead land a heavenly look. The group marvelled at the site of the different lights fracturing into all the colours of the spectrum.

'*Ah, that would have taken your attention,*' Silver said.

'*Long ago there were weapons that dealt massive destruction. It is unknown whether this particular sight was targeting the Anunaki or other humans who you love to fight yourselves. This was once a desert. The humans back many cycles created far more potent weapons than they originally had which would burn like the radiance of a thousand suns and, as you can guess, that's more than a summer heat many times over. When sand gets hot, it turns into glass to my understanding. This whole place used to be a desert and now it is nothing but a barren wasteland of radiated glass spirals, such a shame, not that a desert is a barren wilderness anyway, at least some creatures could exist within its boiling environment,*' Silver finished, sitting on all fours to admire the sight with the group.

'Must have been some blast,' said Boris, amazed by the view that seemed to stretch at least eight to ten miles.

'Aye, if we had weapons back in the city like that, well I'd rather not give it another thought, it's such a shit,' replied Neveah.

'I think the world's psycho enough as it is,' said Crazy John.

'But then again this shouldn't surprise you, the world was once a green and blue beautiful planet. This is why Meridia is trying to rectify so many mistakes,' said Angelite leaning on her staff, a tear rolling down her cheeks.

Maledream said nothing but just stared at the bright spectacle as the sun began to refract the light into his eyes from the glass more harshly.

'*If you look into your ration sacks, you'll find some useful goggles. I suggest if you value your eyesight you wear them now before it hits noon, and Angelite please start using Catalyst to shield us from the heat and radiation. We do not want to bake. One more thing when we are walking make sure you avoid the bright sun spots, otherwise you will burn into flames because the rays of the sun are magnified to such an extent that you will not live if you stray too far from Angelite's protection which can only offer so much.*'

Nodding in turn, the group reached into their bags to find another surprise from N'Rutas. Strapping the black Onyx goggles onto their heads, the complaints of discomfort began to sound from the group, too much of Silver's distaste as Maledream had to strap a similar one onto Silver himself at his order, even the wolf couldn't get away with wearing no protection.

Growling, Silver's thoughts raced to the others.

'*Stop complaining I know it is very black and dark, but trust me, when we get down there it will look as if it is as bright as a normal day, but*

also watch out for your feet, even with Angelite's protection it isn't uncommon to get blisters on your feet.'

Neveah himself had one specially made with an eye patch attached to it that gave his other eye protection as well. A nice change, he thought to himself cheerfully tightening the thick leathery straps behind his almost bald scalp.

'Aye,' replied Neveah.

'Stop bitching and everyone head out. The faster we get through this the better.'

The group felt strengthened by his strong voice.

'We made it this far and I don't count on dying Neveah, besides this shit is getting weird and you know how I hate weird shit,' Crazy John whispered to him.

'I don't lie, mate. Just do as I and the wolf say and you'll make it out alive,' Neveah whispered back, trying to reassure Crazy John.

'I hope I have your guarantee on that. I won't lose my only love either,' replied Crazy John.

'Look mate, don't do this to me now, or your lady, just stay with it,' replied Neveah, gripping Crazy John's arm in an iron hard grip while whispering it with gritted teeth.

'What's up?' Maledream asked, wondering why they were whispering.

'Aye, let's move on,' replied Neveah.

Maledream raised an inquisitive eyebrow towards Crazy John as if to ask, "what's was going on?"

Crazy John ignored Maledream and shifted his way back to Boris silently.

Angelite spoke a few incantations lighting up the staff, before everyone began to climb down the steep slope protected by the enchantment that had covered everyone in a seemingly cold, hazy, blue glow. At the bottom of the slope, the group navigated their way through the vast glowing hot spires of glass that inhabited the once barren yellow sands.

'So, this place was once a desert?' asked Maledream.

'Yes Maledream it was, nothing but sand for as far as the eye can see, and now it is nothing but crystal looking glass,' replied Silver.

The Tribal thought deeply about the place, his feet slipping from time to time on the once heated surface, as the group penetrated deeper in the bright abyss. Angelite expected to strain from the pressure but her new gift, Catalyst, seemed to alleviate most of the stress caused by her using the Resonance energies from the ether.

It felt as if she were covered in a pocket of cool air with a sense of spiritual attunement that she felt that she could accomplish anything, although she did need to maintain her concentration.

Something still did not feel right to her. She had thought the beast in the cave had explained her earlier foreboding but still she felt uneasy. Something seemed to be eating away at her very soul but she could not put her finger on what was wrong.

She brushed her fears to one side and concentrated on following the others weaving in and out of the cool and hot spots that threatened to burn them alive if Angelite's shielding was not strong enough to withstand the power of the magnified giant glass spires towering above them like city buildings. From time to time, she could swear she could hear spirits whispering to her, their language garbled like an out of tune radio frequency as they continued their long walk through the sun.

'Wait,' said Neveah, halting everyone in his or her tracks, his well-trained one eye latching onto something.

'What is it, mate?' replied Maledream.

'Look closely around you, and look up,' Neveah said.

All around them, they could see ashen shapes of human skeletons preserved in the glass, giving it a dirty look on closer inspection.

All of them seemed to be in awkward positions, as if they had flown through the air to land in a mangled heap.

Everyone was lost for words or gasped, while Angelite stared at the skulls above trapped within the glass looking down at them from the strange spirals of their glass prison.

Angelite stared into their eye sockets and the whispers she could hear began to increase in her own skull.

'*Help us…*' the first clear spirit said, giving Angelite chills down her spine as Catalyst started to hum in her palms. The voices began to fill her head at an alarming rate, blocking out even her own thoughts, as if a thousand strong crowd were speaking to her at once…

It was then that Angelite's consciousness left her. Her companions that were with her had disappeared in an instant as her eyes scanned her surroundings. The priestess seemed to be walking along the sandy plane that was now free from all giant glass spires. Children brushed passed her playing games, their laughter ghastly echoing on her senses. She stood still, in complete shock as she watched hundreds of refugees for as far as the eye could see walking passed her. Some were travelling in vehicles or others simply trekking along the soft sands that she now felt beneath her feet.

Whispers within her mind began to intensify.

'*What are we being attacked by?*' asked a child to a parent.

'*I don't know my princess, but we must hurry.*'

Angelite watched the small family continuing past her. Looking up she could see strange snaking smoke trails in the sky racing back and forth. Missiles screamed death from one end of the continent to other through the blood red clouds.

Her eyes refocused on the refugees taking cover on the ground as large flashes of light appeared in the distance followed by explosions that sounded on the horizon. Screams sounded from all around her as parents covered their children's ears whilst covering them with their own bodies. Gazing up she watched one of the smoke trails began side winding in a confused manner as if out of control.

'***It's coming straight for us!***' one refugee screamed at the top of his lungs.

Whispers haunted Angelite as she watched the missile in every agonising moment, misfire from the heavens towards the hundreds or even perhaps thousands of refugees that traversed the desert sands. She stood still watching, unable to move in the sheer terror that she felt around her.

'*It's ok baby, always remember that we've always loved you, nothing will ever take you away from us, nothing in this world will ever separate us,*' the parents cried, as they clutched onto the children they loved, forming a ghastly echoing chorus.

Angelite stared at the people's hopeless hysteria, tears streamed from her eyes as she witnessed the powerful explosion before her. The heat surged through her very bones in an instant, her skin feeling every agonising atom tearing her apart. Hot molten sand swept through her body as if it were a wave of water in an ocean.

Terror etched onto the refugees faces for all eternity, trapped in the glass to forever stare at their demise. The parents were right to tell their children that they would never be separated.

She let out an almighty scream...

Everyone turned to see Angelite screaming, confused looks etched on their brows. Maledream and Neveah were the first to her side shouting at her to calm down as she injured their eardrums with her hysteria.

'What the hell's wrong Angelite?' Maledream asked as he stared her directly in the eyes through the screaming.

'Hey, lass, what's up?' Neveah tried asking above the hysterics. Angelite panted, screamed, and cried uncontrollably.

'Hold her down before she hurts herself' Boris said, the two men nodding and holding down Angelite's hands and feet that were dangerously close to leaving Catalysts protecting aura.

Silver walked up to her and let off a fierce howl. So fierce in fact that it made the earth tremble beneath the group's feet.

Angelite stopped screaming, wrestling free from Maledream and Neveah to hold her eyes shut tight, her hands covering her ears.

'It's me, Angelite, Silver. I can hear them too, but you must block them out. They are spirits forever trapped until they realise they have to move on. They only want help, and we cannot provide that. Just block them out, Angelite.'

Silver spoke to her with thought form hoping she heard his voice. Angelite slowly opened her eyes, trying to keep back the tears, realising that she had dropped Catalyst. She nodded to Silver slowly looking into his wild eyes that seemed so deep and understanding.

Next, the priestess slowly crouched to the floor picking up Catalyst that still hummed with its protective enchantment.

'Block it all out, all of it...listen to my voice only, focus on me Angelite,' Silver repeated.

Long moments passed as Angelite sat upright, her breaths sporadic, gradually calming down as she centred herself.

'Keep blocking it, do not let your guard down. It seems you are susceptible to hearing the spirits more than most,' Silver said.

'Thank you,' Angelite replied, kissing Silver on the nose, making him recoil slightly.

'You okay, Angelite?' asked Maledream as he watched Neveah pick her up slowly by the hands.

'Yes, thank you. Let us not speak of this again. Let's carry on moving,' she said, trying the best she could to concentrate, wiping away the tears that crawled through the goggles.

Neveah shrugged, wondering what all the fuss was about but he decided to ignore the commotion. It was the first time he had seen Angelite pull off such a worrying stunt.

With hardly any words and reassuring pats on the back, they continued to pass through the skeletal graveyard of glass.

'I do not think we have far to go,' said Angelite, breaking the long silence of the group, and feeling the need for some friendly voices out in the barren glass land.

'Aye, I certainly hope so, lass,' replied Neveah as he grabbed a carrot out of his ration sack crunching it satisfyingly.

'You know,' Neveah continued, speaking with his mouth full,

'This reminds me of the time me and Maledream had when we were younger, when we had to walk through many places just to even get to the city, before we lost each other in that mad place...my legs are starting to feel like rocks again. Its good exercise I reckon,' he said, finishing his carrot.

'Bah, this thing tastes like crap but spose I shouldn't complain though. We should be out of this place by the end of the night shouldn't we Silver, aye?' Neveah asked in a tired tone.

'Of course, as long as we don't slow down, or come across any surprises...so far I'm surprised, I smell a tainted scent on the hot air but I can't place where it is coming from.'

'Indeed. I've had a slightly clouded intuition ever since we entered the cave,' said Angelite.

'I wouldn't worry,' Silver replied.

'I expect your energies are at their most potent and that staff N'Rutas gave you will heighten your senses in more ways than one. I expect your human senses still need to adjust to its energies.'

Angelite smiled at the large wolf's wisdom.

'I guess you are right. I have not meditated with it yet or attuned myself properly to it, so I should expect some instability' she replied in a daze staring at him.

'Yes Angelite, I assure you, you will be fine.'

Silver's words of reassurance made her melt as she grinned, but then her attention was caught by the sunlight that had split into rainbows from the glass.

'It is strange,' she said.

'Our Chakra points are the same colours, but also they are the same in the order they go down in the chain.'

'What are you saying?' asked Maledream turning to look at her with a raised sweaty eyebrow.

'Chakras come from an ancient language called Sanskrit which means "Wheels of Light" or "Vortex" and are a part of us all, so I have been taught by the elders back home. They all have different colours to represent your emotions within yourself, which we all share. If you feel something deep inside of you when you get that feeling, it could mean that your "heart" Chakra is speaking up inside you as it were. For example, the first colour in the Chakra system is Purple, and is meant to represent consciousness, infinite consciousness, and that is also the

first colour of the rainbow, or this fragmented light.'

Neveah butted in:

'Aye, although I don't quite follow you, are you saying we are just like rainbows? And is fragmented light the same thing?' He scratched his scalp, feeling hot and sweaty.

'Yes,' she replied smiling at him.

'To simplify things I'll leave them at just rainbows,' she cheekily giggled, giving the group a slight morale boost seeing her take her mind off of earlier events.

'Shall I continue? All right now it gets easier from here, the second Chakra inside you is of the colour blue which is your "third eye" situated in between your "physical" eyes, your psychic powers or other such spiritual potency wherever you place your faith can be expressed through this Vortex. The third colour is of a lighter sky blue and represents your expressions and how you let the world see how you are, and how some people could learn to view you. It is more of the socialising energy point, as it exists in between your throat and shoulder blades it would make sense!'

'Now, the fourth which is the colour of green, is your heart Chakra, which I would say is actually you, if you decide to express who you really are of course, but it really stands for more than anything how much "heart" you have and how you can express love and other such emotions or much deeper feelings.'

'Very, uh, educational, Angelite,' replied Crazy John.

'I think you said something about this before but I didn't really understand it,' Maledream asked, ignoring Crazy John.

Angelite continued speaking enthusiastically about the subject. She seemed to grow stronger as she talked.

'And so! The fifth Chakra, Vortex, Wheel of Light is the colour of yellow and it is situated within your stomach. It stands for willpower.'

She smiled looking at the prismatic gigantic spikes fragmenting the lights for what seemed several miles in all directions, as if the whole place was a spider web of light in the sun.

'Only two Chakras left! Then I shall stop and have a drink.'

She sighed, returning to her thoughts away from the awe of the beauty of the place they entered, and the haunting spirits she had shut out of her mind.

'Number six is the colour of orange and I think it stands for your appetite, but more importantly it focuses its energy within your body, it is situated by your, uh,'

'Spit it out woman!' Neveah butted in nudging her with his elbow gently and jokingly.

'Groin,' she whispered.

'What, you mean our balls?'

Neveah bellowed loudly, his voice bouncing off the many glass spires high in the sky.

'Fantastic!' he cried, others in the group were mildly amused, especially Maledream who shared Neveah's sense of humour.

'No wonder I glow orange when I've had a good one!' he said, while flexing both his arms in an upward fashion and humping the thin air for a moment.

'What a gorilla!' Boris sighed in disgust.

'What? Best joke I have heard all day!' he continued to laugh sporadically.

The Tribal could not help but smile and laugh with the Pack leader, while the humour was not to Crazy John's liking.

'Yes, it does stand for sex, and rather how much energy you have for it,' Angelite finished, her innocent cheeks blushing a pale pink.

'Aye woman its good stuff. I expected Maledream to beat me at crunching the joke off but looks like he is too sweaty after last night.'

Neveah jabbed Maledream hard with one arm and slapped Angelite's arse with the other before grabbing them both around the waist like a big lout, insinuating that the pair had been extra close during the night, embarrassing both of them, relishing every moment.

Spirits were now high. Angelite took the joke well, glad that he was around to lighten the mood.

'*Orange aura, honestly,*' she thought to herself with a smile.

She never did finish off the last Chakra now that Neveah and Maledream continued to joke about them for the rest of the afternoon.

'*About time these humans lightened up,*' Silver thought.

Chapter Thirteen

Dread Rising...

'The dread of evil is a much more forcible principle of human actions than the prospect of good.'

John Locke

Unknown to them, they were being followed by the presence of an Anunaki Blood Adept bearing rich red robes lined with silver and a potent looking staff made of gold and adorned with many symbols that resembled those of the Great Halls of the Anunaki Council.

Protected, its presence cloaked with a huge amount of psychic prowess, it had watched from afar, the heat doing nothing to the powerful Anunaki as it levitated just above the glass surface.

Its powerful, dark eyes, resembling those of a hawk, transfixed on Angelite and her staff while also gazing towards the other group members to evaluate their potential threat. It was particularly interested in Maledream's sword and blinked rapidly at the sight of the powerful relic of Anunaki bane. He closed his eyes, sending the information within his mind to others scattered around wherever they were. Craftily the Blood Adepts began linking through their thoughts to put together a plan.

The Blood Adept that had found the adventuring group continued to follow them, knowing their probable destination. He and the other Blood Adepts intended to lay a trap for the party. Gradually the sun passed its highest point in the sky as the group carried on with a relentless spirit. Before them rose two mountains with a pass straight through their centre.

Crazy John said in his gravelly voice:

'Looks like a canyon or something, maybe a league away or such?'

'Aye, it does look like it,' Neveah said, stretching his legs, which had begun to ache.

Silver raced his thoughts among them:

'I sense Anunaki, we should quicken our pace.'

His feral eyes beamed into the distance and around the surrounding area of the remaining glass desert, while sniffing the air maniacally.

'Well if there are any, I doubt we will have to wait long to find out,' Maledream said.

'Look on the bright side, if they appear and we kill one then we will have fresh meat to eat,' said Crazy John, smiling at the prospect of cutting up a lizard and baking it for dinner within the hot temperatures of the glass.

'For a start that's just wrong...' replied Maledream.

'Of course it isn't, we can be on top of the food chain as well,' he replied.

'Boys will be boys,' Angelite muttered, chirpily breaking the ice a little to prevent the tensions rising.

'We have been travelling a long time I know, but please remember we are not that far from safety now,' Silver said.

'Aye everyone, keep it down, no bickering. We can soon settle down and rest before anything else happens,' said Neveah.

With that, the group carried on their trek gradually moving outside the glass land, leaving behind the strange terrain to step onto the hard dried rock and mud, which led to the canyon directly in front of them. From left to right, apart from the narrow escape from the glass spires, was nothing but a cliff face, which seemed to circle around the desert they had walked through.

'Some sight isn't it?' murmured Boris.

'Aye, looks like the only way is straight forward, may as well take off these goggles now the brightness behind us is fading in strength. The sun is setting quickly as we approach winter.'

'Don't say winter, mate, I'm starting to feel cold already,' replied Maledream.

'Well, I would keep them on as the levels of light are still not safe, trust me. It seems like it is getting darker but it is far from it. Until we reach the canyon, do keep on the goggles. Once we are in the shadow you may take them off.'

'Aye, fair enough,' said Neveah, as the group travelled into the mouth of what was left of the sunlit Canyon.

The air was dry and almost suffocating as the air could not circulate properly so the group members still felt hot and sweaty. Fortunately, Angelite continued the protections through her staff, Catalyst.

Old bones of creatures and humans littered the ground all around them as if they had died in great numbers, perhaps while trying to escape from the blast. Some were even carbonised into the walls for eternity at the beginning of the canyon, their bones painting a powerful yet sad ending for the living creatures and refugees that passed through here. Clothes were sparse, save for old shoes that crumpled and crunched from the touch of the adventurers standing on them as they passed the dead walls.

'This place is terrible, not something I'd enjoy walking through more than once,' said Angelite, her voice shaking from it all.

'I'm glad,' replied Maledream.

'This place certainly isn't for anything living, only the dead, as hard and harsh as that sounds.'

'Aye, mate,' agreed Neveah sharply as he surveyed the scenes with his one good eye and tensing his huge arms in an animal instinct.

Maledream paused where he was walking and for a moment could feel a chill. He looked back at the glass fields that were now losing light incredibly quickly through his black goggles. He could feel something was watching them closely.

'*Maledream,*' suddenly sounded within his head, but it was not Silver's telepathic gift, it was something else. Something he had heard before many nights and days before.

Without any thought, he dropped his backpack and pulled out his heavy blade that had sat in his shoddy scabbard for most of the journey. He scraped it on the floor before finding the strength to heave it behind his shoulders causing everyone to turn around in stunned fashion as Maledream continued to hear the voice within his mind.

Paranoid to what it was and confused, he took off one goggle and looked all around the canyon.

'**Who are you?**' he shouted, his blade seemingly activating its runes on Maledream's survival instincts turning the sword into a soft humming resonating light that seemed to breathe, his voice echoing around the cavern while all were in silence.

No matter where he looked he could not see the intruder of his mind state and started sweating profusely out of his control.

'*Maledream, Maledream, Maledream, Maledream, Maledream,*' the mysterious voice sang as if it came from a serpent's throat.

'What's wrong?' Angelite said with a worrying frown on her brow at seeing Maledream seemingly suffer from some unknown intent on him. Silver could sense it, but could not lock on to where the communication was coming from.

His ears keened the best he could get them.

'Where are you?' he shouted once more while ignoring Angelite's caring question.

'Aye, mate, what's up? Come on settle down before you scare us shitless,' asked Neveah in a stern voice.

He put his hand on Maledream's shoulder stopping him from swinging the large weapon and doing anything stupid. The Tribal ignored him as he continued to read every rock and every crevice within the rocks. Gradually his eyes took him up the canyon cliff walls almost hypnotically in a trance as his mind felt like exploding from the shear pressure. Voices from the others were being drowned out from his mind, while the intruding voice repeated his name in a louder and louder chorus cutting through his head like razors.

The pressure was so relentless that he feared he would pass out. He gazed up at the top of the canyon and, through his Onyx goggles, he could see a dark shape of a robed figure standing there. Heat waves from above made the creature look as if it was a mist shimmering like faint shadows on light and being blown and billowed as if cloth to wind. Feeling paralyzed on the spot, he could not open his mouth nor look away staring into the large black eyes of the Anunaki Blood Adept who seemed to be melded into another dimension altogether.

Maledream's eyesight began to fade into a darker world as if he could see through the eyes of the Anunaki. His Onyx goggles were cracking from the sheer pressure of the small protection it could offer him. Time seemed to stand still as Maledream stared at dread itself and felt completely overwhelmed, his sword glowing dark abyssal colours that could be seen by all, along with his goggles cracking.

Neveah tackled the young man to the ground, which seemed to break the spell as he punched Maledream in the face whipping him out of the daze, his sword landing in the hard stone surface next to them, corrupting the dead earth for but a moment until the glow of the runes faded. Maledream ripped the goggles off and shivered. His face as white as a ghost, he screamed letting out the dread that had built inside him, almost shaking the canyons walls causing small debris, dust, and stones to fall peppering the ground.

'It's okay, mate. I'm here with you, what's wrong man?' Neveah said shaking Maledream.

In answer, the Tribal pointed up towards where he had seen the being as Neveah gradually let loose both his arms on Maledream before staring upwards with his specially crafted Onyx eye patch.

He was shaking and before he could say anymore pushed himself aside from Neveah and vomited bile onto the dry rocks while

recovering from the huge headache that started to rapidly dissipate.

Neveah looked up to where Maledream had pointed to see a dark shape but, before he could see it properly, it had moved out of sight.

'Shadow beings again?' asked Neveah.

'I doubt it, not in this light. There is enough death but this area isn't a major energy grid to give them enough physical manifestation,' said Angelite as she wandered over to Maledream, resting her hands on him while pulling him away softly from the spot where he had retched.

She picked up a cloth and rested him on her lap while she wiped his lips and wet his head with some water from a flask.

'I have a more major concern,' said Silver.

'It must be the Anunaki, and after targeting Maledream they must be after one thing I regret to say, and that's his blade, the ancient Relic of the Creators. They need him as a vessel to use it,' he added, wandering over to Maledream's sword. He sat by it and gave it a slight sniff.

'Strange, it's as if Maledream resisted being possessed.'

'Or I snapped him out of it, just by fluke and instinct. I felt something was strangely wrong right before this happened,' the Pack leader replied.

Neveah looked over at Maledream being comforted by Angelite with a sincere care in her eyes. She stroked his hair and face, whilst keeping one hand on his chest and concentrated on healing his soul and body from the strange psychic attack.

'Oi, Neveah, let me and John check it out, we'll cut the bastard down for that,' asked Boris.

'I've needed to spill some blood,' Crazy John added enthusiastically, whipping out his large polished knives.

'It's too dangerous. Our best bet is to carry on. I don't want any one getting taken out or being used against us, especially what Silver just said,' he answered with worry.

He clutched his large pole arm ready for any danger.

'That's right, although I am assuming that if it is the Anunaki and I am sure it is, they are probably planning something far worse. Be on your guard and whatever you do, do not stare into their eyes, the Anunaki which we have fought before are soldiers and do not possess such mental capacities but great strength instead. These are far more cunning. They are frail but they are not something to be reckoned with, if N'Rutas were here I'm sure she would have been able to figure out what to do, but this is our test.'

'Some bloody test,' roared Neveah, his temper beginning to get the better of him.

'I ain't risking my skin for no test,' he said, striking the butt of his weapon on the floor several times to take out some of his anger.

Angelite raised her voice:

'Look, just help Maledream walk. He is going to need more than my healing as the encounters have left him physically exhausted.'

'I'm okay,' he muttered and coughed rising slowly from Angelite's lap and standing up.

He wavered slightly until he could steady himself gradually.

'Let's just go. Let's get out of here,' he coughed.

'Aye, good suggestion, mate,' said Neveah.

The Pack leader helped Maledream collect his sword, his strength returning surprisingly quickly as he stretched his aching back.

The group began walking at a quick pace, it was now growing darker as they approached the abyss that lay before them. One by one, the group members took off their goggles as now the sun had almost set, leaving little light seeping in to the canyon.

'Let's create a little light,' Angelite said.

With a few gestures and playful words, Angelite tossed a few crystals from her hands, the stones emanating a soft light. Controlling them with her mind and a mental grace, the crystals lit the path as they floated around the group like neon comets.

'This should help me attune to Catalyst,' she thought.

Silhouettes of the shadows created by the movements of the flying light crystals made Crazy John jump from time to time.

No one blamed him as they all had their eyes cast for any sign or presence of danger. All went silent except from the occasional foot scuffling there was silence.

Maledream thought back to what he had seen and still the thought of losing himself within those large black eyes from that shadowy Anunaki made him feel cold.

He wondered what had happened to him, feeling slightly different as if he had a great gaping hole inside his chest like an unlocked door that had been flung open and left unlocked waiting to be entered again. Reaching into his pocket, he withdraw the damp cloth that Angelite had used to dampen his head as he had recovered from the vision of the figure and had felt it try to tear into his soul.

Gripping the cloth tightly he looked over at Angelite who led the way with Silver. Just seeing her in her coloured robes, her long red flowing hair made him feel a little calmer.

Maledream became aware of the ache in his face from where Neveah had punched him but he felt grateful for it, he knew that the Pack leader probably saved his life. He began to wish, as he stared

towards the slightly cloudy sky that covered the moonlight, that he was back at home with Larkham in what had been a more peaceful existence. He missed waking up in the early morning and gazing up at the rising sun of every new day, while sitting around with the Tribals in complete safety.

'How I miss it,' he thought.

'I've come so far and met so many new or old friends, it's a great thing to have.'

This new thought made him smile. It was what he needed after having the life drained from him. The group travelled through the canyon for half a night, not even stopping to eat. They relaxed in Angelite's soft light spell that seemed to ooze warmth around them.

'There are some gates up ahead,' Boris spoke, but not too loudly as to wake the dead.

'Shine a little more light in front of us if you can,' replied Neveah, his eye gleaming with hope.

'So it will be!' Angelite's light pressed on up to what was left of the straight section of canyon as she throttled more energy into Catalyst.

'Does this mean safety at last?' Maledream sighed with relief.

'It certainly does, the Watchman are great in number and professional warriors from Meridia, we've made it!' she replied excitedly.

'Damn...just when we had the prospect of killing something...' Crazy John quietly muttered to himself.

'We did it lads and lasses! To Meridia we go!' Neveah cheered raising his pole arm skywards.

'Thank the spirits,' Maledream thought, letting out a deep sigh of relief.

Softly illuminating the wooden and corrugated iron frames ahead of them, the group almost instantly started running towards salvation the gates had on offer. They crashed in unison against the great barrier while they took a breather, while Angelite shone her light back towards the darkness from where they had walked almost the entire night.

'I'm fecking tired, I tell you,' puffed Boris, unlatching her studded leather chest piece slightly to let more hot air escape.

'Indeed,' replied Maledream falling to his knees, staring at the tall thirty feet high and thirty feet long doors.

'Right, how do we get in?' asked Neveah.

There was a long pause. Silver sniffed the door for a short moment.

'*Well,*' he said thoughtfully, before Neveah butted in:

'Shit! I've said it for you, no one is alive behind there?'

'*I cannot sense any thought forms.*'

Neveah shouted and punched the thick oaken doors.

'For fuck sake!' he roared.

'Now what?' he asked, breathing heavily, wishing he could do something.

'*Normally they opened the gates long before we got within thirty paces, I knew something was up back in the mouth of the canyon. In addition, another thing, there is no noise coming from the other side. It is a small Watchman port by any standards but they make enough noise as it is by loading supplies and the like. Aside from that the only light present is Angelite's.*'

Everyone sat down in a slight despair, only realising that when they did, that they were standing or sitting in muddy puddles that seemed to seep from under the doors.

'Why water?' asked Maledream, wiping his wet ass and getting back up.

'The lock mechanism's broken,' said Crazy John as he examined the steel lock in between the old corrugated iron framework with the little light he had to observe in the tiny crack.

'Very strange' Neveah added.

'Right, everyone get by me and help push this bastard open,' he ordered.

Gradually and slowly with the aid of all, the gate began to shift and move across the wet surface of the mud. The large door moaned and groaned loudly as all bodies pressed against it.

Angelite's light shone through the darkness beyond the door as she pointed her staff to reveal a terrible sight in the dock area.

Bodies were strewn across the small bay area including the open wooden sheds and the loading areas of the port. From the looks of it, whatever had attacked them had been a fearsome foe.

Neveah led the way forward, followed by Silver and Angelite, while the rest followed cautiously, all weapons drawn from their respective places.

Maledream dragged his blade along the sandy muddy terrain showing that his physical strength was still drained from the encounter earlier in the canyon.

'This is unexpected,' he said in a low tone as he examined a well-armed guard. He touched some pieces of solid steel and chainmail armour torn from what looked like Anunaki warrior talons.

'Looks like scorch marks on this body, and his armour is ripped to shit,' the Tribal added.

'It must have been an ambush, probably from the sea near where the boats are kept over by the docking area,' Angelite theorized.

'Whatever they were, they certainly knew the humans weak points,' said Crazy John, gazing into the gaping holes of the corpses. In one victim, he could see the arteries had been severed acutely.

'Cleanly cut, similar to how we did it back in the city,' Boris remarked.

'Aye, I know what you two get up to,' Neveah said looking across to the sea one hundred paces away.

'By the spirits...look at the sea' Angelite cried out.

The scene was poorly lit by the moonlight, but was just enough to make out a glimpse of corpses floating in the water, crashing against rocks or sand as they floated back and forth with the tide.

Angelite could barely contain her stomach at the carnage. She could see spilt, dry blood lying on the sand, noticing Silver had backed away from the sight. Blood was still wet and thinly spread across the beach where the red waves crashed. When the moon showed itself fully, Angelite could see more of the slaughter scene. She stood closer to Maledream as if hoping his presence could comfort her.

'If only we knew they were attacked,' said Maledream, stooping over a corpse and examining its armour.

'Aye, it was also our only exit too,' Neveah replied, staring at the bloated floating corpses, the blood shimmering in the moonlight.

Angelite looked away from the corpses and towards some of the wooden and iron ships that were still sitting in the docks as if they were untouched, just floating there minding their own business.

Some ships in the distance lay on their side as if they had been used as a likely escape, but had failed in the attempt and were either smashed or capsized.

'Well the boats are still here, some by the looks of things tried escaping this horror.'

A tear slid down Angelite's cheek. Boris made her way to Angelite and put her arms around her, giving her a hug.

'Don't worry, sweetie,' Boris whispered.

'Well, I reckon we should start fixing one of those ships up, aye Crazy John?' said Neveah.

'I'll give it a go,' Crazy John replied, whipping out his personal fixing tools from his backpack.

'Right, which ship do we think is seaworthy enough to fix up?' Maledream asked.

'The ship in the centre of the piers looks like a good start,' said Angelite pointing in its direction. Carefully, the adventurous group followed Maledream towards the ship, their footsteps sounding heavy on the old wooden pier as it creaked with each step.

The ship only had one broken mast out of the three it sported and the hull was the least damaged from the rest of the ships either docked at port or broken in half just out to sea.

'By the looks of things this attack was just a one off,' said Crazy John.

'Although I would not like to put it past the Anunaki that we had encountered earlier to have something planned for us. Be on your guard,' replied Silver's thoughts.

'Those things are rather tenacious aren't they?' Boris whispered, staring at the carnage on the beach from the wooden pier.

Maledream shut his eyes and listened to the sweet sound of the waves gently hitting the shore and the rocks, allowing it to soothe his racked nerves. The smell of the ocean, salt water, and the cool of the breeze added to the sensations he was feeling. He felt a strong longing to travel over the ocean.

Angelite and Neveah also had a longing to leave, just to escape the scene of carnage. Crazy John disappeared into the bowels of the small sleek ship to have a gander at what he could find and fix, while Boris examined the upper deck for anything that could prove useful.

'Think I'm going to look around and salvage equipment and weapons,' announced Maledream, opening his eyes to gaze at the pale moonlit bloody beach once more.

'I'll go with you mate. Angelite, stay here with the mutt. You need a rest so find somewhere and sit down and eat something,' said Neveah, patting her on the shoulder and giving her a smile.

'Mutt...' Silver's thoughts raced, Neveah giving him the thumbs up.

Weakly smiling, she nodded her head and put her hand on Silver's fine furry coat as they walked up the small gangplanks onto the deck of the ship. She lit some candles with a click of her fingers nearby, lighting up several candle lamps instantaneously.

'That's better,' she sighed.

Neveah and Maledream walked slowly back off the pier to the beach, leaving Angelite to rest for a moment in Silvers company.

'Poor bastards,' cursed Neveah staring into the many dead eyes that lay before them.

'Not much we can do,' replied Maledream.

'Aye, they have some fine looking armour and weapons strewn

about the place as well. If I find any knives, I'll hand them over to Boris and Crazy John.'

'I'm just interested in food which isn't vegetables,' said Maledream.

'But, if I do see some useful armour or any daggers, I'll pick them up. The ones that I have hidden in my coat are a bit rusty to say the least.'

Maledream spotted some loose silver looking gauntlets adorned with many symbols on it attached to a man that was ripped in half with his intestines ripped out. Trying not to vomit, the Tribal walked on the sand where it softly padded under his worn boots to get a closer look.

'Wow, mate, have a look at this thing. Is it to keep your weapon on you?' he asked, staring at the gauntlet that had an iron looking chain attached to a small sword that had broken in two.

'Aye, it's a failsafe, you attach it to your gauntlet which this poor bastard has done here, so if you lose your weapon in combat it would keep it within quick reach. It's basically a life insurance. I'd grab it off him, mate! Very handy that is.'

Maledream smiled:

'I've lost my weapons in the past a few too many times so I think I shall.'

He put the gauntlet on his own wrist and attached the chain to it. Maledream was quite pleased with the find. The runes on the gauntlet lit up briefly in a hazy crimson before disappearing altogether, making Maledream and Neveah nervous.

'You see that?' said Maledream.

'Aye, I'd ask Angelite about that,' Neveah replied.

'I expect it's nothing to worry about, if they come from Meridia then I expect they have stuff similar to Angelite.'

'Yeah your probably right mate doesn't help us when we're on edge though!' Neveah chuckled ironically, both smiling.

'This chain is great, a bit long but at least it won't be ridiculously out of reach if I drop it,' said Maledream.

'Aye, that's the idea mate,' replied Neveah, as he stared around trying to find other pieces of armour to wear.

They could see that the bodies had been severely disembowelled and much of the armour had been damaged.

They did manage to collect some small arms fire that Crazy John could use but there was very little else that could be of any use.

'Aye, Maledream! Look in this hut. I've hit the jackpot.'

'Why what is it?'

'Armour plating, shoulder pads, cloaks, and hoods! Oh...and the

jackpot of them all...I've found **tobacco**,' he cheered.

The list was endless and it pleased both Maledream and Neveah who jumped around like little kids at the treasure they had found in the shadowy storage cabin.

'Finally, I can have a good smoke,' smirked Neveah, getting his pipe out and filling it with some sweet smelling tobacco before realising he would need to find a light.

'Save some for me then you big shit,' Maledream chuckled.

He began sorting through the cloaked hoods, and some chain mail and scale mail armour with some light chest plate pieces lying around.

'Right, I'm going to strap some of this on!' said the Tribal.

He took off his old coat for a moment and discarded his smelly old tops, replacing them with brand new knitted ones that were made out of silk or wool. Interesting patterns were inscribed onto them, which added to their charm. Both changed their appearance drastically, smashing many locked crates with their weapons to get what looked like the better stuff. They delved deeper into the storage finding yet more robes, which would suit Angelite and would look more impressive than the purple and green she wore now.

'Looks like the Anunaki are good at killing, but that's about it,' said Maledream, adjusting his new shining plate armour and chain mail links with his clean and soft dark purple cloak and hood flowing over the Runic metallic shoulder pads.

'Aye, its damn hard putting all this on in the crap lighting I know that much. There's very little here for Crazy John, and Boris though, but they usually stick with no protection and rely more on their agility in combat any way.'

Maledream strapped on his new prized boots, casting away his old ones hastily. They had caused him enough hardship and grief in the past and he was very glad to be rid of the death traps.

The Tribal replied:

'Yes, right let's bring some of this stuff for Angelite and be on our way. Are you sure Crazy John can find something to fix the ship?'

'Aye, he is the greatest mechanic I know. There's not much he can do with wood, but that boat's made out of thick metal as well, so he will have found and fixed something.'

With that, the two of them exited the storage area of the beach port of the Watchman and headed quickly to the pier. Both were clinking and clanging from the new armour they had donned. They were proud of their new look, thinking of it as a much needed improvement, leaving them with a feeling of more cutting edge power.

Walking onto the wooden pier towards the ship, they noticed the third mast that had been broken now stood tall again, helped by Angelite working her magic upon the vessel. They could see that Catalyst hummed with raw power as Angelite concentrated on melding the wood back together, while holding the giant wooden beam with telekinetic prowess.

Around her were white brightly lit orbs with some gold and green coloured lights circling around her feet spreading out as the power grew on the surface of the wooden decking.

'She's at it again,' said Neveah.

'Brilliant stuff,' replied Maledream as they walked up the gangplanks onto the deck.

Angelite aimed Catalyst at the broken area of the wooden beam, unleashing the magic. This seeped slowly out of the end of the statuette while glowing with a faint green and gold, its energy reaching the break in the wood to meld it solidly into place.

Finishing her spell, she relaxed and the energies quickly dissipated. She let out a sigh of relief and said to Silver:

'Thank you.'

'Do not thank me, I just encouraged you to believe it was possible. That new staff has attuned to you nicely.'

Angelite smiled and as she turned her head towards the gangplanks leading off the ship she stared at a heavily armoured Maledream and Neveah with big grins on their faces coming aboard.

'That is...that's the armour from Meridia!' she exclaimed excitedly.

'Where did you find it?'

Maledream with both hands lifted his blade and sank it into the wooden decking. He leant on it with one hand before saying:

'I found some stuff in a very small wooden hut,' he said.

'What else was in there?' she asked.

'Aye, these robes and other clean clothes. Maledream was quite pleased with his new scabbard for his blade too,' replied Neveah, also looking pleased with himself as he put the robes and other equipment in his arms down on the deck, before walking towards a lit candle on the deck to light his pipe, smoking in the tobacco like it was a comforting heaven.

'You'll have to show me. Did you see any paper lying around at all in that hut? It should have the information for the equipment,' Angelite said, while inspecting the runes and some embedded crystals in the finely crafted armour. She could see that they contained a very soft glow.

'It's on the beach but I don't think...'

Before Maledream could finish what he was saying, she pushed past him and started running towards the beach shouting to them to follow her. Neveah shrugged and then nodded to Maledream to follow Angelite back to the beach.

'What else could she be looking for?' asked Maledream, already sweating in his upgraded half plate and leather armour.

'No idea, mate, but you know what Angelite is like,' Neveah answered, jumping and landing heavily upon the creaking wooden pier.

The two followed her closely but could not keep up with her as their new armour was very heavy, making them pant and puff as they strolled behind her.

Above, high on the hilltops overlooking the beach port of the deceased Watchman, the Anunaki Blood Adepts watched in unison as the three made their way to the beach once more.

'Is it time?' one said in a voice from mind.

'Yes, release them, they have nowhere to run' another different toned voice thought replied.

Silver raised his keen ears for a moment, his eyes slowly rising to the top of the cliffs at the port before releasing a frightening howl from the ship to Maledream, Angelite, and Neveah who had just entered the beach, echoing off the walls of the rocky hill face with great effect.

'Silver?' said Angelite as she paused in her step before feeling the sand underneath her shift slightly.

'Angelite!' screamed Maledream hearing Silver's cry and then seeing the sand shift before Angelite's own two feet as she stopped to wonder what Silver was howling about.

'Raaaaaaaaaaaaah!' bellowed Neveah, throwing his pole arm like a javelin towards Angelite, whizzing past Maledream's skull.

It embedded itself into the skull of an Anunaki warrior killing it outright before it could fully raise itself from the sand.

Angelite shrieked but had the presence of mind to reach for her staff, Catalyst, its runes flowing and glowing around her in a piercing sunlight barring another Anunaki warrior trying to take her life.

Its weapon bouncing off the golden rippling shield as she knelt on her knees in panic as it brought its golden halberd again upon her with intent to take her life. Maledream's eyes widened at the sight, his sword lit with energy, its runes reacting to his nervous response system. The scene seemed unreal as he watched the slowly dancing, circling, spiritual runes protecting Angelite and faced the Anunaki warrior who

aimed to kill her. His sword became a crimson coloured blade, matched in colour by his newly attached gauntlets, attuning his emotions even further to greater strength.

Before he knew it, a surge of power rushed through him and his sword sliced through the warrior. Angelite stared at Maledream, aware that he was capable of such feats of darkness in order to protect those he felt closest to him.

Neveah watched with his one good eye and could tell something was not right, even with the Anunaki warriors that started to number in their ten's and soon to be a close hundred on the beach as he strolled towards Angelite and Maledream. Wrenching the pole arm out of the Anunaki's skull, he stared at the amassing Anunaki warriors.

'I think it's time we departed to the ship and got the hell out of here,' he said, feeling outnumbered from the many Anunaki that lumbered towards them as if they were puppets controlled by an outer force.

Maledream could not hear Neveah. All he could hear was his heartbeat as he stared coldly at the massed, scaled warriors that walked or stumbled towards them, sand covering every crack in their scales, claws ready to inflict death.

Without warning, the Tribal lifted his blade above his shoulders and charged towards the mob.

'**Maledream!**' screamed Angelite as if she could sense he was being guided by a darker purpose.

'Leave him,' snapped Neveah.

'**We have to run, forget him!**' he shouted at her, grabbing her roughly by the arm and then running towards the ship dragging her in tow.

'He will be fine. I have a feeling this isn't his end and not ours so we have to go,' he barked.

Angelite watched Maledream charge into the mass of scales. In her spiritual eyes, she could see that he was being fuelled by hate and anger that threatened his life.

Chapter Fourteen

Deceitful Plan...

*'During times of universal deceit, telling the truth
becomes a revolutionary act.'*

George Orwell

'He is a fool,' spoke one Anunaki Blood Adept watching the
scene from high above.

*'I agree, but do not dare underestimate the weapon or the potential of
that bony human,'* spoke another, as they all concentrated their psychic
power on manipulating the ancient Anunaki super soldiers.

*'We must start the corruption from what this Maledream has
equipped,'* one ordered, while the rest nodded in unison focusing their
great psychic powers...

Blood red and black spots were all Maledream could see before
his eyes. Dark voices whispered to his soul to protect those he loved
and to destroy his enemies, clouding out memories of his childhood
and lost memories of his parents that had tried to surface in order to
confuse and weaken him.

His spirit felt a longing to be reunited but his rage threw that
longing to one side so he could put all his energy into charging deeply
into the mass of scales. He sliced his sword through all opposition
toppling any enemies that came towards him.

Footsteps were heavy on the wooden floorboards of the pier as
Neveah and Angelite looked back for a moment seeing Maledream get
swarmed by over a hundred scaled Anunaki warriors.

'Please, don't look back,' said Silver's mind as they gazed upon the
carnage, trying to catch their breath.

'Wait, this isn't over just yet,' said Silver, gazing out at Maledream
fighting on the beach.

'Crazy John, Boris!' shouted Neveah.

'Yes!?' shouted back Crazy John from beneath the decking.

'**Are we ready to set sail at full speed and quickly?**' yelled back Neveah as he also stared towards the beach.

'**Just about,**' Boris screamed back.

'**Then go full power, now!**' he ordered.

He could see Maledream wiping out many of the beasts in one go, and yet more kept coming. About twenty Anunaki jumped and toppled him for a moment under a mountain of muscled scales.

In no time at all, the engine began humming from the hull of the ship while Crazy John shouted:

'**I've got it!**'

The ship bolted forth as the propellers in the water began to shift much water at a fast rate of knots catching all but Neveah off his feet as he lurched his weapon with great pose and strength to sever the thick ropes that bound the ship to the docks.

Maledream cut another swathe of Anunaki away in several quick blows, to him strength did not matter anymore, he could not even feel his muscles amidst the blood red eyeballs of the Anunaki he continued to slay.

'*You're saving your friends and loved ones,*' a voice said to him, making Maledream feel that the sword was speaking to him.

It was burning his hands yet he could feel no pain. Instead, he felt connected to an amazing power.

Maledream deflected a blow from a swipe of a claw as the Anunaki warrior covered in radiated pus ridden boils tried knocking his head away from his spinal column. With a sharp upstroke after the parry, his Relic Sword cut through the warrior like a ribbon.

Everything was in unison, as he barely had enough time to look at each of his foes but swiped at them all the same. He cut through them swiftly and was unaware of the tear rolling its way down his cheeks as his spirit cried to him to stop. All he could focus on was the need to be victorious.

'*Why, Maledream, why are you fighting?*' Angelite thought, staring at the battle from the ship.

'*Look, on the hill tops, I could feel what those things were thinking. It's why I howled a warning,*' said Silver.

His words drowned out by a huge bolt of resonating energy that arced in a nova knocking all the warriors on the beach down on to their knees as Maledream used more of the blade's potential.

'Whoa,' said Neveah.

'Is there anything we can do?' Boris asked as she looked far onto the hilltops seeing the shadowy figures watching from high above.

'I'm not sure although it would explain where all the radiated warriors disappeared to when we travelled here...those psychic Anunaki have mass mind controlled them, and by doing so wiped out our only exit. Let us hope we can just set sail. I was meant to be going back to N'Rutas but it looks like I'm fated to travel with you,' said Silver.

'Aye, looks like Maledream's travelling spirit has that effect on some people,' replied Neveah.

Angelite struggled to come to terms with what she was seeing. She could feel the strange dark magic coming from those extremely powerful and potent psychic Blood Adepts. She was aware that the ship was almost ready to go.

Crazy John and Boris were rushing into positions, following Neveah's barked orders. She felt a jolt rock the ship and yet, she still focused on Maledream still fighting the mass of dark scales and claws.

'Are we setting sail without Maledream?' asked Boris.

'We have no choice,' Neveah said between gritted teeth.

'What can we do against those odds?' he asked.

Angelite gripped her staff with an anger that grew in her that found a solution to Maledream's predicament.

In a rush, she ran onto the bridge of the ship and climbed up steep, iron steps gripping Catalyst with a renewed vigour.

'I'm coming,' she shouted. As she ran, her green and purple robes whipped in the wind.

'No don't,' shouted Neveah.

Angelite stopped when she reached the bridge. She looked at Maledream on the beach and then towards the hilltops sharply.

'Angelite, don't,' Neveah shouted again, tripping on the last step of the iron stairs, his jaw slamming into the metal grating.

All he could do was grunt, rubbing his sore face as Angelite called out to Maledream.

'I will be fine, keep the ship moving, but keep it at the end of the pier,' she barked back.

Angelite got up and stood on the wooden beam seeing the waving water below her.

'Is it deep enough? Spirits help me,' She thought, gazing back to the beach and then the water.

She swept her long red hair back from her eyes as the winds of magic picked up around her, the robes she wore started to pull on her

and threaten her balance, but she stood firm on a wooden beam. Catalyst began to light up as she smacked the butt of the rod into the beams before raising it with both hands and chanting:

'Water and Air guide and protect Water and Air guide and protect. Feel the anger of the tides, feel the fury of the winds.'

'Dona'rils Kuna'shaka El'noran til'donadnan Teilmarie Shakshillusin.'

'Water and Air guide and protect Water and Air guide and protect. Feel the anger of the tides, feel the fury of the winds.' Answer my call, answer me.'

Her staff's different coloured crystals glowed brightly as she channelled the energy of her spell through herself, her eyes glowed a rich cosmos purple as something within her commanded the very essence she sought. White, glowing orbs, circled around her erratically.

The very light of them brushed warmth onto her spirit as the wind picked up around her.

'What's she doing now?' asked Crazy John as she chanted.

'She is saving Maledream,' Silver's replied.

'I'm coming Maledream,' she thought, now totally unaware of the others around her.

Cutting through another red-eyed beast, Maledream's strength was beginning to weaken even though the sword now seemed to weigh nothing. The Tribals soul felt like it was being drained and he could not stop the bloodshed before his eyes. Only one more moment and he knew that he would die.

A blow knocked him from behind causing him to lose his balance as he jolted forward into a huge swinging arm from another warrior that flung him through the air before landing with a crunch on his back. His blade was almost lost save for the chain link that kept it close to him as he yanked on it and grabbed the handle again before raising the blade into the roof of an Anunaki warriors mouth that tried biting his face clean off. Blood and pus leaked over his small form and armour as he struggled to get his wind back.

The Tribals world started to turn to darkness as he watched many Anunaki jump above him in order to land a killing. His life, or what he thought was his life, flashed before him like a storm, until he heard a voice reach inside his mind that sounded to him like Angelite.

'Run to me Maledream, run as fast as you can.'

Barriers of life and death shattered before his eyes as strength returned to him, hearing her voice of clarity within the storm of chaos that surrounded him.

'I'm coming,' he shouted in return, as he stared into the eyes and minds of the warriors that wanted his blood, almost upon him from their leaps.

His blade turned instantly from crimson to a soft purifying gold that eased the pain of his burning wrists and hands and hummed with high energy of spirit, as if something awakened inside him and the sword. The Tribal raised the weapon high above himself only to stab the soft sand beneath him.

'Get out of my way,' Maledream roared defiantly as the sword gouged itself into the granules of sand, a powerful shockwave sent ripples across the ground, the energy exploding in a nova around him.

Sand and Anunaki warriors went flying away in opposite directions from the powerful crack of energies from the blade. Each tiny grain slowly began to fall creating a shower of sand, as well as Anunaki warriors, clearing a path for Maledream.

'Run to me, Run as fast as you can,' her voice was strong and fed him with a loving hope.

'I'm coming,' he cried and ran as fast as he could over the dead severed heads, spilled intestines and other such guts from what remained of his insane carnage of survival.

He ran, and ran, while all seemed like slow motion as he looked back with the granules of sand falling like snow before his eyes while many a dark mass of warriors gave a slow motion chase as they got back onto their rotting thick scaled legs roaring with fury and insanity.

'Now is the moment,' Angelite muttered, thanking the spirits that she had gotten through to Maledream.

'Go,' her sweet voice resonated within his skull.

Maledream watched Angelite fall from the bridge of the ship towards the water. He reached his hand out towards her but again heard her voice.

'Run as fast as you can,' she continued.

Her hair rising as she fell towards the ocean below her feet as she clutched Catalyst, the lights of the spiritual Orbs falling in free flow like neon with her. Neveah rushed over only to look over the deck and watch her fall. She raised her staff high above her head and, at the right moment, released the power she had stored within Catalyst and then hit the tip of the staff, the Swan, into the water.

The ocean reacted, a boom sounded like a clap of thunder as the water beneath leapt up in front of her that encompassed the whole beach's length. Millions of gallons raced towards the beach as the tide turned into a gigantic tidal wave under Angelite's power.

Maledream raced towards the end of the pier where Crazy John had a rope waiting for him. He was in time to see Angelite fall into the ocean and to hear the crack of thunder hit the gentle waves, turning it into a torrent of water before him.

Aware that the wind had picked up strongly behind him, pushing him even faster as he watched the wooden pier's planks rise and fall like a serpent before his eyes as the water grew higher and higher towards him.

The right moment was everything as the ship was within ten paces and the planks were jumping almost as high as his head. Looking down between the large gaps of the planks, he could see seaweed on the surface of the water glisten in the soft sparse moonlight, as he took a breath and jumped towards the rope, gripping it with all his might.

'Pull him up, dogs,' yelled Neveah, as he grabbed another loose rope on the bridge hastily wrapping it around his waist.

'After you're done, pull me up!' he yelled, feeling the wind pick up and hit him as he plummeted towards Angelite to clutch her from the waves before they returned from the beach to swallowed her.

Angelite was focused on the tsunami of water racing towards the beach, breaking the piers and swallowing any ships between Angelite and the blood harvest to which she wrought.

Still with no fear, the Anunaki warriors charged into their demise as the large wave carried them back to shore and swallowed them up. Maledream could hear the warriors roaring with defiance as they were crushed beneath the massive waves. Catalyst hummed within Angelite's hands as she lost concentration from using so much energy.

'*I didn't think this far,*' she thought, biting her lower lip and watching the torrent of water fast approach her from all sides, the ship itself beginning to move with the ocean above her.

Hearing a roar from above, she looked up helplessly as Neveah's large form crashed into the water beside her making her shriek as he sank for a moment before breaking the surface of the water again.

The Pack leader gulped some fresh air before smiling at her as the ocean came back in on itself

'Come here, hold your breath woman,' he said, grabbing Angelite quickly with his huge arm.

'That water and wind is going to swallow us! **Pull us up!**' he yelled back up towards the ship but no one replied.

They turned around to see the water coming back into the ocean at a fast pace from the debris stricken beach housing the old broken ships in the harbour.

'Hurry, dogs,' he yelled once more, feeling a tug, his prayer was answered as they were hurriedly yanked up back onto the decking of the ship. Angelite was chucked over the side. As the priestess got up from her knees, she was surprised to see it was Silver holding the rope in his mouth, easily pulling Neveah over the edge. Landing on his already bruised jaw, he let out a roar of pain as he looked up into Silver's kind eyes.

'I'm a wolf, not a mutt,' Silver spoke.

Neveah laughed weakly, before replying:

'You can be a cheeky bastard can't you,' he said, patting Silver's fur as he got up from his knees.

Huge bursts of wind whipped the masts of the ship, sending the vessel forward at an incredible speed.

'We made it,' Neveah said with relief, looking back onto the deathly beach. Scratching his eye patch and wiping the salt water from his good eye.

Angelite raced down the deck in her wet robes and, before Maledream could say a word, she slapped him so hard that she almost knocked a tooth from his mouth.

'Idiot!' she cried and broke down, clutching at his hot crystalline armour and clothes.

'You do that again...and...'

He was shocked but also relieved and grabbed her gently giving her a hug.

'I'm sorry,' he said.

'Something...had some power over me...'

'I know,' she sobbed, slamming a clenched fist repeatedly into his newly acquired armour.

'I don't care anymore, Maledream. I just want to take you and everyone else home with me where we will all be safe from this crazy land...and I don't want to lose any one again! You know...you above all else should understand that!'

Angelite cried and cried with relief as Maledream continued to grip her tightly. Silver watched and smiled. He did not know everyone personally but felt it was perhaps destiny that all of them were together on this journey. Below them, soft humming began as Crazy John started the arcane engine up, speeding the ship even further into the huge open ocean. Something made Silver and Neveah gaze back towards the beach, something was stirring on the wind.

'Madness!' exclaimed an Anunaki Blood Adept as they all watched the mass of Anunaki warriors that floated helplessly on the ocean surface after being crushed by the huge tidal wave.

'We still have time, only a little further out to sea and we will unleash the next weapon.'

'I cannot wait,' spoke the one in charge.

'I will utilise it now. I want a Possessed Agent to corrupt that Cattle, Maledream. There is a gaping hole in his soul, we almost had him,' spoke the leader of the few watching the remnants of the battle.

'Once we have control of him, we have control of the weapon,' said another Blood Adept.

'It seems that the red haired breeder has much control over him. We will need to step up our powers and wear him out further. Remember, we need her captured soon after we find any trace of the Cattle's breeding ground.'

'Get ready my minions,' the leader spoke, clasping his hands together.

'This time we shall not fail. She will not interfere with us...'

The group smoked the fresh supply of tobacco while they drank alcohol and enjoyed the food they had left. Angelite and Boris went below decks to change into clean clothes while the men watched the flames of three lamps that sat on the centre of the main deck.

'I tell you, this is some journey,' said Crazy John, as he inhaled more tobacco, breaking a long silence.

'Aye, my lad,' Neveah replied, scratching his groin before smoking more tobacco from his favourite pipe and drinking more alcohol from an ancient posh looking pint glass he had found within one of the cabins of the ship.

Maledream sighed and looked up at the patched clouds. He wanted to say something but felt he needed to rest, trying to come to a conclusion to as his hands brushed the cold wooden seating that he was sat on.

Silver stood at the brow of the ship being ever watchful and away from the others so he could try to centre himself. His head was getting confused by the barren sea with no lush greenery or dry earth to set his weary eyes on.

'Well, we have lost many good friends, lads, and once we get to this Meridia place we will honour their deaths to the spirits, aye?' questioned Neveah.

'If you're lucky,' replied Crazy John, his tongue toying with the tip of his knife.

'Then that's sorted...what the?'

Silver howled as he watched the water rise before the ship alerting all the passengers aboard the lofty vessel.

'This isn't possible!' yelled Neveah, getting up and out stretching his arms in dismay.

A huge beast rose from the ocean at such a speed that it threw up a big wave that rocked the ship, almost causing the humans to lose their balance, Silver's jaws bit onto a nearby rope as his four paws slipped for a moment.

'It's a Behemoth,' yelled Maledream, staring upon the giant ocean insect, the hairs on his back rose as he recalled his vision.

The moonlight shone into the beast revealing its insides as its skin seemed to be made of transparent like muscle and sinew.

'It's disgusting!' yelled Crazy John, his voice drowned out by the low deep roars from the Behemoth.

The beast eclipsed the pale light of the moon causing a slight shadow. The sound of its erratic heartbeat could be heard thumping away rapidly. Seeming to be in pain from not being under the pressure that the deep ocean offered, it advanced upon them.

Thud, thud, thud, its heart raced as it roared with a low tone again drowning out all voices as it moved into the attack. Its insect slippery body made its way towards the ship at a fantastic demonic speed.

'Brace yourselves!' yelled Neveah, not noticing that Angelite and Boris were emerging from the depths of the hull.

Angelite was wearing the new robes that Neveah and Maledream had gathered for her. The women shrieked as the ship was bashed so harshly that the vessel almost turned onto its side and onto its belly. If it had not been for the strong wind, then they would have capsized. The group regained their balance and drew their weapons but it was difficult to know what to do next.

The huge beast took its place by the stern of the ship, and looked at the humans and the wolf while emitting a series of rasping clicks. It began to reach out towards them with its many tentacles.

'Cut them down,' yelled Neveah.

In doing so, he breathed in some of the creature's appalling salt-water breath, which was so foul it almost knocked him out cold.

Boris and Crazy John tried to cut through and dodged the clumsy tentacles that were the width of their height but to no avail. Silver stood back while the others dodged anything that tried to grab them.

Neveah, although strong, found it hard to even cut through one of the lumbering mountains of transparent flesh.

Angelite shrieked as one grabbed onto her, soaking her clean robes and her through to the bone. Thud, thud, thud, the constant heartbeat of the Behemoth growing even faster as it exerted more energy as it raised Angelite off her feet.

'**Get off!**' shouted Maledream.

The Tribal rushed forward with his blade to cleave the tentacle in two with a welcoming thundering smack, his Relic Blade's runes glowing a welcoming soft Resonance of humming light.

He reached out to Angelite, trying to reassure her but her eyes were fearful as she looked at the scene before her.

Distracted by his desire to help Angelite, Maledream failed to see he was in danger until a tentacle wrapped itself around his waist, yanking him with great speed off the ship and high into the air as if he were a rag doll.

He used his sword to swing and cut through it in mid air, slightly catching his breath from having his ribs crushed only to be caught by another tentacle and to repeat his erratic slicing as he was juggled from one tentacle to the next. His friends could do nothing to help as they battled for their own lives, slipping on the now water-laden deck, as the sea thrashed waves on board from the giant behemoth that sought their blood. Being squeezed constantly by the tentacles was weakening Maledream and he lost his grip on his sword. It dangled on his chain gauntlet as the strong transparent tentacle wrapped tightly around his chest plate and gradually cracked the strong metal.

Meanwhile, Angelite had grabbed an unbroken candle lamp. She aimed the lamp towards the direction of the transparent behemoth and began to sing to the flame seemingly making it glow brighter.

'Flamash, Flamash, Flamash, Gionistisa triatus.'
'Fire light the beacon, fire be my light, fire be my guardian.'

'Fire be my Sun, Fire be my creation, Fire give breath to the Ether.'

'Flamash, Flamash, Flamash Gionistisa triatus.'

Neveah cheered on hearing her use magic. It reminded him of the time he and his gang had met her back in the city. Now he was grateful for her powers as the inferno grew in the air as the fire nova circled and blew around her.

In one hand she held the lamp aloft while, with her other hand, she held up Catalyst, augmenting the crystal energies into effect.

> *'Like a droplet of water to the ocean, like a candle lit flame to the sun.'*

> *'Elin'shana dookilla shuen Allina Canshanna, Flamash, Flamash, Flamash,'*

She chanted, the flame grew until it resembled a gigantic ball, easily six feet in diameter and roared with fierceness against the wind.

The gloom was now no more and the transparent beast could be seen in all its glory as the ship continually rocked against the growing windy waves as a storm fast approached on the horizon that brimmed with menace. They could see the many hearts of the behemoth beating down its flimsy but tough body, while its veins pumped gangrenous blood through its body and intestines. The eyes glared white with a tint of red as the constant chattering continued as they blinked.

Angelite began to shriek as the power surged through her own body into Catalyst itself. She spun on the spot, her robes catching in the wind. The runes and crystals stitched onto her clothes shimmered and shone as they reflected light from the bright fireball as she launched the inferno at the behemoth. For a split moment, as the fiery ball closed in and smashed into the wet beast, all were blinded as the explosion rocked the ship with a bright light.

'That should have sorted it surely!' yelled Neveah, as he gained his footing again after slipping on some tentacle flesh, rubbing his bruised chin for a third time.

Before anyone could answer the muscled man, a loud groan was heard and, as the group's eyes adjusted to the gloom once more, they could see Angelite down on one knee, a tear running down one cheek as the energies threatened to consume her conscious mind again and cause her to black out.

Shaking it off and standing up with her frail form, she watched the beast thrash the hull of the ship knocking everyone to the floor from the impact, while all they could do was grab onto anything to stop them from falling off.

Tilting almost vertically and then back down again from the weight of the beast's attack, the ship steadied itself but only just, its sails catching the full breath of the wind and creaking harshly above the sounds of the giant behemoth's heartbeats.

Maledream, still in the clutches of a tentacle high in the sky, lost consciousness from the heat for a moment but opened his eyes again to see a gaping hole in the injured Behemoth's skull, its brain fluids leaking profusely, and its eyes going red with pain and anger.

The momentum of the thrashing tentacle that kept a stiff hold of him worked to his benefit as the blade waved up and the hilt brushed his palm allowing him to grab his sword once more.

'**Get away,**' he shouted with fear and anger.

The sword's runes turning from a soft resonating light to a darker toned red, which was all too familiar to the Tribal but he seemed to have no choice, he barely knew how to use it the right way.

Wriggling as much as he could through the tight pressure that held him, he lifted his blade up enough to let it slice through the beast in quick moments, before again falling free fall speed through the air towards the behemoth's gaping skull. It roared.

Below it, the group could see the faintly red blade heading towards the beast but then it knocked into the ship once more, its tentacles grabbing hold of the masts, trying to snap them with vengeance.

'*One chance,*' Maledream thought, continuing to shout:

'**Take this down with you.**'

His cries echoed to the decks below. All they could see was Maledream landing the blade into the behemoth's skull, causing it to let go of the ship and groan once more as the tens of tentacles it had left raced from its underbelly to try and swat the insect that injured its scorched mortal wound.

'*Steer us away from the beast now,*' Silver spoke to Neveah in a private message.

'*Or we won't make it, he is going to finish it*' and, before Silver could see where Neveah was, he was already racing up the wet iron steps.

'**We're leaving, no questions,**' Neveah yelled.

'What?' Angelite asked but her question was drowned out again by another deep groan from the monster.

'I said we're leaving, we aren't going to make it otherwise.'

The ship turned a sharp fifty degrees to the starboard and began moving at a fast pace of knots as Neveah steered the wheel away from the beast. Meanwhile, Maledream scrambled on top the behemoth's skull, striking it hard. The sea storm seemed to be picking up even more strength and rain started to drizzle softly on the ship as Angelite looked beyond the beast and to the horizon where strobes of lightning could be seen illuminating the dark clouds.

Her feelings were of sorrow as she gazed up at the monster and Maledream, feeling a loss of the friendship that she had made. She knew there was nothing more she could do to help him, feelings of hopelessness sank into her already heavy heart. Maledream struggled on against all odds. He began to strike at the skull repeatedly. His hands started to burn with energy as they had done earlier on the beach making him cry with each blow. At the same time, he was trying to dodge its tentacles with swift agility.

'Not long now, old man,' he muttered, striking again.

'Until I'm one of the spirits you talked about.' He lashed out with another stroke.

'I wish I had stayed at home, watching the stars,' he said, anger and worry seeped into his words, his mind tormented with emotions and fear, he felt like just being swallowed whole by it and his resistance dwindled rapidly, when he became aware that the ship was leaving without him. More anger rose within him.

'So this is all it meant, Neveah?' he said, gritting his teeth, his robed armour and cloak swaying frantically in the wind threatening his grip but he didn't care, sticking his blade in the behemoth and using that as a balance worked just as well for him.

'So this is all it meant, Angelite? What am I saying?' Pulling the blade out from the groaning beast's skull he side swung the blade quickly many times in the spot.

Great chunks of bone, green and blue blood that shone in the pale glow of the red blade and pale moonlight were hacked away.

'I...' he gazed back at the ship again which was now even further away than when he had last looked, time seemed to be flickering on and off to his senses.

'Damn you all to hell,' he yelled, before a tentacle managed to at last grip him, but not before Maledream let out a blood curdling scream, striking the sword with all his furious emotions to finish the beast once and for all.

A flash of light hit his eyes before the dark took him, he felt the breath being squeezed out of him, the armour he wore finally crushing like a tin can, cracking under the immense pressure. Screaming, Angelite was held back by Crazy John and Boris as she tried to jump into the giant waves to swim towards Maledream.

She could only watch as a flash of lightning ripped from the sky into the beast with a boom, causing it to fall back into the ocean, almost completely ripped apart by the force of the Resonance energies released from the blade.

'He is dead!' she screamed.

'I bet he hates us, that's not what I wanted,' she continued hysterically before at last fainting from exhaustion. All the Packers and Silver could do was watch from afar as the tip of the behemoth in the distance finally disappeared below the surface.

The air whipped silently at the masts as the soft drizzle fell on the group's faces with a deep and dark sorrow as silence fell to the sound of the oncoming storm.

'It's good to dream isn't it,' came a voice within Maledream's mind.

'You're in a world where no one can touch you and you have the will to create anything you want.'

The strange voice continued as Maledream opened his eyes but all he could see was a cage surrounding him made of thick shadows and blurs that served to confuse him. It occurred to him that he was in a dream but he was conscious of everything around him, even if it was a little surreal to him.

'You're in a world also where you can't control or take control for yourself, you feel scared, petrified in fact,' continued the male sounding voice.

'Which is why we will take care of your dreams for you Maledream, the world is full of pain and is a horrible place for Cattle such as yourself. We will guide your hand of murder and sorrow and take care of those that abandoned you.'

Behind the bars, he could see a brown robed large black-eyed figure standing tall, watching him. His world of dreams turned into a dark abyss as he watched shadow people dance around him whispering and talking sinister dialects. The Tribals eyes grew dark and a pain racked his heart as he cried on silently.

Chapter Fifteen

Safety of Meridia...

'There will be no end to the troubles of states, or of humanity
itself, till philosophers become kings in this world,
or till those we now call kings and rulers really and truly become
philosophers, and political power and Philosophy
thus come into the same hands.'

Plato

Many nights and days passed as the crew let the navigational
crystals and technology guide the ship back to Angelite's home through
many sunsets and moons as each day passed. The Packers, and even
Silver himself, tried cheering Angelite up but to no avail. She lay on her
bed in the cabin and slept constantly.

Maledream had disappeared from their lives. Neveah stood on
the bridge watching the sun high in the sky beam down onto the clear
blue waters wondering if another one of the beasts may attack. It had
left him feeling slightly on edge. With their numbers down a further
one person, it did not lighten his mood, especially as he had abandoned
his childhood friend less than three weeks after meeting him again.

No one dared go near him, as he would just bark orders or shout
some nonsense to put the blame on to someone else, so they let him
stew, and he was glad. Peace and quiet was all he could tolerate while
they sailed through the barren ocean. His one good eye watched the
horizon hypnotically as the ship bounced on the waves, the water
thrashing the side of the crippled port side with sloshing sounds.

Crazy John had sealed it enough to fix it as they made their
retreat before they risked being sunk or came across anything else
lurking deep down in the depths of the sea. Neveah could not put his
finger on why things had gone so wrong. First, there had been the
Anunaki ambush, second, the giant insect squid like Behemoth
popping up out of nowhere.

He did not like such surprises, especially when they came with a sinister robed figure on the hilltop overlooking the beach. The Pack leader reflected on what had happened, each time shrugging, thinking, and shrugging some more.

'I sense very strong energies,' said Silver, his silver fur catching Neveah's good eye as it shone brightly in the sunlight, shimmering like the ocean itself.

'Energy...' Neveah weakly replied, adding:

'What's it good for?'

'No need to be so pessimistic, Neveah, you really should celebrate about the lives you saved and not the life you lost.'

'Shut the hell up,' Neveah barked back.

'You have no idea, Silver, so just keep your damn level head to yourself.'

Silence fell on the two for a moment as they gazed out to the horizon until Neveah spoke again apologetically.

'Sorry, Silver,' he said, his voice deepened.

'I felt close to Maledream, as if he was a brother, and he is gone because I had to save people, as dark as that sounds. It pains me a lot, and I'm frustrated that I couldn't do anything more to help the poor bastard.'

'That is understandable, I am sorry for being too blunt.'

'Nah, I'll be all right,' he said.

He scratched his eye and then stretched out his arms, crossing them behind his scalp.

'First moment in a while that I've opened my mouth so I should thank you for that, but still I'm just so tired, pissed off, agitated, and want bloody murder at the moment if you get my meaning. Blood is boiling hotter than a flame and thinking just gives me a headache.'

'I've not had a headache, save for N'Rutas hitting me for biting her leg when I was a pup.'

Neveah looked at Silver before grinning at him, replying:

'Aye, she was a weird one, just about eaten all the grub she made for us, not to mention we lost a lot of our bags because we left them on the bastard deck when that giant monster attacked. I'm so hungry and it's the irony of it that makes it worse. No fishing rods and we are in an ocean full of bloody fish. And I say fish loosely, knowing our luck if I stuck a rod in the water I would catch one of those bastard monsters.'

Neveah's stomach grumbled.

'Mother Earth, save my stomach,' he added.

The Pack leader noticed that Silver did not seem bothered that he had not eaten for days. Moving slowly across the sky were small clouds that occasionally crossed the sun and still the two sat on the bridge of the ship staring blindly out to sea.

'So Silver, you were saying something about energy?' he sighed.

'Yes, we are almost at Meridia,' his thought patterns replied.

'Well, you are pretty useless in a fight, but you have other talents,' Neveah said laughing at Silver.

'Ape,' Silver jested.

'Mutt,' Neveah replied.

Below in the cabin, Angelite's eyes were weepy and sore from her miserable state. Her hands clung onto Maledream's old long coat that he had left on the ship. Every passing moment she would smell him and upset herself further for hours on end as she lay on the bed. Hours, that to her, did seem countless and beyond age as she stared meaningfully at his coat, every thread being stroked with her delicate fingers.

Her pale freckled face furled slightly again with swelling tears, but now it seemed as if she had no energy left to even cry. She let out a long drawn breath for a moment clutching on the coat, shutting her eyes slowly before opening them again.

'Home...' she said, sniffing quietly, feeling the ship gently rock from side to side as she eyed up the wooden cabin and sniffed the air.

This small temporary home had been a private place to her for the last few days.

She had spent the time lighting one candle after another in a lamp by her bedside, staring into the candlelight while she reflected on her thoughts.

No other light from the outside world had been allowed in. To her, this cabin was a sanctuary to her mind and feelings away from the others.

Sighing again, she looked over towards the key in the lock and remembered the first time back home when her teachers had taught her how to use Resonance at an early age. Open the door and the door after that to keep advancing they would say to her.

Never fear or look back to the pain that you left in the last room, never hesitate or be lost within your pain and sorrow. This was a hard lesson to learn, many feelings of her past kept trying to reach through to her but she would not let it happen, she would not return to the first door she had opened.

The candle again caught her eye as she sat upright, her head tilted down slightly as she sighed again and looked around the gloomy room trying to find some sort of sign or compensation within her mind subconsciously. Brushing her long red hair behind her back, as she finally found the courage to stand she stared at Catalyst which lay resting against the wooden wall in the corner of the small cabin.

She hesitated for a moment and did not want to let go of Maledream's coat.

'*I wish you were here Maledream, you would of loved my home,*' she thought, further upsetting herself as a tear left her eye as she lay his coat to rest on the bed begrudgingly.

The priestess walked over to Catalyst, squinting at the ornate staff. She cradled Catalyst in her smooth palms and, for a moment, it hummed and sang to her before the sounds disappeared from her ears.

She did not know whether to smile or look even sadder at the cold silver like object she now held in her hands.

'Best go up and see everyone,' she said, walking over to the locked door. Angelite was wearing new robes that were adorned with many patterns containing runes and crystals, as was Meridian fashion.

She hesitated to unlock the door for a moment, the rich silk comforting her skin.

'With each step through another door, another one awaits to be opened,' she said to herself thinking back to her teacher's philosophy.

'**Land Ho!**' A voice from above the decks sounded.

Angelite upon hearing this was anxious now to join the others.

'*Don't cry again,*' she thought.

'**Check it out!**' yelled Boris.

'Aye it's amazing,' said Neveah raising his pole arm with his arms above his head holding it and shaking it like a trophy as the whole group celebrated the sight of land ahead.

'*That's definitely Meridia,*' said Silver.

'*The energies are very strong, I can feel magic in the air about this place.*'

'Aye,' replied Neveah.

'I can smell food already!' he laughed as he continued to wave his weapon high above his scalp.

Walking onto the top deck of the ship, Angelite joined the group to see what was making them so happy. She did smile with them but still felt a continuing deep sadness.

'It looks better than I imagined, I thought it was like the city we used to live in,' said Crazy John.

'Still, doesn't look like I'll be able to cut anyone while I stay there though,' he added.

Crazy John hit the floor as Boris landed a punch in his cheekbone, beating him on the floor as he squirmed and begged for forgiveness.

'Only a joke woman!' he cried, covering his face with his arms as she finished punching him.

'Do not make jokes like that when Angelite's around you idiot,' she snapped at him with a whisper.

Crazy John stared across the decking to see Angelite lost in thought. He smirked and nodded in agreement to Boris.

'Aye, you two, stop it,' ordered Neveah as he gazed at them before kicking them both with his boots, his shiny armour clinking occasionally as he did so.

'*Nice of you to join us, Angelite,*' smiled Silver, noticing she had crept up behind them.

'Girl, are you okay now?' asked Boris leaving Crazy John who squirmed on the floor while tending to his bruised wounds.

'Yes, I'm fine thank you...' she said quietly.

'We should be at the docks of Meridia soon, I will probably be taken away to be debriefed by my peers but you shall all be fine and looked after so don't you worry, feel more than welcome to wander around the place,' she said.

She smiled but her eyes seemed to have no emotion existing within them. Instead, they seemed lost, disturbed, eyes that looked as if they were looking inside and not out.

In the distance was Meridia, and from what they could see, it was constructed out of many tall spires, and vast pyramids made of ancient stones that shimmered with a hint of silver and other colours.

Neveah gasped:

'It's certainly something...and to think we only thought of this place as myth.'

'Well...' replied Angelite.

'You can now call this home, it's very different from the dangers I have traversed through, and that you have lived through.'

'Not too peaceful, I hope,' said Crazy John.

'I wouldn't want to get bored,' he added, under the hateful gaze of Boris.

'Well, I'm sure there is plenty to do there, aye?' replied Neveah, grimacing at Crazy John's words.

'You will love this place, as much as I do I hope,' said Angelite, placing a hand on Silver's back, reassured by the wolf's presence.

Sleek ships were on the horizon and did not seem to move very fast or at all, as they seemed to be just off the shoreline. Other ships, similar to their own, could be seen travelling next to them at far distances.

'Well, I guess we should just wait. We should be there very soon,' said Angelite.

'Aye,' replied Neveah.

'Gather your things everyone, we are getting ready to depart this floating sham.'

Soon enough the group's ship entered a harboured area, its beaten hull attracting attention from Meridian's inhabitants who eyed up the new strangers as they stood upon the bridge.

It had been known for people to arrive with just half a surviving ship or even a shoddy raft that made it through the harsh storms that surrounded the ancient city. High walls hid the bottom halves of the tall pyramids and shining building spires that had, on closer inspection, bridges interlinking most of them, while many exotic and different plants draped from their sides. The smell of incense floated in the air, reminding the group of N'Rutas' hut back in her mountain lodge.

Singing and music echoed from the distant city centre beyond the high walls and through great marble doors that were adorned with runes and thousands of crystal shards. The ship docked itself with its navigational system while the Portman chucked the group ropes to tie around the ship to keep her steady and in place.

In the distance, several men could be seen adorning robes similar to Angelite approaching the Portman from the ancient stone docks. Angelite turned to the excited group to tell them once again that they would be well looked after and of the several men that were almost upon the ship.

'They are my teachers, the one wearing the red robes is called Elric, he is the friendliest, and the most down to earth person you will ever meet. Do not let your eyes deceive you though, he can fight with a pole arm just as well as you Neveah, with the added bonus he can use Resonance.'

'Aye, is that so?' Neveah replied, tensing his muscles with a slight jealous undertone.

'I bet my bear like biceps would crush him,' he said, laughing, while flexing his arms comically raising a small smile on Angelite's lips.

'Now where was I? The other gentlemen wearing the purple and blue, slightly similar to these new robes I am now wearing, is my other

teacher, his name is Eldred, and no Neveah he can't use a pole arm.'

'Well, what a shame,' Neveah replied cheerfully, grinning as he wiped his forehead.

Finishing their talk, Angelite led the group down the wooden ramp to meet up with the two Resonance teachers.

'Greetings, Angelite,' said Eldred.

His face was clean-shaven, his hair short but not too short, as his hair sported fashionable curtains that blew gently in the wind of the harbour.

'Hello, Master Eldred,' she replied, steadily gripping Catalyst slightly not sure what to expect from her teacher.

Elric broke the ice:

'Welcome back, and welcome to your...new friends?' he said.

His hair was short and spiky and he had an unshaven thick black five o'clock shadow, but it was his friendly smile that endeared him quickly to the group.

'Aye,' replied Neveah, shaking his hand.

'We're glad to be here, we have travelled from a city far across the ocean, we're tired, lost a lot of friends, and we are very, very hungry, mate.'

'I see,' Elric replied as he leaned on a smart, shiny weapon containing silver plating adorned with many honours, crystals and runes which seemed to glow on and off like a soft heartbeat.

'Well Angelite needs to be debriefed and that could take a while, so why don't I show you all around while Eldred looks after her?' Elric asked.

'That would be a good idea,' answered Angelite's soft voice.

'I need to borrow the Grand Circle immediately for Resonance evacuation,' she said, looking at Eldred.

'Of course Angelite,' he said nodding in agreement.

'Come with me and we'll get the debriefing done quickly.'

He began to walk out of the harbour with Angelite in tow. She waved and called goodbye and said she made a promise to Maledream's tribe, which confused the group but they waved back as though they understood.

'Right now that is all sorted...wait a minute, is that a wolf?' Elric said, asking:

'May I ask what his name is and how is so tame?'

'*You could call me a spiritual accident. My name is Silver,*' Silver said thoughtfully, staring oddly at Elric's charming grin.

'And you can speak through mind, I have heard of your kind before, fascinating. I take it you have not been here before?'

'Of course not, N'Rutas was the only one that came here and that was around a decade ago by the suns and moons.'

'I see, one of the Nephilim by the sound of that name. I believe I met her a long time ago, but there are stranger sights here now than when Angelite left well over five or six moons ago. We have been worried as we expected her back around last month or so. When we spotted your ship, we zoomed in to see her on the deck! Made our way down straight away...but I'm sure she had her reasons as to why she took longer than expected...I do not see her original companions with her, for now friends, let me show you this place further behind these great walls, follow me,' Elric finished.

The group followed him, breathing in the strange exotic smells of incense, food, and wine coming from the many places and shops dotted about the port. Doors that were much smaller than the giant marble one were scattered around the great wall but they passed through a door that stood much taller than Neveah.

He could feel the walls were cold and clammy as they walked down a passage that seemed to spread for fifty or so paces. On closer inspection, the walls had many ancient sea creatures big and small fossilized into the ancient stonework's architecture.

Swiftly passing through the tunnel, they entered a huge area containing a beautiful sight of wonders. The tall pyramids and spires had stairways leading all the way to their top. They looked far more arcane and wondrous than the bleak ruined cityscape they used to live in, in the Dark Age lands. Birds of many varieties sang in the falling day's sunlight high above them over many passageways. People were everywhere, drinking and eating outside on stools among areas of rich well cut grass.

Crystal clear water sprayed from fountains that reflected the sun off each other, created many dazzling different colours from the different huge crystals embedded in them, making it look like the fountains were full of rainbows. The very air seemed to tingle as though it contained some magical quality. Everywhere looked perfect, no illness, nobody eating mouldy food or drinking muddy water. Feelings of being slightly cheated rose up inside the Packers' hearts, as they looked on with envious jealousy that their lives had not been so fortunate to indulge in such luxuries.

'This place is wondrous indeed,' said Boris, so moved that she linked her arm with Crazy John much to his surprise.

'Now, before I go on,' said Elric, turning around facing the hungry Packers.

'There are a few rules, I'm afraid...'

'Aye, spit it out mate,' cheerfully replied Neveah, his good eye still looking around at the many different cultured peoples that co-existed peacefully, laughing, singing or playing many musical instruments that filled the streets with a tranquil chorus.

'I must ask you to attend the college here in Meridia, this is a special place, once an ancient city that was split asunder in old times, but I will be happy to tell you more about its history later while we get a drink in one of my favourite taverns. I expect you have many questions about the history of this city and now its present inhabitants.'

'It all sounds slightly confusing to me, Elric. All I remember is being a refugee and then killing for a living, so pardon me for not knowing my history,' Neveah joked.

'The rules are simple. Number one: free will, that stands for your free will and the free will of others. Please respect everyone here and they will respect you back. Rule number two: love yourself and those around you, give it to people who you don't know and you will get it back. Rule number three: absolutely no violence. Rule number four: live peacefully. Rule number five: learn a little philosophy that we can teach you...we teach everything here and we do not try to enforce it, as remember the first rule is free will so it is entirely up to you to take it on my friends, but I do ask you try. It can be difficult to adjust to such a culture shock.'

'So you're saying we can do what we want in basic terms?' asked Crazy John.

'Yes, but please do bear in mind that the rules are only there to help you settle in. The transitions you will experience here will shock you and some have gone insane in the past from it. Moving from life in the Dark Age lands to Meridia can have unexpected consequences. Some have searched for this place all their lives but cannot cope with the memories from their past. You're lucky that you have stumbled upon Angelite as she can guide through a new beginning here.'

Neveah butted in.

'Understood mate, we will learn a little while we are here, hell we've got to, after all we are still young and hungry! And if any Packers break these rules, I'll break their necks personally!'

'Free will!' replied Boris.

'Snap our necks and it's against the rule!' she said cheekily, undermining Neveah's authority to which he wittily replied:

'Aye, but I've not gone through the transition yet. I am still your leader and I will break your bones if you're not careful! That's what my free will is all about,' he chuckled, slapping her on the back gently.

'That is why you need to learn some philosophy while you are here friends. It's all well and good everyone claiming they have free will, but unless you have the knowledge and the know-how with the philosophy of Meridia you will take it the wrong way and intrude on one another's wills. You will learn a great deal,' continued Elric heartedly, scratching his unshaven five o'clock shadow for a moment.

'Now, I take it that these rules are understood? I understand you have had it hard. I was once a refugee myself many, many cycles ago. I experienced a similar life to you, a life of hardship. Angelite had no real clue about the outside world until she got restless and demanded the chance to explore, an example of free will, what lay outside Meridia. We let her make her own decisions, but enough of that for now.'

Elric continued:

'I will now tell you how this city is structured before we settle for a drink. We are at present in the outskirts but, although much of the city looks the same, you can tell which part you are in by the style of the buildings, the different vegetation scattered throughout, and most importantly the different circular walls that separate each area. This sector of Meridia is called the "Port" sector, and if you follow the roads going further into the city you'll find the first small circular wall that spans for miles. Do not be alarmed though when you come across it, just look out for small doors to enter each sector. The second area is called the "Social" sector, which also spans for many, many leagues in a grand circle and is the most beautiful in my opinion, not to mention the music and night life is much better along with the alcohol and food than what exists here in the Port!'

'Sounds like my kind of place!' added Neveah.

'I thought so,' Elric replied raising a smirk.

'Many, many fun and games I have had there. Do be careful though as it is considered rather raunchy but I will leave you to find that out for yourself,' Elric said.

'Now, the third circular sector is the "Craftsmen's" sector and has many great skilled artisans and crafters the likes of which you have never seen. They make many things ranging from the staff pole arm I have right here to some water powered vehicles...still in early stages though mind you.'

'Water powered?' asked Boris.

'Yes, water or rather hydrogen, a base element of water, we believe in a clean and friendly environment, and not to disturb the world's balance. We believe in healing the planet, and the best way to do that is to use the most abundant resource on the planet that goes directly back to Nature herself.'

'But that's impossible surely?' asked Crazy John.

'I take it you have been using the last of the oil to use your crude vehicles back from where you first came from?' asked Elric inquisitively.

'Aye, mate,' answered Neveah.

'Well, they only recently just now managed to make a few prototypes of these water powered vehicles because of our expeditions into the Dark Age lands where we rediscovered this technology that was left abandoned when the darkness fell on humanity. Not only out in the Dark Age lands mind you but also here. We rediscovered this city when it was spat up from the oceans. It has taken many years to rebuild this place to the way it was but with the additional thanks to the resonating frequencies that merged with our dimension it has made morphing stone and steel a lot easier, mind over matter and all that.'

'Very interesting,' said Neveah looking in wonder at the pyramids and the tall spires with slightly frowned eyebrows thinking about the large history of this place that he still would have to learn over time.

Still he could not get his head around it.

'So yes, the Craftsmen's sector is a good place to go if you want any armour or weapons, then head to that sector. I do say Neveah, are you wearing the latest Watchman batch that we sent to shore?'

'I uh, yeah I am, bad story if you ask me to how I got it. You can blame those bastard lizards.'

Hearing this did not seem to surprise Elric, he merely raised an eyebrow and sighed.

'Hmm, I sense dread within your emotions friend. We will talk about it in detail later…but if it is what I am thinking then they did not last long. It was a shame, we were trying to tie our bonds more closely to the Dark Age lands with that port as well.'

'So I guess you know what happened?'

'You could call it that.'

Elric's smile disappeared for a moment before he continued his lecture.

'Anyway, later we shall discuss that event. The fourth sector is if you haven't guessed it already, the "Philosophical" sector or "Educational" sector where you will spend some of your spare moments, if you're not sightseeing, learning with many teachers. They teach not only the mind, but the body, the spirit, medicines such as alchemy, or the resonating arts. It doesn't matter what you choose. You can learn martial arts, fighting with spirit, body, and mind, which would probably interest you the most from the look of your rough rugged fighting forms,' Elric laughed heartedly.

'No offence,' he added.

'None at all mate. I wouldn't mind learning some of that martial arts stuff if it makes me a better fighter.'

'Same here,' added Crazy John feeling the edge of his dagger with his spare hand in his pocket.

'It is the most revered sector, as it stands for the whole foundation of what the people live here for, very important and is the most guarded by everyone that lives here. Knowledge is power my friends and it is safely guarded by all that live here. That is another duty of all the people. Now the last and final fifth sector is the Core of Meridia itself, it is ironically called the "Core" sector, and houses many ancient scriptures and artefacts from the old world. It is guarded by not just the Educational Sector, but also by people such as myself. There are some closely guarded things in there, such as old skeletons from ages past, small to giant size human beings, and other such strange "peoples" that still exist with us today.'

'You mean the reptile creatures?' Boris asked.

'The Anunaki, yes,' Elric replied.

'There is history of this place that will shock you to the core, you can learn it all of course. This city does not allow for secrets.'

'Aye, so giant human beings then? Are we talking a little taller than me?' smiled Neveah.

'Well, no, about six times taller actually.'

'Bull,' Neveah said, thinking Elric was pulling his leg for a moment.

'I'm not joking, I assure you, you can see for yourself after we get something to eat and drink. You can't touch them though, they are held in the museums for protection but you can look at them,' Elric added.

Neveah looked concerned at the thought that huge humans once walked in this city. It made him feel small and inferior as he stared at the giant city once more thinking whether or not the place was built by giants.

'Not just humans mind you, but other such races and experimentations that took place eons ago before this city was buried underneath the waves. We have some large ocean specimens too.'

'You mean behemoths?' asked Boris in a sweet placid tone.

'Behemoths?' asked Elric.

'Yes, Behemoths...one attacked us on the way here. It was at least half way as tall as the first walls outside the port. It was huge and was the size of six or seven ships added together,' she exaggerated.

'Hmm...Ah ha, I know of the creature you mentioned, it has been

229

given a name by our archaeological teams but I have not heard of that one before, cannot think of the name now but I am sure it will come back to me. Now sorry for keeping you this long without food or drink it has been very rude of me, but it is my duty to tell new visitors about Meridia.'

'Aye mate, lead us on to the tavern,' said Neveah.

'Indeed I shall! It's called the Goblins Tap, very nice tavern, very nice music, food and beers, it's only a short walk after we hit the Social Sector,' replied Elric.

'Goblins Tap? Odd name if you ask me,' said Crazy John.

'I do agree with my man,' said Boris.

'What's a goblin?' she asked.

'A dimensional being,' Elric replied jokingly.

'Okay? I'll stop with the silly questions,' she said.

Elric simply smiled at her and then at the rest of the Packers and Silver who had remained quiet throughout the talk, instead just scratching behind his ears from time to time while listening carefully.

'Right, follow me,' he said, leading them towards excellent food and good alcohol after their long voyage.

Meanwhile Angelite followed Eldred through the many sectors for what seemed hours, as they navigated around the city of Meridia, making their way forward to the Grand Circle situated on the top of a pyramid. It was here, almost within the Core sector of the city, where the planet received the main influx of energy from the cosmos.

'So this young man, Maledream, he was swallowed by the sea after fighting one of those gigantic beasts you say?' said Eldred carefully.

'Indeed, teacher, he protected me for most the journey and I felt a huge connection with him. I hoped to bring him here to see our beautiful city but it was not meant to be I guess,' she replied sombrely.

'Not all things in life can be worked out the way you want them, dear Angelite, but rest assured life is full of mysteries and magic. Who knows what the universe has in store for you? Perhaps it was meant to happen, perhaps it was not. I am sure you will be all right in given time.'

Eldred brushed his short hair back for a moment. He focused on Angelite's staff and eyed it up hungrily.

'And that weapon, dear Angelite? I take it some fallen one crafted it for you?'

'Yes?' she replied, adding:

'A Nephilim called N'Rutas.'

Bells rang inside Eldred's mind for a moment, but he was not sure why he felt so worried. From that moment however, he had stopped staring at Catalyst.

'And did she have anything interesting to say? She is free to visit but has not in many years now. Did she give you any artefacts or relics that you should hand over to the established guilds in this city to research?' he asked.

'After I have read them, then yes teacher I shall. She did give me maps of the old world, but I'd like to make copies first,' she said sternly. She did not want Eldred to take over the study of her information, already she felt he was trying to take control, even the sound of his voice was beginning to irritate her. She wished Elric were speaking to her instead.

'Nothing like home sweet home,' she thought, a small smile twitching on her lips.

'Of course you can make copies,' he replied.

'However, please let me have them next! I would like some copies myself.'

'Of course teacher...'

'Whatever you say,' she thought.

Angelite paused outside the pyramid steps that went up half way to reveal the door at the entrance to the circle. The two thousand feet tall pyramid itself was adorned with many ancient symbols that were carved into great ancient stonework's that had lasted over the last millennia. Thousands upon thousands of old sea creatures, some of which still existed in the shattered world, were etched into all the stones, fossilized forever upon the surfaces.

Some of the giant runes and writings that were carved long ago were rubbed off or eroded, but only slightly, which had surprised many a scholar when Meridia was discovered after the Dark Age fell, as erosion should have had its way after thousands of years beneath the ocean.

'There it is,' said Eldred.

'Thank you, teacher' Angelite sighed, staring at the steps and how far she had to climb.

By now, her legs were aching from the stairs.

'Who is it you want to summon? A man called Larkham and his Tribals?' he asked.

'Yes, teacher, I made a promise to him to contact him and to seal my promise. I left him with one of my most valued and most powerful crystals. It was the only way I could think to help him. Then I left with Maledream, as I agreed with Larkham that all the tribe moving at once

would be too dangerous, two of us travelling together would be less noticeable. It was a gamble and perhaps too much of a risk for…Maledream.'

'Hmm I see, dear Angelite. Because of your connection with the crystal, you intend opening a rift in the dimensions very good,' he said.

'You are certainly going to pass many of the highest graduates that use resonating energies, Angelite. I am very proud of you and yet also so envious, but still you have a long way to go before you can match my powers.'

Angelite could have flamed him on the spot for being so pompous and arrogant but she let it slide.

'*Yes I will out do your powers, Eldred,*' she thought, hiding her emotions well so as he would not notice.

'Indeed, teacher,' she cheerfully replied.

'I have mastered many gifts and abilities and my staff, Catalyst, will help me open such a rift.'

'I shall watch, dear Angelite.'

He smiled at her, looking at her with eyes that reminded her of a greedy snake. Eldred was a lot older than Angelite, and she knew that he had feelings for her.

All she could do was pretend she had not noticed to keep a lid shut on things. She did not want to give him any encouragement.

'Right, well you lead the way, teacher, I guess.'

'Of course, Angelite, follow me,' he replied walking first up the stairs.

'*What a perverted teacher,*' Angelite thought, glad he was in front of her as she did not like the idea of him watching her from behind.

Soon they had reached the entrance and had entered the cool shadow of the tunnel network that led down into the giant chamber.

Small glass globes burning rich, incense oils, were hanging from the side of the crumbled entrance and along the walls deep within the pyramid, providing a sense of comfort and giving strange sensations that were designed to open up the third eye's psychic abilities.

Angelite was feeling woozy from the steep climb but, after smelling the strong and different exotic smells, it seemed to restore her and give her a much bigger energy boost. Now, she was eager to speak to Larkham so she moved more quickly racing ahead of her teacher.

She sped past bright glowing runes, leading the way through the spiralling labyrinth until finally she entered the opening above the circle on a balcony that overlooked it. Grand lights that burned forever on the power of the dimensions lit the huge would be dark chamber forever keeping it lit.

Many Watchman were stood around chatting but took little notice of Angelite's and Eldred's sudden appearance on the balcony.

'I shall watch from up here, Angelite. Now, take your place within the centre of the Grand Circle, so you can carry out your task. I shall stay here so I can assist you if you need any extra energy.'

'I will be fine,' she said firmly.

'You have not seen the acts I have done since I left,' she added, quickly moved away from Eldred.

'I'll show him how it's done,' she said quietly under her breath as she walked quickly down the steps from the balcony towards the circle.

She stood at the centre of the Grand Circle, took a deep breath, brushed back the sleeves of her robes, and placed her long red hair back behind her shoulders. She was ready. Catalyst sang to her like a chorus within her mind as she made mental preparations.

'You have to be alive, Maledream,' she whispered.

She stared up at the giant lights above her. She could see there was also a large circle at the top of the pyramid that could be used to view stars at night. The circle was covered in a thin layer of dust that suggested it had not been used within the last moon or two which was unusual. However, she had more important things on her mind as her keen eyes stared at the crystalline matrix of lines and symbols that lay etched on the floor waiting to be activated from where she stood.

Closing her eyes, she channelled energy through her body activating Catalyst. A soft humming resonated and was duly felt as the Watchman crossed their arms and watched the young priestess of the Order of Spirit do her magic.

Gradually a chorus of choir singers could be heard around the chamber as she closed her eyes and focused greater Resonance into Catalyst. The Swan on the tip of Catalyst began to glow a rich violet energy that snaked its way carefully down the shaft activating the runes into multi-coloured energies.

Its wings began to spread out and up in an arc as if it were going to take off, the strange metal, and crystal, morphing before Angelite's eyes.

'*So beautiful,*' she thought.

Onlookers gasped, as they had never seen such a staff work so quickly, nor release such sounds. Eldred looked on with a jealous fever.

'I summon forth from my spirit a rift through the gateways of the mind and body, to set free the wills and energy. I call upon a Vortex within this mighty temple of ancient spirits to do as my energy commands.'

Her voice picked up momentum, her adrenaline rising as she could feel her spell being augmented by the staff N'Rutas gave her.

It began to sing with her, mimicking her voice with what sounded like thirty clear voices as the swan on the tip glowed darker and lighter as it did so. The Watchman looked on with fascination, as they had never seen such magic done before while Eldred narrowed his eyes, looking on with envy at the seemingly limitless power she seemed to possess as she sang.

'Minutus cantorum, minutus balorum, minutus carborata descendum pantorum.'

'Catapultam habeo. Nisi pecuniam omnem mihi dabis, ad caput tuum saxum immane.'

'Si hoc signum legere potes, operis boni in rebus Latinus alacribus et fructuosis potiri potes!'

She continued to sing sacred words with Catalyst in tow, the words echoing far and loud through the deep labyrinth of the pyramid.

Now was the time to use the energies that now circled Angelite. Bright orbs of many colours raced around her voluptuous elegant form taking up most of the Grand Circle with their odd dancing flight patterns. She lowered the butt of the staff, ions of what seemed like crackling electricity danced off the crystals and runes, and she could feel the high charge within it bursting to be expelled.

Slamming the staff into the centre of the circle, she released the energy pouring as if it were a waterfall. The Grand Circle itself lit from the huge amount of energies but it was only a matter of time before it would dissipate so she had to act quickly.

'I summon forth from my spirit a rift through the gateways of the mind and body, to set free the wills and energy.
I call upon a Vortex within this mighty temple of ancient spirits to do as my energy commands.'

The crystalline structure of the Circle pulsated like a heart as she poured more energy through the staff to keep the energy going. Her hair flowed while her robes seemed to levitate and defy gravity.

'Just a little more,' she thought, and a little more she provided.

'Fac ut gaudeam!'

234

Angelite finished, her spell's Resonance rising through the air as the floor shone every colour known to man, while the people who watched closed their eyes as protection from the extreme brightness that lit up the whole place. She lay out her hand and channelled a beam of light from her lit up fate lines towards the thin air in front of her.

The false lights above shattered and began to float slowly towards the earth in slow motion as the great resonating energies pulsated within the Circle. In front of her eyes, she could see a Vortex opening, where time and space were all deficd and unknown to the dimensional gateway she began to tear in the fabrics of reality. Sweat dripped off her nose but she pressed on with her determination to do it.

'Just a matter of tearing through the constant,' Angelite thought on.

Eldred watched as Angelite opened up a gigantic black hole that sucked in the energies from her hand and of the circle while her staff hummed. He looked into the hole and saw an ancient city. Leaving it were many people walking towards Angelite.

It took barely moments before everyone was through the gateway. An old aged man was the last to come through in dirty white robes and a dirty matted black and grey beard. Once he was through, Angelite stopped the channelling energy flowing from her hands and closed the portal.

The Swan atop Catalyst began to shrink in size again, the chorus of the echoes that resonated inside the large chamber beginning to subside. When she opened her eyes, she was met with many refugees all cheering and applauding for what she had done for them. Angelite fell to her knees before Larkham. She was pleased to see his familiar well-worn face.

'Well done, Priestess Angelite Rose,' he said kneeling down beside her to add:

'Thank you.'

'It was as we arranged,' she dryly coughed.

'Here, have some water,' Larkham said but, before he could pass it to her, Eldred tapped him on the shoulder.

'We will look after her,' he said calmly but his eyes showed his displeasure.

'However,' he added:

'I must ask you all to accompany these dear chaps here so they can get you all washed up and find you something good to eat.'

The thoughts of Angelite surpassing him so soon were annoying him greatly. Eldred stared at the staff Catalyst, his eyes glazed at such a potent staff gifted to Angelite for reasons yet unknown to him.

'Why did that cursed Nephilim give a novice such a potent gift? How dare it?' he thought.

'Thank you very much, young man,' replied Larkham, wondering who had spoken to him.

'Meet the others at the Goblins Tap,' Angelite said.

'They will tell you everything. Find Elric, he should be there,' she said, collapsing slowly onto the floor.

'Best get her some water boy,' spoke the old man coarsely,

'Because if anything happens to that petal you will answer to me understand?' Larkham said, his eyes piercing into Eldred's own glazed eyes.

'Ah, yes okay, so who do you think you are exactly?' remarked Eldred to the stern old spiritual guru.

'I'm Larkham, an angry old man,' he replied with a rasp.

'I can see you like her staff,' Larkham thought as he watched Eldred consistently eye up Catalyst.

'I see,' replied Eldred finding it impossible to look directly into the old man's eyes.

'Well, you dirty Tribal types must be tired and in need of rest,' he said pompously.

'You can find that old pub, old man, in the social area...people in the street will direct you.'

'Now that I'm here boy, I'll use my own intuition. Now get Angelite to bed and get her some water before I take her to this tavern myself.'

Eldred clicked his fingers and some healers and Watchman came in to carry her away.

'I'll look after this for her,' Larkham said, hearing the whispers of the staff trying to attract his attention.

'I'll look after that,' Eldred said quickly.

'This staff wishes for you not to touch it boy, sorry' replied Larkham.

There was something within the young man that he did not understand, nor trust. The two men glared at each other.

Some Watchman turned to them with interest, they knew Eldred was used to having his own way.

'It needs to be studied. It is no good in your feeble hands!' exclaimed Eldred grabbing onto the staff, however it let out a shriek and within a heartbeat burned his palms.

Eldred yelped then cursed aloud as the staff let out a slight humming sound.

'You are not trusted by the spirits, or the staff for that matter,' Larkham said coldly, eyeing Eldred's cocky eyes up with contempt.

Eldred did not say a word and backed off with his tail between his legs as he motioned to the group to follow him from the circle and out into the open air.

'Bastard of an old man, who does he think he is? Some guts for just arriving in my city,' Eldred thought deeply, anger coursing through his arrogant pompous veins.

Larkham smiled at his fellow Tribals and followed Eldred out to the top of the pyramid structure. He inhaled the smell of incense, glad to have escaped from the Dark Age lands and felt satisfaction that he had fulfilled his followers' trust in him. They had waited a long time to find a place of safety. As the Tribals walked out onto the balcony behind him and witnessed Meridia shining within the last embers of day light, many of them fell to their knees weeping at the sight of it.

This was indeed heaven to them, a place of peaceful existence and sanctuary. Many citizens awaited them as they exited the mouth of the entrance, bearing clean clothes, food, and sparkling clear water. Larkham bid his Tribe a farewell with a promise that he would return soon. For now, he had to make his way to this tavern.

'Something does not feel right,' he thought.

Chapter Sixteen

Reunion...

'People always seem to like reunions, to see those friends from all those years ago. All those bad and embarrassing moments resurfacing for you to face again, the very thought petrifies me.'

Author

Sitting on finely crafted oaken stools with drinks at a table, the group of Packers, Silver, and Elric sat in the corner of the pub, smoking tobacco and drinking from mugs containing many various beverages.

They were becoming quite merry as they regaled Elric with tales of their acts of heroism and their many adventures. Elric was fascinated making him an ideal audience for their stories. Neveah was the loudest and most boisterous but then again it was the one-eyed pack leader's style.

'Those bastard Vasps were bloody huge,' he said.

'Crap your pants in the process?' asked Crazy John with a dark laugh to follow suit.

'Aye, I would have been their grub if Maledream hadn't turned up. I miss that sod you know.'

'Come on, Neveah, don't depress us already, you've been a miserable bastard for two or three weeks now,' Boris answered in a low tone.

'Aye, I'm sorry, but that bloke was a good pal, those bastard lizards, I bloody hate them...one way or another I'll make them pay.'

'You mean the Anunaki. I think I mentioned something about them earlier as we were walking towards here,' said Elric.

'Whatever they are, I just call them bastard lizards, seems to suit them. I had heard myths about them back in the city, along with my fellow Packers here, rumours you see. Too close to the water and bam! They take you into the ocean and feast on your flesh or so they said! But never thought I'd fight some on the way, those shadows were something else as well I'll tell you,' Neveah said, swigging a healthy dose of alcohol down his gullet with a satisfying grunt at the end of it.

The human conversation bored Silver as he stared into a fireplace, watching the roaring fire with orange and yellow flames, the smell of wood barely catching his keen nostrils as he examined the pub while breathing in everyone else's passive smoking. Behind the bar hung up high on the walls were old armours and weapons that had been worn away by the ocean of this risen city.

Some looked as if they had been powerful weapons thousands upon thousands of years ago that there were some who had said that they had been used more for evil intentions that to defend the good ones. Many people of all societies and cultures were gathered in the tavern, some the Packers did not recognise, and the room hummed with the noise of chatting, laughing, and generally the sound of people having a good time.

Although to Silver's distaste, some of the crowd would look over at him from time to time, not used to seeing a wolf in their company as many of them had never ventured outside Meridia, the wild life of many creatures seeming more myth or legend than reality to them.

Sounds of instruments could be heard around the unseen corner of the Goblins Tap from musicians playing different styles of folk music, changing from culture to culture from time to time at different intervals. The song would end and applause could be heard from the other end of the tavern and then another style of music would start leaving an altogether good sense of unity from a race that was once damned for finding silly excuses to kill each other in ages passed.

'Anyway,' said Elric,

'Now you have had something to eat and drink, I'll tell you a bit more about this city and its foundations.'

'Please do,' said Boris looking for a good history lesson while rubbing Crazy John's hand affectionately, leaving Neveah and Silver feeling slightly sick at the sight.

'Okay then!' exclaimed Elric, getting into the history as dusk settled in on the glistening city.

'Our records show that around thirteen to fourteen thousand cycles ago that mankind was created by a race of Elders and that they were not totally physical like us right now. They were called Creators and were mainly of a celestial origin, similar to the spirits that are around us today. The theory goes that they wanted to feel what it was like to be physical, to enjoy all the senses of the brain such as pain, pleasure, being "real" or "solid". So they decided to cross the dimensions breaking the universal rule of free will and so took native races on our world and turned them into a more substantial being so they could experience life in to these beings, sort of like shallow Creators if you will. Of course, we cannot know true their motivations but we do have evidence that our race changed. Bones have been discovered that were of our old species and we were very primitive and animal like, but were also dying from a defect within the blood, or what you would technically call DNA, the building blocks if you will friends, of what makes us who we are. The defect meant that our bones such as our skull were growing too large, leading to problems with the females giving birth. The baby's head was far too large for the pelvis so the mothers and babies were dying in labour.'

The group listened inquisitively.

'Aye, but so, uh, it is slightly confusing...haven't us humans been the same as we always have?' asked Neveah.

'We used to be primitive cavemen called Neanderthals, without speech, without knowledge of technology, had only recently discovered fire and how to use simple tools and to hunt wild game. Before the Creators turned us from that path, we had no spiritual beliefs so no religion. We did not even practice magic because we did not have the knowledge, capacity, or DNA to achieve this. Strange thing was because of the big brains we had we used to use telepathy with the rest of the animals on the planet in order to communicate, but we are still researching more into that matter. Hope you are listening carefully because it is complicated. When the Creators messed with our DNA, they added a sample to it, which restructured us so we had a crystalline structure in place. It is why me, and Angelite for example can use crystals to work with Resonance so well, therefore augmenting our new human powers that have been re-awakened since the Dark Age arrived.'

'So they did not know how to make weapons? And, instead of speaking normally, do you mean they could read thoughts like Silver?' asked Crazy John, raising an eyebrow.

'They may have. We have not yet unearthed any real evidence of this. There is so much we don't know because it all happened so long ago,' said Elric, drinking his fine wine, and then relighting his tobacco in the pipe to take a big drag.

'So, maybe then,' asked Boris.

'They would have known such things, after all you said that their brains were getting bigger, which meant their skulls got bigger.'

'Which must have been painful,' added Crazy John.

'Exactly,' Boris said.

'But also they must have learned something out of all of that?

Like an animal instinct maybe?'

'Aye,' replied Neveah.

'It does explain why Angelite can Witchcraft stuff and understand how to use crystals.'

Elric smiled at each of them and then took another sip of his wine. He cleared his throat with a harsh grunt before replying:

'Indeed, that is what our "core" societies believe who investigate history and I believe it myself. You could say Mother Nature did not create man "perfectly" like many other species on this planet, however we will never truly know if evolution had intervened before the Creators interfered...and yes it is why we can use crystals.'

Elric sipped more wine as he finished.

'Yes, Neveah, it means I'm better than you,' Silver's thoughts raced, joking with Neveah.

'Aye, it does Silver, but I quite fancy wolf kebab if you don't keep your clever moments to yourself!' Neveah laughed joyfully patting Silver hard.

'Always wanted a dog, a man's best friend, and all that,' he slyly added.

Silver ignored him, lowering his bored face to the floor whilst groaning.

'Right, I shall continue. As I was saying, spirituality, or the sense of a spirit, never occurred to the "primitive" man and so the beings redesigned the human blue print. They did this by possessing the babies of the newborn populations to experience life themselves. To keep this sense of spirit, religions were set up by ancient powers a sort of a containment issue to help balance the human creations. Once the old humans were replaced by beings now possessed of spirits that wanted to experience 'life' on this plane of existence, they started to teach philosophy to, and develop technology for the new human beings. And there was not just one type of human being, there was variation so the people would learn that you can be different and yet live together because we all come from the same origins of the energy of the cosmos. They would learn to set aside differences and to live in peace and harmony. It did not succeed very well at first but now every man, no matter what his background, has had to unite under common survival circumstances.'

Neveah's good eye was staring blindly at his pint of alcohol thinking long and hard about all of this.

He was not sure he understood all this talk but he was happy to listen and enjoy the relaxing atmosphere in the tavern.

The songs of the Goblins Tap carried on peacefully in the background adding to Elric's story, giving a more emotional feel to the group. They themselves felt something of a definite spiritual origin gradually awaken in them which they could not explain but had this feeling that they knew this information somehow deep down.

Ash and embers were replaced with firewood when the bar keeper had the chance to keep the warmth going in the growing cold of the autumn outside the tavern.

Smoke floated and formed various shapes as people carried on smoking and drinking, having another good time. It was as if they did not care of any danger that existed beyond the walls the city, yet of course, they were not ignorant of the fact that evil did exist outside the walls, be it a man, shadow or other such beings.

'Religions, never heard of that before, they sort of like the Tribals?' said Neveah adding to the conversation as he stared at Elric.

He elaborated:

'Back from where we were from, there are people called Tribals. These people adopted Maledream too, luckily, for him I ended up on the rough edge of the stick eh? Anyway, they have such spiritual beliefs but, before I met Maledream again for the first time in cycles after losing him in an attack on our friends and family and watched Angelite perform what we called "Miracles" or "Witchcraft", we are very superstitious. Sometimes being around this place scares the crap out of me in some way, and at first Angelite scared the crap out of me, and everyone else!"

'Well,' replied Elric,

'Religions are a spiritual practice to support whatever beliefs their followers hold. There are still some religions about the city but they have been in decline since the Dark Age arrived. Most people now don't know what to believe, but know deep down that there is something spiritual in the universe. Their beliefs are none of my concern and certainly you are free to do as you wish, in accordance of the first rule of free will.'

'Aye, I think I'm getting it now.'

'Indeed friend, you'll find it easier as the days go by. There were many differences but the Creators forged on in their endeavours ever certain that they could create the perfect life to exist. Now you may find this the most interesting part and the most confusing, there were several Creator races, but the primary one that created us originally are called the "Creators" or more accurately the "Sky Gods" to which the ancient peoples called them around five to six thousand cycles of the sun ago. These ancient peoples are often called the Amarucians and

with the help of the Creators made fantastic cities after the destruction of this one, but not so huge. I'll lose you if I skip by to that history so let's stick to the basics of the foundations as I'm getting far ahead of myself, so please forgive me,' Elric sighed softly taking in some needed air.

'It's great mate,' replied Neveah.

'I'm surprised you can remember all of that to be honest,' he added.

'I've reread the historical scripts a lot,' Elric said with a chuckle, scratching his five o'clock shadow.

'Well basically, they created this city in ages past, these Creators. In fact, this is where the start of the new humans began, they say, and so the celestial Creators taught the newborn great things, mind over matter, philosophy. But, because of their ignorant flaw and breaking of the universal right of free will upon a species, they in all their wisdom began to create weapons of mass power and devastation, claiming it was their right to defend themselves. However, "from whom" I asked myself when I read the scripts? I read on further and it mentions this Anunaki race. Back then, there was an alliance between the Creators, Humans, and the Anunaki that spanned many a millennium from what I have learned. Of course under the rule of the Creators, the city was itself the centre of this grand alliance.'

Elric finished for moment taking a sip of his drink.

'So those monsters were allied with us?' Boris gasped in shock.

'It appears so, young lady,' replied Elric, darkly.

'Of course tensions grew between all the races who started breeding programs to increase "Genetic" stock I believe if memory serves rightly, which basically means mixing DNA together or more commonly blood of both races. As you can see this city has two very distinct building types. The pyramids from the Anunaki and the tall rounded spires built by the Creators, that we, the humans tend to favour. To that end it is why they all have bridges linked between them, it does not just signify easy passage between places but it also stands for an alliance of ages in the past that died long ago, it stood for unity and reassured all the populations that used to live here, our ancestors...their ancestors.'

'So, wait a minute, we could be related to these things?' asked Neveah.

He was showing his alarm by staring at Elric with his bewildered and confused eyeball with his creased forehead and eyebrow raised, his jaw had dropped also.

Elric laughed at the sight but reassured him:

'No,' he said.

'Those beings are what you could call half and half, they were the result of experiments which both sides tried mastering, but ended up with these "experiments" not trusted by either side. To the Anunaki they were used as weapons to hide within the newborn societies to steal more secrets than they should have, and to the Creators, near the end of the days of this ancient place, they were not trusted in the slightest. These beings were called the Nephilim or "Fallen Ones" in ancient tongues. The reason for that was because they were hunted or eventually killed off by both sides. Some of them have survived even to this very day. They try to make amends for their past "transgressions" even though they were not to truly blame for their own creation or actions. N'Rutas is one such being, my friends.'

The Packers gasped in unison. Neveah spilt his half pint of beer at hearing this news.

'You what?' they all asked.

'News to us, I thought she was a human who practiced magic or such,' said Boris.

Neveah and Crazy John nodded in agreement, they squinted at Elric.

'*I could have told you from the very start of course,*' said Silver.

'Well, if there are such things as half human and half bastard lizard then what are you?' said Neveah to Silver eyeing him up.

Silver just shook his head.

'*You bore me, don't be ridiculous,*' the wolf replied.

Elric laughed.

'No, no, no. Silver is not anything that unnatural. It is what the planet has done and what evolution has done that has made Silver the way he is, friends.'

'Aye...maybe, just maybe,' said Neveah who began to smile again, the look of worry fading as the reflection in his eyeball revealed him lighting another pipe swelled with tobacco with a match.

'That reminds me though,' said Boris.

'That old "lady" gave a new staff to Angelite,' she added.

'Ah!' said Elric.

'I did notice her holding it and thought that it was slightly different from the original staff she had before she left, a lot more different in fact, but she was in a rush so I did not have the right moment to ask of course. It does not surprise me though. The Nephilim are the only ones with the vast knowledge inside their deep insane minds to construct such an item. It can normally take many centuries of human artisanship to even get halfway to what the Nephilim can create in just a decade or so. They are very potent objects. However, even the Nephilim with the knowledge they pass over to each of their generations, do lose the touch and feel of their more human qualities such as the Creators themselves. That was the Creators most prized possession along with DNA advancements and breakthroughs where they mixed crystalline structures into carbon based structures...The Creators made weapons long ago that do not break or age, even if they appear to.'

'Like what sort of weapons?' asked Neveah crawling ever closer to the edge of his seat wondering where this story was going.

'There are legends of weapons so powerful and deadly that were made by the Creators, that when this city was formed in the alliance the Anunaki demanded knowledge for the crafting of these weapons but the request was denied. They were created for close quarters combat. Or at the very least used in close vicinity to an enemy. You remember me telling you about the newborn humans that were two or three times the size of a man of today? They were the ones that utilised them in the Great Sundering of Meridia, but of course weapons like that, and they are rumoured by the way, to be like daggers to them because of their huge size, but they would be the size of, let's say for example...a double handed sword to a normal human of today.'

'Maledream,' Neveah said, the word broke from his lips.

'Maledream?' asked Elric having his history lesson abruptly cut by Neveah.

'My long lost friend, he found a sword that could split lightning from the clouds, it could cut through anything that stood in its path and it turned Maledream into a killing machine.'

Elric was speechless and did not know what to believe.

'You're having me on, Neveah, that isn't funny. Nephilim can make weapons that resemble them but none are known to exist today...'

'*No, it is true,*' said Silver in a firm tone.

'*Maledream had found such a blade, and N'Rutas advised him not to over use its potential power...she feared the blade was awakening the more it was used.*'

'No, it can't be true,' Elric protested politely.

'We would have found one by now surely?' he said.

'Elric listen to us,' said Boris.

'We can all tell you the same thing, you believe in things that might not have happened so long ago but you have to believe us about

this. If anyone has any knowledge on this it is you!' she finished, drinking more wine as the conversation got more serious.

'Well,' Elric replied.

'I shall take your word for it, I feel no lies from any of your lips. How big was this sword?'

'Let's just say that Maledream had difficulty swinging that heavy bastard. It would glow strange colours, weird symbols would ignite under its surface, and a host of other things to boot,' answered Neveah.

'I see, this is serious,' said Elric, his hands finding their way to support his hairy chin as he thought over the matter carefully.

After several moments of silence in which the group continued to smoke and drink, Elric found the courage to speak again.

'Now, after careful thinking, I believe it could be possible. There are legends of such weapons back at the Core that hint of such objects. It is why I mentioned them, they are weapons that were made by the Creators themselves but there were no mention of them after that, it is as though they were wiped off all the records...which could only mean something, someone or maybe some secret society held on to these weapons for safe keeping. It is entirely possible.'

'It is mind boggling, mate,' said Neveah.

'Indeed it is, friend. It is a shame. Why is this Maledream not here now, dare I ask? You mentioned his name earlier but no other details?' Elric asked.

'Aye, he would have been but something seemed to possess him to go down into the deep ocean with that giant behemoth sea creature. He had courage and a will like no other when he had that sword. I don't get scared easily but when over a hundred bastard lizards jump out of the sand and Maledream races towards them I knew the odds were stacked against him. Angelite saved the poor bugger. I have no idea how she snapped him out of his blood frenzy but he was like a machine. That is when we thought we could make a getaway on the boat, but when it attacked, whoever it was who wanted him dead got their wish...they really did not want him to get away, sorely miss the bastard he was a cheeky bloke sometimes but I liked him, and I did give him a lot of stick too.'

Crazy John pushed his luck slightly with a patronising sigh.

'You sound like you fancy him Neveah, just marry the guy.'

Neveah did not take this very well, punching his knuckles together, glaring at him with the look of killing poor Crazy John.

'Sounds like you all lost someone you knew very closely. After all, surviving dangers with the company you keep develops a special instinctive bond for survival,' said Elric looking at Neveah with a

woeful heart and feeling ever so sorry for him.

'Aye, he was a good mate,' Neveah said swigging down more alcohol.

'Well, legend has it that there were around thirteen such weapons,' continued Elric.

'Obviously we have none in possession of course and if we did who knows, we would probably heed the legends and keep them locked away, as surely only destruction would once again rain upon this civilisation which we now desperately want to hold on to. The thing is if that is one of the Ancient Relic blades of legend then it makes you wonder what happened to the other twelve.'

'I know I'd be king of the old city if I had one...' coldly uttered Crazy John, his mind constantly on murder in cold blood.

'Aye, if I had one I'd shove it up where the sun don't shine Crazy John so keep that mouth of yours hushed,' growled Neveah keeping Crazy John smiling and tame.

'Scary when you think about it...wonder if we'll ever find out what happened to the other weapons,' said Boris.

Silence swiftly fell across the table for a moment as all began to contemplate this information, despite their intoxicated minds.

Elric broke the silence.

'There is so much more you need to learn about this place, but I think that's enough for one day as dinner is just about to be served, along with another round of alcohol!' he said, lighting the mood up.

'Aye sounds great,' Neveah said as they watched the waitress bring in their food in turns.

Most of it was cooked vegetables but also fish was a staple part of the menu that got Neveah excited as he hastily put down his pipe of tobacco and tucked in almost giving himself indigestion. Rice and noodles were also on the large plate covered in many exotic spices to make it taste that much more satisfying as it whet their taste buds.

'Well, everyone,' said Boris.

'Let's have a toast! We made it under the leadership of Angelite and Neveah!'

Everyone raised a glass in celebration, gorging themselves on food that was not stale, rotted, and green or otherwise.

Larkham walked on his weary old wrinkled legs, resting on both Angelite's staff and his rickety cane as he approached the Goblins Tap.

The spirits whispered to the spiritual leader that he would meet the individuals who met Maledream and Angelite, but who exactly these were he would have to find out for himself.

Smells of ale and rich food caught his dangly haired nostrils as he sniffed the air.

'Smells like the place,' he muttered, walking passed many smartly dressed and clean-clothed people.

He was aware that they were watching him as he walked up to the thick oaken doors of the pub, he himself looking a state from the poor living conditions he was accustomed to. Sounds of music inside also caught his ears.

'Not heard that in a long while,' he whispered, pushing the door open, almost coughing from the smoky atmosphere.

His eyes caught those of the barman, as he edged closer to the bar and looked around trying to find a clue to show him who exactly he was looking for.

He heard roars of laughter from the darkest corner of the pub that was lit with faint candles above their heads. A wolf was situated with them, it caught eyes with Larkham and locked a sense of friendliness with his own.

'Odd,' Larkham remarked with a cheerful smile.

'Excuse me, sir?' said the barman.

'Want a drink?'

'You have water, kind one?' asked the old man.

'We certainly do. Are you another refugee, old geezer?' he asked.

His hair was long and knotted, stubble covered his face, giving him a rough edge. Larkham noticed that his clothes were almost as dirty as his own were after his travels and yet he cleaned a mug carefully with his clean apron before pouring Larkham a mug of clean water.

'Thank you bar keeper,' said Larkham.

'I'm looking for other such refugees. Have you seen any here, by any chance?' he asked.

'Certainly sir, over there in the corner talking to Elric.'

His accent was strong but Larkham was unable to distinguish where it was from, the barman possibly being a refugee himself.

'Thank you, kind sir,' the old man said, nodding as he walked away with a pint of water in one hand and two staffs in the other.

As he approached the group sat around in the corner, they eyed him up. Larkham was carrying Angelite's distinguished staff, Catalyst.

'Hey old man! Where the hell did you get that staff?' Neveah barked.

His voice was on the verge of anger, thinking the old man had stolen it. He stood up, planting his hands firmly on the table with almost gripped fists.

Larkham stared at him and merely smiled, spending a moment as if to prepare himself for some mighty speech.

'Hello. I am guessing you know dear Angelite?' he asked calmly to the group, resting his pint of water on the table, all eyes following his every move.

'Aye, we may well do, who are you?' replied Neveah suspiciously.

'I am Larkham...also a friend of dear Angelite. She told me to meet you here,' he said answered confidently.

Neveah's nerves calmed down while Elric decided to lighten the subject a little.

'It seems you have been travelling long and hard too, old man. Come and sit with us,' he said cheerfully.

'Don't mind if I do, kind sir,' Larkham said, pleased by the young man's manners unlike the other similar robed Eldred he had met.

'So, I guess we should all get properly acquainted before someone gets hurt?' said Crazy John.

After much discussion, Larkham and the Packers found a truce with one another within the pub. Much talking was floating in the air, they all became acquainted and started to talk about the long journeys they had experienced since leaving their homes.

'So, I feel something is wrong,' said Larkham, his voice low and husky.

'Where is Maledream? Is he taking it easy somewhere?' he asked causing a silence within the group.

'We have talked about him too many times today,' said Boris drinking her fresh glass of poured wine.

'Why? What has happened to him?' Larkham asked, squinting his good eye towards Neveah and fearing the worst.

'Aye, listen to me closely old man as this may take you by surprise. Along the journey, Maledream went down into the depth of the abyss of the ocean while defending us from a giant monster of the deep...a behemoth.'

Neveah sighed, having to relive the thought of it once again.

'I see,' said Larkham taking a swig of his water carefully thinking for a moment, and for the shock of the news to settle in briefly.

'But to my knowledge of what the spirits say, he is not yet in the spirit world. This seems troubling...'

'His soul has not joined with the Great Spirit?' asked Elric.

'No,' Larkham replied bluntly.

The Packers seemed confused by this statement.

'I believed him to be well and safely with Angelite but the spirits can't tell me everything, only that he is not a part of the energy,' he

continued, his voice growing a tad darker from the troubling thought of what could have happened to him.

'That boy is a trouble isn't he?' Larkham continued to mutter.

'There was no teaching that boy, I wonder where he is,' he added.

'So Maledream is alive then?' said Crazy John almost pessimistically.

'Aye, shut up, that's what the old man Larkham said, idiot.'

Neveah's one eye shined at the thought that Maledream might still be alive even if his voice did not make that vocal expression in the serious conversation.

'I don't believe that the little bastard is alive though old man, if you had been there, you'd have no doubts.'

Neveah seemed angered by the old man's thoughts that Maledream was still alive. He felt that the old man was having him on in some way.

'Neveah's right, Maledream had no chance! It can't be possible,' Boris added.

'And I get told to shut up at the thought of this?' asked Crazy John staring coldly at Neveah for a split second.

'Aye...shut up...' Neveah fell into silence for a moment.

Nothing that he had witnessed thus far could be disputed.

'Do not lose faith, trust in the spirit,' Larkham said, catching Neveah's ears, giving him a small light of hope for his friend.

'Then what can we do? Look for him?' asked Elric, his thoughts wanting to meet the young man and his Relic blade.

'Aye, that sounds like a damn good idea to me!' said Neveah.

'Yes,' added Boris.

'But, how are we going to search the depths of the ocean for him...if he is in the ocean?'

'It sounds mighty confusing to me young ones, but I would say just give the rescue mission a rest for now. There's one thing you youngsters are good at and that's rushing into trouble!' said the Tribal leader, as he stared at the happy patrons in the pub laughing, drinking and smoking without an idle clue about what lay beyond Meridia's walls.

'Perhaps dear Larkham is correct, my friends, it would be foolish to assume we could hold our breath under water and swim to the depths to find him' Elric said.

'Aye but if he is alive then that means I can take the piss out of him again!' Neveah said, his voice reaching a happier pitch.

'Sounds good to me,' said Larkham.

'I've missed that too.'

He chuckled with Neveah.

'Larkham is an older version of Neveah without a weapon,' Silver thought, watching the humans ever more closely in the bar.

Then, as his eyes arced across the pub, he noticed that Catalyst, which lay against the table close to Larkham, began to glow lightly of purple and crimson. His keen ears were raised so he picked up what he thought sounded like some sort of choir of human singers chanting.

Getting up, he wandered closer to Larkham and Catalyst getting a better glimpse and sound. This of course did not go unnoticed, as Silver had sat prone for hours with the group by the dark oaken table.

'What's the matter?' asked Neveah as he poked Silver.

'This staff, it's activating and Angelite's not here,'

'Huh?' came from the group as they all got up and stared at the staff, its runes, symbols and crystals still softly glowing.

'Can you hear that?' asked Silver, the glow reflecting off his eyes as he got closer.

'It's singing,' said Larkham.

'I'm not sure why but it does talk to you but only as if it's singing,' he added.

'This place and all these things are strange,' said Boris.

'I agree with my woman,' said Crazy John, due to his superstitious beliefs he was eyeing it up as he believed it was a great deal more evil than it was.

'I can assure you its fine,' said The Tribal leader.

'It hasn't glowed before, purple and crimson...purple is a sign of knowledge, mind power, the psychic abilities, and crimson for anger. I do not know what this means though,' said Larkham, picking up the staff with his hands and examining it more closely.

'The Runes and crystals are a natural part of Resonance to aid casters,' said Elric.

'A lot of these symbols were once lost knowledge, however we have a whole archive on what they mean but this staff has so many and it was created by a...'

'Nephilim?' Larkham said, cutting Elric's conversation short but all he could do was nod and smile in agreement.

'I know of old legends of these creatures of the past, stories of such Creators that made weapons such as these...which I may have to ask now. You said Maledream went down with a giant monster in the sea?' asked Larkham.

No answer could be heard but all nodded in agreement as Larkham's rough old hands rubbed up and down the Catalyst's cold

smooth metallic surface, feeling the energies within flow like water, his ears close to the staff as if listening to it.

'Then may I ask how he did such a feat? I noticed he kept a sword hidden away from me, however, I could feel the weapon's presence. I take it he used a similar weapon such as this to accomplish such a task to kill the giant monster?' continued Larkham, still he only received nods in agreement as the Packers continued drinking and smoking with the occasional belch from the good food they had all eaten.

'Your wisdom and intuition is something to behold, sir,' said Elric, sounding suitably impressed.

'Cycles of practice and of knowing thyself, my friend,' he smiled.

'So, he found one of these…that boy got himself into this, but I do admit I knew he had something up his sleeve when he left with Angelite over a moon or so ago now. I did not worry so much but I had many strange visions about Maledream, times of shadows and regret. Almost like a soft depression which you could not unearth within his soul for he was the only one that knew himself, bah I'm losing you all with my babble.'

'Aye you are, old man,' cheekily replied Neveah with a smile.

'Your sense of humour is like Maledream's isn't it? You remind me a lot of him,' said Larkham. Neveah did not know what to say so he grinned as he rested and began to relax on his seat's backrest.

Silver sat by the staff and continued to feel the strong spiritual presence of the energy that flowed softly.

It seemed to soothe everything around its mystifying aura. The group started to relax once more and talk about other dark topics that came to mind.

The moon began to rise higher into the night sky as Angelite walked calmly through the streets of Meridia, on her way to meet the group at the tavern so she could finally have glass of fine aged wine which she had not had the pleasure of having for a while.

She was glad to get away from the Core where the healers had helped her back to health telling her to stop overexerting herself otherwise there would be a chance she would never wake up.

'What a relief to get away from Eldred. It seems I've lost the respect I once had for him, or that I forgot what he was really like over the cycles of the moon,' she thought.

Wind gently brushed her as she passed through the city streets that shone and reflected the pale moonlight.

Animals had long ago gone into hibernation as the city grew ever more silent save for the Social Sector where life was only just picking up once more in a city that knew no bounds of where fun could stop, especially for the younger generations.

Smells of incense and oils were almost gone as the traders stopped trading and bartering their goods and were instead replaced by the natural smells of the many different varieties of plants and trees that littered the city which were fed healthily from the energies the many assortment of giant ancient crystals gave freely.

Dreams were all she could focus on and the lengthy journey she had travelled. Making her way to the dark world to lose her old companions and then discovering new ones.

One of them was Maledream whom her heart wanted to get to know more, but it only seemed like a dream now and he was gone forever. Angelite looked at the moon beyond the tall shining spires and large pyramids wishing that events could have worked out differently.

Entering the Social Sector, she made her way hastily towards the tavern where she could feel the strong presence of Catalyst. Alerting her was her intuition as she stopped dead on the cobbled path, the wind picking up strength for a moment blowing her hair strongly before disappearing as she looked towards the port district that lay to her east.

'What are you telling me?' she asked blindly to the winds.

'What is it…no I'm being silly' she whispered eyeing the direction with a sense of great questioning as if she knew something was there waiting for her. Laughter caught her ears from the Goblins Tap that lay around the corner from where she was stood.

Legs carrying her once more, she walked around the corner and looked at the many people going about their own business as the night life began to pick up with alcohol and music illustrated with bright lights that burned fiercely in many colours.

Pushing the door open, she made her way through the busy tavern noticing that everyone she knew well was having a merry time.

'Over here!' yelled Neveah, his voice so loud it could almost rock the foundations of the place everyone drank in. She smiled and quickly made her way to the table hugging all friends affectionately while being poured a large glass of wine by Boris.

Finding a place to sit next to Larkham and Elric, she began talking with them far into the night. Darkest events were soon forgotten as everyone did not like to talk about them. It had been a long journey and they all thought they deserved a good hard-earned rest.

Chapter Seventeen

Release from Darkness...

'Darkness is only driven out with light, not more darkness.'

Martin Luther King, Jr.

'I've had far too many wines! I best leave now before it gets too late,' Angelite said with a blush.

'That's fine by me, aye!' said Neveah, stumbling as he got up to give Angelite a giant bear hug almost crushing the poor girl.

'Now if anyone bullies you, Angelite, just come to Neveah and I'll sort them out,' he said, letting go of her so she could catch her breath.

'I shall. Don't worry,' she said smiling.

'I've had a nice time. Shall we meet up tomorrow around noon and have another drink and something to eat?'

'Most certainly, dear priestess,' answered Larkham and had another sip of water.

'I'll be here again tomorrow as we all need to have a serious talk. After all, this is such cosy place,' the old man added.

'Don't know if I'm up for more serious stuff, but I'll drink to that!' said Boris, raising another glass.

'Okay, then, it's settled. Now I must go before I drop,' she said, giggling softly.

'Elric, I take it you will look after my friends while I am away?'

'Of course, my wonderful student,' he answered.

'It's an honour for these fine people.' Elric heartily chuckled.

She grabbed her staff, thanking Larkham for looking after it and, with a wave of goodbye. She left the Goblins Tap as the rest of the nightlife carried on, as it would well into the morning.

'Something is making her on edge,' said Larkham to Elric in a quiet whisper.

'Indeed, Larkham, I'm sure that once she gets some rest she will be fine,' Elric whispered back, although loud enough to be overheard by Silver.

'Larkham, Elric, I shall follow her in a few moments and keep a close eye on her, If anything is the matter, you'll hear me.'

Elric and Larkham smiled at the large, silvery wolf.

'You do that, my friend,' said Elric.

Larkham, edging closer, nodded with a smile towards the wolf.

Soon Silver left the pub to begin his surveillance, using his better senses to follow Angelite undetected.

The night was loud until she walked east towards the Port Sector ever wondering why her senses were drawing her closer to the sea. A part of it was curiosity as she stared at the moon asking her friends to forgive her for lying to them when she said she needed sleep when her true motive was to follow her heart.

Catalyst's runes and crystals were faint in the gloom of night, as she carefully made her way to the Port Sector of the city in her elegant windswept robes. The staff hummed with energy, more so than it did when it was not within the boundaries of the city, as if it were more alive than usual. The soft, cold, spiritual grip Angelite had on it gave her some peace of mind.

Sea breeze touched her nostrils strongly again as she passed through the large tunnel way where she had come through first thing this morning with Eldred. Watchman lined the walls sparsely with their weapons and armour as they kept guard by the port. Damp was all she could feel as she followed the large tunnel to the other side, while glowing orbs darted back and forth in front of her spiritual eyes as she felt a stronger presence about the port.

Gazing out to sea as she got into the open docked area, she looked over to their ship that was still where they had left it, rocking on the small and steady waves. Angelite sighed, relieved that she could not see anything out of the ordinary but could not help but think of Maledream and the Port of the Watchman back on the Dark Age lands where she had travelled.

'Better get his coat and head back,' she thought.

Anger, pain, and sorrow began to fill her as she focused on the pier, recounting Maledream's act of bravery and the last time she was in his comforting arms.

She had never been sure if Maledream felt the same way about her, but now it seemed useless to speculate, so instead she stared at the reflection of the moon on the sea. The wind picked up again, blowing her loose robes and long red hair again and brushing her cheeks with a soft cold feeling.

Sometimes she hated these moments of digressing over her feelings and thoughts.

Suddenly, a chill ran down her spine, her premonition kicking into action as she turned her head slowly to a small stretch of beach to her right away from the pier onto the dim golden sand.

In the gloom of the moon, she could see someone or something crawling on the beach, her eyes squinting painfully to try to see more detail. Dread seemed to seep into her but at the same moment she could not blink or look away from what it was and instead started to approach the strange shadow on the beach.

She called out 'Hello? Are you hurt?'

There was no reply except for a moan in the distance, Catalyst began to sing a low chorus for the first time reinforcing the omen that seemed to dawn on Angelite's fear, as she got closer and closer to the beach.

'Hello?' she called out again.

There was no reply in return but she could see the shadowy figure was getting up, looking as if it were some sort of puppet on strings from the movements it gave as it clambered clumsily to its feet holding something long and thick in its arms.

Instinct caused her to react by holding her staff in a defensive pose while with one hand tracing symbols in the air and muttering a few magical words quietly to prepare for whatever it was coming her way. Feelings of being alone and maybe being unable to defend herself did not help as the fear started to creep in.

Catalyst began to respond in kind with its crystals lighting up the area around her like a torch. Pausing in her tracks again, she let the being walk towards her into her light. Utter shock terrified her as she stared at a ghastly appearance of Maledream, who clearly was not himself. Angelite's heart fluttered and thoughts began racing through her mind as to how he could be here in Meridia but, before she had a chance to ask, the puppet of Maledream ran towards her with demonic speed.

Now with only ten paces between them, she looked at him in total disgust and horror as she noticed that his eyes were pitch black, while his dark aura seemed to strangulate the air.

'You and all your kind are ours now breeder,' an echo raced inside her head almost making her faint, the cracked armour Maledream he wore was soaked, unnaturally rusted through, while shadow energy seeped from the cracks lighting the old crystals attached to the armour with crimson energies. He raised the sword ready to decapitate her in one fell swoop.

'**Maledream, please!**' She screamed raising her staff, she ducked her head hoping the blade would miss her flesh.

Catalyst sang and activated on its own accord to protect its user, letting out a blinding golden barrier of Resonance energy that surrounded Angelite, roaring like a fierce flame. Smashing the Relic blade into Catalyst, she successfully blocked the blow. With her adrenaline now running, the priestess darted to one side from another clumsy swing from the dark entity that possessed Maledream.

'**We'll see about that!**' she screamed in defiance, her eyes lighting with a bright violet as she readied herself against another blow and then another, sparks flew from both the blade and the staff.

'*You cannot possibly defy your masters, you are all Cattle, and we are your birth right,*' the voice yelled inside her mind but, although shaken from fear, the priestess was now filling with courage and conviction.

Battering another blow from Maledream's possessed swing, Angelite gathered energy in her hand, channelling it through her quickly tiring body and blasting him away by several metres in a ball of bright multicoloured lights.

Landing heavily and picking itself up off the floor it laughed insanely, his eyes blacker than the void as he glared back at her.

'*You cannot stop this vessel, this blade will be more powerful the more I slaughter you all with it,*' it carried on, Angelite gathered more energy into the staff as the possessed Tribal charged again.

'**Maledream, I know you're listening,**' she screamed.

'You have to break free, snap out of it!'

She parried another blow but landed on the soft sand from the force of the hit. As she tried to get a footing to get away, she saw Maledream attack but managed to escape with a roll as the sword cracked the earth, dark energies polluting the grains of sand with red cracks as it struck, seemingly melting the crevices into glass.

'*You cannot stop my new found power,*' it said, dragging the sword out the sand in an upper cut like fashion causing Angelite to block it from below.

A flash of light signalled a small energetic explosion and, as it faded, Angelite flew limp in the air as she was hurtled tens of feet in an arc landing on solid earth and away from the beach.

Pain hit her spine and winded her stomach, but thankfully, her weapon was still with her. Catalyst kept its chorus high, healing Angelite's wounds in a slow fashion.

Her staff had giant scrapes in it, however the special metals began to remould back into its original shape as if it were never damaged. Before she could react and recover her breath, the big sword almost swiped away her head again, as the possessive being used Maledream as a vessel for murder.

She could not let that happen. Blocking another blow, she enacted the exorcism rights of such supernatural beings.

'Illumani' Penetrana Sheol dagadan, Illumani' Penetrana Sheol dagadan.'

Gold energies surrounded her spare hand as she caught Maledream within the Resonance frequency of the spell, similar to when she had last used the spell on the ancient battlefield.

'Be gone, beast,' she yelled, spinning on the spot smashing the charged Resonance of Catalyst into Maledream's torso, releasing another explosion that sounded a boom as the air shook the ground that she stood on defiantly.

The creature's cold abyssal eyes stared at her moments before it was blasted away ten yards back onto the beach. It did not end there though as the being steadied itself in mid-air, landing in the sand on its feet, blowing millions of particles of it into the air as if a meteor hit the beach.

'Is that all you have?' it asked mockingly.

'You are truly pitiful, we should not have overestimated your empty powers.'

Maledream's tired and withered body prepared for another charge, his sword glowing with a crimson fury as he lurched the blade forward, releasing an arc of energy, followed by a loud crack of power.

Angelite's pupils dilated as she watched the energy of it crash into her protective barrier before inevitably overwhelming her. Screaming in agony from the bolt, she hit the floor as Catalyst struggled to keep her alive with its consciousness absorbing most of the blast.

It glowed with a hot molten red within her hands for a moment sending the ancient relic's powers into the ground to act as an earth.

'And now to end you,' it said.

Raising the blade up towards the sky, the sword's energy created another batch of ions across its ancient metallic etched surface, its silicon crystalline pathways glowing red hot from the use of it.

Angelite muttered a silent prayer as she held Catalyst as if clasping her hands together.

'I used so much of my power by opening the portal in the afternoon, I can't keep going,' she thought.

Catalyst seemed to go silent, its surface still cooling down from the large energy it had to dissipate, its power spent for the moment until it had recharged, but it would not be in time.

'Spirits help me,' she said closing her eyes, tears beginning to leak down her cheeks.

She watched the Relic blades potency gather more energy, the runes lighting up along its surface as it charged for a final energy strike.

A howl sounded that seemed to surround the entire city in its fury as the shadowy entity looked to see a large silver object run with infinite speed, crashing into it, sending it reeling across the ground. It howled again before repositioning itself between Angelite and the possessed Maledream.

'I am sorry, Angelite, I followed you. Hurry and get your strength back, I cannot hold him back for long,' Silver said.

The shadow entity formed itself for attack by arranging itself like a stringed puppet once more, its aura of abyss growing ever larger as tendrils began to grow outward from its aura. Maledream held the sword aloft, trying to attack Silver's agile form but failing to do so, frustrating the being. Angelite thanked her stars as she looked up above, and now with Silver here fighting by her side, she felt she had to try even harder. She struggled to stand but began to focus her healing energies on herself in a deep meditative state while Silver bought her more time.

'A mangy wolf, I thought we had eaten most of you in the end of this world's days.'

Silver simply hopped to one side, ignoring the intrusive thoughts, jumping out of the way of its clumsy sword stroke but also dodging the tendrils of dark snaking energy that tried to grab him.

'Maledream, wake up you stupid fool, wake up,' Silver called out.

Angelite watched the two fighting, her eyes now glowing a golden green colour as her true energy was reaching out from her soul, her higher self. Catalyst's symbols now lit up properly as she focused her energy correctly in order to activate the staff's true potential.

Crystals lit their way up the staff as the resonating manifolds recharged and gained higher powers, a low-pitched hum grew louder as every moment passed.

'I have no time for this,' the shadowy being said as it lifted the blade in the air for a moment with both hands and then stabbed the blade into the sand.

A crack of thunder sounded as Silver was caught by a strike of crimson lightning, blowing his four-legged form into the air as the ions exploded and arced out from the ground like an earth quake, seemingly defying all science. The form of the Tribal raised the blade above his head, the large wolf fell helplessly onto the sword, impaling him. Silver roared in defiance howling with a blood rage to suit but was powerless to do anything as his spine fractured instantly.

'Angelite, find him, his soul is still here.'

It was the last thing Silver said as Maledream with great demonic strength smashed the wolf into the ground, sending sand high into the air, a crack of power signalling the defeat of Silver. Angelite looked on, her rage barely contained at the sight she had just witnessed.

'No!' her voice echoed like a chorus, her aura glowed a bright vibrancy of light manifested. Deep down inside something was awakening within the priestess.

'No?' it echoed back with a dark chorus choir of its own in its foul tongue of incantations, laughing maniacally.

'Well, let's see what you got breeding scum,' it said, leaping high into the air, defying gravity with the sword raised high.

The possessed Tribal fell in an arc, swooping the blade down and letting out another shot of crimson energy that struck in unison with Angelite's staff.

She held Catalyst high above her, blocking its passage to harm her, creating another shield to hold Maledream in place as his feet landed on the staff. Catalyst absorbed the blast of potent energy, the shock of the sharp edged Relic blade, in turn adding the power to its own repertoire of energy.

The energies of conflict wagered on as Maledream's feet rested upon Angelite's protective shield that rippled against the dark tendrils, but her legs could only take so much and, without warning, her knees buckled in with a crack as both kneecaps popped out of socket. She screamed as she could feel the entities dark shadowy energies pushing her further into the earth, causing a round crater to form the more they held their powerful weapons in a lock, such was the weight of raw power.

'Maledream, hear me now, please listen to me. It's Angelite, you must wake up.'

She stared into his dark eyes while watching the dark tendrils close in around her from his back.

'Please, Maledream, listen to me' she began to cry, the black eyes seemingly showing no emotion to her yields.

'It is no use breeder, this feeble man never cared for you or any one. I have shown him real memories of what he is…of the great deed's he shall bring us.'

'You liar! He is kind and gentle,' she screamed, her arms almost breaking from the pressure now as she kept her muscles as best locked against her wrists and elbows the best she could muster.

'You have no idea, he loves nothing…not even you…he considers you just another breeder.'

It cruelly laughed.

'Lies,' she screamed again, not believing a word it said at all, even though her doubts were there she could not let this thing get the better of her. Another strong wave of emotion further opened up Catalyst's real potential. As the shadow tendrils closed in around her, she wept.

She could hear singing in all the madness of the dark moonlit night, speaking to her as the energies that protected her began to fade as she weakened and struggled under the supernatural being's wrath.

'Trust me, and trust in yourself, Angelite, let me work with you now. I am ready,' the staff spoke humming with every word echoing inside her mind.

Without needing to say a word, and acting on a gut feeling, Angelite gave in for a moment, letting Catalyst control the flows of energy.

Flashes of bright orbs almost with lightning quick speed raced around Angelite and Catalyst brightly, building up into a ball of energy and then releasing itself into Maledream, throwing his body back to the beach in a violent push, crashing violently back into the sand with a resounding thud.

Angelite began to slowly and weakly float off the ground, her hair lifting as if gravity was turned upside down while her robes blew as strong winds took place. A white blinding light enveloped her.

The reeling shadow got up, turning its shadowy tendril like wings around and gazed upon the new form Angelite was taking as Catalyst transformed her being into something quite unexpected.

'What manner of foolishness is this now breeder? Where did this power come from? Impossible!' the entity uttered.

Raising its wings with a shriek, the Swan on top of Catalyst sprang into life, seemingly becoming a living entity as it fluttered its wings and grew in size atop the staff. Its tail feathers grew in length to entwine itself down the neck of the staff. Feathery wings of multi colours sprang from behind Angelite's back, her spirit used as a

weapon, free from the physical laws of her body. An aura of bright white then gold surrounded her as her wings grew six times the length of her body on either side. Her skin shone with a soft light that seemed to purify her body of all ailments, her legs snapping back into place with no pain as the staff fed her unstoppable power now she had the trust and tune needed to release its potential.

'I know your weaknesses now dark one,' she whispered.

Her violet eyes brightly shone as she floated above earth, her spiritual feathered wings flowing with the wind like soft gentle velvet curtains that shimmered in the light of day.

However, Angelite recalled quickly from N'Rutas that Catalyst could only keep this power going for three minutes. She was short on time, and every second counted...could she do it?

'Breeding scum,' it yelled, running towards her and raising the blade maniacally, its shadowy tendrils growing in size to match those of Angelite, ready to strike at her again.

'Illumani' Penetrana Sheol dagadan, Illumani' Penetrana Sheol dagadan.'

Angelite sang with the sound of a thousand voices as she raced towards him, her gentle wings in pursuit as she flew. Light and dark crashed into each other, gigantic bangs of power sounded as staff and sword cracked each other. Angelite seemed to have gained supernatural strength and qualities.

Now free from limited physical bonds, while being one with Catalyst, she made the shadow possessor strain under her power as the light of her power burned Maledream's possessed crippled form. Holding the staff in a parry, she deflected the blows that Maledream's clumsy body flung at her. Elemental sparks of ether danced through the air as the sound metals clashed supernaturally.

Each time she counter attacked after the parry, hitting the shadow of him with great bangs and thuds of pure multicoloured energy square in the chest with finesse, her red hair and robes brightly glowing in the light of day as they flowed within the great winds.

Its dark tendrils caught her off guard for a moment, grabbing her staff with great pain, trying to reach her soul in order to corrupt. It was then that Angelite with a spin of her wrist and a quick lock of weapons came eye to eye with the beast. Angelite's eyes spewed forth ethers of hot bright energy like candle flames, while the possessed Maledream's eyes seeped the very darkness of the void.

Her wings tangled with the shadows, metallic screeching echoed aloud as the weapons waged war upon each other with great resonating energies.

'It does not matter if you destroy me,' it raged.

'More will be coming to claim back this city,' it added.

'We shall see about that,' she calmly replied, locking the staff and sword together with a twist of her arms with a great speed and agility as the beast tried to free itself from her bond.

'We shall meet you three fold,' she said, a thousand voices backing her like a chorus as she sung the rights of exorcism for a third and final time.

'Illumani' Penetrana Sheol dagadan, Illumani' Penetrana Sheol dagadan.'

She roared as her spiritual feathery wings fought the dark tendrils of the shadow being, pulling her free hand back to build up the power Resonance.

'Be gone, beast!' she screamed, opening her fist to reveal her palm.

The Anunaki Blood Adept could see her hands fate lines shining with a powerful light, helplessly watching her slam the energies into Maledream's chest with an echoing thud of power. A rush of air silenced the fall of the Anunaki as her hand blasted the beast into oblivion, littering the air with silvery ether.

The dark shadows that had fought Angelite's own spirit dissipated as the dark spirit of the Blood Adept was knocked back from its core plane of existence. The corrupted armours, especially that of the red-hot gauntlet that Maledream wore shattered into dust, his body stood for a moment from the spiritual blast that passed through his body.

The priestess sighed for a moment as power coursed through her body, the staff Catalyst singing a choir of a thousand voices as it hummed within her hand as she watched Maledream slump gently to the floor. Still in her higher state of being, Angelite stared back towards Silver, to his shattered body. She rested Maledream onto a wing of hers, carrying him as she effortlessly strolled towards the brave animal.

'You saved my life friend, and for that I shall return yours,' she said, softly resting her main hand on Silver's body as she concentrated on reuniting the spirit with body. She healed the broken vessel with brilliant rays of light that emanated from her own spirit and Catalysts power.

Silver's wounds seemed to knit together, his fizzled hair returning to its original state as she performed a resurrection of a life.

'Awaken,' she uttered, before her higher form began to disappear and her spirit began to join her physical prison once more.

Maledream slumped to the earth, his once heavily wounded and burned body now also healing at the speed of which Silver was. From afar, the Packers, Elric and Larkham watched in awe with a few Watchman, could not believe what they had just witnessed.

'She has surpassed her teachers,' Elric said as they all began to move quickly towards Angelite.

'Indeed,' said Larkham.

'Although it was a shame we didn't get here sooner, we will have the chance to ask them our questions later. For now, let's get them back home.'

'Maledream, It's good to have you back,' Neveah thought, rushing towards the three with great speed onto the shifting sand of the beach.

Chapter Eighteen

Grave Matters...

'You won't find a solution by saying there is no problem.'

William Rotsler

Several days within Meridia had passed, news spread quickly throughout the city like a wild fire of rumours that a great battle had taken place. The Port Sector was closed off until further notice by order of the Watchman Guild, who worked closely with the Order of Spirit on the matter. It appeared that Maledream's possessed person took a ride to Meridia on the back of the Behemoth that washed onto the beach the next morning after the fight between him and Angelite took place.

Rumours that powers of old were once again rallying to take out their beloved city was creating much fear amongst the populace who now started to craft even more weapons of various kinds to make a last stand if needed. The Order of Spirit told the populace that there was nothing to fear for wards were being set up to protect against such a scourge against them, quelling some, but not all.

Deep within the Core Sector of Meridia, Larkham and the Packers stood within a small council room discussing issues of importance. They were concerned that wards of protection were far from completed without certain crystals that were needed for such a viable defence. Elric and Eldred were also present and led the council in the decision-making as the group struggled to come to a conclusion. Eldred told of the grave news and encouraged them to think of ways to solve the mess Meridia could be in for.

A small turquoise round room made of marble etched with many ancient writings that seemed to hum gently as if energy was being transferred around the room. One arched door with strange metallic steel signalling the only entrance and exit to this private room where they sat discussing the issues.

'We have told the population that there is no need to worry, but this is the first time in the history of this city that such an act against free will of a person's passage from the port into the inner districts has taken place, and of course this has sparked outrage from everyone. They do not know all of the facts but, for the moment, not even we have a bearing on what is going on,' said Eldred twiddling his hands as he thought deeper on the matter.

Elric replied to everyone:

'Indeed, but as I'm sure you know that we are in a predicament. Your friend Maledream has brought with him a great Relic, which we have left where Maledream dropped it on the beach, everyone is afraid to go near the weapon.'

'Aye,' replied Neveah sternly, his lips uttering a good question.

'If what you say is true about the bastard lizards knowing the whereabouts of this place now, isn't it wise to keep it as a defence? You speak ill of it, like it is an omen.'

Elric frowned with worry, something he did not want to think about, and at first hesitated to reply.

'Indeed,' he said.

'We are unsure of its potential, and that of the user's ability to resist such possessions to indirectly use its power. Through the fragments of the obliterated armour he wore, much like your armour Neveah, it was found to be corrupted. Which part of the armour, we are unsure, do you have any clue?'

Neveah moaned as he thought back to the beach where they found the Watchman's armour.

'Aye, there was something Maledream picked up which I didn't mind him having at the time, it glowed a crimson colour as well, strange letterings on it, not like the strange ones you all have around this place or one your staffs or other such weapons, of course we both didn't think much of it at the time. We don't understand any of it.'

'Of course not,' answered Eldred painfully sarcastic and obnoxious in his reply.

'It was the ancient language of the Anunaki, true, our alphabet looks similar but only because of the alliance the Creators and the Anunaki shared in this ancient city's time. However, there have been many differences since then. You can say it's a more racial trend between both of our races. Only the Nephilim dabble in such language, for they do share Anunaki bloodlines,' Eldred finished with a sigh as if boredom of preaching history had started to set in within him.

Elric merely glanced at Eldred and shook his head as if even he couldn't put up with him half the time.

'It is not Maledream's fault,' said Larkham, his new purple robes shining and shimmering under the lights of the room that pulsated brightly.

'He is a curious young man. It has almost killed him in the past, and there is not a doubt in my mind that there is something special about that young, cheeky man, after all, to survive a possession of an Anunaki and manage to survive and breathe again is not a feat anyone can accomplish without great spirit...a strong spirit.'

The Packers looked in amazement as the old man defended Maledream sternly.

'Aye, I second that,' said Neveah, slapping the marble table with his palms in quick sessions like a drum before listening again to Larkham.

'Who knows what Maledream's spirit had to endure while his vessel, his vehicle was abused for more sinister purposes. Angelite, I believe, is the key to his success, and she has attended to his bedside since she fought for his soul and body. She is attracted to his spirit.'

Larkham sipped some water before uttering what some would convey as nonsense in the room.

'They are soul mates,' he said.

Neveah bellowed in laughter:

'That little squirt? It wasn't long ago that I was mocking him for not sticking it in her yet...now that's connection.'

Larkham winked at Neveah smiling back and chuckled in turn. Elric smiled and in fact so did everyone else but Eldred was stewed at the old man's comment.

'I cannot believe we are wasting time talking about soul mates. We have more depressing and important matters to talk about,' Eldred reminded everyone.

'My people are in grave danger because of you peo...' he began, but was cut short by Larkham.

'Choose your words carefully, Eldred. There are a few in here that will not take kindly to your next words,' he said firmly.

Eldred was silent, slinking back into his chair and avoiding eye contact, letting out a brief sigh.

'Aye, fine have it your way, we'll talk about important things,' replied Neveah cracking his knuckles, already having a gut feeling that Eldred fancied Angelite in some way by the way he always seemed to act whenever Maledream and Angelite were spoken of in the same sentence.

'Eldred is right,' soundly replied Elric sticking to a neutral stance.

'The Anunaki now know where we are and this is why we must think of a way to protect our fair city. I am all for a joke, however we must get down to some ideas and trade knowledge on what we know and what we can do about our situation.'

The group chatted for hours over ideas, coffee, tea, and pipe weed that were in abundance as the Pack, Larkham, Elric and Eldred piled on theories coming to some conclusions but not many. The old Tribal leader focused on his thoughts, passed on the pungent smelling tobacco and caffeine that saturated the air around him as he silently asked the spirits for a sign.

All he could see within his mind were crystals in the shape of different human-sized skulls. He pondered over it for many hours thinking it was nothing terribly important over the confusion of the arguments that were bound back and forth but remained patient throughout, knowing in some way they were a clue, whispers speaking to his ears. It was by chance that Elric mentioned these objects in conversation about the museum.

'There are legends of these crystal skulls that were said to have the power to save the world back before the Dark Age arrived, old prophecies that were not fulfilled in time they say. Again we think it's another myth as the skull we possess just seems dead, however our researchers do note that it was not made by human hands, its craftsmanship is elite to say the least, possibly a Creator artefact.'

Larkham responded casually to Elric and in a light tone:

'Indeed, but most of you are young fools. You have not yet learnt to stay in touch with the sound of spirits. It was fulfilled this prophecy, but not as imagined,' Larkham's voice was getting lower and lower as he went on in a trance staring at the clear crystal water within his glass as he hunched over the table.

'They want to be re-united, these Skulls of Meridia, or rather Skulls of...Atlantis?' Eldred and Elric were shocked to hear Larkham utter the last word for it had not been spoken of in a long time.

'Stop it now, old man, don't you **dare** speak that word again inside this city,' ordered Eldred loudly, standing on his feet and placing his hands on the table with a slam. Neveah got up in turn along with Crazy John and Boris, squaring off against Eldred.

'Aye, carry on Larkham, Atlantis? I take it Meridia was once this Atlantis? Why re-name it?' asked Neveah, his one good eye staring angrily at the pompous man.

Elric got up, trying to calm the erupting conflict:

'Eldred, sit down, you lot sit as well...it has been a few hours since we have been cooped up in this room so I would advise we all just take a breather. I will tell you that we re-named the city because it isn't the same place it once was. In the past it was used for war by the Creators, Humans, Nephilim and the Anunaki.'

As they listened, the pack settled down, smiling at each other in contentment.

'We decided upon the name Meridia because it is derived from the word meridian or Ley lines of the energy flows of the planet, of Mother Earth. That is how the new name was inspired. It is now the centre focus, the main point, from which the cosmic energies flood into our planet. These energies are the magic of Resonance, the power and essence of the spells we breathe. The former name of this place is well known, but we would rather not call it the same place...it has changed much like anything else. Hence why also some choose to call this city Sanctuary instead of Meridia, as some people say that name is also an ill omen, although only a few think so. This city has many names and for a good reason. We are all different peoples living here, and we all share it. Nevertheless, we all in this city agreed not to speak of the word just mentioned. You can read about it, you're free to, that is after all first decree, but it is said to bring bad omen to those that mention it too often or very loosely.'

That was all Elric thought they needed to know for now. He sighed, wiping sweat from his forehead in the hot room.

The Packers were satisfied with the answer they had received, and instead continued smoking or drinking their hot tea or coffee as whispers were abound.

Larkham felt the subject of the skulls needed to be a primary subject, so he continued to annoy Eldred with much delight, his cheeky old wrinkles quivering with mischief as he carried on throughout the rest of the afternoon.

'I have a feeling that if we can find all these skulls, then maybe...just maybe we can fulfil an old prophecy properly. I have a feeling the spirits wish this.'

'So then, everyone, what is our best choice of action? Does anyone know of any skulls that exist outside of Meridia?' asked Elric to the pack.

'Now that you mention it...' said Boris.

'Me and Crazy John did a little information trading, at the time I thought it was totally useless if you ask me, a load of crap for some good supplies which I traded here and there with my man. We heard of the most powerful Pack Leader in the city that had such a skull. Rumours were passing round that gave him abilities no witch or mortal could possess, sorry I did not bring this up sooner, this was around five cycles of winter ago. I swear there is something else we have heard recently about them but I can't quite think of it.'

'Aye, it's okay. You ain't proposing on sending us back to the city?' asked Neveah.

'What? We've only just got here...' said Crazy John.

Eldred replied to the idea joyously:

'It would be a great proposal! The best I have heard all evening. Something supports your claims about a skull Boris. Angelite found journals that I have deciphered easily from the old languages, and the author of one of the journals mentions a friend owning such an object, before the Dark Age arrived. It is possible that some brute has such an object of old.'

Eldred clasped his hands, resting them under his chin with a patronising smile.

Elric cut in:

'Well, would you mind going then if that's the case, if Eldred and Boris are correct, what do you think, Neveah?'

Silence gripped the table, as all eyes turned to Neveah for a final decision as he smoked his pipe weed before giving an answer.

He leaned back on his chair, placing his feet on the table and crossing them relaxingly. The Council leaned in their seats further and further expecting him to say anything, any second. He moved his arms, the table almost gasped as he casually put his hands behind his head, further relaxing himself, staring at the ceiling.

Finally, he spoke after the long silence...

'Like fuck we're going.'

'What!?' replied Eldred, almost in a whimper, a nervous chuckle erupting around the table.

'You made us wait for that long? With a foul tongue also?' Eldred added, tiring of the group of Packers that used such words in their everyday vocabulary.

'Aye,' Neveah replied, eyeing up the cocky, posing magician.

'I lost basically my whole gang. The Packers you see here, Crazy John and Boris, are all that is left. It's a month's travel time, maybe more depending if some of us live or not so what I'm trying to say is, what's in it for us, you pompous twat?'

Elric smiled along with Larkham as Eldred stewed at the comment, turning his head away from the table. Neveah eyed him up with his only eye, knowing Eldred would not dare touch him if he tried.

'Well,' Elric said,

'You will be thought of as heroes. There is not much I can possibly offer you, except it would be a good deed to yourself and everyone else you know. If this wondrous city is attacked many millions will perish, women, children, destroying everything we have strived to

rebuild. Please help us for humanity's very existence.'

'Aye, I guess...'

'We will do whatever you want,' offered Elric.

'Anything?' asked Neveah.

'Anything,' replied Elric.

'Well...I'm not too sure...' the Pack leader jested.

'That means we can kill lizards?' he asked further.

'Well, I guess if any cross your path,' Elric replied.

'What about armour for my Pack? New weapons? This martial arts combat stuff...you can teach us all there is to know?'

'You can have it...all of it and more,' replied Elric with a smile.

'I'm going wherever Neveah will, and so will John,' Boris replied happily, Crazy John gave the entire table dirty looks.

'I'm sure we have more than a few "forbidden" objects you can take with you. We can also teach you all the magic of Resonance if needed? It would be formidable artillery,' Elric said.

The pack fell silent after hearing this.

'Sorry to say this but no,' replied Neveah.

'Everything except that stuff...we Packers are kind of well, we don't like it at all. We don't mind Angelite blasting things, but that's as far as we would venture. Just get us some hard ass weapons and we will do the dirty work for you.'

'Fair enough,' said Elric.

'Then it is settled,' said Larkham, leaning forward on the table rubbing his now clean, long, black beard.

'Give them training for a month, time to relax and study. Meditate the ways a little more. And then they can set off, and if Angelite and Maledream are up for it, perhaps they will join you.'

'Aye old man it sounds good to me, besides me and the pack love this place, but it ain't quite the same as our old home. So going back there and taking down the biggest boss in all the ruined city would be a pleasure. I have an old score to settle with him,' Neveah sinisterly remarked in a low tone.

'I was unaware you had an old score with him,' said Crazy John, the only one who dared speak up.

'Aye, for a woman I lost to his hands many cycles ago.'

All around the table were astonished, especially Eldred.

'Why a woman would choose you for a mate I have no idea', he sensibly thought to himself, not letting his venomous tongue slip.

'I wondered why you didn't want a woman,' said Boris sweetly.

'Aye, love eh?' Neveah replied his one good eye filled with sorrow.

It was not known for Neveah to shed a tear but he was close, giving his blind eye covered by his eye patch a good scratch. The eye he had lost could have had even deeper meanings than it once did.

'Now we ain't promising anything,' he continued.

'If we find these skulls, we will be as quick as we can to return...how many are there? How many skulls should we be looking for?' he asked.

'Good question,' said Elric.

'Legends say thirteen such skulls existed, but apart from that and what I mentioned slightly earlier about them, that's all I can say about them. We don't have much knowledge on them.'

'It's a start. Can we take the one you mentioned for reference? Angelite could probably look after it?' Boris asked.

'Agreed,' Elric said, nodding his head frantically in agreement with Neveah.

'It's been a long afternoon,' said Eldred.

'I have more pressing matters to attend to, and I must address the rest of the different Guilds on the matter. It's a long shot but it's our only one protection from all out defensive war that will more than likely kill us all.'

With that, Eldred left the room in a rush, pushing the seemingly heavy doors with ease as his rich threaded robes arrogantly flowed through the air with his stride.

'What a damn shame, he had to leave us...why hasn't any one chucked his ass into the ocean? You want me to save Meridia from the likes of him as well, Elric?' Neveah said laughing.

'Well naturally we have been waiting for a hero such as yourself Neveah,' Elric returned the jest with a chuckle.

'Right gang, let's get some rest, and start getting ready for our training tomorrow to make us into better killers!' announced the Pack leader.

Elric smiled and thanked the spirits for a minor chance of salvation against the oncoming darkness that was sure to pounce upon the last strand of human civilisation that existed upon the face of the earth, in a great scourge upon the ancestors of the Creators.

Larkham joined Elric to chat more as they left the room while the pack decided to go and tell Angelite the news, or rather Neveah himself while the three remaining members of the pack travelled to the Goblins Tap for a night out.

Angelite stroked Maledream's face softly, staring at him with a smile as he lay in bed silently snoring. His chest rose and fell slowly, as he continued to heal deep in his mind.

She chose not to adorn robes but instead wore a long black skirt, with many fancy symbols that appealed to her stitched up and around it, not least the new tights that kept her legs warm. Her top was a frilly pink shirt made of fine velvet that she could feel caressing her skin as it moved slightly in the soft wind that crept through the window of their apartment within the Social Sector. Catalyst was not far from her reach as she slept next to Maledream every night hoping that by chance he might wake up.

The priestess lost count of the tireless hours she had tried healing him with her curing magic but it seemed to have no effect. Larkham had suggested that Maledream would probably take a few days to recover but it did not stop Angelite worrying about him.

She recounted the battle that had almost killed her and Silver if it were not for Catalyst taking control of her focus, turning her into some kind of being that prevented the possessed Maledream from entering the city. Now Catalyst leant against the bedpost next to Maledream as he lay in the oaken room. Flowers were scattered everywhere from Angelite's homemaking skills, the room was bright thanks to Angelite's womanly touch.

She kept stroking him, the thought of him waking up gradually starting to fade within her.

'At least he is back, and safe,' she thought.

Getting up off the bed, she walked calmly across the room to the open window feeling the cool autumn ocean breeze pass her welcomingly. The smells of incense were also carried upon the breeze adding further to the pleasant aroma of the room making it feel a comfortable place to relax in.

Sparse clouds traversed the skies slower than snails as her green eyes gazed on them, their silver linings shining brightly from the afternoon sun. Her eyes looked down into the streets below and she saw that Neveah was approaching her apartment room with speed.

She looked back towards Maledream, his tired form still sleeping. From time to time, he would have nightmares or worse as he wriggled in his sleep, sometimes muttering strange words of the Anunaki or something else other than his own as he sweated a lot.

All she could do was to keep a wet flannel over his forehead when that happened. Sure enough, Neveah knocked on the oaken door of the bedroom. Angelite beckoned him to enter softly, her voice seemingly void of hope.

Creaking open the door, Neveah smiled at her not saying a word, shutting the door quietly, and trying not to be loud. It was hard to imagine that Neveah could be anything but loud.

'No use yet, sweet?' he asked, his leather patched clothes all washed and polished since Angelite had last seen him.

'No,' she replied hesitatingly.

'Sorry I did not come to the meeting, but I'd rather look after Maledream.'

'Aye, that is understandable. Not much has happened except that within the next full moon, we, or rather my pack, will be heading out back to our ruined home city. I was hoping that you might join us.'

Angelite's eyebrow raised as the soft wind caressed her cheeks as she sat on the window ledge wondering about Neveah's offer.

'Excuse me?' she asked.

'What? Why? Why would you want to go back?'

'Aye, the Anunaki now know that this city is being rebuilt and exists once more or something, so the council came to the decision to send us back to look for a chance to save this city. We have to find these Skulls of Meridia.'

'I see,' she answered.

'What of Maledream?'

'Well, if he awakens then he will be more than welcome to come back with us. I don't think he knows you have brought Larkham and his fellow Tribals here either so that will be a great shock for him when he wakes up.'

Neveah smiled, hope seemed endless in his one eye and that lightened her heart a little

'But,' he continued:

'We will be training in this "martial arts" that they have here to make us into better fighters. We only have a full moon to do this in, and by then we will stand a better chance. The dark nights will help us travel more safely.'

'Not to mention it will be freezing,' she said with a smile, her head turning away from Neveah as she watched the sun beam its warm rays onto the city, well aware Winter solstice was fast approaching.

'Aye and that, although I would like you to learn some close combat yourself Angelite, as we have had some close calls. I fear that if that ever happens and we will not be with you then it would be easier for you to defend yourself. Remember that time back in the city when some of my Packers attacked you, well these martial arts could have helped you.'

'Yes.' Her eyes widened, her anger rising as she remembered that night horribly well, the terror of that evening was not easily forgotten. Neveah's idea was a good plan for her to undertake.

'I will Neveah, worry not. How will we travel back to the old

city? And why are these skulls of Meridia so important?'

'Aye, well um, we didn't talk about how we would get back there, but I'm sure Elric has a way. He went off with Larkham to talk more privately about something. Also, something I have to ask you before I talk more about these skulls, have you seen Silver?'

'I did this morning,' she answered.

'He hasn't been the same since he was struck down by Maledream but I think his spirit is still healing. He may be in the Social Sector resting in a park.'

'Good,' he replied.

'I think he misses the woods where he came from to be perfectly honest. He might even be missing N'Rutas. I will have to find him and tell him the news. As I was saying though, Eldred found your journals or something when you went to the city, and it supported what Boris said about a crystal skull existing back in the city. There are thirteen skulls like this and apparently we have to try and fulfil an old prophecy from what Larkham was talking about...these skulls are the very key to surviving.'

'I see,' she said, staring back at Neveah as her ears flinched slightly from the news.

'He was very quick to read my notes, but this time it is a good thing that he did, as I struggled to read the old language. Then I guess we don't have much choice, the Anunaki surely know that we are here. After all I banished the Anunaki that possessed Maledream, I think it would be wise to assume it slithered back to its masters like the snake that it is.'

'Aye, we only witnessed the last moments of the fight you had with it and, by the spirits, you turned into something more unnatural than the spells you cast yourself!'

Angelite smiled.

'It was the first time I've experienced limitless power like that, but I really should thank N'Rutas when I meet her next time. It was Catalyst that helped transform me into that higher being.'

'Aye,' Neveah replied, reaching for his tobacco and pipe out of his chest pocket as he walked closer to Maledream wondering when he would wake up.

'Poor bugger,' he said with a sigh.

'We believe that some of the armour he wore from the beach was tampered with from what I understand and that's how the Anunaki managed to possess him.'

'I thought as much,' replied Angelite.

She walked slowly and casually towards the bed sitting down on a chair next to Maledream.

'His armour was glowing like the blade was, in a crimson colour, but Maledream only had that once when he was angry. That happened back in the city when he stopped the Packers from...well you know...it glowed with his anger, but on the beach, it was not a natural anger. I felt something was manipulating him. And it seemed to work very well.'

'What do you mean?' he asked, his match striking the box as he puffed away with his pipe. He had sat down on a chair opposite to Angelite.

'Well, I am guessing that they wanted to use Maledream as a weapon, as he had the sword on him which was crafted by our great ancestors thousands upon thousands of millennia ago. I presume they wanted to destroy Meridia with him, but to no avail. Now, as we think, they will use force against us.'

Angelite paused, a brain wave struck her mind so fast that she gasped.

'Wait!' she shouted excitedly.

'N'Rutas told us about those skulls. Do you remember!?'

Neveah dropped his pipe.

'You're right,' he said loudly, remembering it all like a flashback.

'That old bat went on for so long I think we forgot totally. Great Spirit,' he added.

'Go and tell Elric, Larkham and Eldred. Tell them what she told us and taught us. It will be of great significance to them and us!' she said, speaking quickly in her excitement that she had remembered some information that could be so crucial.

'Aye, I'll be back soon,' Neveah replied, his large form getting off the chair, picking up his smoking, smouldering pipe off the floor before legging it outside the room quickly.

'*Thank you, N'Rutas,*' Angelite thought deeply, staring at Catalyst, the staff seemingly humming into her ears again softly.

Maledream began to stir and writhe within his slumber as Catalyst started to sing.

Angelite watched closely, clasping her hands on his.

Torment racked his mind, guilt, punishment, being a slavering puppet to his master as he watched the shadows of the Anunaki in his dreams. Faint lights could be seen now and then in the darkness that fell on him since he had last felt Angelite's spirit touched through to him. Choir singing could be heard barely above the rasping dark whispers as he tried breathing against the pressure around his neck.

No voice could escape from his vocal chords as he watched crimson eyes blink at him from different angles and never in the same place within his field of vision. Strange ethereal writings like neon lights would rise and fade in front of him, his spirit feeling a gruelling cold touch every time that somehow made his spine shudder dead cold.

Headaches rocked his sick head occasionally as he wondered how he would break free. All he could feel was fear and anger, images of his friends leaving him alone when he went down with the Behemoth creature, it was then that his vision darkened and that his soul was imprisoned.

A huge impact it had on his psyche it seemed, as he battled still for his sanity. He struggled against the darkness, trying to awake from a nightmare from which he had no control. It was then that he witnessed appearing in front of him out of the gloom of this darkened space, a skull. Entirely made of bone, and of human origin it looked at him, its surface glowing faintly as it came to him from the darkness, crawling it seemed, silently.

Feelings of more fear were inspired within him as he struggled within his mind, its hollow eye sockets piercing his mind slowly and surely as it just floated towards him, its jaw dropping and rising occasionally. Guilt from his life surfaced, like it was being ripped from his soul to be shown in images, embarrassing him, making him feel small, insignificant, and insecure.

It closed in, growing larger and larger opening its jaw. Human teeth growing into fangs, a laugh tore his mind feeling it would split any moment from this strange surreal torment. It grew in size opening its mouth, before it placed its jaws around Maledream. For a moment, it felt as if it was a horrible death, but then, for a split moment it lifted.

He found that he was in a field, looking around in wonder as the headache lifted from him, his insecurities, and guilt fading from his emotions. Still confused, he looked around, and it was indeed a strange world this skull had swallowed him into.

It seemed to be daytime, save for a lilac aura surrounding everything. Tree's seemed to disappear and reappear, and some seemed to be buried upside down, the roots floating on ends into the air.

The faded grass he stood on constantly grew in and out the ground like a reverse forward motion. Maledream did not know where to stand, on what he then realised were his own ethereal feet. Dizziness took him after he peered up at the ozone layer, birds flying forward but upside down and some flying backwards, their songs in a strange reverse to what they should be.

It was then that he tried to retch, but he could not. He watched the moon circulating the earth every three seconds above him, going through the monthly cycle of crescent moon to full moon, his thoughts boggled.

'*A dream,*' he thought.

'*It's all a dream, it has to be.*'

The moon seemed to hypnotise him as his dreary eyes watched the moon passing over his pupils again, again, and again.

'I'm afraid not,' came an old soft voice that seemed vaguely familiar behind him, he sat upwards off his knees.

'This place is wonderful isn't it? You are an unfortunate being to have been dragged here. Luckily, for you I have friends here who keep me informed. You are here as your spirit Maledream. If you can guess who I am, you may have found your way home.'

Maledream wondered as the moon passed repeatedly around his pupils, an answer trying to escape his lips.

'*N'Rutas?*' he thought without expecting his thoughts to be read, as he did not know what to do.

'Correct,' she answered, turning his head around to see something he did not expect.

In her Anunaki form, her spirit totally ethereal and free from the weathered effects of physical time, her scales glistened gold's and silver's.

Robes she wore were difficult to see, but they looked fantastically rich in detail with runes that danced off the seams as if they were attached but not all at the same moment.

A staff she wielded seemed displaced and backwards, confusing him immensely as its form continually shifted into different letters of her Nephilim alphabet on both ends of the rod.

Glistening white eyes glowed from her skull, and were not big or black unlike the true Anunaki he had experienced.

Seeing her apparition seemed to calm him down, as if her spirit was similar to Angelite's own healing touch.

'Do not be alarmed however as you know my intentions are good ones. It was hard work dragging you out from the elsewhere referred to Heavens between Heavens where you were almost trapped for eternity. I could not idly watch a soul suffer torment at the hands of those unborn or otherwise souls of shadow. I could not restore you to your body in that harder dimension without first freeing your soul from a negative dimension. It would surely have had dire consequences on your health, my poor child.'

Maledream looked on, he could not grasp entirely what she was talking about, save for that time on the Battle Hammer, the images of his memories flickering in front of his eyes. She continued, her soul walking towards him as she continued to talk.

'You are here in what is called the fourth dimension. You could say that this is where the powers of the Resonance manifest into your world. It is free from space, the material...the constant...save for the spirit. This is not heaven, but rather Earth's reflection of the mirror of itself. A contradiction to what you or your physics say how the world works back in your harder dimension that you call home. Since the second Dark Age, humanity is now aware of its great gifts, my dear Maledream. Use the strength you have within you to use the infinite power offered by this dimension. This plane is the bridge to the higher planes, but you will not visit there yet until your body is totally free of will and you are ready to venture further than this...and do not worry when you die, it will not feel like this again. You are here experiencing these feelings now because you still have a vessel to go back to, as you my young Maledream, still have a soul link. It is a weak one I do admit, but existing in this place when you still have a body to thrive in is actually only achieved with Great Spirit.'

Maledream's eyes shifted. He began to realise he was connecting with something higher than what he was used too. Ideas began to swim in his head wondering if he was like this before he was born.

'I will now reconnect your soul properly friend. You have someone who cares greatly about you still waiting on the other side of this place...this plane of existence,' she said, kneeling down a few feet away in front of Maledream. A question struck into Maledream's mind.

'So does that mean you and even Angelite have limitless power connecting here? If this is everyone, is this infinite energy?'

She smiled at Maledream with his question, moved nearer, and he could see her scaly, pale skin close up.

'Yes it is infinite energy, although Angelite does tire her physical form out a lot in doing this process, but she will get stronger. I was like her once in my "younger" days. This dimension feeds your spirit and physical forms with the energies of the universe, but this dimension is also responsible for your dreams Maledream. It is here where creation takes place within one's mind. You could say that this was once the plane where the Creators first came before they ventured even further to the denser dimension. Of course they do not reside here now or ever will again.'

A vast consciousness seemed to awaken within him, realisation teaching him a thing or two.

Before he could ask another question, N'Rutas changed her mood and seemed to be in a hurry.

'It has been nice talking Maledream, but something is coming, breaking the universal rule of free will. I will deal with this personally. For now I shall reconnect you, and do not worry this will not hurt one bit child.'

Her form shifted for a moment, a look of concern on her face.

'They have found my anchor, we must be quick.'

The world around Maledream began to shift as N'Rutas raised her ethereal hand towards the sky while closing her eyes before uttering incantations.

'Larszarish Zandrishth Zuthell'el Carntanooria Zandalaar Naria'lith.'

As she sang, Maledream could see the land and sky shifted and rippled under her loud voice. Birds that were flying upside down began to shift like an ocean, turning up the right way as Maledream's soul began to feel the weight of denseness grapple his soul. Feelings of surrealism began to lift as his spiritual Chakras lit up around his body, his soul glowing from all the colours.

He stared at N'Rutas, finding the strength within himself to rise up to his feet. She smiled at him, questions burned inside of him yet it seemed maybe another moment to meet this strange being would come around again for him to ask. Gaping underneath him, he peered into a hole that began to open in between him and N'Rutas, staring at his tired physical form.

He was thinking of maybe not going back, that broken, skinny and useless body of his. Yet he stared at Angelite, her sweet hands wiping his puke from his mouth as she tended to him. Nothing he could see in that hole shifted, yet everything else around him kept shifting and dancing, the two comparisons between the dimensions fascinated him even more.

N'Rutas' staff twisted madly into a different letter each time as the energy fluxed, the runes on her staff jumping off and floating around them both as they glowed multi neon colours that acted as if they had a mind of their own.

'You must go, Maledream' she calmly uttered, yet seemingly anxious to go somewhere. He nodded at her and then took one last look around him in the wondrous place he was, falling into the hole.

'*Thank you for everything,*' he thought.

He could see a smile appearing on N'Rutas' lips as he disappeared from the strange dimension.

Chapter Nineteen

Back from Dreams to Reality...

'Keep your dreams alive. Understand to achieve anything requires faith and belief in yourself, vision, hard work, determination, and dedication. Remember all things are possible for those who believe.'

Gail Devers

'You're awake!' Angelite shouted with joy as she watched Maledream jump upwards with a big jerk. She hugged him tightly as he coughed and spluttered taking in a big breath of air as his soul slammed back into his being.

For several moments, he could once again feel his heartbeat, every pulse within him, and the constraints of his muscles as he attuned with his body. It felt good to be back.

'Angelite, I've missed you,' he whispered, gaining his voice back.

'And everyone else,' he added with a sigh of relief.

'Thank the spirits, I was afraid you'd never wake up. We were all so worried, Maledream. Please don't do it again,' she said, her tone breaking into a cry.

Maledream hushed her as she hugged his aching ribs tighter, almost squeezing the air out of his lungs, air he badly needed! She looked up at him, her lush deep green eyes blurry and filled with tears as she smiled with happiness at him.

'I promise,' he said with a struggle, his voice croaky.

'Here have some water, sweetie,' she insisted, handing him a glass.

She felt deliriously happy. He drank down the pint of water in within moments. She instantly got him another one and then another glass before he insisted he was okay as she tried forcing it down his throat.

'I'm all right, woman!' he said loudly, giving her a cheeky smile.

'I'm just looking after you! Drink!' she would not take no for an answer as he drank down the last gulp from the glass.

He took a moment to observe the room as Angelite told him to lie still while she got him something proper to dress in. He could feel energy, as if he were holding the sword.

'I feel something inside you has opened up Maledream,' Angelite said, looking carefully through the wardrobes that stored various assortments of rich looking clothes.

'If only I could tell you the half of it,' he replied with a groan, rubbing his sore eyes that had not been open for a long while.

'It was very strange...a very strange dream. N'Rutas was in it, and among other things from what I learned it was not a dream but something else. N'Rutas saved me from the Heaven between Heavens.'

Angelite's jaw dropped before slowly turning around with the clothes in her arms.

'Are you sure, Maledream?' she replied, a serious look on her face, as if the jaw dropping was not enough.

'I am certain but I will tell you and everyone else later. Are we going to meet up with them?' he asked.

'Of course,' she said.

'Let's get you dressed. I cannot wait until you tell me!' Her face lit up with excitement.

'N'Rutas in your dreams...or rather, I guess spirit? I am dying to hear more about this, Maledream!' She hastily chucked Maledream his clothes that had been washed, the armour was polished to the highest of quality, and there were new mail links covering vital areas.

It all looked upgraded even his old torn and patched coat had been fixed with the matching material instead of being roughly sewn.

'Wow,' he said looking at his stuff in top quality condition.

'Where did you get this from?'

'Well we're in Meridia, Maledream if you hadn't guessed.'

His eyes squinted, his eyebrow raised at this news.

'Never mind you will learn more in the next month before we set off from here again. A lot has happened, Maledream, there is so much to tell since you were away and since you were sleeping.'

'I'm sure it has' he replied, thinking back to how he saw the boat leaving before he blacked out.

Angelite caught his deepening sadness and so took her place by his bedside sitting next to him on the mattress placing her fingers on his lips and raising them to a smile.

'Maledream, you were brave and courageous. You are so strong so please do not feel stupid or inferior. I think you're amazing.'

Then she surprised Maledream by softly kissing him on the lips, her kiss locking them together as he closed his eyes, barely able to have the time to ask any questions he had that quickly disappeared from his skull. It felt like an age as she kept her soft lips moving against his as they both enjoyed the heart racing feeling as flirtatious adrenaline flowed through both of their veins.

'You should get dressed,' she whispered breaking the long kiss.

Her cheeks had a slight blush, her eyes shone and there was a faint smile rising outwards and upwards towards her cheeks, her light soft freckles making her look even more cute.

'You're right,' he said, embarrassment taking over Maledream's feelings as he too blushed. For a moment, Angelite stopped him thinking of his troubles and for that, he was glad.

'I'll wait outside for you to get dressed, and then we must go and meet up with the others. I bet they are dying to see you!' she said, excitedly clasping her hands as she jumped to her feet off the oaken bed. Without saying a word, she left, closing the door softly.

Maledream relaxed for a moment to collect his thoughts. His body felt very exhausted yet he was fully awake and hopeful of events yet to come.

Excitement rose in him as feelings of exploration of something new, an experience set within his mind. After a while, he got out of bed, his leg muscles strained while his back and neck creaked unhealthily as his ligaments stretched out with his arms.

Shaking it off with a satisfying grunt, he gradually put on his old, cleaned clothes and armour, his coat he carried behind his right shoulder. Noticing a mirror he looked into it, his skin was slightly pale as he stared at his scrawny form with a smirk, even his hair was un-knotted and brushed, slightly cut around the front while a band kept his long black coarse hair in a ponytail.

'Never knew I could look this good,' he chuckled to himself, before eyeing up the door through which Angelite had exited.

'Better get going,' he said. He opened the door to see Angelite expectedly waiting for him.

'Feel any better in all that?' she asked smiling.

'I do thanks,' he bluntly replied, yet he smiled, he felt it was a pleasure and an honour to have met her.

'Follow me,' she said.

Maledream nodded before following her down the dark oaken stairs that had strange runic symbols and crystals etched into it.

Candles flickered and burned as the night scene cut in.

Meanwhile Neveah met up with his Packers, while also catching Larkham and Elric on the way to the same location, and so they decided to all have a drink to talk over the matters at hand concerning the Skulls of Meridia.

The pub was quieter than it had been during the Packers' first visit. Talk and rumours were on every patron's lips. People were discussing first the arrival of outlandish Packers, and then the Tribals and the strange event, on the same night, of a shadow being that had rocked the night at the Port Sector leading to a battle between Angelite and that strange Tribal known as Maledream.

Low lighting lit the scene, and only the smoke of pipes filled the air. Tensions were high while some musicians still played trying to take people's minds off the bad omens.

'Well,' said Elric, pondering over the information given to Neveah and the rest from N'Rutas.

'It seems that we should pay heed to her wisdom. Maybe she told you this by accident, maybe not, but if what she says is true, then...you will have a long journey ahead of you. We estimate that the Anunaki will not attack during the Winter Equinox period, as any soldiers they have will not take a liking to the freezing elements. Nor can they withstand such resonant magic users who can control such elements as ice and snow. No, they will attack mid time next cycle. Nevertheless, we shall stay on guard around the city walls and build our defences. It was naive of us to think that we would be very safe living here.'

'It was folly,' said Larkham rubbing his hands together, his elbows on the table separating the conversation with the Packers as he drew Elric's attention for a private natter.

'Through oral traditions I have taught my Tribals about the beings that live under the Earth or even, for that matter, live within the deep ocean.'

'Indeed, my friend Larkham, I guess we have had a lot of arrogance running through the city. It is because we have retained so much technology and knowledge from those who first discovered this ancient place that arose from the ocean itself. As the generations passed, we discovered so much that we believed ourselves to be advancing fast, but it seems we are not fast enough,' Elric replied.

'Sorry to sound patronising, young man,' Larkham continued:

'But it is the true history of what happened that will save us, not technology. Remember that the Mother Earth crushed us once and could do so again, in whatever way she chooses, whether it by cataclysms or simply through some creature that exists here also. You must not place your faith in Dark Technology like our fated ancestors

285

did. Only wars and destruction can follow suit. It almost killed Maledream,' Larkham sighed, taking in a swig of water.

'This technology will more than likely save us this time, now that we have you here to help guide us, Larkham,' Elric replied with a smile.

Larkham choked, almost spitting out his drink.

'Boy, I am a Spiritualist, not a true leader. I just look after those that wish to follow by my example. There are many fine people here in Meridia that can take my place. I am getting old...too old now. Tired is the word for it. You need someone young, someone who has the potential, and someone who knows how to fight for the spirit of the people. That I do not have.'

Larkham shiftily eyed Neveah who smoked his pipe and drank his beer while chatting nonsense to Crazy John and Boris, paying little attention to Larkham's and Elric's private conversation on the other side of the table.

Elric looked on in the old man's directions pondering over his words for a moment to try to scale his true meaning. He whispered his reply:

'You do not give yourself credit my old friend...and you do not mean Neveah? For sure?'

Larkham laughed staring back into Elric's eyes, a wrinkly grin rising from his mouth.

'Yes, he has a spirit of a true leader. He would be a good choice, but he has a long path to tread before he takes up such ideas or choices. Maybe, just maybe, he is the one, my young Elric.'

'Hmm, perhaps, I've not seen it quite in him, maybe I have joked to him about it a couple of days ago, but not anything serious. Right, I think we need to make a summary.'

Elric got to his feet, asking for the attention of others to speak of the quest but, without warning, Neveah jumped onto the table almost as swiftly as a monkey, leaping past Elric to meet some newcomers into the pub.

'Maledream, you little shit!' he bellowed getting his arm around poor Maledream's aching neck while pressing his knuckles into his to rough up his scalp.

'All right, all right!' he yelled.

'Get off me you big ass.'

'Aye, have it your way! Take a seat you two.'

He let go of Maledream slapping him on the back hard, almost causing him to throw up from the impact.

Angelite smiled and stared at the smiling table, while others in the pub grew quiet.

Whispers again being heard as heads turned to look towards them and then looking away again. A feeling of being unwelcome set in, but it was something Maledream ignored trying not to feel insecure.

How could he be when friends surrounded him? It was then that his gaze rested on Larkham.

'Old man!' he said aloud.

'Angelite said a surprise but this I did not expect!'

'You had better believe it boy,' he said, staring at Maledream's posh looking clean armour and clothes that were meshed together.

In return Maledream eyed up Larkham's new attire with a head shaking grin.

'But you still need a good ear clipping, you little bastard,' Larkham said, chuckling over times long ago.

'It's been too long,' replied Maledream, walking over to the old man, his adopted father and, for the first time in his life, shook his hand to Larkham's surprise.

'How do you like it here?' asked Elric.

'I've had a strange month...and it only gets more surprising.'

'Well met, Maledream. I am Elric,' he grinned.

'Well met yourself,' answered Maledream.

He could not help but smile and think of getting a bit of smoke himself as he stared at the Packers lit pipes.

'Well, sit down next to everyone here and I'll go and fetch you an alcoholic beverage,' said Elric.

'Thanks a lot. I need it, it'll taste good knowing it isn't piss like back in the old city,' Maledream replied, sitting on a chair next to Neveah and Angelite to face everyone else as they began to catch up over smiles and stories.

Maledream's gaze was full of wonder. While walking through the night time streets of Meridia, his soul had made him feel compelled to love every inch of the place they had struggled and fought to reach.

Now he relaxed with his drink, enjoying the laughter already floating over the table as excitement from Maledream getting to Meridia and waking up finally removed everyone's dampened mood that had surrounded the past couple of weeks.

Angelite was in the best of moods, being ever so flirtatious with Maledream as they all talked and relaxed before Elric had to drag the evening back to business.

'Now before Neveah leapt over my head,' Elric said jokingly, getting a smile or laugh from group.

'I was about to break some news. First I must welcome Maledream and I am glad he has made it to our wondrous city.'

Everyone cheered.

'However, I digress, we the people of Meridia need all of your help, including you Maledream, against the Anunaki threat that we fear will soon arrive on our shores to attack us.'

Maledream did not know what to make of this but eyed Elric carefully, slightly nodding with curved eyebrows awaiting more from the smartly dressed magic user.

'You may remember blacking out? Your friends have told how they saw you fighting the Behemoth. From my detective work, I believe that some of the armour you wore was designed on purpose, perhaps through the chained braces, to give the Anunaki a chance to possess you and take control of your blade.'

The news cut into Maledream as flashbacks from the battle and the voices inside his mind raced through him.

His headache was coming back slightly but he put it down to the beer he was drinking rather than his emotions, or rather, it was what he liked to believe. Maledream cast his mind back to the blade realising that he did not have it on him. Elric continued as the table sat silently.

'With the blade, you went down with the beast, disappearing from your friends. Do you remember what happened?' he asked.

'No, I woke up after some disturbing...nightmares,' Maledream answered.

He did not want to disclose yet what had happened in those dreams, although he had told Angelite on the way to the pub.

'You ended up on the shores,' continued Elric.

'It was then a few nights ago that you and Angelite bumped into each other, her intuition telling her of an omen no one else knew was about to happen. To cut a long story short my friend, Angelite banished the creature from your body. But she did not kill it, so we are hazarding a guess that it crawled back to its masters...the Anunaki.'

'I see. It all fits, I guess,' Maledream replied sombrely.

'Indeed, my friend, but not to worry, you are here now. The blade you have is linked to you in some way and no one has been brave enough to pick the weapon up so it is still on the beach. That is one reason why we have blocked the Port Sector off. It could be a danger to someone, especially children. It is lodged in the sand sticking out, which I am hazarding to guess awaits the return of its warrior.'

'I see,' he replied not wholeheartedly believing the warrior nonsense, the others around the table sensing it in his voice.

'How are you going to stop the Anunaki attacking this city?' Maledream asked.

'We have asked Neveah and his pack, and I would like to extend

the invitation to you and Angelite to set off on a journey to find some artefacts to possibly fulfil an old prophecy to protect the last lawful settlement of humanity?'

Maledream's ears winced for a second as he thought it over quickly. He had only just awakened from his coma and arrived at the city, and now it seemed he had to be thrown back into the fray.

However, he could not let his friends go back alone. In some way, the young Tribal man felt deeply responsible.

'I'm in,' he said reassuringly.

'And I also,' Angelite returned.

'What do you want us to do?' Maledream asked.

'You will need to go back to the Dark Age lands and find twelve artefacts that I've branded the Skulls of Meridia. It will not be an easy task and we can only direct you back into the city where you first met everyone here,' Elric said.

'Are the skulls we seek like the one in the museum?' Angelite asked inquisitively.

'Yes,' his short reply sounded.

'I can see where this is going,' she replied.

Larkham chuckled before waving his hand to Elric to continue.

'I know...but do you remember what N'Rutas told you?'

'Of course, .you mean of the Maya and such?' Angelite asked.

'Aye, little lady,' replied Neveah, finishing off his mug of booze.

'So I see...we need those skulls for a defence?' she asked, facing towards Elric again.

'Indeed, my fair Angelite, indeed it is so. I have with me that one skull from the museum.'

Elric lifted up an object onto the table, unwrapping the taut leather strings and straps that held the skull and its jaw piece together. All eyes were on the Quartz human looking skull as they gazed in wonder at it.

'It is quite something,' remarked Boris.

'Must be worth a pretty penny especially to the Pack Baron back in the city,' said Crazy John.

Everyone gawped at the attention to detail. Not a mark seemed to show it was chiselled with heavy or light tools. It seemed that not even the best artisans in Meridia could make such an object without spending perhaps hundreds of generations refining and defining it.

'The Order of Spirit has tried tapping into this object but it seems dormant which is why we just left it collecting dust in the museum,' continued Elric with a smile.

'We believed it was once of an important significance, even

though we doubted the legends and myths of such objects. But, of course, we have learned more recently through the old documents collected by Angelite.'

Angelite interrupted:

'Elric, listen, N'Rutas said that the skulls were created from mind out of matter.'

'As I thought,' he said, smiling.

'You are my star pupil, Angelite. Keep it up!' The compliment made Angelite blush slightly but she returned his smile.

'Angelite is correct. These were gifts from the Creators. It seems that we may be in a position to, for once and for all, fulfil what are ancestors could not. The prophecy has yet passed and has faded so it is a long shot to try and re-unite all of them,' Elric said.

'But,' spoke aloud Crazy John:

'What if the Anunaki possess some of these skulls?'

The question rocked the table with silence making them all feel fearful.

'We can only hope they don't,' Elric replied, a sigh escaping his lungs at Crazy John's valid and intelligent question.

'Why do you always have to dampen the mood?' shouted Boris, giving Crazy John a battering.

'We must try,' said Maledream, although to him it was the least he could do to stop the guilt raging inside him.

If he had not been possessed and ridden on the back of the Behemoth that was on its last legs then perhaps it may have been different. The group calmed down and carried on discussing the skulls throughout the evening, considering what N'Rutas had said about them.

They knew that the more information Elric had, the better he could assess the situation and try to see what else he could muster before the end of the month.

'Now I will show you some maps,' Elric said.

The crystal skull's eyes beamed a small amount of light from its sockets reflecting the soft lighting of the pub. It was a serene object that slumbered. Anyone that gazed upon its surface or touched it felt something of a certainty, a magic, about it.

Elric reached below the table wrapping his hands softly around some old parchment that was still intact but only from years of care.

Larkham made a space on the oaken table for Elric to roll out the maps, using everyone's hands to hold the corners carefully on his instruction.

Maledream tried using his mug but was severely clipped around the ear by Larkham for being so lazy.

'It has been decided by the Guilds of Meridia to open an ancient tunnel network that has existed underneath the city for a long time. Since the shift of the continents, they have either collapsed or worse. It was thought that by using our Resonance skills we could quickly and clearly build a way back to the city you all came from,' Elric said.

'Aye, so I'm guessing it would take you a while to clear the way anyway? Would a boat be far too dangerous?' asked Neveah.

'Indeed, my friend, we do not know how many beasts they may be controlling to guard the waters until their possible attack.'

'Then what happens after this tunnel is clear?' Neveah asked, pointing at the ancient map of the world that was spliced together from bits and pieces from other maps to make the clear picture on the brown rumpled paper.

Elric's finger traced a line, and the trajectory of where they were to where they would be travelling. The group smoked their pipes looking at the map wondering if it was at all accurate, but Angelite said it was, so they went with what she said in confidence.

'We must travel back in a straight line if we can as it will be the fastest way. We may reach the city in under a week in that case, maybe even sooner with transport. It was once an ancient labyrinth underneath the city used by the Creators, according to what we have written down back in the History of Meridia,' Angelite said.

'I see,' replied Neveah.

'Does that mean that the Anunaki have knowledge of these tunnels? What if they don't attack by sea but by underground? You did say they lived in this city once. Even if it was a long time ago, they would surely have kept records of it like you have,' he said anxiously.

'It is a possibility,' conceded Elric.

'It is more likely that they would attack by sea and we intend to keep it closely guarded, don't you worry.'

'You had better,' said Larkham,

'Because if you don't protect both your back and your front with a long weapon of wisdom and knowledge your city will not be standing if Neveah and the others do not get back in one piece.'

'Gee, thanks old man!' replied Maledream.

'I'm sure we can get them all back here before anything such as that happens.'

'Don't get too cocky, boy,' Larkham replied.

'Remember, these are dangerous beings, not to mention other dangers that exist elsewhere in the Dark Age lands. Remember all my

tales Maledream, I'll quite happily repeat them as you know I do all too well.'

'Spare me,' Maledream quipped with a smirk.

'Larkham is right,' said Elric.

'We will have every possible front guarded. However, until then focus on your quest for the skulls. You all have a month to train, and I am sure Neveah or Larkham can update you, Maledream, in your spare time. Leave the defences to Eldred and me. We will work with everyone in the city to ensure its safety. Angelite, look after this skull and make sure you pay close attention to it. In addition, everyone, keep this map keep it safe. We have other ancient copies, but not in such a good quality, so please try to look after it.'

All nodded in agreement to his words while drinking and smoking more from their pipes as Elric wrapped up the map tightening the leather straps softly around its coiled body.

'Maledream, I recommend you pick up that sword of yours tonight, so we can reopen the port. The sea is one way for us to harvest food before the winter, and every day is costly as we need to prepare for a siege.'

'I will,' he replied, staring blindly at the skull. Larkham watched him, wondering what his adopted son was thinking.

'Well, now that this business is settled...hmm...' Elric pondered getting his facts straight.

'You all know about the skulls now...and anything I have missed you can all fill each other in. I've made you aware about the tunnel you can directly travel too, which is being excavated as we speak, Eldred is overseeing the work himself.'

'I for one am glad he is,' butted in Angelite harshly, making Neveah grin, his one good eye creasing from a soft chuckle as he smoked.

'So am I, my star pupil,' Elric laughed.

'Now, I think have covered everything, any questions?'

No one spoke as the group looked at one another, happily resting in the smoky atmosphere and dim lighting that seemed to reflect their mood.

'Training starts tomorrow for all of you interested in becoming better fighters. I suggest you take this up, Angelite.'

'I will now. I'm not so naïve,' she smiled.

'Right,' Elric said.

'I am tired, and so I bid you all a good night. Remember to pick up your sword, friend. Farewell all and look after the skull and map that I have given you,' he added.

He got up, shook hands before departing, leaving the group to finish their drinks before closing time.

Neveah started one more conversation for good measure.

'So, old man, are you not joining us?'

'I will remain here and make sure the fools who look after this city don't get carried away with weapons of war,' Larkham replied, stroking his immense dark beard whilst thinking of Eldred's possible actions as he did not trust him.

'Aye, sounds like a plan, besides you might slow us down!' Neveah jested.

'You be surprised boy! You're just as cocky as Maledream, but I guess in time you will learn the error of your ways much like him,' Larkham replied.

Neveah and Larkham traded bouts of laughter, helping to alleviate the tension from planning the mission that lay ahead of the group. Maledream watched Angelite strap the skull back up.

'Where's Silver?' Maledream asked.

Everyone shrugged.

'Hmm...' Maledream grunted.

'I'm going to the beach, I'll see you all later. Angelite, is it okay if I go back to that apartment of yours?'

'Of course, Maledream, go for a walk and clear your head!'

'I may just do that.'

'Aye, it'll be the best thing you've done mate, relax by the beach. Tomorrow we start training.'

'Thanks,' Maledream replied.

'Catch you all later,' he finished with a drab tone.

Leaving the tavern, he put on his long jacket and raised his hood as the chilly wind cut into his face with a slight bit of drizzle from the clouds that had crept over during their stay in the pub all evening.

'*So much has happened,*' he thought as he trod through the streets in new boots that were finely made.

With gripping solid soles to his shoes. It made all the difference as he traversed through the streets following the smell of the ocean on the breeze. Being unable to read made it difficult, but luckily he was good at memorising streets in a city.

The Social Sector had fallen quiet, everyone staying inside as the drizzle set in, winter was coming closer every day that passed slowly but surely. He travelled along paths formed from crystals that lit his way with their soft glows of lights. Silver was nowhere to be seen which troubled him, but what could he do?

Maledream found the Port Sector guarded by Watchman who let him through almost as though he was expected. He crossed underneath the huge circular wall that surrounded Meridia, noticing the old fossils that were etched onto the walls and buildings around the place.

To him, they represented evidence that life existed even before his ancestors were even thought about, and from what he had learned that was not too far from the eerie truth. Before him lay the docks, and as he stood in the soft drizzle and breeze that he welcomed so much. He caught a glimpse of the moon behind the soft pale clouds for a moment. Strange lights made from old technology burned away to light the area for miles around the city along the docks that amazed him further still.

Not sure where to look first Maledream began to take a long walk around the docks which went on for an age as his thoughts raced back through the entire events that he had experienced and unfolded within his life. He regarded his life as just one star in the heavens, and if so much had happened to him, then what about the other stars themselves? Like a droplet to the ocean, he wondered and pondered the vastness of all the lives that have ever existed and what would happen if the experiences of all those lives and souls were merged into one mind.

It seemed that, since he had visited another dimension, his questions of the world grew more and more as intrigue lit his soul on fire with burning wonders. His eyes gazed out into the distance, seemingly all alone save for the Watchman that hid in dark holes on the sides of the great wall trying to shield themselves from the cold elements of the winter.

The Tribals eye caught Silver sitting on the beach and staring out towards the ocean, his silver and white damp fur blowing gently from the breeze. Maledream left the stony, cobbled path lit by the crystals and moved onto the sand to reach Silver. He noticed that the sand in this area looked disturbed unlike the rest of the calm beach. Glancing over at the piers leading in to the sea he noticed the number of ships docked in the huge circular outer harbour.

'Glad you have woken up, come join me Maledream, it is a pleasant night isn't it?' Silver's thoughts raced as the Tribal drew closer to the large wolf.

'It is,' said Maledream, sitting down next to Silver.

He could see his blade sticking out in the sand several metres in front of them both. It was covered in wet sand and the waves were brushing gently against it, most of it was buried at an awkward angle, the shaft was the only thing that stood out properly.

'It has been there for days, I've been watching over it personally for you. Do you remember what happened?' Silver asked.

'I'm afraid not...it is all a blur.'

'Then it is best left forgotten for now,' Silver added.

'It was some fight you had with Angelite, or should I say battle with the Anunaki that controlled your being.'

'So I'm told. Thanks for everything Silver, if I haven't thanked you before.'

'No need to thank me, it was a trip worth making, although I do long to be home. You are the only one I have spoken to in a while...sometimes I just need space away from you humans.'

Maledream smiled before saying:

'Well, friend, it has been some journey. I have heard that we are once again going to head off...because of me, the Anunaki now know of this city.'

'Oh be silent Maledream,' Silver replied, the Tribal turned and raised one eyebrow at Silver.

'You humans either blame yourselves then get upset about something or you blame others for your mistakes. You never quite see it from a third "person" perspective. It is because of your natural selfishness, which is your downfall, just go with the flow, Maledream. You know it's your style, besides that's how it should be, it's called natural and it's very simple.'

He stared at Silver almost wanting to slap the large wolf on the snout, but knew he was correct.

'I guess it was my mistake for being a human,' he replied with a chuckle.

'Don't start, Maledream. I had a rant with that ape Neveah just a few days ago,' Silver groaned.

If he could laugh ironically or sigh he would. Maledream, without saying a word, got up and walked towards the Relic blade. The breeze and drizzle of rain blew into him, his coat flowing slightly, his hood rippling.

'Then that will all change,' said Maledream to the wind. Silver caught the words easily with his keen ears. The Tribals palms gripped the hilt and, with a groan and a tug, he tore the blade out of the wet sand, lifting it up far enough before resting lightly on the hilt. Both he and Silver stared into the distance of the cold deep ocean in silence.

Meanwhile, deep within the earth's crust, Quetolox had learned of the troubling human's new settlement.

He ordered an army to be raised to finally wipe out the last free pocket of human resistance.

His anger was great, and it did not take much to convince the Royals at the drop of a whim to once again gather an army, the likes of which that had not been seen in almost two centuries.

'Next mid cycle we will begin the attack,' Quetolox said, his tongue rasping the warm air as he stood within the Royal Highness chamber speaking with the Queen.

'Then it is so,' she replied.

'Make sure Quetolox that you do not displease me, or you will have more than the Cattle to worry about.'

Her supple albino skin glinted from the blood red candlelight in her temple as she relaxed her writhing body in her blood red High Throne.

'As you wish your highness, the Red Sect has begun their warrior breeding,' Quetolox said, barely able to keep his tone as the Royal guards eyed him, his anger silent.

'And then you will have your feast of true victory my Queen,' he said, turning on the spot and leaving the room with speed.

'*I will deal with that breeder then this Maledream personally,*' he thought.

His one eye glowing crimson as his highly decorative regalia clinked and flowed with each step down the dark brooding hallways of the Anunaki Chambers...

'You will all perish...'

[Continued in: Approaching the Dark Age - Orchestra]